AN ECHO IN THE SORROW

SOULBOUND VI

HAILEY TURNER

Don't miss out on sneak peeks, exciting news, and more!
Sign up for Hailey Turner's newsletter
to stay up to date on her upcoming books.

WELCOME TO THE WORLDS OF HAILEY TURNER

Urban Fantasy
Soulbound

Science Fiction Romance
Metahuman Files

Steampunk-inspired Epic Fantasy
Infernal War Saga

1

Special Agent Patrick Collins crouched down and glared at the offending bag of chips hanging by a corner from the vending machine's metal shelf. He smacked his fist against the glass, only half listening to what Sage Beacot, his god pack's dire, had to say on the phone. The chips didn't move.

"You have the time off at the end of the month, right?" Sage asked.

"For what?" Patrick asked as he hit the glass again, trying to shake the chips loose.

"My *wedding.*"

"Oh, yeah. I have that day off. I put in my request back in spring."

Sage and her fiancé, Marek Taylor, were due to get married at the end of August. The preparations for the event had steadily increased, and Patrick had done his level best to escape them whenever possible. Sage wasn't a bridezilla by any stretch of the imagination, but she was *meticulous* when it came to details and expected everyone around her to be the same when it came to wedding decisions—whether making them or obeying them.

"What do you keep hitting?"

Patrick gripped the top edge of the vending machine and tried to shake it with one hand, which didn't really work. "Break room vending machine ate my money and won't give me my chips."

Sage laughed in his ear. "You sound like Wade."

"Unlike Wade, I'm not going to vandalize the damn thing."

"Are you sure about that?"

Wade Espinoza was a nineteen-year-old fledgling fire dragon they'd rescued a year ago from vampires and brought into their god pack. Keeping him fed definitely put a dent in their pack tithes. He was known to buy out the snack aisle in Target on the regular when he wasn't hoarding the latest shiny object to catch his eye.

Patrick hit the vending machine one more time, and the bag of chips finally fell into the catch tray. "Ha! Got it."

"I'll leave you to your lunch. Don't forget you have a suit fitting tomorrow."

He retrieved his bag of chips. "I should be able to make that."

Someone cleared their throat behind him. "Collins?"

Patrick straightened up and looked over his shoulder. The executive assistant to Henry Ng, the Supernatural Operations Agency's Special Agent in Charge for New York, stood in the entrance to the break room on his work floor. Tiana Martin raised an eyebrow at him, and Patrick sighed. The fact that she'd come down to locate him rather than wait for him to get back to his office and return a voicemail or email didn't bode well for the rest of his afternoon.

"Uh, I may have to postpone that fitting," Patrick said.

Sage sighed. "We'll work around you. But you *will* go to a fitting. I'll talk to you later."

She ended the call, and Patrick shoved his phone into his back pocket. "What does the SAIC need?"

"You," Tiana said.

Patrick looked down at his chips, knowing he wouldn't get to eat them anytime soon. "Lead the way."

He followed her out of the break room and to the bank of elevators, taking the first one to arrive up to the thirtieth floor. Henry's corner office was guarded by Tiana's desk. Patrick discreetly left his bag of chips on her desk, intent on retrieving them afterward. He waited while she knocked on Henry's door, then poked her head inside for a quick check-in with him.

"I found Special Agent Collins," Tiana said.

"Let him in," Henry replied.

Patrick slipped past Tiana, who closed the door behind him with a quiet click. He crossed the office to stand in front of Henry's wide wooden desk. The furniture was still the same as when Henry had taken over the office and SAIC position last summer, but there were a couple of new commendations hanging on the wall.

"You wanted to see me, sir?" Patrick asked.

Henry was a warlock in his late thirties who had an affinity for elemental magic. Pulled out of the San Francisco field office last year to head up the New York City one, he'd eased into the role well enough. Henry was stern but fair, and his loyalty was to the SOA, not the Dominion Sect like his predecessor. What's more, he generally had no problem with how Patrick ran his cases, a position which had earned Henry SOA Director Setsuna Abuku's backing in other areas of his job as SAIC.

Henry gestured at the pair of leather chairs in front of his desk. "Take a seat."

Patrick sat, the cross-guards of his gods-given dagger pressing into the soft cushion. He wasn't wearing a suit, despite being desk-bound since returning from Paris in early July. Henry had yet to remark on his break from business casual.

The reason Patrick's caseload had lightened considerably was due to the focus of the media into his actions in London and Paris. He and his pack had followed intelligence leads to London, where the Morrígan's staff had been up for sale at the Auction of Curiosities and Exceptional Items. Lucien had been the one to go undercover at the request of the federal government and help retrieve the staff. In exchange, the master vampire had received a century of what basically constituted diplomatic immunity while within the United States.

The trouble Lucien could cause in one hundred years made Patrick want to drink, but ultimately, it wasn't his problem. He wasn't the one who had signed off on the agreement, and he'd most likely be dead by the time Lucien's future actions—whatever they might be—required intervention.

But Lucien had gotten them into the auction, even if the master vampire hadn't retrieved the Morrígan's staff. It had subsequently been stolen in a fight where most of the auction attendees had ended up dead and then become the walking dead due to necromancy.

Ilya Nazarov, a necromancer who was the Patriarch of Souls for the Orthodox Church of the Dead, had run off with it. Patrick and the others had followed Ilya to Paris, where the necromancer had forsaken his position in the end, sacrificing the god he'd worshipped to the Morrígan's staff's hunger in order to raise millions of Parisian dead. Patrick still wasn't sure if Peklabog's godhead had managed to escape the sacrifice, even if his body had not, or if his worshippers would be enough to undo what Ilya had wrought.

Again, not his problem.

Ilya had ultimately emptied the Paris Catacombs and sent the walking dead to attack the City of Lights. Fighting zombies on summer solstice had been a nightmare, and only the blessing of a goddess of fate enabled them to stop Ilya.

They'd won the fight but not the war, coming away with a broken-off piece of the Morrígan's staff while Ilya got away with the rest of it and half an army of the undead. Ilya and his zombies had disappeared through the veil, carried away by the weapon's magic to some allied hell most likely. His loyalty no longer resided with the god the Orthodox Church of the Dead had worshipped, but with the Dominion Sect and Patrick's father, Ethan Greene.

It was an alliance no government was happy about.

Patrick clenched his left hand into a fist, remembering how Srecha's blessing had burned him, though it didn't compare to the way the Morrígan's staff had hungered for his soul. Her blessing had turned into a prayer, one the Morrígan's staff had answered with the resurrection of the mother of all vampires.

The carved raven Patrick had broken off from it was currently hidden away in his nightstand drawer, along with the last Greek coin from the ones Hermes had given him last summer as payment for the dead. It wasn't the best hiding spot by far, but both artifacts remained quiescent.

Patrick hadn't told anyone at the SOA the Morrígan's staff was broken, nor that he'd kept a piece of it. Even with Setsuna in a position of power, Patrick didn't trust the government to do right by what was, in all honesty, a weapon of mass destruction. He'd reported that breaking up Ilya's spellcasting and magical support had been enough to put a stop to the zombie invasion.

Putting into his report that he'd had help from the gods wouldn't have been believed by the people handling the fallout. Gods might walk the earth, but their worshippers weren't the ones in power these days. Patrick's case report had been as detailed as he could afford it to be, but there were obvious gaps people were still arguing over in three countries.

Setsuna had done her best to keep Patrick out of the political line of fire. On her orders, Henry had restricted Patrick to mostly desk duty since his return to the States last month. Desk duty was abhorrently boring, and Patrick was itching for work outside the walls of his office.

"I know Setsuna wants you to remain within New York City and keep a low profile, but Casale asked for you specifically on the phone call I just got off of," Henry said.

Giovanni Casale, Chief of the NYPD Preternatural Crimes Bureau, was someone Patrick had worked closely with on several cases in the past. As far as relationships with local police went, he hadn't yet burned that bridge.

Patrick tried not to look eager about finally getting to leave the office. "What did he want?"

"He's currently at the Metropolitan Museum of Art. Apparently there was a break-in over the weekend, but the museum director didn't see fit to call the police until today."

"Why is Casale's department involved if it's a case about stolen art?"

"Because the item in question was an artifact."

Patrick bit the inside of his cheek and swallowed a groan. He could've done without another missing magical item to track down. The Morrígan's staff was enough of a headache.

"What kind?"

Henry shrugged. "Casale described it as part of a traveling exhibition but wouldn't say more than that. If it didn't have any magical properties, the case would've gone to the FBI. Since it *is* of a magical nature, he's requesting some federal help. You, specifically. I told him you'd be there in thirty minutes. Someone will be waiting for you at the museum's main entrance."

Patrick tried not to wince. Despite the low profile he'd been forced to take due to the zombie invasion in Paris, he hadn't been able to stay out of Casale's way when it came to pack politics.

While in London, they'd confirmed demons were working with hunters to take over god packs and break their power. Without stable god packs to fight for the rights of werecreatures, the packs who looked to them for guidance would lose protection, opening them up to discrimination and quite possibly outright murder.

Hunters allied with werecreatures was anathema, but werecreatures sharing their souls with demons was worse. It was a problem that had been growing in New York City since February when Estelle Walker and Youssef Khan, alphas of the rival god pack, had contracted with the Krossed Knights. Patrick had been in Chicago when the bounty on Jonothon de Vere was activated. Since then, they'd been fighting guerilla-style battles in all five boroughs as the civil war in the werecreature community spilled out of the shadows. The PCB wasn't thrilled with any of that.

Alliances with the fae and the Night Courts helped guard their territory borders, but Patrick knew they couldn't rely on that support forever. Their god pack held half the city now, territory twisted like gerrymandered districts through Estelle and Youssef's. Casale had warned Patrick last month rumors were reaching the police about his personal involvement.

He doubted those rumors had died down.

They'd played off Jono's involvement in Europe as being one of Patrick's criminal informants. The story was thin, but they were sticking to it. They all knew that wouldn't be believed forever, especially if some enterprising reporter dug up their lease information.

"I'll leave now," Patrick said, realizing he wouldn't get a lunch.

Henry pinned Patrick with a look. "If the case takes you out of the five boroughs, it will be reassigned."

Patrick bristled at that order. "It's my case."

"And the director was clear on your current limitations."

Patrick had half a mind to call Setsuna and tell her to lift the restrictions, but he had a feeling she'd ignore his call. "Fine."

"Keep me updated. That's an order, Collins."

Patrick nodded, knowing better than to antagonize someone who was in his corner. Henry had let him run his cases how he saw fit and backed him in moments other SAICs might not have. His predecessor definitely wouldn't have. Henry's loyalty was to the agency, but it helped that he believed in Setsuna's quiet eradication of Dominion Sect supporters and sympathizers within the SOA.

Patrick left the office and grabbed his chips off Tiana's desk. He ate them quickly on the elevator ride down to the lobby, bypassing the floor his office was on completely. He left the SOA's New York

City field office with his dagger strapped to his right thigh, tactical pistol holstered to his right hip, and badge tucked away in his back pocket. The second he stepped beyond the warded walls and air-conditioned interior of the federal building, he was met by a wave of humid heat that had him sweating before he even finished crossing the street.

Summer in New York City was as bad as the ones he'd lived through growing up in Washington, DC. They were both swamp-like in their own way, and no amount of cold charms in his clothing could fix that. It's why his leather jacket had a permanent spot in the closet now until the weather cooled down.

His Mustang was parked in the adjacent warded garage, in need of something more than a detail job from getting clawed by a werecreature over the driver's-side door the other week. Patrick hadn't had the time to get it seen to between work and pack problems.

Getting behind the steering wheel, Patrick started the engine and then turned the air-conditioning on full blast. Sighing in relief at the coolness blasting him in the face, he pulled out and drove toward the exit, mentally mapping out his route. The Metropolitan Museum of Art was located at the edge of Central Park. Heading Uptown on Madison Avenue was going to take some time. Tourists were out in force, and Monday traffic was always the worst in his opinion.

Being the height of summer, one would think Central Park would be a riot of greenery. Driving past it on his way to the museum, Patrick noticed the trees didn't seem as thick as they should for the season, and the flashes of lawn and bushes he caught glimpses of looked thin and brown. It looked as if autumn was coming early despite the hot weather.

Sage and Marek had a view of Central Park from their home, and she'd commented on the change the other day, noticing it happening in other parks across the city as well when she went to meet with some of the packs under their protection. Nothing out of the ordinary on the magic front had come through the SOA regarding the flora change though. Local opinion seemed to think it might have been leftover damage from last summer, but Patrick wasn't so sure. Central Park had looked fine in spring, and the wilting of the plants was more recent.

The issue wasn't one he could focus on right now though, not when he had a missing artifact to deal with. Patrick put it out of his mind and kept driving. The museum had its own parking garage, which was full, but a security spot was open on the ground floor when he finally arrived. Patrick claimed it, knowing the government plates on the Mustang would keep it from being towed.

He scanned Fifth Avenue while he waited to cross, nothing out of the ordinary pricking his attention or magic. Patrick's damaged soul and magic meant he could more easily track demons and monsters than other agents, but his magic made everyone who could sense it uncomfortable. The anchors for his personal shields had been set into his bones by Persephone, and they helped to hide what he was, letting him pass as a mundane human.

With everything going on right now, he wasn't willing to make anything easy for the enemy. Hiding in plain sight was an ingrained habit after so many years of doing it, but that wasn't a guarantee of safety.

The summer crowds flocking to the Metropolitan Museum of Art were a mix of tourists and locals alike this time of the year. Patrick cut his way through them as he hurried down the sidewalk toward the front entrance of the grand building. The smell of hot dogs and pretzels wafted from the food carts situated on the sidewalk in front of the steps leading to the museum. It made his stomach growl.

Colorful banners hung between stone pillars over the museum's façade, one of which showcased *An Eastern Spiritual Journey* summer exhibit. The image used for it was that of a stone Buddha statue, the limited dates of the exhibition listed below it.

"Collins," someone called out over the noise of the crowd.

Patrick rocked to a halt midway up the stairs, scanning the area through his sunglasses. A slight, dark-haired woman in a dark pantsuit caught his attention, and Patrick waved at Detective Specialist Allison Ramirez.

"I thought I was only meeting with Casale," he said in greeting as he approached her.

"Dwayne and I are lead on the case, but the museum director refused to talk to anyone but Casale," Allison said.

"Oh, he's one of those types."

Allison snorted. "Seems like it."

"Where's your partner?"

"Interviewing some of the museum workers involved with the exhibit in question. Casale is with the director, but he told me to bring you to him."

"Then lead the way."

Patrick had worked with Allison and Dwayne on cases several times before and got on well enough with the detectives. Allison led him up the rest of the stairs to the entrance, flashing her badge at the security guard on duty to bypass the long line of patrons eager to get in. They were waved around the metal detectors, entering the Great Hall beyond. The neoclassical space echoed with footsteps and hushed voices of visitors.

The information desk was crowded, but Allison bypassed it in favor of approaching a slim blonde woman dressed all in black with a museum lanyard hanging from her neck. She stood near the wall, out of the way of the foot traffic. A walkie-talkie was clipped to her belt, and she was studying an iPad held in one hand. She looked up from it when Allison cleared her throat. The discreetly disdainful once-over the woman gave Patrick made him raise an eyebrow.

"Is this who we've been waiting for?" she asked. Her ID card listed out her name as Cynthia Fox, a curator for the museum. She felt human to his magic.

"SOA Special Agent Collins is here to assist the PCB with your problem," Allison said mildly.

Cynthia shook her head. "The SOA really didn't need to get involved."

"Chief Casale thought otherwise. If you'll take us to him and your director?"

Allison was polite enough, but the request was firm. Cynthia sniffed delicately, clutching the iPad to her chest. "Very well. Follow me."

They were escorted out of the Great Hall and into a side alcove where an employees-only door was located. Cynthia scanned her access card across the sensor to unlock it and allow them entry into the maze of corridors and offices that made up the museum staff's work area behind the scenes.

It took several minutes for them to make their way to the museum director's office, needing to take an elevator to a higher level. The office area was cramped, but the director's was the largest Patrick had seen on their walk-through. It didn't come with any windows due to the building's architecture, but the walls were covered in artwork and credentials.

Casale stood in front of the director's desk, but he turned around at their arrival. He wore a business suit rather than a white-shirted uniform, probably to help blend in with the crowd. Patrick had a feeling the director wanted discretion over anything else if he'd waited days to report a crime.

"Collins," Casale said.

Patrick nodded in greeting. "Thanks for getting me out of the office. What's going on?"

"Apparently the Met had an artifact stolen from their summer exhibition this weekend. Director Phillippe Weiss finally reported it missing today."

Phillippe was a slim man in a sleek suit with stylishly cut brown hair of a particular shade that spoke of hair dye. He bristled at Casale's statement, a flash of annoyance crossing his face.

"As I informed you, we needed to report the loss to our insurance company first," Phillippe said.

Patrick shrugged. "Insurance companies will always advise reporting the crime to the police or a federal agency. What's missing?"

Casale gestured at a file spread out on Phillippe's desk, colorful archival photographs and insurance paperwork lined up for perusing. "The Trishula of Shiva."

"My SAIC said it was an artifact."

Phillippe irritably waved aside his words. "It was *barely* an artifact. It held lingering traces of magic that were so miniscule our archivist witch said it didn't need wards. Representatives of the Louvre agreed when we gave them a preliminary report on our security efforts."

"It still had magic. It probably should have been warded."

"It's a priceless piece of art, not a weapon. The Met is already warded to protect the collections."

Patrick bit his tongue so he wouldn't say something he'd regret about how anything with magic could become a weapon. He was living proof of that. "When was it stolen?"

"Friday night sometime. We've been given security feed of the exhibit room from Friday through Saturday, when it was discovered missing. Ramirez will be going over the security feed when we get back to the PCB. According to these screenshots, it was there one second and gone the next," Casale said.

Patrick approached the desk and peered down at the two sheets of paper depicting the screenshots in question, the time stamp separated by a single second. The Trishula of Shiva was propped up behind a tall glass case, the soft light angled at it causing the gold to shine, the exhibit room empty. The next screenshot showed an empty case and still no one in the room at the time.

"Did anyone check the wards surrounding the room for tampering?" Patrick asked.

"The sorcerer in charge of magical security is one of the people Guthrie is interviewing right now," Allison said.

Patrick frowned, catching Casale's eyes. "I'll need to speak with them and see the exhibit room in person. Can you get me a copy of the security feed as well?"

"It'll get reviewed back at the PCB with some facial recognition software. We'll make you a copy after we get those results," Casale said.

"Does the trishula have any history of conflicting ownership?"

Phillippe cleared his throat. "No. It was donated by a private owner to the Louvre twenty years ago. Its historical background is not at issue."

"We'll need copies of those records."

"They're already being pulled at Chief Casale's request."

Patrick nodded. "Then I want to see the exhibit room."

Phillippe sighed in obvious irritation. "Cynthia can show you. I ask that you don't make it obvious you're there for a crime."

"I'll come along. Ramirez can take it from here," Casale said, nodding at his detective.

"We aren't closing the exhibit down while you're there. The museum is open, and it will be too noticeable if we attempt to close off that area right now," Cynthia warned as she opened the office door.

Casale stared her down. "We already lost possible evidence by your delay in reporting the crime. That isn't helpful. We'll handle this review as we see fit."

"What did you do with the display case?" Patrick asked Phillippe.

The director waved a hand at them. "It's still in the exhibit room. We left a placard stating the trishula has been taken off exhibit for the time being."

Patrick caught Casale's eye and shook his head in disbelief. The things some people did to try to save their own ass. Not that he had any room to talk.

"Let's go," Casale said.

Patrick was glad Casale had opted for a suit over a uniform. It meant neither of them stood out when they finally made it to the special exhibition gallery in the center of the museum. Cynthia walked them past the timed-entry line, leading them to the room that had held the Trishula of Shiva and currently still held other artifacts.

The second Patrick stepped into the exhibit room, recognition cut through his shields, the warning burning through his magic. Patrick's head snapped to the side, gaze skimming the nearby crowd. His attention settled on a man who made his lips curl into a snarl.

"Excuse me," Patrick said curtly.

He left Casale and Cynthia without explanation, sliding through the small crowd, never taking his eyes off Youssef Khan. The alpha of the rival New York City god pack watched him come with a sharp smile, amber eyes bright in the dim lighting of the exhibit room. He hadn't bothered with sunglasses, which ensured everyone gave him a wide berth.

Youssef was in his forties, stocky and dark-haired, and married to Estelle. Patrick was of the opinion their marriage was a power exchange rather than one built out of love. They'd kept a stranglehold on the packs in New York City over the years, but Patrick's pack was rapidly changing that. Niceties had long since been left by the wayside between their packs. The fact that Youssef was here didn't bode well. It made Patrick hyperaware of his space, knowing other werecreatures could be in the Met. Aside from that, their paths crossing right now was decidedly not a coincidence.

"Come to gloat over your crime scene?" Patrick asked lightly, unable to keep the venom out of his voice.

"I have no idea what you're talking about," Youssef drawled.

"Right. Because you aren't making deals with devils, except for how you are."

"Again, you're making accusations that have no merit."

"How long have you been following me?"

"I wasn't, but even if I was, you're easy enough to track."

"I doubt that."

"You leave a lot of damage behind wherever you go. Here. Chicago. Paris."

Youssef's smile settled somewhere in the vicinity of a smirk. Patrick's magic wasn't picking up any hint of hell from the older man, but that didn't mean he hadn't been around any hunters carrying demons in their souls. After everything they'd uncovered in London, Patrick knew it was only a matter of time before the demons came out.

"Stalking is a crime, especially when a federal agent is the target," Patrick said.

Youssef stepped closer, not bothering to keep his voice down. "But you're not just a federal agent, are you? Stands to reason you're fair game in your other capacity. I've always been curious if your superiors know of your true allegiance and how it affects your cases."

Patrick fought against clenching his teeth, trying to keep any physical tells to the bare minimum. "If you're here to fight—"

"I'm here to enjoy the fine arts." Youssef's gaze briefly flickered over Patrick's shoulder before returning. "The Met is open to everyone."

"Is there a problem?" Casale asked from behind Patrick, voice calm and easy.

Youssef rocked back on his heels, never taking his eyes off Patrick. "No problem, Casale."

"Then you might want to move along. We're working."

It wasn't a suggestion. Youssef seemed more willing to listen to Casale than to Patrick—whether for ulterior motives or otherwise, Patrick couldn't tell. Considering what was going on, Patrick would leave the Met later as if he were heading into a war zone. He didn't trust Youssef not to try to ambush him out in the open.

Youssef left the exhibit room at a lazy pace, secure in the

knowledge that Patrick couldn't do anything to him. Patrick wasn't sure how far the other man would really go, so he pushed magic out of his damaged soul and conjured up a tiny mageglobe. He closed his fingers around the softly glowing pale blue sphere, filling it with a silence ward. Static washed over the space he and Casale stood in, bringing with it an all-consuming quiet.

"I didn't think you liked being so popular," Casale said after a moment.

Patrick turned to face him. "What's that supposed to mean?"

"Don't play dumb. You know exactly what I'm talking about."

Patrick fought back a scowl. "Youssef is an asshole. So is his wife. It's not a crime to hate them when they're shit at their jobs."

"The fights breaking out between packs are a crime when innocent people get caught in the crossfire." Casale frowned, the lines around his mouth deepening. "What's happening won't be good for your job in the long run."

Patrick knew that, but his pack wasn't something he could or would walk away from. At some point, his personal and professional lives were going to collide. But that was in some future even the Fates couldn't control, and all Patrick could do was walk toward it.

"Lucky for you all I'm doing today is dealing with a stolen piece of art and not a dead body," Patrick said.

Casale eyed him for a moment before shaking his head. "Word of advice, Collins. Estelle and Youssef won't back down. Things are going to get ugly."

"Uglier than hunters with demons in their souls making a mess of the city? You know what they've done."

"Knowing and proving are two separate hurdles."

It was an argument Patrick couldn't afford to have in public, even with a silence ward wrapped around them. His position in their god pack wasn't known yet to the public, even if Casale was tacitly aware of it. The longer he could keep that fact hidden, the safer his pack and his job would be.

"We've got a case to work on," Patrick finally said.

Casale allowed the change of subject without a fight. Patrick drew down his magic, the silence ward fading away around them. Sound hit his ears again, and Patrick shoved aside his worry about pack problems in favor of doing his job.

2

"ANOTHER SCOTCH?" THE GUCCI SALESPERSON ASKED WITH A POLITE smile on her face, crystal decanter in hand. She smelled only slightly of fear, which was a refreshing change considering Jono usually got overwhelmed with that scent in close quarters whenever he went somewhere without his sunglasses.

Still, it tainted the alcohol.

Jono glanced over at the cut-crystal glass resting on the stylish table by the sofa he sat on in the private fitting room they'd been escorted to upon arrival. He'd drunk almost all of the first glass he'd been offered, the taste of the expensive drink still on his tongue, souring in the back of his throat.

"No, thanks," Jono said.

She nodded and moved on to ask the same question of Leon Hernandez, who had no compunction about taking another glass. Marek's was only half-empty since it was his turn up on the tailoring dais for the final fitting of his three-piece wedding suit. Patrick would've been there, except he'd been assigned a case yesterday and was currently working. His final fitting would have to be rescheduled, but Gucci's fashion director had said it wouldn't be a problem.

Apparently money could make the world revolve around you, as Jono was witnessing when it came to Marek and Sage's upcoming nuptials. Being a tech billionaire meant no expense was spared for the intimate ceremony planned for the end of the month. That included being able to dictate the schedule of a luxury fashion house designer.

"You should have another one. It's not like it'll impair you from putting on your suit," Leon said as he sniffed appreciatively at his drink.

"Had quite a bit last night at work," Jono said.

Leon nudged the small platter of hearty steak sandwiches Marek had asked be available for today's fitting closer to Jono. "Then eat something. You can't have got much sleep last night."

Jono picked up half a sandwich. "I got enough."

Truth be told, it wasn't much, but the hour-long nap he'd snatched in bed with Patrick that morning after closing up the bar had been worth it. Holding Patrick in his arms always put Jono in a better mood these days.

Leon eyed him, brown eyes full of worry, just like his scent. He was the co-leader of the Tempest pack, and his partner, Emma Zhang, was Sage's matron of honor. Leon would stand with Marek as his best man, and Jono would be walking Sage down the aisle. Their wedding party was small because neither were fans about putting their lives out there for the public to consume.

Unfortunately, privacy was becoming difficult to come by. Ever since Jono and Patrick had delegated Emma as their proxy dire while they'd been in Europe, she'd lost some of her hard-fought anonymity. The encroaching media spotlight was beginning to widen onto PreterWorld, the social media company Marek owned and which Emma and Leon both worked at. The business was profitable, but Jono wondered how much longer it would be before its stock took a nosedive because of their personal lives.

"You're next, Jono," Marek said.

Jono watched as Marek was helped out of his suit jacket, the item in question handled carefully. Assistants divested him of the rest of his clothes, the suit needing no further alterations. Jono eyed where his hung from a rolling rack, assistants already working to take it out of its garment bag. He swallowed the last bit of scotch in his glass and stood.

"Stand here and strip, please," Terry said. The designer pointed at the dais without looking at Jono in favor of loudly directing his staff about as if he were a conductor. Jono could still hear how fast his heart was beating, the hint of fear mixing with his sweat. Terry was good at hiding his fear, but he was still uncomfortable around werecreatures.

Jono didn't mind stripping down to his underwear. He wouldn't have cared if he needed to be naked. Most werecreatures didn't, and Marek had learned not to be over the years after joining the Tempest pack.

He passed his clothes to one of the assistants, nostrils flaring slightly at the brief hint of attraction seeping through a couple of harsher scents. Better than fear, but that wasn't saying much. Jono knew people were attracted to his body until they saw his eyes. Few people wanted him after that realization.

Patrick had never been scared of him, and that had been as much an attention-getter as his cocky smirk had been across the bar counter. Their first meeting last year had been an unmitigated disaster in the face of a soultaker attack, but they'd sorted themselves out. These days, Jono couldn't imagine his life without Patrick in it. Soulbond aside, they were never going to walk away from each other, and helping out with Sage and Marek's wedding had got him thinking about his own future with Patrick. They were already bound to each other, having promised to never leave, but Jono wouldn't mind seeing Patrick wearing a wedding band.

Maybe it could happen someday in an unknown future where

Patrick's soul debt was paid and the war dogging their heels was over.

Jono's mouth quirked a bit as he stepped into the trousers an assistant handed him. *Should probably look at rings first.*

The thought was an idle one, but nothing would come of it right now. Jono let it fade, focusing instead on being moved about by the designer to check the fit of the suit he finally had on. The charcoal-gray color was paired with a natural green tie and hand-kerchief tucked into the breast pocket to match the wedding colors. The style was sleek and classic, with little embellishments. The material was luxurious and didn't itch his skin, the tailoring masterful, and the overall fit pretty much perfect for a wedding.

Just not a fight.

The private fitting room was located on the third floor, in a space designed to cater to rich clientele. The stairs leading up to their level had been roped off from the general public on the first floor. Multiple work areas and several private fitting rooms filled the space, and the door to theirs cracked open, the heartbeats behind it calm. Jono didn't think anything of it until the aconite hit his nose, burning his eyes as he snapped his head around.

"Get down!" he snarled.

Jono didn't wait for people to listen, knowing most people's reactions were delayed if they didn't outright panic immediately. He grabbed the two assistants nearest him and yanked them to the ground, lashing out with his leg to knock the designer's feet out from under him with as gentle a blow as he could. Marek had already dropped to the floor while Leon had body tackled the people closest to him.

Silver bullets dipped in aconite cut through the air where everyone had been standing. Jono rolled off the dais, already shift-ing, his brand-new designer suit tearing open at every seam. The flash of agony disappeared as the werevirus turned off pain recep-tors in his nerves for the shift. That didn't stop his brain from processing the pressure of bones breaking and skin splitting as Jono shifted from human to wolf in seconds.

He'd gotten faster in the last year, but he almost wasn't fast enough. Two Krossed Knight hunters shoved their way into the private fitting room, dressed like upscale shoppers. Except they weren't carrying money, but weapons, the pistols in their hands aimed unerringly at Jono.

He didn't hesitate to attack, charging forward with a snarl that made fear spike in the air around him. The hunters tightened their fingers on the triggers, but Jono was on them both before the silver bullets left the gun chambers. He clamped his jaws on one hunter's right arm, teeth ripping through skin and shattering bone, swinging the man to the side to knock over his partner.

The hunter screamed, a sound that was choked off by something else. The taste of sulfur exploded on Jono's tongue, blood tainted with hints of hell, the same way the hunter's soul was. The demon the man carried in his soul looked out of human eyes, black veins pulsing in his face.

"You won't win," the demon hissed.

Jono gutted the hunter from throat to navel with one deep swipe of his left forepaw even as he twisted his head to snap the hunter's arm off at the elbow. This time the hunter broke through the demon's control to scream in agony as Jono spat out his arm. Blood poured from the hunter's ruined elbow even as his guts slipped through the ragged holes in his torso. He fell to his knees, blood trickling out of his mouth as the demon fled the dying body with a thunderous flash of negative light.

Leon had engaged the second hunter, who had gotten back to his feet with supernatural speed. Leon's wolf form was smaller than Jono's but no less lethal in a fight. He'd bitten off the other hunter's hand holding the gun, but the demon riding the hunter's soul had pulled a silver-and-aconite-coated knife from his belt.

Jono leaped on the man before the knife could find its target in Leon's neck. His weight drove the hunter to the floor with a loud crash. The hunter swung his arm around, looking to sink the knife into Jono's side, but Jono twisted around out of range. He kept one paw on the hunter's head, pressing his weight onto the man's skull in a threatening manner. He wouldn't mind killing the bloke, but Jono had listened to Patrick whinge about leaving someone alive to question plenty of times.

Another flash of negative light meant the demon riding that hunter's soul chose to flee rather than attempt to fight. The smell of sulfur dissipated, fear and pain replacing it in Jono's senses. He eased up on the pressure on the hunter's skull, listening to him breathe wetly. The stump of his arm dragged through the spreading pool of blood beneath the bitten-off wrist. They'd need to tie the limb off so he didn't bleed out.

Jono tilted his head to the side, dialing up his hearing. He didn't hear any calm heartbeats, only the frantic ones of people on lower and higher levels of the building panicking from the sound of gunshots. He didn't take his eyes off the entrance to the private dressing room, the door riddled with bullet holes. The air smelled like blood and aconite, but not sulfur. The two hunters appeared to be the only threat.

Leon knelt in front of Jono, back in human form, skin streaked with blood that thankfully wasn't his. "I'll deal with him. Shift back. The cops have been called. We don't want them to shoot you on sight."

Jono moved off the hunter, and Leon took his place, keeping the man on the ground. Without a demon riding his soul, he was swearing and crying from the pain of losing a hand, shock most likely settling in.

Jono shifted back to human, body twisting and breaking from four legs back to two. He shook his head to clear it, vision settling into normal human parameters. He crouched there for a moment between the two hunters, one dead and the other bleeding out, and tried to choke back the fury.

"They tracked us," Jono said.

Leon nodded grimly. "Yeah. I need a belt if you want this one to live."

"Rather he didn't."

"You know what your other half would say about that." Leon paused. "Well. You know what he'd say if he wasn't advocating murder."

"Fine. I'll get you a bloody belt." Jono craned his head around. "Marek? Are you all right?"

The seer had knocked over the chaise lounge he'd been sitting on and had dragged two people behind it with him. He raised his head over the top, hazel eyes wide. "We're fine. Are there any more hunters?"

Jono got to his feet. "Not that I can hear or smell."

"Doesn't mean more might not come." Marek stood, gaze raking up and down Jono's naked, bloody body. He made a face. "You ruined your wedding suit. Sage is going to be so mad."

"She's going to be bloody pissed about the hunters."

"Well, yeah, that too, but you aren't the one responsible for organizing a wedding."

"You have a wedding planner for that."

"And who do you think oversees the wedding planner?"

Considering Sage ran herd over the pack the same way she ran her cases at Gentry & Thyme, Jono wasn't surprised.

"I need a belt," Jono repeated.

Marek immediately undid his and handed it over. "You need some clothes, too. Both of you do."

"I can…find you some," Terry said hesitantly, looking a little glassy-eyed as he stared around his destroyed and bloodied fitting room.

His assistants were all huddled on the floor crying, none of them moving. Jono tossed the belt to Leon, who used it to create a tourniquet around the hunter's arm to stop the bleeding. He screamed when Leon tightened it down, and Leon growled a warning that sounded more wolf than human to Jono's ears.

The cops arrived a few minutes later. In that time before their arrival, Terry managed to locate a pair of trousers and shirts for both Jono and Leon from one of the adjacent workrooms. He'd even come up with a pair of shoes for each of them before he finally took a seat with his back to the room and started to shake.

Jono couldn't help him, not when faced with police entering the fitting room. He'd ordered Leon off the hunter and to stand with Marek behind him. Jono kept his hands loose to his sides as the police came in, weapons drawn, stepping around the dead hunter and the savaged one.

"Hands where I can see them," the first cop into the room barked out, his gun never moving from Jono's chest.

"They attacked us," Marek said loudly before Jono could speak up. "I'm allocated personal protection by the United States government. My friends performed that function in lieu of a security detail."

The moments following the police officers' arrival were tense and loud as the officers cleared the floor and called for an ambulance for the wounded hunter. Marek's statement of federal protection was ignored by the police, and Jono allowed himself to be separated from the group and ordered up against the other wall. It wasn't anything he hadn't dealt with before, but the anger and embarrassment churning in his stomach was difficult to ignore.

His eyes, along with the firsthand account from Terry and his assistants, eventually required the officers on the scene to radio the PCB and request their presence. The crime was preternatural in nature, and the NYPD as a whole was aware of the hunter problem in the city. Any crime that dealt with magic or the preternatural community was run through the PCB.

Jono was glad for the change in officers because it meant people stopped pointing guns at him.

The pair of detectives out of the PCB who arrived first managed to diffuse the tension in the fitting room between the other officers and everyone else. It wasn't the first time Jono had dealt with the police after a hunter attack, but the dead body prob-ably wasn't helpful.

"I'm told it was self-defense," the older detective from the PCB said. His badge listed his last name as Sanderson.

"My mates and I were here for our wedding suit fittings when the hunters attacked us. What was I supposed to do? Let the bloody arseholes shoot us?" Jono asked, not bothering to keep the anger out of his voice.

"I wasn't suggesting that. It's clear they were the aggressors in this incident. It's the why we're after."

Jono glanced over at the body that was still on the ground. The hunter's partner had already been taken off to a hospital with an officer in tow since he was under arrest. The body had yet to be removed because the ones to process the scene had arrived with the officers out of the PCB and weren't done gathering evidence. He wished Patrick had come with them.

"I'm the alpha of the New York City god pack. There's your reason," Jono said.

"My understanding is there are two god packs."

"Mine is the only one that matters. Why do you think they keep trying to murder me?"

"Is that what you think this was about?"

Jono resisted the urge to roll his eyes. "Why else go where they weren't supposed to be, armed to the bloody teeth, and open fire on innocent people?"

"I don't need your attitude when I'm trying to get all the facts."

Jono's mobile started to ring from somewhere on the floor. He'd had it out on the side table before things all went to shit and was glad to discover it hadn't been damaged. "That's my mobile. Mind if I retrieve it?"

"I still have questions for you."

Jono's mobile didn't stop ringing. Leon's started up, then Marek's. His shoulders tightened at the sound. The only reason people would be ringing them all at once would be because something was wrong.

Marek was the one who finally got permission to answer his mobile, his status as a seer getting him cleared far faster than Jono or Leon. Jono dialed up his hearing in order to listen in on the conversation.

"Sage, listen. We're all right, but we were attacked by hunters, and we're dealing with the police right now," Marek said.

"*What?*" Sage snapped loud enough Jono was sure the officer standing near Marek heard her.

"We're fine, I promise. We're—"

"I've received word five of the packs under our protection were attacked by hunters and other god pack members within the last thirty minutes. Several people are dead."

Marek froze, and he snapped his head around, gaze finding Jono's unerringly. "*Shit.*"

"Hey, are you listening?" Sanderson asked, breaking through Jono's concentration.

"Am I free to leave?" Jono asked, ignoring the question when the answer was obvious.

"I still have some questions."

"Then can you hurry it up? There's pack business I need to handle."

Sanderson tapped his pen against his little notebook. "I'll take as long as I need to."

Jono ground his teeth and took a deep breath, knowing this was something he couldn't walk away from. It rankled though, that the people he'd sworn to protect were hurting or dead, and he was stuck in a fashion store repeating his story for the third bloody time already.

He knew better than to piss off the police though. All Jono could do was follow their orders and hope he didn't get arrested for defending himself. The laws surrounding the preternatural community differed slightly when it came to situations like hunters, but Jono wasn't a United States citizen. Getting charged with a federal crime would be a one-way ticket to deportation after serving whatever sentence was handed down.

Jono wondered, as he went through the rigmarole of answering the officer's questions, if that maybe wasn't what Estelle and Youssef were ultimately after. It'd be easy for them to take back New York City if he was forced out of America.

Years ago, Marek had promised him a future with a pack he'd never have found in England. These days, fate wasn't set in stone, and Jono couldn't be sure the future Marek had seen wasn't changing.

3

PATRICK BANGED HIS WAY INTO TEMPEST SOMETIME AFTER 1800, phone clutched in one hand as it had been for most of the day ever since getting the call about the attacks. He hadn't been able to leave because he'd been working out of the SOA field office. The optics would look awful if the government discovered he'd turned his back on a case for personal reasons, despite those personal reasons making the news. Recusal couldn't happen because the government didn't know he was pack.

Needing to hide his ties to the preternatural community was becoming more and more of a significant problem.

The bar was way more crowded than it usually was on a Tuesday evening, but everyone got out of his way as soon as they realized he'd arrived. Patrick made a beeline for the stairs in the rear that led to the sublevel of the bar. He shoved his phone into his back pocket on the way down, not bothering with a silence ward. The bar was closed tonight to anyone who wasn't pack. Everyone drinking upstairs had come with their alphas.

The sublevel was opened up depending on the night and the crowd, or if there was a private event going on. Tonight, it was as packed as the main bar upstairs, with every alpha of the packs under their protection present for the meeting Jono had called. Tempest was technically neutral ground, but it was also the only public place big enough to hold the people who'd been summoned since he and Jono didn't have access to the legacy territory and buildings currently held by the other god pack.

Like upstairs, people shifted aside so Patrick had a clear way to the table someone had pulled away from the wall to the center of the floor. Without the crowd in the way, Patrick spotted Jono immediately. He didn't care about their audience when he finally made it to Jono's side, framing the other man's face with both hands. Patrick kissed him with a bruising intensity that didn't do anything to ease the knot of fear in his chest.

"I'm all right, love," Jono said when Patrick broke the kiss. Patrick was glad to see he looked it, but the tightness around his mouth spoke of choked-down fury.

"Not everyone else is," Patrick said, taking the empty seat to Jono's right. "*Fuck.* This was a coordinated attack."

"Aimed at the strongest packs under our protection. Two people are dead. One pack member each from the Monterossi pack and the Davenport pack," Sage said.

Her chair was between Marek and Emma, and Marek had his arm around her waist. Wade sat on the other side of Emma, even though technically he was too young to be allowed in the bar. With everything that had happened today, Patrick was fine with breaking the law to ensure Wade was safe. No one in their pack could afford to be alone right now.

Patrick grimaced, reaching for Jono's hand underneath the table. Jono's grip was warm and firm, his thumb dragging over the back of Patrick's hand. The press of his knee against Patrick's was a solid reminder that he was alive.

He'd been caught up at work with the missing artifact case when his phone had blown up from calls and texts from the alphas whose packs had been targeted. Then he'd gotten the update from

Sage about the attack on Jono, and Patrick had very nearly put his fist through the wall of his office. Being unable to leave to check on Jono had been a special kind of hell.

As co-leader of their pack, Patrick should've been there to help handle the aftermath of the attacks. His job as a federal agent tied his hands in ways that were becoming glaringly apparent as Estelle and Youssef stepped up their attacks on disputed pack territory.

Patrick looked around at all the faces turned their way. Amelia Davenport stood front and center, looking tired and angry. She'd approached Emma in their absence back in June, requesting protection. Jono had accepted her loyalty once they'd returned from Europe. Patrick hoped she wasn't second-guessing her support.

Amelia was professionally acquainted with Marek, Emma, and Leon, all of them working in the tech industry. She was a partner in a venture capitalist firm and married to a human federal judge. Her pack was out of Brooklyn, so large that when she chose their sphere of protection, the territory that came with her effectively gave them half of Brooklyn when paired with some of the other packs who'd already joined them.

It had been a body blow to Estelle and Youssef's pack. They'd let their displeasure be known in vicious skirmishes that Amelia's pack always won, sometimes with the aid of the Brooklyn Night Court.

It appeared their winning streak had ended.

"Your loss is all our loss," Patrick said, the saying one Sage had taught him months ago. It was one of many phrases Patrick had learned since they'd staked their claim on New York City. Pack law was archaic in some ways, but it's what had kept the werecreature community alive through the centuries in the face of human encroachment and discrimination.

Amelia nodded, jaw clenched tightly. Patrick was distantly glad he didn't have enhanced preternatural senses to smell the amount of anger that had to be choking the room, judging by everyone's faces.

"The attack came out of nowhere, which seems to be what happened with everyone else today," Amelia said.

"All the hunters carried demons in their souls," another person within the crowd said.

"What about the werecreatures who were present at the attacks?" Jono asked.

"The ones who attacked my pack didn't seem to carry demons in their souls," Amelia said.

The packs under their protection knew about the demonic threat that had infiltrated the London god pack. It was information Patrick and Jono couldn't afford to keep secret, not when it threatened every pack across the globe. Cressida's background as a hunter and willingness to accept a demon in her soul had wreaked havoc in the London god pack. The repercussions had spread beyond the United Kingdom, and they'd come home to the States with the expectation Estelle and Youssef would follow the same path, especially after their partnership with the Krossed Knights.

"Youssef followed me while I worked a case yesterday, and now this. Those assholes are getting bolder," Patrick said.

"What are we going to do about it?" Sage asked.

"They're testing our borders, looking for weak spots. They've lost half of New York City since the beginning of the year. They won't give up the rest without all-out war," Jono said.

"You think that's what this is? War at last?" Leon asked.

"It was always war. They're just finally bringing it into the streets."

"Then how do we win it?" Emma asked.

Her question was echoed by other voices in the crowd. Someone reached between Patrick and Jono to set a beer down in front of him. The sharp smell of Guinness hit his nose, and Patrick reached for the glass. He took a sip, mind spinning through all the options he and Jono had been discussing over the last couple of weeks. None them were easy, all of them were messy, and even with Fenrir secretly on their side, there was no guarantee Estelle and Youssef would back down. Not if they were making bargains with hunters and demons.

PIA Special Agent Spencer Bailey had exorcised Andras out of Cressida's soul in London. The Great Marquis of Hell was a demon allied with hunters, and hunters had no love for anyone who wasn't human. The hypocrisy would be laughable if their kill count wasn't so damnably high.

Considering the Krossed Knights had been working with Estelle and Youssef since February, Patrick wouldn't put it past them to convince their pack to accept demons into their souls. The pair were power-hungry enough to find the risks acceptable, and they had a track record of doing what was best for them above anything else. They'd made shitty bargains in the past with vampires and gods, after all. Demons almost seemed an afterthought.

When it came to a second presence riding a soul, they had their own ace in the hole, so to speak, and Patrick wondered if it was time to break it out. Fenrir was Jono's animal-god patron, having received the immortal's blessing years ago. Fenrir's presence was an approval Estelle and Youssef would never have, but it was one Jono couldn't afford to reveal in the years he'd lived in New York City.

Gods were fickle, but more than that, a pack of four against an entire city, even with a god's blessing, didn't guarantee they'd win the war. Jono had kept Fenrir a secret from everyone until last summer when the god revealed himself to Patrick. Sage and Wade had found out the truth in December, while Emma, Leon, and Marek were made aware of Fenrir back in February.

The revelations hadn't changed Jono's stance over the last year or so, simply because they didn't have the strength in numbers to take on Estelle and Youssef directly. Patrick took in the alphas surrounding them and wondered if the situation had changed enough that they had a fighting chance to take everything from Estelle and Youssef once and for all.

"The only way to win is to take them out completely. That's going to be a costly fight in terms of blood and territory," Jono said.

"What about our alliances?" Wade asked.

Jono shook his head. "Their assistance in maintaining our borders is helpful, but we need to be the ones to push Estelle and Youssef out. This is our fight."

"What about going the direct route and meeting them in the challenge ring?" Marek asked.

"I wouldn't trust any fight that happens in that place," Amelia said flatly.

Other people in the crowd echoed her statement. Patrick had never been to the challenge ring located beneath the god pack home in Hamilton Heights. The underground space was familiar to everyone else from the times all the alphas had been summoned to meetings. He'd seen the aftermath of fights held in other challenge rings to know they were bloody spaces. He agreed with Amelia though—no fight held in a space controlled by Estelle and Youssef could be handled fairly.

"I'm not sure how much help the fae will be able to provide right now. Tiarnán was summoned to Tír na nÓg today on an emergency basis. He's been our liaison for the fae, and I don't know when he'll return," Sage said.

Patrick shrugged. "His absence shouldn't affect the alliance. We—"

A loud explosion in the bar above cut him off, magic crashing against the wards embedded in Tempest's walls. They flashed fire bright for a split second, nearly blinding Patrick. Before the glow faded, Patrick was on his feet and racing for the stairs, Jono right on his heels. The crowd of alphas peeled away from his headlong rush forward, giving them both space.

Patrick took the stairs two at a time up to the main level, seeing patrons pressed against the wall and away from the front of the bar. Someone was dragging the limp body of the bar's doorman out of the line of fire. The smell of burning flesh hit his nose, and he hoped the bouncer was alive. He couldn't stop and check because hellfire was burning across the entrance to the bar with all the ferocity of magical napalm.

The very expensive wards Marek had paid to keep the bar intact against all manner of attacks were holding. How much longer was anyone's guess.

"Bloody *fuck*," Jono growled.

Patrick ripped his shields out from beneath his skin and expanded them to cover Jono. Together, they ran out of the bar, hellfire licking at his magic, the heat of it strong enough to make sweat form on his forehead even through his shields. Their feet hit the sidewalk in time to take another hellfire bomb head-on.

A man sat on a motorcycle, helmet on, a glass bottle held in one gloved hand, ugly hellfire burning in its depth. He threw it in their direction and didn't wait to see it land before driving off, weaving through traffic. Patrick tapped a ley line through the soulbond, siphoning external magic through Jono's soul and pouring it into a mageglobe already burning between his hands. He strengthened his shield, and the hellfire bomb exploded against that defensive barrier in a furious splatter of heat and magic.

Marek's Maserati, parked out front of the bar, took the brunt of the attack this time. Paint and metal melted from the heat as Patrick manipulated his magic to entrap the hellfire bomb. It took most of his concentration, but he trusted Jono to watch his six for the handful of seconds he needed to initiate containment. Patrick's mageglobe burned hot between his hands as he locked down the shield around the hellfire bomb.

"See if you can't catch that asshole," Patrick snarled.

Jono didn't need to be told twice. He ran off like lightning, preternatural speed aiding him. Patrick focused on the hellfire, sweat sliding down his face as he reinforced his shields. He hoped someone with an affinity for defensive magic would come with the first responders.

"Cops have been called," Sage said from behind him.

"Someone needs to take Wade home. He's underage. Emma can't afford to lose her liquor license."

"You mean Jono can't."

Tempest provided Jono with a job, as was required for his green card status. Patrick was certain that if Tempest closed, Marek would hire Jono into PreterWorld, but the paperwork would be hell to clear him with a new visa. In the midst of a civil war, they couldn't afford that kind of setback.

"Just make sure he's safe."

Sage nodded. "I'll send him home with an escort."

Wade didn't protest Patrick's order to get clear of the crime scene, although he looked like he wanted to. Sage stepped away while Patrick did his best to keep the hellfire contained, ugly smoke and sparking heat roiling against his magic. Shields weren't his strong suit, but he'd done this sort of defensive work before when backed into a corner while with the Mage Corps. He'd done it last year when he first came to New York, and that memory left a knot in his gut.

Back then, the hellfire bomb in his car had been cast by Hades. Patrick knew it wasn't Hades on that motorcycle, but whoever it had been had access to the same sort of power, which meant they had access to gods.

Patrick flexed his fingers, magic flickering at his fingertips as he sought to put out the hellfire bomb. Sirens screamed in the distance, the mixed sound that of the police and fire department. Patrick half turned, raising a shield between the building the bar was in and the hellfire licking at the structure. The second he shielded the hellfire stretched across the entrance, people started pouring out of Tempest, fleeing the scene.

"I sent Wade off with one of Emma's pack members. They'll

take him to our apartment," Sage said as she and Marek approached Patrick.

"That was my car," Marek said, sounding equal parts pissed off and scared.

"That was my *bar*," Emma growled as she popped up beside them.

Marek touched her elbow. "It's still standing."

A blur of motion down the street drew Patrick's attention. The subtle tug in the soulbond told him it was Jono, who skidded to a halt in front of him an eye blink later. His clothes were torn in places, blood smeared across one forearm, but Patrick couldn't see a wound. The furious expression on Jono's face promised murder.

"Who was it?" Patrick asked.

Jono's nostrils flared on an exhale, mouth twisting. "Nicholas. I got the bloody bastard off the motorcycle, but I couldn't hold him. He had a demon in his soul."

Patrick tried to ignore the way his heart beat faster. "It's London all over again."

Nicholas Kavanaugh was dire to the other god pack. Youssef didn't have a trace of hell in his aura yesterday, but it seemed the same couldn't be said for some of his pack members. It meant they'd have to counter demon-backed werewolves who weren't shy about collateral damage. Patrick realized they'd reached the point where they wouldn't be able to stay their hand any longer.

"We won't let New York turn into that mess," Jono said in a low, furious voice as the first police car turned the corner and sped down Avenue B.

4

THE SMELL OF HELLFIRE HUNG HEAVY IN THE AIR, LEAVING A BITTER aftertaste in the back of Jono's throat where he sat inside the bar. The Crime Scene Unit out of the PCB was currently processing the front of the bar and the street outside. Patrick was working with the FDNY to put the hellfire out with the help of a witch with an affinity for water magic. Marek's car was a complete and utter loss, but at least the bar had mostly withstood the attack.

"I paid half a million dollars for those wards. Worth every dollar," Marek said as he watched CSU work.

Jono grunted his agreement, arms crossed tightly over his chest. Police milled in and out of the bar, checking in with the people processing the scene. Jono and the others had already given their statements, but he knew their night wasn't over yet.

Leon was in the back room with the police, making copies of the security feed for that night. Emma and Sage were sitting beside Ronaldo on the floor near the stairs to the lower level. He'd been the one manning the door when the attack happened and had taken the brunt of the first hellfire bomb. He'd shifted to his wolf form to heal the burns, but even in wolf form he was wounded. It was taking multiple shifts in order to heal him, and he was exhausted. Sage had wisely taken a slew of pictures of Ronaldo's injuries in the beginning and had promised to email them to the detectives assigned the case as evidence.

Paramedics with the FDNY were waiting off to the side, asking Emma and Sage quiet questions about Ronaldo's physical state, but so far weren't interfering. Jono half thought they weren't getting closer because they didn't want to get infected with the werevirus, despite being masked and gloved up.

A tall figure stepped through the bar's entrance, Casale's familiar scent hitting Jono's nose. He was dressed in a suit rather than a uniform, the lingering hints of an evening meal drifting about him. Must've had a lot of garlic in the recipe.

"The PCB taking a statement from you twice in one day is not what I was expecting," Casale said as he approached.

"Not how I wanted to spend my evening either. Or my morning, for that matter," Jono said.

Casale came to a stop in front of where Jono leaned against the bar. Marek casually hiked himself up onto the closest barstool, making it clear he wasn't going anywhere. Casale's gaze flickered over to him, but he didn't try to get Marek to leave.

"My detectives tell me no one died."

Jono's lip curled. "Not for lack of effort on Estelle and Youssef's part."

"You'll need proof if you're going to go around accusing people of attempted murder."

"The hunters making a mess of New York since February aren't enough?"

"Considering there's a civil war happening within your community, there are two sides to blame. I warned you months ago about how badly this would go if you let it get this far."

Jono glared at Casale. "My pack and the ones under my protection aren't going to roll over and show throat at every hint of provocation. It's within our right to fight back."

"Is it worth the collateral damage to the city? To innocent citizens?"

"My side isn't the one who hired hunters. We aren't the ones throwing hellfire bombs at a packed bar. We aren't the ones making bargains with demons."

Casale's lips pressed into a grim line. "I know. But if you had hoped to keep this fight out of the media, that's not going to happen. The attack on you at Gucci this morning and the one tonight will make people question the underlying reason of *why* you're a target. Your background as a god pack alpha won't be overlooked."

"You're not telling me anything I don't know."

"Any chance Marek has seen something different?"

"If I had, I wouldn't even make the city pay for the cost of the vision," Marek said.

Casale glanced at him. "Is that a no?"

"In case you didn't notice, that's my very expensive Maserati that got fucking torched by a hellfire bomb. Estelle and Youssef don't know it yet, but I'm going to sue."

"Again, you're going to need proof. Give me something to work with here."

"Nicholas was the one on the motorcycle. I smelled him," Jono said.

Casale shook his head. "That's not good enough. The courts accept a lot of preternatural evidence, but scent isn't one of them."

"Then pull the fucking traffic camera feeds on him. I'm sure something will come up."

"We'll look into it." Casale sighed and rubbed at his forehead, frowning at them both. "Can you think of any reason the attacks against you would double in a day?"

"If I had a reason, I'd discuss them with an attorney first."

"How'd I know you'd say something like that?"

Jono inclined his head in Sage's direction. "I learned from the best."

"New York City can't afford a civil war between god packs."

"Bit late for that, innit?" Jono straightened up, letting his arms fall to his sides. "As I said, it's within my right to protect my territory. Are your people interrogating Estelle and Youssef the same way you're interrogating me?"

"We're aware of their pack's actions over the last few months."

Jono's lips curled. "But not their actions, specifically, is that it?"

Casale met his gaze with a steady intensity. "The only side I'm on is the city's. Consider this a friendly warning that the mayor knows what's been happening and isn't thrilled. We've been told to start cracking down."

"Are you only warning me?"

"You and Collins."

"I don't know what you're implying."

Casale shook his head, keeping his voice low. "Don't play dumb. It's a crap look on you. We both know his place in your pack. I've already warned him people are starting to question his presence with you every time something goes down. Tonight isn't going to stop people from thinking otherwise."

"It's a public bar. Everyone is welcome," Marek said.

"It's a bar that caters to the werecreature community."

"Nothing illegal about that."

"I'm not saying there is." Casale took a step back. "My detectives will pull your security feed, and we'll work on the traffic cameras. We'll be asking for witness statements of anyone we find on camera. Things will go quicker if you give us names."

Jono couldn't warn Casale off without good reason, and he didn't have one, not with hellfire bombs having been tossed at the bar. It was an opening salvo no one could ignore, even those whose identities as werecreatures were kept a closely guarded secret. But neither could he simply give up the privacy and anonymity so many of the alphas who had been there tonight tried to keep for themselves and their packs.

"We'll see," Jono said, unable to offer complete cooperation.

Casale jerked his head at the front of the bar. "The media is camped outside. You may want to get a ride home with someone else."

It was a subtle, pointed suggestion to not be seen walking away from the mess tonight with Patrick. For all that they were openly together within the werecreature community, their relationship was a secret from everyone else because it had to be. Jono knew that was going to change. When and how badly was anyone's guess.

"We're free to go?" Jono asked.

Casale nodded. "For now. We have your statements. We'll be in touch."

Casale left to deal with the mess outside. Jono pushed away from the bar and walked over to where Sage and Emma were trying to coax Ronaldo through another shift. He was in wolf form now, panting hard and whining softly in the back of his throat.

"We're going to take him home with us," Sage said.

Jono crouched in front of Ronaldo, reaching out to stroke a careful hand over the other man's still-healing head. "Need you to shift back to human, mate. We've some clothes for you to change into, but you can't walk out of here on four feet. Got too many cameras outside for that."

Two feet wasn't much better, but he'd be more maneuverable if he passed out in human form. Ronaldo whined again. Emma looked at Jono, the extra clothes taken from the employees' room resting over her thighs.

"You'll have to force the change," she said, shoulders slumped in defeat.

Jono sighed, not liking to use that power on someone so obviously wounded. God pack alphas were capable of calling packs to them or forcing werecreatures to change from one form to another. The call was rarely used these days, what with everyone having a mobile, but Jono's pack ties were far more extensive than they had been even six months ago.

Control wasn't something Jono cared to force onto someone else, but they had very few options here. Ronaldo needed to change forms, not only so he could leave, but so his wounds could continue to heal.

Jono gripped the thick scruff of Ronaldo's fur with gentle fingers. Ronaldo licked his teeth, staring at Jono without fear in his eyes or in his scent. It was that lack of fear that drove away the guilt Jono felt at imposing his will on someone else.

"*Change,*" Jono growled.

The command in his voice was one which Ronaldo could not ignore. It wasn't magic, but something more primal that pulled at the pack bonds tying Jono to the people under his protection. It forced Ronaldo to shift from wolf to human, body writhing as bone broke, skin split, and muscles realigned themselves.

The shift was slower due to exhaustion, but soon Ronaldo was lying on the floor between them, naked and shivering. Large swaths of his skin were pink like a bad sunburn, but nothing like the ugly, painful third-degree burns he'd been sporting until Sage and Emma started cycling him through shifts.

Ronaldo blinked at him tiredly, dry lips parting, but no words came out. Marek thrust a water bottle over Jono's shoulder, and he took it with a nod of thanks. Jono twisted off the cap before pressing the rim against Ronaldo's mouth.

"Small sips," Jono said.

Ronaldo obeyed, looking a little bleary-eyed. When he'd drunk all the water he could, Jono let Sage and Emma take over getting him dressed.

The female EMS stepped closer while her partner remained where he was. "Does he need medical attention?"

Jono shook his head. "He'll be all right."

His assertation was enough for them to leave, taking their medical kit and gurney with them. Jono stood, the slow burn of anger still simmering inside him.

Sage caught his eye as she and Emma helped Ronaldo to his feet. "You heard what Casale said about the media?"

"Yeah."

"Don't drive home with Patrick."

Jono scowled, his instinctual response being to argue that point, but Sage was their dire for a reason. "Fine. But Emma's car won't fit all of us."

"I'll get a police officer to drive me and Sage home. Emma and Leon can drop you off, Jono," Marek said.

Jono could only nod and agree to the decisions made on his behalf. He'd argue against it, but it wasn't worth the bloody headache involved.

Sage tucked a lock of hair behind her ear, meeting Jono's gaze. "Come to my firm tomorrow. This is something we need to discuss with the fae concerning the alliance. Tiarnán's partner can tell us what they can safely offer in terms of support."

"Will he be okay with someone else making decisions in his absence?" Jono asked.

"Yes. Deirdre always speaks for him when he isn't present."

He trusted Sage to provide accurate information for the safety and benefit of their pack. She'd never steered them wrong, and he knew she wouldn't start now.

"All right. Let's get everyone home safe."

———

JONO HEARD Patrick's heartbeat before he saw him. Getting up from the sofa, he padded over to the entrance of their flat on bare feet, hauling the door open before Patrick could fumble for his keys on the landing.

"You look absolutely knackered," Jono said.

Patrick made a face as he stepped inside, bringing with him the thick smell of hellfire and smoke that completely buried his own bitter scent. "I had to stay until the scene closed."

Dawn was a couple of hours away on a far too early Wednesday morning. Jono didn't want to see the sunrise. "Any problems getting home?"

"No. What about you?"

"No attacks."

"Two in one day is a few too many."

Jono waited until Patrick finished locking the door and strengthening the threshold before pulling him close. Jono wrapped his arms around Patrick, face tucked against the curve of the shorter man's shoulder and neck, breathing him in. The hellfire stench made his eyes water, but a couple of deep breaths helped him to make out Patrick's comforting scent. The bitterness Jono drew into his lungs had never bothered him.

"You need a shower," he mumbled against warm skin.

Patrick slid his fingers beneath the soft sleep shirt Jono had pulled on after he'd arrived home, the heat of them against the small of his back a comforting touch. "You don't."

"Could have another."

"Mm." Patrick sighed, pulling back. "Come on."

Jono followed him to the bathroom attached to their master bedroom. Jono set about turning on the water and getting it to the right temperature while Patrick removed his weapons and stripped out of his clothes. Jono shed his own sleeping clothes, stepping into the tub beneath the spray of hot water.

Patrick joined him seconds later, and Jono maneuvered them so Patrick stood beneath the spray. Jono reached for the soap, running it over Patrick's shoulders and down his back. They both had space to move around in, but not a lot, and Jono's elbow kept brushing against the shower curtain as he slowly washed the sweat and grime and lingering traces of hell off his lover's body.

The muscles of Patrick's back were knotted, and Jono took his time to work them out with hard presses of his fingers and thumbs. Soap eased the glide of his hands as he cleaned Patrick, steam from the hot water filling his lungs. The hellfire stench swirled down the drain until all Jono could smell was Patrick.

He dragged the tip of his nose up the curve of Patrick's spine as he rose to his feet, letting his lips linger over warm skin. Jono pressed a kiss to Patrick's shoulder, wrapping his arms around Patrick, hands skimming over smooth skin and the ridges of scar tissue. He stepped back, pulling Patrick with him, until the water beat against his scarred chest.

Patrick tipped his head back against Jono's shoulder, dark red hair plastered to his skull, lashes spikey from the water. Jono nuzzled his cheek, breathing him in. Patrick's mouth parted on a quiet gasp when Jono wrapped his hand around Patrick's cock, slowly stroking him. Water eased the motion, and Jono splayed his other hand over Patrick's stomach, holding him close. His own cock was nestled at the top of Patrick's arse, and he rolled his hips, grinding slowly against slick skin.

Patrick arched against the pressure and the touch, humming softly, eyes still closed. "Gonna have to clean me up again if you continue."

Jono kissed the corner of his mouth, rocking forward. "Travesty."

Patrick's laugh turned into a moan when Jono tightened his fingers and stroked him harder. The steam in the shower made every breath thick as he worked them both over with steady motion, aware that the water wouldn't stay hot for long but unwilling to move them out of the shower.

Holding Patrick in his arms and getting them both off would never grow old. The way Patrick responded—hitched breaths, fingers digging into Jono's skin, need and desire saturating the air around them—made Jono never want to let go.

It was easy to draw pleasure out of Patrick, whispering encouragement against the shell of his ear. Patrick came with a quiet moan, spilling over Jono's fingers as Jono ground against his arse, cock sliding over warm, wet skin. Jono wrung every last drop out of him before fitting both hands to Patrick's hips and taking one more step back.

The space gave him just enough room to dig his thumbs into the meat of Patrick's arse and spread him open. He slid the thick length of his cock into the crease, enjoying the sensation. He ground against Patrick for another minute until he came, sticky white ribbons spattering over Patrick's arse and back.

Jono kissed Patrick on the side of his neck before turning him around to kiss him on the mouth. The water was still warm, but only just, the lingering steam a heavy blanket in the air around them. Patrick kissed him back lazily, the water washing away the mess Jono had left behind, though it wouldn't ever erase the pack scent buried in his skin.

When they broke apart, Patrick let his forehead drop to Jono's shoulder, the water starting to finally cool. Jono ran his hand up and down Patrick's back a couple of times before gently putting distance between them.

"Come on. Let's finish up and go to bed," Jono said.

They didn't spend much more time in the shower, only long enough for Patrick to wash his hair. Jono turned off the water before they got out and dried off, pulling on sleeping pants for bed. The air conditioner was running, the coolness of the apartment a relief.

Jono picked up Patrick's tactical pistol and dagger still in its sheath from the dresser and brought them to Patrick's side of the bed. He set the dagger on top of the nightstand. Opening the drawer, he placed the pistol inside, fingers brushing against the old Greek coin that Patrick kept there. The broken-off piece of the Morrígan's staff was hidden inside a small iron box that was shoved in the back of the drawer, leaving enough space that the pistol still fit.

Jono closed the drawer and went to his side of the bed, getting under the covers and pulling Patrick close. He rested his chin on top of Patrick's head, holding him tight.

"We can't let this attack slide," Patrick said quietly.

Jono drew in a breath and let it out slowly. "I know."

Patrick's hand on his hip tightened, but he said nothing more. Jono closed his eyes, thoughts spinning, hoping for at least a couple of hours of sleep. He tried not to think how moments like this, lying in bed with each other, might be limited.

Deep in his mind, Fenrir stirred, the god's presence drifting through Jono's awareness. *This war was always inevitable.*

Jono knew that. It didn't make it any easier to accept.

5

Jono stared at the driver white-knuckling the steering wheel, fear a rancid smell filling up the car. "'Course you don't."

"That's rude," Wade said from the seat beside him, brown eyes narrowing as he glared at their driver.

Jono shook his head. "Leave off."

Even with his sunglasses on, some people still got a glimpse of Jono's eyes. The brightness labeled him as *other*, and Jono normally wouldn't care, except he didn't want to be late for his meeting with Sage's fae partners. Patrick had taken the Mustang to work today, and Jono had been on conference calls with all the pack alphas ever since they'd woken up.

Sage had dropped Wade off at the flat before heading to work. She'd arrived a couple of minutes before Patrick had left but hadn't come up. Jono only knew Wade had arrived when the nineteen-year-old had let himself into the flat and made a beeline for the fridge.

Jono had ordered them an Uber to take them downtown because it was quicker than the subway or trying to flag down a taxi. Apparently, they were taking the subway after all. Sighing, he got out of the vehicle. Wade climbed out after him, grumbling under his breath about arseholes all the while.

The door had barely shut before the driver sped off with a squeal of tires. Wade raised both middle fingers at the car as it disappeared down the street. "He was a rude asshole."

"He was scared," Jono said. He stepped back onto the sidewalk and started walking, not bothering to call another ride. It wasn't worth the hassle.

"He can be both."

Jono waved at Wade to follow him as he pulled out his mobile to text Sage. *Taking the subway in.*

Jono didn't get a response for half a block, half listening to Wade still muttering about how they should give the driver a one-star rating. When Jono finally did get her response, it came as a call rather than a text. Sage's name flashed over the screen, and he answered immediately. "We won't be late."

"Weren't the two of you getting a ride?" Sage asked.

"We were until our driver saw my eyes. He kicked us out of the car and canceled the pickup."

"The news is rife with werecreature stories right now, and none of them are positive. That's still a rude thing to do."

"See?" Wade interjected. "Even Sage thinks he was an asshole."

Jono rolled his eyes. "I wasn't going to have a row with the bloke when it's his car."

"I can send someone to pick you guys up," Sage said.

"We'll be fine."

"You'll be at risk."

"I understand that, but they've proven we're at risk no matter what we do. Hiding won't change that."

"I wasn't talking about hiding, but about being cautious."

"We'll be fine. You know why."

Sage ignored his subtle reminder about Fenrir. "Are you falling back on your do as I say, not as I do idiocy? Because we've discussed your stupidity in that area before."

Wade cackled loudly at that and smirked at Jono.

Jono shook his head. "That's more Patrick's state of being."

"You both hold the title of idiot when it comes to personal safety sometimes. Traveling outside right now isn't safe. I thought yesterday was enough of a reminder?"

"I'm aware of that, but I don't want to be late. We should be fine on the subway." Jono sidestepped a woman walking her dog, ignoring the way the dog growled at him. "If we keep arguing over this, Wade and I will be at the office by the time you end the call."

Sage sighed heavily. "Your names are on the security list to be let up. Text me as soon as you reach your stop downtown."

"The second the train stops."

Jono ended the call and tucked his mobile into his back pocket. Wade linked his hands behind his head as he walked, side-eyeing Jono. "Can we stop at a bodega on the way to the subway?"

"You're not supposed to eat in the subway," Jono reminded him.

"I'll finish the food before we get there."

It was a promise Jono knew Wade would have no trouble keeping. He shrugged. "All right."

Wade grinned widely and raised an arm to fist-pump the air. "Yes!"

"You act like I didn't make you breakfast."

"That was hours ago."

"Barely two."

"*Hours.*"

Jono snorted and quit arguing. There was no winning with Wade when it came to food.

He kept his senses dialed up as they walked, gaze skimming the area ahead of them. The walk to 34 Street-Penn Street Station was an easy one that Wednesday morning. The humidity was high already at half past ten in the morning, settling into another hot August day, but it didn't bother Jono or Wade.

Summer in New York City reminded him of the sweltering days growing up in London. Despite the heat, Jono had dressed in dark jeans and a white button-up with the sleeves rolled up to his elbows, sunglasses firmly on his nose. He wasn't one to show up to an important meeting with their allies in casual clothes if he could help it, no matter his job as a bartender. Wade, on the other hand, was dressed like a typical teenager.

Halfway to the subway station, they ducked into a bodega to pick up half a dozen egg and sausage sandwiches with cheese. Jono kept an eye on the people who entered the bodega and those meandering outside, while Wade practically vibrated in place as he waited for his order to come up, not paying attention to anything except his food. Once he had his bag of sandwiches, they started on their way again.

As promised, Wade finished all six of the sandwiches before they even made it to the subway. He brandished the empty paper bag at Jono, cheeks bulging as he rapidly chewed the last of his food.

"See?" he mumbled. "All done."

"You're ridiculous. Toss your rubbish in the bin and let's get below," Jono said.

Wade did as he was told before following Jono down into the subway. The morning commuter rush was over, and the ticketing level wasn't too crowded for a summer day. Jono tagged his MetroCard on the sensor pad to get through the turnstile, Wade following right behind him. They headed for the stairs that led to the C train platform, going at the pace of the small crowd.

Despite being underground, Jono kept his sunglasses on, scanning the area when they finally arrived on the platform. A discreet sniff brought with it the general stench of the subway—piss, garbage, sweat, and the metallic taste of old magic he only got when below.

The protective wards encasing the New York City subway were embedded in the tunnels and the tracks, lining the platform edges and walls with discreet power most people never looked twice at, if they could even see it at all. The magical anchors were invisible until activated by whatever they perceived as a threat.

Pickpockets never triggered them; neither did fights between mundane humans. Only when magic was slung about, or artifacts brought into the fray, did the wards wake up. The fringe of the veil could be found underground in places, and most of humanity had learned to guard against what lived in the shadows.

Wade fidgeted beside him on the platform, eyes glued to the screen of his mobile as he played a game. "Do I need to sit in with you during the meeting?"

"You aren't wandering downtown, if that's what you're hoping for," Jono said.

"What if Sage's office is out of Pop-Tarts?"

"Then you starve."

"That's cruel and unusual punishment."

"You know the rules. No running off on your own right now."

Wade scowled down at his game. "Ugh."

Jono ignored Wade's sulking, too busy keeping an eye on everyone else around them. He kept his guard up, not trusting the people scattered on the platform. Jono didn't smell anything out of the ordinary, but that didn't mean they were safe. Yesterday had proven Estelle and Youssef were now eschewing indirect, under the cover of darkness attacks in favor of direct hits targeted for maximum damage.

The C train rolled into the station with a rumbling engine and the squeal of brakes some ten minutes later. Faces of people inside the train flashed by as it came to a loud stop. The doors slid open, allowing passengers to exit and enter the cars. Jono and Wade stepped into a car, and he guided Wade toward the middle, sliding past other passengers who barely shifted out of their way.

"Excuse me," Jono muttered politely.

Wade elbowed people aside and ignored the dirty looks thrown at him. Jono despaired of him ever learning manners.

The benches in the train car were all filled, so they were relegated to standing, holding on to the overhead bar to help keep their balance. The train started up again with a rattle on the tracks, lurching forward. Jono swayed a little where he stood, scanning the train car, gaze flicking over faces. Nothing seemed or smelled out of the ordinary as the train headed downtown, but he didn't trust the sense of ordinariness. Wade kept his eyes glued to his mobile, playing his game with one hand.

The train car was almost too warm, even for Jono, though Wade was obviously fine. Almost every subway he'd ever ridden didn't have air-conditioning, but the stifling heat was manageable for short periods. With no delays, it wouldn't take long for them to get to their stop downtown.

The train rolled through two more stops, with people getting on and off, the shift in scents washing through the enclosed air. The busker who came on board at the last stop was very clearly fae going by scent, even if his glamour was that of a human. Jono had gotten better over the months at sniffing out fae due to their alliance.

Jono picked up hints of magic users and other people of the preternatural bent in the car they were on. Nothing worried him until they left the 14th Street Station and the shadows of the tunnel beyond the windows sparked with magic when they shouldn't.

Jono tightened his grip on the overhead bar, going tense as he stared into the dark, emergency lights occasionally streaking by. The smell of magic got sharper, tickling his nose. Few others seemed to notice the shift in the air—Wade, whose head snapped up, the fae busker, and a teenaged girl at the other end of the car. Everyone else was minding their own business, and all Jono wanted to do was get off the bloody train.

"Something feels weird," Wade said as he put away his mobile.

"Should've got a bloody ride," Jono said under his breath.

Someone slipped through the crowd to stand beside Jono, carrying with them the crackling taste of ozone that burned the back of Jono's throat when he breathed. Strange yellow eyes he'd seen only once a year ago stared back at him in a weathered face framed by two thick braids. The immortal's jeans were faded, and Jono couldn't make out the design on his T-shirt since it was hidden beneath a breastplate made out of white bone beads.

No one else on the train paid them any attention at all, though Jono wondered if humanity would ever recognize the gods who walked amongst them.

"It's a shame the spirits of my children don't get along," Áłtsé Hashké said, mustache twitching above his lips as he smiled.

Wade grabbed Jono's arm with tight fingers, but Jono held up his hand to ward off whatever the teen was going to yell about. "Shut it."

It didn't work.

"He smells like lightning!" Wade hissed.

"Well aware of that. Shut your gob." Jono kept his attention focused on the god. "What do you—"

The train lurched to a sudden halt, brakes squealing so loudly Jono had to dial down his hearing. The force of the stop pitched people out of their seats and onto the floor with no warning. People standing staggered about, trying to stay upright, while others fell on top of people sprawled on the dirty floor.

Jono's feet skidded over the floor as Wade clung to him, nearly taking them both down. Jono tightened his grip on the overhead bar to the point he dented the metal. They managed to stay upright through sheer stubbornness.

Áłtsé Hashké was unaffected, standing amidst shaken people with a calm expression on his face. Dozens of voices yelled out in confusion as people picked themselves up from the floor, looking around for answers that weren't forthcoming.

"What the fuck? Is this your doing?" Jono growled.

Áłtsé Hashké shook his head. "No. I came to warn you."

Jono could feel Fenrir waking up in the back of his mind, clawing at the deepest edges of his soul. He ground his teeth against the sharp tug on his awareness that he knew could easily swallow him whole.

"What's going on?"

Áłtsé Hashké didn't speak. The god merely turned his head to the side, and Jono followed his gaze. Dull light burned beyond the train windows, tracing sigils Jono couldn't understand. Lines of magic flared up in the dark, sputtering in a way he didn't like.

"Are those the protective wards?" Jono asked.

"That can't be good, right?" Wade asked, refusing to let go of Jono.

"Hey, what's going on out there?" someone called out from the other end of the car.

More and more people were looking out of the windows and pointing at the magic peeling away from the subway tunnel walls. Gray mist floated past the windows, sending a chill down Jono's spine.

"Are the wards breaking?" Jono asked, heart rate picking up.

"The veil grows thin," Áłtsé Hashké warned.

Jono breathed harshly, and on the second inhale he got a whiff of sulfur that made him want to gag.

Áłtsé Hashké looked Jono in the eye, but it wasn't Jono the god spoke to when he opened his mouth. "I'll keep watch on the veil. Stay hidden, cousin."

"What do you mean—"

Jono broke off when the train lurched again, as if someone had shoved it. The lights overhead flickered in a way he didn't like. A high-pitched sound rent the air, one that made Jono's teeth ache. Metal screeched as it twisted and broke somewhere near the front. The entire train *shuddered,* and the lights went out completely, plunging them into darkness.

People screamed and scrambled toward the emergency windows, trying to get them open. Flashes of light from mobiles came and went as people panicked. Outside the train, the glow of the protective wards was dying out as the sigils disintegrated off the walls. Jono knew enough about magic these days that a breach in the protective wards lining the subway could only end badly.

Jono ripped off his sunglasses and tossed them aside. "We need to get off the train."

"Don't need to tell me twice," Wade said, his brown eyes glinting gold in the dim lighting coming off people's mobiles.

The train lurched again, sliding down the tracks in a way that almost made Jono lose his footing. People screamed—not just in their car, but in all the others, the sound echoing back to him. Some of the passengers lost their balance as they tried to climb out, falling out of the train into the dark. Since it was still capable of moving, Jono hoped no one lost any limbs.

Witchlights flickered into being in their car, cast by a teenager whose wide eyes looked like dark holes in her face. The extra light allowed everyone to panic more now that they could see. Jono swore under his breath as passengers fought each other to climb out of the broken windows first, heedless of the jagged pieces of glass sticking out of bent frames. No one seemed to realize that leaving the train didn't mean they were immediately safe.

Whatever had slipped through the veil and broken the protective wards wasn't going to stay confined to the subway train.

Jono looked around, but he didn't see Áłtsé Hashké anywhere, the god having slipped away in the panic and darkness. Fenrir bit at the edges of his thoughts, but Jono ignored the god. Passengers struggled to safely exit the train, freezing in fear every time the train moved along the tracks as metal crunched farther down the train. The sound was getting worrisomely closer.

Wade yanked on Jono's arm. "Are we leaving? Because it sounds like when I crunch a soda can, and I don't want to be in the middle of that."

"Yeah. We're leaving."

Jono headed for the crumpled sliding doors, using his preternatural strength to rip them apart. The teenager who had cast the witchlights scrambled out of the train through the doors rather than an emergency window, taking most of the illumination with her. Jono helped a middle-aged woman out the same exit and would've followed, but the sudden eruption of cold fog behind them had Jono twisting around, putting himself between the threat and Wade.

"Oh man," Wade moaned. "You guys really need to teach me how to drive after this."

Jono ignored him, eyes on the new arrivals. Fog drifted away from Zachary Myers' tattooed and glowing hands as the Dominion Sect mage stepped through the veil into the damaged car with a trio of hunters and half a dozen god pack members led by Nicholas. The rotten stench of sulfur hit Jono's nose, burning his lungs. The blackness of the Krossed Knights' and god pack werecreatures' eyes was proof enough of the demons they carried in their souls.

Jono didn't smell any immortals traveling with the lot, which told him it was probably the demons that had banded together to rip open the veil. That wasn't a comforting thought. He knew from Patrick and his own experience that crossing the veil took a lot of power and wasn't easily done.

"Maybe we should run?" Wade asked, one hand slipping into Jono's pockets to nick his mobile and keys.

"You won't get far if you try," Zachary said.

Jono's attention zeroed in on the hunter standing to Zachary's right. He'd seen the man back in February when the hunter had exited Estelle's SUV during her ill-fated attempt to pressure Jono and his pack at Tempest after they'd returned from Chicago. The hunter was tall, ruddy face washed out by the glow from Zachary's magic. The light couldn't hide the scar that bisected his brown eyes over his nose, nor the blackened lines that traced the veins in his face.

He smelled familiar—like Cressida had back in London when she'd been trapped in Spencer's magic as the mage sought to exorcise a Great Marquis of Hell from her soul.

Oh, bloody fuck.

No wonder Zachary and the others were able to travel through the veil. They had help from a high-ranking demon. Jono supposed it had been too much to hope that Andras had fucked off somewhere else that wasn't here after the mess in London.

Red-black magic crawled over the tattoos on Zachary's palms, cuts splitting open over the ink. Blood trickled out over his palms and down his wrists, dripping to the damaged floor of the train. The runes tattooed on his skull glowed with the same colored magic, but those ones didn't bleed.

Jono yanked on the soulbond, flooding it with anger to warn Patrick. Neither he nor Wade had any magic between them, though Wade was certainly immune to most of it. Right now, his suggestion about running was the only route they had, even if Jono didn't like it. But running would keep them alive, and that was all that mattered.

"Could've asked for a meeting rather than ruin everyone's commute," Jono said, bracing himself for the fight he knew was coming.

"Where's the fun in that?" Zachary asked.

Jono couldn't shift faster than a mage could cast magic. He *knew* that.

He still tried.

Jono shifted in the face of a maelstrom of magic that never reached him. Zachary's attack spell crashed against a shield that smelled curiously of the fae, all bright, woodsy notes that were out of place in the subway. The force of the magic was directed elsewhere, blowing through the walls, floor, and roof of the train car as if they were nothing. Metal shattered as the train car jerked apart, splitting in half.

Jono couldn't look to see who had come to their aid as his body twisted and broke from one form to the next. Agony lit up his nerves for a second before the pain abruptly disappeared. He lost his clothes in the shift, but better fabric than his life. Fur pushed through muscle as bone reset itself. When Jono finally settled on all four feet less than a minute later, he craned his head around to see who had cast the shield.

The fae busker from the last stop was leaning into the train through a broken window, one arm outstretched, magic twisted around his arm and hand like tiny rivulets of power. He'd shed his glamour, and an impossibly beautiful face looked back at them. He could've run, but he hadn't. Jono would be forever thankful for his pack's alliance with the fae.

"I can't hold them off forever," the fae warned, hand shaking.

Wade tugged on Jono's fur, his fear sharp in Jono's nose. "Let's get out of here."

Fighting in an enclosed space wouldn't give them space to maneuver, but taking the fight out onto the tracks would put everyone else at risk. They'd have an escape route though, so long as Áłtsé Hashké stitched the veil closed so nothing else could come through behind the broken protective wards.

That still left Jono with Wade, who couldn't shift mass this far below ground, and a fae whose magic would always be weakened because of iron, facing off against demons, werecreatures, and a mercenary mage.

Let me out, Fenrir snarled through his mind.

Áłtsé Hashké's warning rang in Jono's head, and he hesitated as he swung his head back around to stare through the shield at the enemy arrayed before them.

If the Dominion Sect had allied itself with the other god pack, there was a good chance Estelle and Youssef already knew about Fenrir because of Ethan. It would explain the uptick in attacks against Jono's god pack. Animal-god patrons rarely gave blessings in modern times. Carrying Fenrir in his soul was proof of his claim to territory Estelle and Youssef couldn't afford to let be known publicly within the packs.

But any bargain those two had made with the Dominion Sect would put them at a disadvantage. Information about Fenrir could be something Ethan would keep close to his chest to undermine them.

As for Andras? It was fifty-fifty if the demon recognized Fenrir in Jono's soul. The Great Marquis of Hell had been far too distracted by Spencer trying to exorcise him back in London to take much notice of anything else happening in that fight.

All of which meant Jono couldn't give up Fenrir if it meant there was a chance, however slim, that the god could be used against Estelle and Youssef later on.

Wade yanked on Jono's fur again, actually capable of moving him. "Let's *go!*"

"Running won't save you," Zachary said as he conjured up a mageglobe.

Zachary's next attack spell was a strike one, the raw, brutal power behind it strong enough to break through the fae busker's shield. The fae screamed in pain as his magic shattered, but the attack never got the chance to do any further damage.

Wade opened his mouth and *roared*, spitting dragon fire over Jono's head at the spell, breaking up the magic. The sound echoed ferociously all around them as the protective wards lining the subway tunnel flared in warning. The air became heavier, fraught with defensive power that ate away at Zachary's next attack.

Nicholas and the other god pack werecreatures lunged forward, dark blurs in the fading light of dragon fire. Jono shook free of Wade's grip and met their charge with one of his own, not holding back. In the damaged, tight space of the subway car, Jono tore into the werecreatures with a brutal swiftness that sent blood and pieces of flesh flying through the air.

He took his own hits, but the pain was negligible. Jono was larger than the other werecreatures, driven by fury, with an immortal clawing at his soul and urging him on. Even with demons riding their souls, the others only had so much space to maneuver in and had to contend with Wade as well.

More dragon fire erupted around them, singeing Jono's fur and outright engulfing one werecreature. The agonized howl he let out was followed by the flash of negative light as the demon left its host. The werecreature slid into the ragged gap between the two broken sides of the train car, a mass of glistening red and singed black skin bleeding all over the place.

Wade breathed fire again, forcing Zachary and the hunters onto the defensive. The other werecreatures regrouped, dodging the flame aimed their way as they targeted Jono once again. Despite leading the charge, Nicholas and whatever demon rode his soul pulled back at the last second, letting the others get within reach of Jono's claws first. Jono went for their throats, twisting around smaller bodies to tear into flesh. Hot blood splashed over his tongue, coating his teeth, as Jono left bodies in his wake.

Those demons that rode werecreatures' souls escaped with explosive speed before their hosts died, the sound of thunder heralded by no lightning echoing in the subway. Jono snarled a warning at Zachary, Nicholas, and the remaining hunters, their group's numbers halved in a few minutes' worth of wrath.

The werecreatures' deaths could be grudgingly allowed by law, but killing a possessed man was still considered murder in many states. The subway was no one's territory, and self-defense some-times wasn't enough of a legal shield. Despite the legal risk he might have opened himself up to, Jono wasn't thinking much about the law as he focused on Andras, the Great Marquis of Hell staring out of the hunter's eyes.

"Did you think I wouldn't find you and ruin you?" Andras asked through the hunter's mouth.

Jono couldn't speak, not in his current form, so Wade did the talking for him.

"Big words for an ugly-ass meat suit I can crispify in two seconds," Wade said right before he let loose an explosion of dragon fire so hot it melted metal.

Zachary raised a shield between their two sides that buckled beneath the vicious heat. Jono stepped forward, ignoring the way the subway train shifted beneath his feet. As the flames faded, he nearly got shot in the face by a barrage of silver-plated, aconite-dipped crossbow bolts.

The threat disappeared in midair, turning into an explosion of butterflies as Áłtsé Hashké appeared in the space between the broken halves of the subway train.

"You would be wise not to send my children to their slaughter," Áłtsé Hashké said, staring at Andras.

The hunter's mouth twisted into a mocking smile, but Andras didn't reload the crossbow. "Your children are only good for dying. You chose the wrong side."

Áłtsé Hashké didn't rise to the bait, an unmovable force standing between Jono and Wade, and those who allied themselves with the hells.

Gray fog twisted around Zachary and the others who remained, the vastness of the veil between worlds ripping open with obvious effort. Jono could see how it cost Andras to tear through the veil while surrounded by the subway's protective wards. The demon was still strong enough to slip away, dragging his group's survivors through the veil.

The only light in the dark came from the fading brightness of the protective wards and the fire in Áłtsé Hashké's eerie yellow eyes when the god turned to look at them. "That one will keep coming."

Jono flexed his claws and lashed his tail, before licking blood off his teeth. He couldn't smell any more sulfur, nothing but magic and the sickly sweet scent of fear that permeated the subway tunnel.

He shifted back to human form, body breaking apart until he crouched precariously at the edge of the magically ripped in half train car on two feet instead of four. Even Jono's enhanced vision made it difficult to see in the dark. Wade reached out to steady him with one hand, bringing the scent of fire with him as he coughed to clear his lungs.

"Can we go now?" Wade asked plaintively.

"Yeah," Jono promised.

Áłtsé Hashké's yellow eyes disappeared, as did the hint of ozone on the air. Jono didn't know where the god had gone, but he didn't have time to wonder about Áłtsé Hashké's interference.

They scrambled out of the train car as quickly and safely as they could. Jono's bare feet hit the cold, dirty wooden slats of the tracks and the broken glass scattered everywhere. He winced at the pain but kept walking despite the debris that cut into the bottom of his feet.

Wade blew out a thin finger of flame, providing some light in the dark. It was enough to see the fae busker sprawled in the narrow space between the train and the side of the tunnel, one arm flung over the track itself. The train was no longer lurching on the rails while being crushed by magic, but Jono didn't want to risk the fae getting his arm cut off. He lifted the unconscious fae onto his shoulders in a fireman's carry.

It left little room to maneuver in the tight space, but Jono kept walking, ignoring the pain that radiated up to his knees with every step he took as Wade led the way forward. Some of the train cars had jumped the tracks from the force of the stop, making him worry about the structural integrity of the subway itself and the buildings above.

The cars lay at odd angles, some blocking the way, with clusters of panicked people crying because they had no way to get out. The group they'd come upon was visible because someone had cast witchlights. Jono scanned the area before handing the fae busker over to Wade with a grunt.

"Keep ahold of him," Jono said.

Wade hefted the fae onto one shoulder as if he weighed nothing. "What are you going to do?"

"Find us a way out."

"What about when the police get here? What do we tell them?"

"Tell them you ran for cover and didn't see anything."

It was a lie, but one they had to stick with. People didn't believe in gods anymore, and Wade's status as a dragon wasn't something the police as a whole needed to know about. His part of the fight in Paris was still making the rounds on social media in recorded videos, but his identity had been something Patrick had fiercely fought to keep out of the public domain.

Jono approached the crowd, and a couple of people shrieked at his appearance. Jono couldn't change the fact that he was naked and covered in blood, and he was too tired to try to smile to ease their fear.

"Give me some space to work. I'm going to move the train car," Jono said, raising his voice.

People stepped aside, getting out of his way. The teenage witch stayed up front, increasing the number of witchlights that hovered in the air. She stared at him determinedly, face washed out beneath the shine of her magic.

"Let me know if you need more light," she said in a voice that shook only a little.

"Thanks, love," Jono said.

The train car blocking their way sat at an angle across the tracks. It had been forcibly uncoupled from the car behind it, which had crashed into the one currently in the way. Jono could smell blood emanating from both cars, and he knew not everyone had escaped alive.

He couldn't tell if the subway tunnel itself had been damaged or not, but staying stuck wasn't an option. Approaching the train, Jono pressed his hands against the side of the car and readied himself.

Fenrir sank claws into his soul and mind, growling low enough Jono thought he could feel the vibration in his bones. *You should have let me loose.*

I'll let you loose on Estelle and Youssef when the time is right. For now, stop being a twat and lend me your strength.

Tossing a car was one thing. Moving a subway car or two was

something else entirely. Even with preternatural strength, that would be difficult. Gods were different though, and Fenrir lent Jono the strength to shove the two train cars aside far enough to make room for the trapped passengers to pass through. Sparks flew as the train scraped over metal tracks, but they faded in seconds.

Jono looked over his shoulder at the mass of scared faces staring back at him. "Come on. Let's get out of here."

Everyone surged forward, desperate for safety after the horror they'd survived.

6

JONO PICKED AT THE SET OF SCRUBS HE'D BEEN GIVEN BY AN EMS crew in the subway, the stiff fabric itching his skin. He flexed his bare toes against the cold floor of Interview Room 1 at the PCB where he'd been sitting for hours, wanting desperately to leave.

The group of passengers he and Wade had escorted through the tunnel had been intercepted by police and other first responders. Most of the passengers had been allowed to leave with their hands over their heads after the first frantic minutes. Jono, however, had been treated like a threat because of the state he'd been in—naked, bloody, and very obviously a werecreature.

Wade had tried to warn them off, as had the teenaged witch, but their protests had fallen on deaf ears. Jono had gone to his knees, hands over his head, staring down drawn weapons as the police approached. He'd been handcuffed and hauled out of the subway tunnel behind everyone else.

Only when they made it to the shutdown West 4 Street/Washington Square/6 Avenue Station did his situation change. That station had been evacuated and turned into a staging and triage area for first responders. By the time they exited the tunnel, police from the PCB had made it onsite, and Jono was remanded into their custody. Due to the nature and location of the attack, Casale had shown up on the scene to oversee it. The moment he'd caught sight of Jono, things had gotten slightly more comfortable, but not easier.

The plastic cuffs had been cut off, and someone had found him an emergency foil blanket to wrap around his waist. His initial statement was taken on the platform, but he hadn't been allowed to leave. Jono had lost track of Wade in the aftermath, and he hadn't seen him since. Wade had Jono's mobile and keys, so there was no way for him to contact anyone except through a PCB line, which limited what he could speak about. Worry gnawed at his gut as badly as hunger.

Casale had ordered Jono taken back to PCB headquarters for a more in-depth interview. He'd been ensconced in the interview room under the watchful eyes of the police behind the two-way window since he arrived. Someone had brought him water but no food, and Jono's stomach rumbled loudly. He'd been allowed to ring one person, and he'd chosen Sage at the time so there wasn't a record of Patrick's number for the PCB.

"I'm not a criminal lawyer, but we're in good standing with several top-tier law firms here in Manhattan where we've done referrals. I'm working on getting you representation," Sage had told him.

He'd known she couldn't represent him; her specialization was civil litigation and pack law. Not to mention, the conflicts of interest were huge. "Cheers."

So far that promised lawyer hadn't arrived, and Jono was honestly ready to walk out of the PCB and damn the consequences.

The door to the interview room opened, and Jono watched Casale come inside. He looked exhausted, the crisp white shirt of his uniform dusty from overseeing the crime scene in the subway tunnel. He carried two bottles of water in his hands, one of which he set in front of Jono.

"Am I being detained?" Jono asked.

Casale sat in the chair across the small table from him. "At this time? No. Someone should have already told you that. The subway train was derailed by magic, which you don't have because of the werevirus."

"I gave you my statement at the scene. Why wasn't that enough?"

"A statement which proves you were probably the catalyst for the attack. After the attacks yesterday and the one today, a lot of people have questions."

"I told you yesterday Estelle and Youssef are behind the attacks. They've *been* the problem for months now. You lot haven't done anything about it."

"Our investigation is still ongoing."

Jono shoved his chair away from the table, more than ready to leave. "I invoked my right to a lawyer, but since I'm not being detained, I'm leaving."

Casale steepled his fingers together over the table, not taking his eyes off Jono. "We asked you to stay for further clarification. You seemed willing enough earlier to do so."

"That was before I had to wait over five hours for someone to show their bloody face in this room."

"The entire subway system has been shut down for the next twenty-four hours. The protective wards were damaged in the section where the crash happened, which is going to require a lot of money and magic to fix them. The streets are gridlocked at the moment, people are in a panic, and the fact that a god pack civil war is the reason behind the attack is not going over well with the public at all. So, yes, you can leave. But that won't help your case any."

Jono stayed put, jaw twitching. "I didn't know Estelle and

Youssef would send their dire and their contracted hunters after me, or that they were working with the Dominion Sect."

"The SOA was notified of that portion of your statement. The Dominion Sect is federal jurisdiction, and the SOA assigned a special agent to work the case with my department."

Jono wondered if Patrick had been assigned, and if so, why he wasn't at the station. "Good for them."

Casale reached for his bottle of water and unscrewed the cap. "Do you have any idea why the Dominion Sect would partner with the New York City god pack?"

"They haven't partnered with the New York City god pack. They've partnered with interlopers," Jono stated flatly.

Casale sipped at his water before setting it aside. "Your statement was bare-bones, Jonothon."

"I explained what happened."

"I think there's more to these acts than you're letting on. It would—"

The door suddenly opened, a detective Jono didn't recognize coming inside with an apologetic look on his face. "Sorry, Chief."

Casale half turned in his chair as a tall, stately Black woman strode into the interview room behind the detective. The navy pantsuit she wore was precisely tailored, and her high heels added even more inches to her height. Her thick, natural curls framed her head like a dark halo. A delicate strand of pearls was draped around her throat, and a square-cut diamond ring sat firmly in front of a plain gold wedding band on her left ring finger.

She could've been in her thirties or forties—it was difficult for Jono to discern her age by the flawlessness of her medium-dark skin. She carried herself with a confidence that told him in no uncertain terms he wouldn't want to be on opposite sides of her.

"Chief Casale," the woman said in a voice that could've iced over a car parked on the street on the hottest summer day. "That will be enough talking with my client."

"Danai," Casale said, sounding mildly displeased. "It's been what? A month since you've graced our department with your presence?"

"If your officers would do their jobs without needing me to file civil rights cases against the NYPD as a whole, then perhaps you wouldn't see me walking through your doors on a regular basis." Her dark brown eyes flicked away from Casale, catching Jono's gaze with laser-like intensity. "Jonothon de Vere, I'm Danai Belvedere of Belvedere & Elliot, your counsel of record."

He'd been friends with Sage long enough to know that a name partner from a law firm taking on a case was a big deal, even if he didn't recognize the woman's firm at all. "Lovely to meet you."

Danai's gaze raked over his body, lingering for a second longer on his bare feet. "I see the PCB didn't adequately clothe you."

"The EMS at the scene—" Casale said.

"I was making a statement, not talking to you, Chief Casale. It's my understanding that my client isn't being detained. If that fact has changed since my arrival in this room, please tell me. If not, we'll be leaving."

Jono could smell Casale's annoyance, but none of it seeped into the expression on his face. "He's not being detained, but we weren't finished taking his statement."

"You can call my office tomorrow to inquire about finding time in my schedule for that." Danai raised an eyebrow at Jono, and he rather felt like when he was a lad and getting in trouble with his mum in that moment. "Let's get you home, Jonothon."

"It's Jono," he said, getting to his feet.

She graced him with a smile that was kinder than the steel in her voice. "Jono."

He went to follow her out of the interview room, pausing at the doorway to look back at Casale. "My pack isn't a threat and isn't the problem. You know who is."

Casale said nothing to that warning. Jono hoped the months of reports of pack fights instigated by Estelle and Youssef, the hunters who hadn't left the five boroughs, and the arrival of the

Dominion Sect would be enough for the PCB to finally go after the ones responsible. The subway attack was a strike at the heart of New York City, and Jono refused to let his pack be painted as the guilty party for it.

"The media is out front but cordoned off down the block due to the wards on the PCB's building having been activated. You will be on television. Questions will be shouted from a distance. Do not engage with the press," Danai said as she led him down the short hallway.

"Wasn't going to," Jono told her.

"Your home address has been leaked. You have a media presence near your apartment building. The gargoyles are keeping everyone at bay so far, but you'll want to keep your curtains drawn and be wary of anyone buzzing your call box asking for access or announcing deliveries."

Jono's stomach clenched, and not from hunger this time. "Bloody hell."

Danai seemed to know her way around the PCB well enough not to need an escort. She led him to the lift bank, and they waited for one to arrive. Jono wanted desperately to ask about Patrick, but he wasn't going to say his lover's name where the police could overhear it. Sage would smack him if she knew he broke attorney-client privilege by speaking about things he shouldn't in public.

Jono followed Danai into the lift when it finally arrived, and then through the secured door that led to the PCB's lobby after they took it down. It was late, but the cement on the sidewalk outside the building was still warm under his bare feet. As Danai had warned, the media was clustered down the sidewalk at the property edge of the PCB building, watched over by police. Cameras were pointed in their direction, and as soon as they appeared, journalists started shouting questions.

"Ignore them," Danai reminded him.

Jono nodded and kept his gob shut. A black Escalade was parked right out front, hazard lights on, tinted windows making

Jono strain to see who was inside. He could hear Sage's heartbeat, and the familiar sound was enough to fractionally loosen his shoulders.

Danai held the back passenger door open, and Jono climbed inside to sit beside Sage on the middle bench. She immediately wrapped her arms around him in a tight hug, face tucked against his neck as she breathed in deep.

Jono ran a hand up and down her back. "I'm all right."

"They tried to crush you in a subway train. Forty-three people are dead, twice as many are injured, and our pack is trending on social media, but not in a good way," Sage muttered.

Danai climbed into the driver's seat and closed the door. "It's going to be a long drive home, but that will give us some time to discuss the situation at hand."

"Casale said traffic was bad," Jono said.

"Bad is a horrific understatement. The MTA is running every bus at their disposal, but that's not enough to replace the reach of the subway system. It's going to take at least an hour to get you home, if we're lucky."

Jono's stomach growled in protest. Sage pulled away and reached for the reusable bag at her feet. She pulled out two deli sandwiches wrapped in soggy paper and handed both to him. "I have more, but start with this."

Jono gratefully took the food and unwrapped the first sandwich as Danai drove off. The street they were on was cleared for police access, but they met gridlock half a block away. The one upside was that it would hopefully make it harder for the media to follow them. Then he remembered the press knew where his flat was.

"Where's Patrick?" he asked around a mouthful of food.

"At your apartment with Wade. He was assigned with other SOA special agents to work the subway scene because of the damage to the protective wards."

"Is he taking lead on the case?"

Sage shook her head. "No. Patrick said Henry is handling it directly because of the Dominion Sect's interference and the target. He's home right now because we all need to be present for the meeting with Danai."

Jono glanced at the older woman. "Doesn't that make a mess of confidentiality?"

"I'm representing your pack as a whole and all of you individually," Danai said, looking back at him in the rearview mirror since they were stopped several cars back from an intersection.

"I'm not sure if Patrick should be included."

Sage frowned at him. "He's pack."

"He's also an SOA special agent. We risk his job if he's named in any sort of defense."

"It's a little late for that," Danai said, a touch caustically. "He's been part of your pack for over a year now, and you can't simply erase that fact or his actions. You can't afford to be blindsided when his position is revealed. You can only hope it's revealed on your terms."

Jono hated that she was right, only because it stripped away what privacy they'd struggled to keep since forming their pack. He knew being god pack meant they would be front and center to deal with the public, but so far Jono had been the face of that. Patrick had stayed working behind the scenes, but it seemed that thin separation was no longer feasible.

Sage passed him a third sandwich, a tiny, tired smile curving her mouth. "Eat. We'll talk about this at home."

Jono ate, because there was little else they could do in the unholy mess that was Manhattan traffic when the entire subway system was out of commission. It took an hour and a half for them to get from Downtown to Chelsea, and another thirty minutes searching desperately for parking. They ended up three blocks away from the apartment building, which proved to be a problem as they walked home.

Jono stood out in his borrowed scrubs amidst everyone else

around them. Walking barefoot on New York sidewalks ensured the first thing Jono would do when he got home was shower. At first he thought it was his appearance that caused people to do a double take, but then he realized they were staring at his eyes, and he remembered what Casale had said about the story the media was running with.

A god pack civil war, and he was the only god pack alpha werewolf in the entire city with wolf-bright blue eyes.

Sage lengthened her stride to put herself on his right, glaring at anyone who looked at Jono with clear recognition on their faces. When they finally reached their corner and turned down their street, Danai swore heatedly under her breath. It only took a second for Jono to see what had caused her irritation.

Hunkered down near the brownstone that held his flat was a dense group of journalists and reporters, cameras pointed at the entrance. Some of the gargoyles clung to the side of the building around the door, their stone-dry screeches a warning aimed at the media.

"Don't say a single word," Danai warned him.

"Wasn't going to," Jono muttered.

Sage dug out her set of keys to the flat, and she clutched them so tightly her knuckles went white. They were halfway down the block when the media finally caught sight of them, and from there it was an absolute scrum. Reporters ran to meet them, encircling them as they walked, thrusting microphones and mobiles set to record in their faces, shouting questions at him.

"Were you responsible for what happened in the subway?"

"How can you justify the attacks on innocent people?

"Are any other werecreatures coming from England?"

The questions came loud and furious, to which Danai calmly replied, "My client has no comment."

Jono pressed his lips together and stared straight ahead, trying not to let any of his annoyance or anger show on his face. When they finally broke through the small crowd, he saw the remaining half of the gargoyles had positioned themselves on the stoop to guard the way in from trespassers, snapping stone teeth at anyone who got too close. The gargoyles let them pass, and Jono spared a brief moment to pat one on the head.

They climbed the steps, and Sage let them into the building. Danai made sure to firmly shut the door behind her until it locked before they trudged up five flights of stairs. The door to his flat was already opened when they turned the landing on the floor below.

Patrick stood in the entrance, expression blank, but the worry in his green eyes came through clear enough. His gaze raked over Jono's body, lingering on his bare feet. "You need a shower."

"I know," Jono sighed.

He had dried blood stuck to his body beneath the scrubs, making his skin itch. He smelled like everything that had happened in the subway, and Jono wanted to wash it all off.

"We can wait until you've showered before we begin," Danai said once they were all safe inside the flat and behind the threshold.

Patrick traced a sigil over the front door, casting a silence ward. The rush of static in Jono's ears quieted the world beyond the flat. Wade sat on the sofa covered in crumbs and the detritus of what looked like six Pop-Tart boxes.

Patrick followed Jono's gaze. "Wade's been stress eating."

"*You* almost get crushed like a soda can where the train you're in is the can and tell me how you feel afterwards," Wade retorted, opening another silvery foil packet.

"Clean up your mess," Jono said on his way to the bathroom.

Jono grabbed clean clothes out of the dresser and spent less than five minutes beneath the spray of hot water. He was looking to get clean, not soak away the stress. He didn't have time for that. When he made it back out to the living room, Jono could smell that Patrick had made him a cup of tea doctored precisely to his tastes.

Patrick came out of the kitchen with the mug in hand. Jono took it, leaning down to kiss him softly on the mouth. "I'm all right."

"We couldn't reach you," Patrick said.

"Wade nicked my mobile before I shifted. I didn't get a chance to retrieve it before we were separated."

"It's on the coffee table."

Jono nodded and went to sit on the sofa Wade had vacated and thankfully cleaned up. Patrick sat beside him while Danai had already laid claim to the armchair. Two of the dining table chairs had been carried over for Sage and Wade. Danai had spread out some paper on the coffee table and had a slim laptop open on her lap.

Danai gave Jono a welcoming nod. "You look better."

"I don't feel better," Jono admitted as he slung his arm around Patrick's waist.

"That's to be expected." Danai pointed at what looked like a multiple-page letter on the coffee table and the pen holding it down. "That is your retainer letter. I'll need all four of your signatures on it, as well as yours and Patrick's as representatives of your god pack as a whole."

"Are you sure that's a good idea?" Patrick asked.

"For attorney-client privilege? Yes, it's necessary."

Patrick ground his teeth hard enough Jono could hear it. He still picked up the pen and signed. They all did. Sage handed the executed letter to Danai, who slipped it into a manila folder and placed it in her leather tote bag.

"I'll send you all copies via email tomorrow. Now, as to what happened today, I will need the entire story," she said.

"Uh," Wade said, blinking at Jono.

Jono gulped down his tea, not caring how it burned his tongue. "Give her the statement you gave the police, Wade."

Danai arched an eyebrow. "I need the entire truthful story. You aren't the first set of clients who have tried to hide something from me."

"Jono hasn't been charged with anything," Patrick pointed out.

"Not yet, but that doesn't mean the DA's office won't bring charges of some sort in the future. You're in an open civil war with a rival god pack in a major metropolitan city. That alone would be a problem, but the spillover has damaged the subway. People are going to want to blame someone, and even if you didn't directly cause the damage, you were the reason the damage happened in the first place. Now, tell me what happened today."

Jono shared a long look with Patrick. "Did Wade tell you what went on?"

"Yes," Patrick said, mouth twisting.

Jono repeated the statement he'd given the police and left it at that. Danai looked at him, fingers resting over her laptop keyboard where she'd been taking notes, and arched an eyebrow. "Anything else?"

He didn't know how to explain about gods, mostly because that meant giving up secrets that Patrick had carried alone for years before they became a pack. Despite being smack in the middle of the mess, it wasn't Jono's story to tell.

Patrick stayed silent on the subject matter, and Jono followed his lead.

"No," Jono said.

Danai made a contemplative sound in the back of her throat. "I may not be able to smell the difference between a lie and a truth, but I know when clients are holding back information. Not disclosing the truth to me will only hurt you in the future."

"They're trying to protect me," Wade said.

Patrick groaned. "Wade."

"What? That's what you guys are doing. Jono told me not to tell the police I was there when all the fighting happened, but I was the one who melted part of the train. They're gonna ask about that, won't they?"

"We'd have figured out a way to keep you out of it if that happened."

Wade scowled. "But what if it got you guys in trouble? You can't protect the packs if you're in jail."

"A charge would also put your visa at risk, Jono," Sage pointed out.

"We don't know her," Patrick said, jerking his head in Danai's direction.

"I'm on your side," Danai reminded them.

Patrick let out a hollow little laugh that made Jono tighten his grip on Patrick's hip. "That's not good enough."

"I've spent my entire career advocating for those in the preternatural community who are disenfranchised. I'm not here to betray you."

Patrick said nothing to that, and Jono sighed. He wouldn't ever pressure Patrick to disclose personal information, which meant he had to treat Wade with the same sort of respect. Catching Wade's eye, Jono gave the teenager a nod.

"It's up to you," Jono said.

Wade sat up straighter in his chair. "I'm a fire dragon."

Danai blinked at him. "Excuse me?"

Red scales pushed through human skin, flowing up Wade's neck and over his jaw to cover his face. Brown eyes turned gold, pupils elongating to black slits. Danai's eyes went wide, her laptop nearly sliding to the ground. She quickly pulled it back, but other than the surprise seeping into her scent, that was the only giveaway of her reaction.

"Human magic doesn't have any effect on me. I stopped the mage's spells while Jono fought the werecreatures and hunters." Wade glanced at Jono, wiping his fingers on his jeans. "He told me not to tell the police that."

"I see," Danai said slowly. "I don't think I'll be putting that into my notes."

"I told the police a fae and the protective wards held off the

Dominion Sect long enough for me to get out of there before they broke. That's the story we're telling to keep Wade safe," Jono said.

The red scales faded, and Wade's eyes returned to normal. He dug out the last foil packet of Pop-Tarts from the box on his lap and ripped it open. He didn't hesitate to bite into the strawberry-flavored snack.

Danai stayed for two more hours, jotting down notes and taking in a sanitized history of their fight with Estelle and Youssef's god pack. They didn't tell her everything—nothing about the gods, their soulbond, or Patrick's past—but enough for her to build a possible first defense on if the police came after them.

"You'll call me before speaking with the police," Danai said when they finally saw her to the door.

"Of course," Jono promised.

"I highly recommend hiring a crisis PR firm. I'll email a couple of suggestions to Sage if she doesn't have one on retainer already."

"It's something I was thinking of, but no, I haven't reached out to anyone yet," Sage said.

Danai nodded. "I'll contact you tomorrow."

They said their goodbyes, and Jono shut the door behind her. Normally he'd have offered to walk Danai to her car, but the media was still parked outside their home, and Danai had assured him she'd be fine. She seemed the sort to eat the press for breakfast with her morning coffee.

Jono looked at Sage and Wade. "I think both of you should stay the night. Who knows how long the media will stay camped outside."

"We never did have our meeting with the fae today," Sage said tiredly.

"We can have it tomorrow. Wade and I will go into work with you."

Patrick rubbed at his eyes, already turning around to head for their bedroom. "I have a meeting with Lucien and Ashanti tomorrow about this whole fucking mess."

"Do you want me to go to that one as well?" Jono asked as he followed after Patrick.

"No. I'll be going on my lunch break, whenever I can take it. Besides, we really shouldn't be seen together right now."

The words came out reluctantly, and Jono's knee-jerk reaction was to protest, but he knew Patrick was right. Despite co-leading their pack, revealing Patrick's position right now would only make their problems worse. Everything that had happened in the past forty-eight hours was proof of that.

Jono closed the bedroom door behind him and got into bed. Patrick stripped out of his clothes and turned off the light before crawling under the covers in a pair of sleep boxers. Jono wrapped his arms around the other man and pulled him close.

"We'll get through this," Jono murmured against Patrick's lips, kissing him softly. "Together."

Because that was the only way they'd ever stand against the world.

7

Traffic in Manhattan was slightly better on Thursday, but that wasn't saying much. The MTA had shut down the subway line the C and two other trains traveled on to replace the damaged protective wards and repair the tracks and tunnel. Patrick wasn't part of that team doing the ward repairs since he'd do more harm than good. Defensive magic wasn't his affinity, and besides, nearly everyone in the SOA still considered him a mage in name only these days.

Work on the missing Trishula of Shiva case had been momentarily sidelined while the SOA focused on the new Dominion Sect threat. Patrick hadn't been given lead on it this time, despite his past history with the group. He couldn't exactly say he was displeased about that, if only because the SOA was looking into the god pack civil war as well, and wasn't *that* a mess just waiting to be spilled.

All of that meant Patrick desperately wished for a cigarette for the first time in months as he drove to Ginnungagap during a late lunch break. He was taking the long way to the club, traffic making his time slower than usual, but considering he'd left the apartment that morning under a look-away ward because reporters were still camped outside the building, Patrick wasn't taking any chances. Getting followed by a reporter wasn't something he could afford right now.

By the time Patrick pulled into the small alley adjacent to Ginnungagap, he wasn't in the best of moods. Lucien would probably make it worse. Dealing with the master vampire of the Manhattan Night Court was an exercise in bruises most of the time. That hadn't changed, even with the mother of all vampires' return.

He locked the Mustang with a push of a button as he approached the door to Ginnungagap. Testing the handle found the door unlocked, and he pushed it open, stepping over the threshold. Crossing through the primordial power that lived inside the walls made Patrick twitch as the world beyond became muffled.

With the air-conditioning off in the building, Patrick started sweating within seconds. He walked past the toilets into the club proper, finding everyone clustered at the bar on the ground floor. Carmen, dressed in a strapless minidress and high-heeled sandals with laces that wrapped up her calves to her knees, sat on the bar counter. Her long legs were crossed at the knees, and she held a martini glass full of a pink fruity drink in one hand, a smudge of gloss on the rim from her lipstick.

She'd dropped her glamour, the horns curling back over her skull and cutting through her thick, curly black hair a marker of her kind. Her red-pupiled eyes watched Patrick's approach with something close to amusement in them. Carmen would always be beautiful and dangerous, and the sexual desire drifting about her like strong perfume was one more reason why Patrick always appeared before them with his shields locked down tight.

Naheed, Lucien's favorite human servant and Carmen's daytime protector, stood behind the bar, probably having been the one to serve up the drink. She was busy cleaning up, her ever-present pistol close at hand.

Lucien sat on a barstool, elbows resting on the counter behind him. He was dressed in ripped jeans and a dark T-shirt, the old leather jacket he wore cut through with spikes, the attire too hot for the summer day. The master vampire's familiar black-eyed gaze never strayed from Patrick, the color a match for the mother of all vampires, who stood beside him.

Patrick's attention never wavered from Ashanti. The goddess watched Patrick close the distance between them with an impassive expression. Her black eyes were holes in her dark face, no sclera showing, and her tightly curled hair was twisted into Bantu knots. Rather than black, her hair was a deep, bloody red which had never faded in all the time he'd known her, the myth of her making seeping into her physical form.

She wore a sleeveless blouse tucked into a floor-length skirt that hid legs which didn't end in feet, but rather bone hooks sheathed in iron caps. Ashanti existed how she had always come into the world—beautiful and dangerous and monstrous in kind.

Ashanti was as much a predator as she was a goddess, and sleight of hand went a long way toward luring in her prey. She was never one to hide the truth of herself behind glamour, but clothes were something else entirely. Dressed like this, she could walk among humans, but the citizens of New York would never treat her kindly. Human instinct wouldn't let them. Humanity might have carved out a life lived beside the monsters in the world, but they did so reluctantly.

Ashanti would always be a living horror in a world trying to forget her.

"I understand the Dominion Sect is making a mess of things," Ashanti said, her rich voice echoing in the nearly empty club.

Patrick came to a stop within arm's reach of her and shrugged. "When aren't they?"

The words felt like an apology on his tongue—meaningless in the face of her return.

It'd been four years since the end of the Thirty-Day War. Four years since Ashanti had delivered the gods-given dagger into his hands and willingly sacrificed herself to break Ethan's spell. The guilt Patrick had carried since then hadn't faded with her resurrection by way of the Morrígan's staff. Weeks wasn't enough time to come to terms with the hidden details of Ashanti's myth and a grief that had been ultimately misplaced.

Maybe he should've looked harder at her history, but he'd been a child when Ashanti came into his life, and gods were meddlesome and uncaring in the face of immortality. Ashanti was no different than Persephone and all the others who tore Patrick apart with their demands in that way. But in some ways, she was kinder. She had never treated him as anything but what he was—a weapon to be used until his soul debt was paid in full.

The lessons Patrick had learned at her hands had taken root in ways that would never die off. Ashanti had taught him to always question what was demanded of him and never put his faith in the gods, even her.

Her teachings had shaped him as surely as his soul debt had. Ashanti had honed him like the blade he eventually carried, and Patrick had always been cognizant of the way she'd carved him up in his younger years. Between her and Setsuna, they'd given him a foundation to survive on; it just wasn't one conducive to living.

He had Jono for that.

"Here to beg for help?" Lucien asked, lips curling over jagged fangs.

"Here to *ask*," Patrick shot back. "Your Night Court holds a treaty with our god pack still. Joint defense of our territory borders is still ongoing."

"Treaties don't mean we're obligated to save your ass every time you lose a fight."

"The other god pack used hellfire in their attack Tuesday night, which means there's a strong chance Hades is back in town. The attack yesterday proved Andras is here in New York. Jono said the demon was riding the soul of a hunter in the subway yesterday. Do you really want to face a Great Marquis of Hell allied with the Dominion Sect alone? Because we don't."

Lucien's eyes narrowed. "You should've dealt with the hunter problem months ago."

"You could've helped with that. They don't just stick to hunting werecreatures, and now there are high-ranked demons in the mix."

"Whose fault is that?"

Patrick opened his mouth to argue, but Ashanti lifted her hand in a commanding *shut up* gesture they both automatically obeyed.

"I had hoped the two of you would have outgrown this pettiness. I see I was wrong," Ashanti said.

Lucien tilted his head at an arrogant angle, but he said nothing in the face of his mother's chastisement. Patrick kept his mouth shut as well.

Ashanti raised an eyebrow at them both in supreme disapproval before gesturing imperiously at Patrick. "Ward us."

Patrick conjured up a mageglobe and pushed his magic through the focus sphere, casting a silence ward around their immediate vicinity. Static hummed in his ears for a moment before fading into an all-consuming silence. Ginnungagap should've been enough of a defense, but with demons running amok, one could never be too careful.

Ashanti stepped toward him, the click of ironshod bone hooks ringing in his ears. She was shorter than him, carrying with her a subtle hint of ozone and something more earthy, like freshly turned grave dirt.

She studied him for a long moment, and Patrick met her gaze easily enough. She didn't scare him; whatever fear he used to have of her had been trained out of him. He knew she could kill him in half a heartbeat, but he also knew she wouldn't. Ashanti had chosen her side in this war of belief when Persephone had brought him to Washington, DC, all those years ago. Patrick was a means to survival for her children, and she wouldn't break him simply because she could.

There were plenty of other prey in New York City for her to do that to.

"I haven't seen you as much as I expected to," Ashanti said.

"I've had a lot of eyes on me since getting back from Europe. I didn't think you'd want that spotlight," Patrick said slowly.

"But you'll come around now to beg?" Lucien drawled.

"Ethan can come after me all he likes. We have the Fates fucking with us because we're all of the gods' proxy. I take offense to him going after Jono."

"The wolf is soulbound to you. Him becoming a target was inevitable," Ashanti said.

Patrick pressed his lips into a hard line, thinking about his words for once. He'd always been less knee-jerk in his responses when standing in front of Ashanti. If she didn't like his answer, she tended to cuff him upside the head. Lucien would punch him in the face. As far as love taps went, he'd take Ashanti's any day over her child's.

"The gods might have given me Jono, but that just means he's mine to protect. I can't keep him safe and fight your war if he's arrested and jailed or deported. Separation means I can't use my magic to tap a ley line or nexus through the soulbond. It means we wouldn't have pack territory in New York, because our claim is run through Jono."

"You'd have your dagger. That should be enough."

Patrick couldn't stop the full-body flinch that hit him at her words. He'd carried her ashes out of the battlefield years ago because of that dagger—she'd *died* because of it—and he still couldn't shake that guilt.

"I wouldn't have Jono, and I'm not fighting without him."

"Sounds to me like that's what the Dominion Sect wants you to do if he is their continued target," Lucien said.

"Then it would be best for everyone if we don't give the bastards what they want. No one in the preternatural community will be safe from a demon-infested god pack allied with hunters and the Dominion Sect. We need support across our territory while we try to take them down."

Carmen sipped at her drink. "You realize none of this would be a problem if you'd done your job in the first place?"

Patrick's jaw twitched. "Either help us or not. I didn't come here for my past decisions to get picked apart by you."

"Your past decisions are the reason we're all in this mess," Lucien reminded him with icy venom in his voice.

"I wasn't the one who lost the Morrígan's staff in London."

Lucien slid off the stool, intent on reaching Patrick to punch him judging by the half-raised fist, but the master vampire immediately stilled at a single look from Ashanti.

"The promise you made to me where Patrick is concerned will remain unbroken," Ashanti said.

Lucien's expression became impossible to read as he inclined his head to Ashanti. "As you will it."

Ashanti's gaze slid back toward Patrick. "You believe Hades is in town?"

Patrick nodded slowly, impressed at the way Ashanti handled the leash choking Lucien but not wanting to push his luck. "The last couple of times we had to deal with hellfire, it was because of Hades."

"If that god is here, then Macaria will most likely be close as well. Hades was never one to stray far from his daughter's side."

Patrick tried not to think about the last thin connection tying him to his twin, buried deep beneath the soulbond. It wasn't one he could open safely for fear of what might happen. He might owe a soul debt, but he'd spent years trying to protect what was left of his damaged soul.

"As far as gods go, we may have a couple more causing problems. I got assigned a case for a missing artifact stolen out of the Met. A Trishula of Shiva is probably in Ethan's hands right now."

Ashanti snapped her iron teeth together, the sound making Patrick twitch. "There are many trishulas in the world touched by prayer. It only becomes Shiva's when he wields it. I would not worry about it."

Patrick wasn't sure how true that statement was, but he figured immortals knew more about each other than anyone else. "If you say so."

If the damn thing wasn't like the Morrígan's staff, then it was one less problem he'd have to worry about. He could do with less of those right now.

Ashanti studied him with those inhuman black eyes of hers, and Patrick never looked away. She didn't make him uncomfortable like she did the rest of his pack, because he knew she was cruel only because she had to live.

"Deal with the demons," Ashanti finally said. "The Night Courts will guard your borders from attacks when they are awake, but they will not put themselves at risk of sunlight. They will not fight during sunrise and sunset."

Which meant his pack would have to rely on the fae for help during the day and when the sun was passing over the horizon. Ashanti could walk in sunlight and not burn because of the godhead that sustained her. She'd carved out pieces of herself when she made vampires over the millennia, gifting that same ability to her direct descendants.

Lucien was the last vampire she had made, and one of her few surviving direct descendants if history was to be believed. Every other vampire in the five boroughs, no matter their Night Court, would be useless during the day. Ashanti and Lucien would always be the exception, but Patrick knew he couldn't count on them forever.

More than that, he didn't want to.

"Thank you," Patrick said.

"Don't thank us for fixing your problems. The sooner you kill Ethan, the better off we'll all be," Lucien said.

"If Hades and Zachary are in town, perhaps you'll get your chance," Ashanti said.

Patrick shrugged, uncomfortably aware that the only way to pay his soul debt was to kill what remained of his immediate family. "Tracking Ethan has proved almost impossible. The SOA is of the belief he goes past the veil with the help of Hades or some other gods and demons. It's where we think Ilya is hiding with his zombie army. Whatever hell they're hanging out in, we can't reach them, and I'm not asking the gods for help."

He'd traveled past the veil more times than he ever wanted to over the past year. Humans couldn't pass through it on their own. It took effort and a lot of power, even by the standards of the gods. Hades had his own set of worshippers, but Patrick didn't think they were enough to give the god power. If that were the case, maybe Hades would've done them all a favor and murdered Ethan in his sleep if the god had the guts enough to do it.

These days Hades was a puppet, guarding his daughter's bound godhead, and isolated from his pantheon. Whatever promise Ethan had given the immortal, whatever coveted place he'd offered up in a new myth, Hades had believed him enough to stay. Patrick didn't think Persephone would ever forgive her husband for that.

"Whether in heaven or hell, it doesn't matter. The fight will happen here, on the mortal plane," Ashanti said.

It would be more than a fight, but a sacrifice—one Patrick might not ever escape from. He'd known that since he was a child.

"I'll do my best to provide you with any information on the Dominion Sect's movement," Patrick said.

He hated being on the defensive, but that's where they were. He and Jono hadn't anticipated Estelle and Youssef attacking so openly. Bargains with demons and hunters, yes, they'd expected that. The other god pack aligning themselves with the Dominion

Sect hadn't seemed like a possibility even after he and Jono returned from Europe.

But if Estelle and Youssef were looking for a way to break them, separating him from Jono would go a long ways toward helping Ethan.

The enemy of my enemy is my friend, as the saying went.

Ashanti smiled slightly, aura brightening around her. She was the only vampire Patrick had ever met who didn't have a black hole where her soul should've resided, only a godhead shining through. "I promised the gods of heaven my support years ago. My reasoning hasn't changed, and it will not. Be the weapon I taught you to be and finish this fight, Patrick."

Easier said than done.

Patrick drew down his magic, breaking the silence ward. Sound returned, muffled by Ginnungagap. He turned on his heels and left without saying goodbye. Patrick could feel Lucien's gaze boring into him as he walked away. The risks of getting stabbed in the back hadn't diminished with Ashanti's return. Lucien would just find another way to make his life miserable.

He found his Mustang untouched where he'd left it in the alley, but Patrick did a brief scan of the car anyway. He remembered all too well getting dragged away from the hellfire car bomb last year.

Nothing seemed out of place, so Patrick got back behind the wheel and started the engine. He sat there for a moment, staring blankly ahead, and tried not to feel like everything he'd worked to keep over the last year or so was slipping through his fingers.

***

"Bloody bastards," Jono grumbled under his breath when he finally made it home that night.

Patrick set aside his MacBook and got up from the couch, absentmindedly casting a silence ward across their apartment's threshold. "Who?"

"The fucking press. A few reporters were waiting outside the bar when I left, and there were some near the flat. The gargoyles were keeping those ones at bay."

"At least those stone rats are good for something."

Jono quirked a tired smile at him. "Be nice, love."

"They're *messy*. They leave pigeon feathers everywhere and try to steal my coffee when I leave for work. They don't even do that to Wade."

"They know Wade wouldn't stand for it."

Patrick would've kept complaining—he didn't like the gargoyles because they considered annoying him a fun game—but Jono kissed the words away. He wrapped his arms around Jono's neck, keeping him in place for a long moment.

Patrick hadn't been able to appear at the pack meeting at the bar tonight *because* of the media attention. He'd joined via video-conference, but it hadn't been the same, and he'd worried over Jono getting home until the other man walked through the door.

"Sage dropped me off," Jono said when they finally separated.

"How did the meeting with the fae go today?"

Jono headed for the kitchen, and Patrick trailed after him. He watched as Jono rifled through the refrigerator, pulling out leftovers to make up a plate.

"Tiarnán is apparently back, though it was longer for him past the veil."

"Typical time difference."

Jono nodded. "Apparently the fae are in a bit of a tiff. One of their higher-ups has gone missing."

Patrick crossed his arms over his chest and frowned. "Who?"

"Tiarnán wouldn't say, though I offered our help in finding whoever it was. We did all right with Órlaith last year."

"Not sure we need to go hunting up another missing fae when we're already being targeted."

"We have an alliance to keep."

Patrick sighed. "I know. Maybe I should reach out to Gerard."

"Couldn't hurt." Jono stuck his plate in the microwave to heat up the food. "Speaking of alliances, how did your meeting with Lucien and Ashanti go?"

"Lucien is still keeping to the bargain he made with us. He's not happy about it, but they'll watch our borders at night after sunset and before sunrise. The hunters are a danger to all of us, especially with Andras in town. I think even Ashanti recognizes that."

"She'd be daft not to."

The microwave beeped, and Jono pulled out the plate. He set it on the counter and ate standing up. Patrick moved to get them both a drink. "Beer or something else?"

Jono waved the fork at him. "Had enough beer at the bar. Water is fine."

Patrick would've preferred some whiskey to soothe his nerves after the last couple of days, but he opted for water as well. If he went for the whiskey, he knew Jono would probably take the bottle away. So he poured them filtered water from the pitcher in the fridge and took up space next to Jono at the counter.

"What did Ashanti have to say about all this?" Jono asked as he twirled chow mein around his fork.

"She's letting the status quo remain."

Jono caught his eye, voice careful in its gentleness. "Are you sure we can trust her?"

Patrick bit down on the reflexive *yes* that wanted to escape his lips. His opinion of Ashanti was tinged by the years she'd popped in and out of his life to help train him and the guilt he felt at her death, however misplaced that might be now. She'd always been secretive, but she'd never lied to him about his predicament. Patrick knew his opinion of her was colored too much by his past, but he couldn't help it.

"We can trust she wants to see Ethan dead, and she'll do whatever it takes to see that happen," Patrick finally said.

"Like dying?"

Patrick curled his hands into fists to stop himself from reflexively reaching for the dagger he wasn't currently carrying. He'd left it on the nightstand after his shower earlier.

"The gods from heaven couldn't breach Ethan's spellcasting in Cairo. Ashanti could. She technically aligns with the hells, and it enabled her to subvert his defense. The dagger made her a target, but she got it to me in time." Patrick listed to the side, letting his head fall against Jono's shoulder. "If you're asking would she die for our side again? I don't know."

Jono wrapped his arm around Patrick's waist, sliding warm fingers beneath the elastic waistband of his sleeping pants. "It's not your fault what happened. Wasn't back then when you didn't know the truth of her myth, and it isn't now. I'll say that as many times as you need to hear it."

His words made Patrick's breath hitch in his throat. He closed his eyes, ignoring the way the counter dug uncomfortably into the small of his back. Jono radiated warmth Patrick wanted to soak up, even in the height of summer.

"We need to strike back," Patrick said quietly.

If another day with incursions in their territory happened, the packs might begin to question their strength and ability to hold New York City. If they lost even one pack's support, it would be one too many.

"I know. So does Fenrir." Warm lips pressed a kiss to the top of his head. "We aren't running away from this."

Patrick nodded, knowing they were running out of time to hold their territory and pay his soul debt. Whatever had drawn the Dominion Sect to New York City, Patrick knew it couldn't be good.

8

PATRICK'S PHONE RANG A LITTLE BEFORE 0600 FRIDAY MORNING. Jono's phone went off at the same time, the surround sound an echo in their bedroom jerking both of them from the depths of sleep. Patrick rolled away from Jono to grab his phone on the nightstand, already kicking off the blankets so he could sit up.

"Collins. Line and location are secure," he got out around a yawn.

"You're needed in Brooklyn," Henry said, sounding far more awake than Patrick at sunrise.

Patrick got out of bed. "What happened?"

"The trishula was found. You need to get on scene immediately."

"Okay." Patrick dragged out the word as he arched his back until his spine popped. "What's the emergency? The Met didn't think it was an artifact of any sort of power, and my review of its history—"

"It was found buried in Youssef Khan's body in Prospect Park."

Patrick froze, a ringing sound filling his ears. "I'm sorry. Did you say Youssef Khan is *dead*?"

"His body was dumped under the Soldiers' and Sailors' Arch in the Grand Army Plaza. A jogger found it sometime early this morning. The PCB is on scene, but they contacted the SOA because of Youssef's standing in the preternatural community. Since the trishula case was yours, you'll be handling the murder as well."

Patrick closed his eyes, breath stuttering in his lungs. He knew he should recuse himself from the case—he *knew* that. But doing so would require giving a reason that would be officially reported. Since the only reason would be he was one of the alphas for the rival New York City god pack—someone with a vested interest in seeing Youssef taken out of the picture over the fight for pack territory—exposing that truth would cause a myriad of problems.

Accepting the case would cause even more.

"Yes, sir," Patrick managed to get out.

"Report in afterwards. I won't leave the office today until I meet with you."

"Understood."

Patrick ended the call, arm falling to his side, his grip on his phone white-knuckled. He turned to look at Jono, who was still on his call, and appeared as shell-shocked as Patrick felt.

"—need to tell all the packs to stay inside today. Don't cross any territory borders if they can help it. It'll be a bloody riot if we cross any of their packs today." Jono tipped his head to the side, grimacing. "Good. You do that. I'll ring you as soon as I finish talking with Pat."

Jono ended the call and stared at the black screen of his phone for a few seconds before lifting his gaze to meet Patrick's. "*Fuck.*"

"Whoever killed Youssef used the trishula. The artifact is apparently still with the body. I've been assigned his murder case," Patrick said.

Worry filled Jono's eyes. "You can't work the case."

"I know. I *know*. The conflicts of interest are a fucking *mess*. But what do you want me to do? I can't waltz into Henry's office and tell him, sorry I can't do my job because I'm pack. I'm a federal agent. We're not supposed to bring bias into our jobs."

Except he had, for over a year now, and that was his mistake from the beginning. His job was a gaping hole in their defense the other side was going to walk right through. It used to be his job—either Mage Corps or the SOA—kept him safe from the Dominion Sect, providing him a screen to obey the gods behind. Now, the badge he carried felt like an albatross around his neck, one he couldn't escape.

Jono stepped closer and pulled Patrick into a hard kiss. "Sage said she's contacting Danai. She'll either come here, or I'll be picked up to go to her office. The press is going to want a statement from me."

"The press is going to think you murdered him."

Jono grimaced. "Yeah."

"I'll tell you what I know as soon as I can."

Patrick got dressed in record time, strapping his dagger onto his right thigh and holstering his tactical pistol to his hip. Despite how hot the weather was, he opted to pull his leather jacket with its embedded charms and defensive wards from the closet. It provided some measure of protection, and Patrick figured he could use all the help he could get right now.

He left the apartment under Jono's worried gaze, stepping outside the apartment building beneath a look-away ward sliding through the auras of the two reporters standing out of the gargoyles' reach. He made his way down the block to where the Mustang was parked, got behind the wheel, and headed for Brooklyn.

Not for the first time did he wish the Mustang had lights and sirens, but it would've been impossible to hear Setsuna over the noise.

"We have a problem," Patrick said when she picked up after their usual manner of calling code to signify who was reaching out.

"I've seen the news," Setsuna replied.

"Not this morning's, I'm betting." He tightened his grip on the steering wheel and tried not to press so hard on the gas pedal while still on city streets. "Youssef Khan was apparently found murdered this morning in Brooklyn with the trishula I've been tasked to find."

Setsuna was quiet for a long few minutes, long enough for Patrick to pull onto West Street going south, picking up speed.

"I told you last year getting involved with pack politics would only cause problems."

"The gods gave me Jono."

"Who was an independent-ranked werecreature at the time. You should've kept it that way."

"No," Patrick ground out. "Jono deserved to have a pack."

"Then you shouldn't have been a part of it."

"He gave me a family. That's more than you've ever done for me."

The words came out bitter and harsh, ringing in the confines of the car. The quiet on Setsuna's side was heavy, but Patrick refused to break it. He refused to apologize for the truth he spoke.

"I did what I had to so that you stayed alive," Setsuna said in a voice that was flat and leached of all emotion.

"By changing my name, boarding me at an Academy, and sending me off to the Citadel to prepare me for the Mage Corps. You hid me from Ethan because the gods told you to."

"I supported you."

Patrick kept his eyes on the road, ignoring the way his stomach twisted in his gut. "Maybe. But a house doesn't make a home if you're a burden to the people in it."

Patrick had driven a quarter mile before Setsuna spoke again. "You were never a burden."

"I find that real fucking hard to believe."

"Believe what you like, but I did what I thought was best for you over the years."

"And now? What do you want me to do about this mess? Because Henry ordered me to take over the crime scene, and while the trishula is my case, I shouldn't fucking touch Youssef's murder."

"Is the PCB running it or the SOA?"

"PCB, but they called in federal support."

"Then let them take the lead on the case. If you recuse yourself, that's going to open up a new avenue of questioning you can't afford."

"I can't afford *this*."

Setsuna made a frustrated sound. "You lost the protection your job could give you when you made your pack. I'll make your excuses if I can."

It wasn't a promise. The choices Patrick had made since last year meant he couldn't look to Setsuna for protection any longer. Not to the extent she used to be able to give it. Too many people were asking questions about his case history already after Chicago and his jaunt through Europe.

"I'll keep you posted," Patrick said.

Setsuna ended the call, and Patrick spent the rest of the drive to Brooklyn trying not to crack a molar. By the time he made it to the police line around the Grand Army Plaza, the sun had cleared the horizon and the air was already warm, indicating the start of a hot day.

Patrick parked the Mustang behind a police car and got out. He hooked his thumb around the chain of his badge to lift it off his chest when a uniformed police officer headed his way to order him somewhere else.

"SOA," Patrick said as he locked the car and started walking.

The officer backed off, and Patrick passed through the police line without being accosted. Traffic was being rerouted around the Grand Army Plaza with the help of traffic cops. Patrick squinted through his sunglasses at the officers and CSU workers milling about beneath the Soldiers' and Sailors' Arch. The monument reminded him of a scaled-down version of the Arc de Triomphe in Paris. This time he wasn't fighting zombies though, but he was still dealing with the dead.

The stone monument rose up against a clear blue sky, the crowning sculpture that of a chariot ridden by Nike. Looking through the arch, Patrick could see a large fountain in the distance, and beyond it, Prospect Park. He frowned, a flicker of recognition running through his magic that spoke of the earth, a subtle sheen of something else pushing through the strangely brown flora of the park.

He shook his head and raised his shields, not sure what to make of that faint hint of magic drifting through the park. He didn't sense a threat, and for all he knew, a coven could've performed a seasonal rite inside Prospect Park. Covens did that all time; all it took was a permit. Judging by how dead the park looked in the distance, maybe they'd done it to revive the plants and trees.

The media had set up on the other side of the wide street that curved in an oval around the plaza. They toed the police line, with every camera pointed in the direction of the Soldiers' and Sailors' Arch. It appeared most of the television reporters were currently reporting live, though Patrick couldn't be sure. Police cars and vans had been positioned to hide the view of the body as much as possible without putting up tarps.

Patrick saw the trishula first, before he saw Youssef's body. It glinted in the sunlight, the gold of its making bright against the stone surrounding it. The artifact's history said it carried magic, but Patrick discovered the Met's director had been right when he dropped his shields. The trishula carried no magic now, but it was a receptacle that could, given the right situation or the right god.

Patrick made his way to Youssef's body, bypassing a couple of frustrated-looking CSU workers. Casale stood near where the body had been dumped, but Patrick only had eyes for the dead.

Youssef lay on his back, nude, the trishula's three long prongs buried in his chest all the way to the connecting point of the spear.

Another wound was in his stomach—three deep jagged holes made by the trishula, the edges torn as if the person had ripped the weapon out in such a way to do as much damage as possible.

Both of Youssef's arms were outspread, fingers curled tight against his palms. Patrick couldn't see any defensive wounds on his skin upon first glance, but he wasn't sure any would show up, not with how quickly werecreatures healed. The fact he carried two major wounds in his torso told Patrick the trishula might have been coated with aconite, or maybe a silver wash.

Or maybe Youssef had known whoever had killed him, and that was why he hadn't fought back.

Both wounds were gruesome and deep. The lack of blood around the body was a strange detail that didn't track with how he'd died. The only blood Patrick could see was dried and streaked around the wounds and coating Youssef's chin and throat. If Patrick had to guess, he'd say the body had been dumped.

"Didn't think the SOA would send you," Casale said by way of greeting.

"The trishula is my case," Patrick replied.

Casale stared at him, a frown deepening the lines around his mouth. He was in his white-shirt uniform today rather than a suit, cap with its braid sitting firmly on his head. Patrick wondered if it was a deliberate choice since a murder like this would require him to go in front of the cameras with people out of the Office of the Deputy Commissioner, Public Information. DCPI was going to have its hands full today.

"You know why I'm questioning your presence."

Patrick met Casale's gaze without blinking. "Are you saying I can't do my job?"

"I know how you do your job, Collins. I just want to make sure this is done fairly."

"You don't need to worry about that. I'm here as support, not to take it over."

Casale arched an eyebrow, keeping his voice low. "You realize that won't look good, no matter how you try to spin it."

Patrick looked away and focused his attention on the body. "Can you tell me what you know about the scene so far?"

He forcibly moved the conversation along, not wanting to talk about all the reasons he shouldn't be standing there beneath the Soldiers' and Sailors' Arch, cataloguing the dead.

Casale shook his head but didn't ask Patrick to leave. "A jogger found the body about an hour ago. They called the police immediately, and we're getting his statement. No one reported a fight last night or this morning in this area. Traffic camera feeds around the plaza have been pulled, but I don't know what they'll show us. Right now it appears to be a dump job."

Patrick nodded in agreement. He didn't ask about Youssef's list of enemies. They both knew who would be at the top of it.

"If it was a dump job and no one saw anything, then magic was probably involved."

"A CSU witch said there's traces of magic on the weapon. Maybe a magical signature, but we can't be sure until the crime lab runs the results."

"You scanned it?"

Casale's gaze never wavered. "Standard procedure if the magic lingers long enough, especially with a high-profile murder like this."

The energy markers on a magic user's signature could be detected on modern equipment. Everyone's was different, like a fingerprint, and the SOA had a national database the PCB could check against. Most criminals tried not to leave traces behind, but if a spell was strong enough, some portion of their magic could remain. Patrick flexed his fingers, wanting to scan the area with his magic—but he couldn't. It could too easily be considered tampering with evidence.

"Has the ME worked on the body yet?" Patrick asked.

"We have an estimated time of death, if that's what you're asking about."

"When?"

"Yesterday, early afternoon. The ME will need to do further testing to pinpoint the exact hour."

Patrick studied Youssef's face with its sightless eyes, wondering if he'd been attacked or sacrificed, and if the latter, if it was willing or not.

"I know the media is going to latch onto the god pack civil war angle, but the Dominion Sect is in town and siding with Estelle and —" Patrick broke off to clear his throat. "Estelle's god pack. That's not something we can discount. Hunters and a mercenary mage were seen working with members of her pack during the subway attack."

"What use would that group of assholes have for a god pack?"

"Plenty, if you're using them as a proxy. Estelle doesn't have clean hands in all of this. You know that."

As far as Patrick knew, the federal government was still working on the case against her and Youssef from their business deal with Tremaine's Night Court and the influx of shine on the street last year. No indictment had come down yet, but cases like that took time.

Patrick knew Youssef's death meant they were running out of it.

"Neither does the side she's fighting against," Casale said pointedly.

Patrick bit his tongue so he wouldn't say anything incriminating where everyone could hear. "Do you need me here?"

Casale studied Patrick for a long moment before shaking his head. "I think it's best for everyone involved if you send me another SOA agent."

Relief flowed through Patrick at Casale's request, but it didn't last. Yes, it was a way to get him clear of the murder case, but Henry was going to want to know why Patrick's relationship with the PCB had suddenly soured. The SOA's relationship with local police agencies wasn't great sometimes, but Patrick had managed a decent connection with the PCB here in New York.

Seemed like it had finally run its course.

"I'll have Henry send someone else over," Patrick said.

He turned his back on Youssef's body and walked away, knowing this only made all their problems worse.

———

"I'M REMOVING you from the trishula case since the damn thing has now become a murder weapon and the PCB requested a different agent for that case," Henry said, angrily signing off on a form before handing it to Tiana. She took it and quickly left his office.

Patrick nodded. "Okay."

Henry leaned back in his chair, a scowl on his face as he drummed his fingers against his desk. "Did Casale give a reason why he wanted someone else?"

"No."

Which wasn't really a lie. Casale hadn't outright accused Patrick of meddling with an active investigation, but the older man would've if Patrick had stayed.

"Maybe he's tired of your tendency toward wrecking cities."

Patrick said nothing to that. The government might not like the property destruction he left in his wake sometimes, but he laid all the blame for that damage at the feet of the demons and monsters —human or otherwise—he was tasked with bringing in or taking out.

Henry reached for his coffee mug and took a long sip. Midmorning sunlight reflected off the building's windows on the other side of the street, shining through the windows behind Henry. Patrick squinted against the glare.

"Am I back to desk duty?" he asked.

Henry set his coffee mug down. "For now. The director hasn't changed her orders regarding your work."

Patrick nodded, thinking of the numerous texts and missed calls he had yet to deal with on his phone regarding the packs. "Understood. I'll—"

Tiana stuck her head into the office. "Sir? Breaking news conference with a statement from the New York City god pack is happening right now. You might want to see it."

Henry opened a desk drawer and pulled out a remote. He aimed it at the television bolted to the wall and turned it on. The screen came to life, already on a news channel, and Henry raised the volume. Patrick twisted around in his chair to better see the screen. The reporter speaking on a live camera feed was in front of a brownstone building he recognized but had never been inside.

Estelle's god pack held ancestral territory in Hamilton Heights. Patrick wasn't surprised to see the media had descended on the location once Youssef's murder hit the morning news. The police could decline to state the identity of the murdered man in Brooklyn until their family was notified all they wanted, but people talked, and reporters were like sharks with blood in the water for a story like this. With Youssef dying so soon after attacks on Jono, the media was apparently following the same line of thought that this was retribution.

A minute later, the front door opened, and the reporter moved out of the way of the live shot so her cameraman could focus on the people stepping outside. A handful of god pack members came down the steps, glaring at everyone. Behind them, a man in a dark suit that screamed lawyer stayed right by Estelle's side as they exited the brownstone. The two walked down the stoop to the sidewalk, escorted by members of Estelle's pack.

Estelle was pale-faced, and a close-up zoom showed her wolf-bright amber eyes weren't bloodshot from crying, but her lashes were spiky from lingering dampness. Preternaturally enhanced healing meant grief didn't show the same way as it did on a mundane human. Patrick could admit the sight of a grieving woman clutching the arm of her attorney as she slowly approached the circle of media was tailor-made to tug at the viewers' heartstrings.

Patrick's phone was muted and in his pocket, but he knew, without even having to look at it, that everyone in his pack was probably reaching out to him right now.

Patrick had dealt with expensive, high-powered attorneys in the past on cases, and the man who spoke briefly to the press probably charged four figures an hour if his attitude was anything to go by.

"My client will give her statement to the press and answer no follow-up questions," Estelle's attorney said.

Then he stepped aside, and Estelle took his spot in the ring of microphones straining to capture every last word. Patrick had to admit she played the grief-stricken wife well, dabbing at her eyes with a tissue, lower lip trembling before she spoke. Her auburn curls were a frazzled mess, a match for the grief she allowed on her face and in her voice.

"The NYPD informed me this morning that my husband, Youssef Khan, was found murdered in Brooklyn. We've been defending ourselves against a pack that has no problem twisting the laws to suit them, and my husband paid the ultimate price. I won't let his death be in vain, not when our job is to protect the people who depend on us to ensure their privacy," Estelle said.

Patrick clenched his hands into fists, heart pounding, already knowing where this press conference was heading.

Estelle raised her chin, blinking back tears. "There are only two people who wanted to see me and Youssef dead, who stood to gain everything with our fall. The police need look no further for my husband's murderer than the foreign pack who seeks to dethrone us, led by Jonothon de Vere and SOA Special Agent Patrick Collins."

"What the *fuck*?" Henry snarled, getting to his feet so quickly his chair rolled back and crashed against the wall beneath the window behind him. "What the *hell* is she talking about, Collins?"

Patrick stared at the television, watching Estelle walk back into her house while ignoring the shouted questions from the press. He swallowed thickly, stomach twisting with nausea that made him feel overly hot in the air-conditioned office.

"*Collins!*"

"You should probably reassign all my cases," Patrick said, refusing to look at Henry. "And call the director."

Patrick closed his eyes, barely listening as Henry erupted into a furious tirade, trying not to get sick as the career he'd worked so hard to attain since leaving the Mage Corps was destroyed in a single morning.

9

J‍ONO WATCHED P‍ATRICK POUR HIMSELF ANOTHER GLASS OF WHISKEY, not even bothering to measure, just filling the glass to the brim. He knew he wasn't the only one watching, but like the others, he didn't try to take the bottle away from Patrick despite it not even being noon on Saturday.

"So you're suspended?" Marek asked.

"My security clearance was suspended. The SAIC put me on unpaid administrative leave yesterday. He took my gun and badge, and said a formal letter was going into my personnel file. They tried to take my dagger, but it's my personal property," Patrick said.

Patrick picked up his drink and knocked back a good quarter of the whiskey. Jono got up and snagged the bottle, carrying it back to Marek's kitchen to hide it in the pantry.

Jono had been holed up with Danai at her downtown office almost all day yesterday after the bombshell that was Estelle's press conference. Sage and Wade had been with him, but Patrick hadn't been able to extricate himself from the SOA's field office until late afternoon. When Patrick had finally shown up there to meet with them, it had been sans gun and badge, shields locked down so tight Jono couldn't smell a bloody thing coming off him.

He still couldn't.

Jono went back to the living room and settled beside Patrick again, wrapping an arm around the other man's waist. Patrick was tense beneath his touch, neither of them having slept well last night after fighting their way past reporters to get inside their flat. The gargoyles had kept the media frenzy at bay, but neither of them felt safe anymore.

Jono looked across the coffee table where Marek sat on the other sofa. "Have you seen anything?"

Marek's hazel eyes were clear of any inherent power, his scent clean without the heavy ozone layer that appeared when the Norns spoke through him. "No. Nothing. I've even tried looking rather than wait for a vision, but I can't see a damn thing."

Sage, who was curled beside him with her laptop resting on her knees, placed her hand on his thigh and gave it a gentle squeeze. "It's not your fault."

"It's mine," Patrick said, taking another sip of whiskey.

"Pat," Jono said.

"What? It's the truth. I'm tied to this whole fucking mess because of Ethan. Our fight, my soul debt, is the reason Marek can't see the future. *No one*, not even the gods, knows which side is going to win."

Jono shook his head hard. "We will."

Patrick's smile was a bitter and twisted thing. "You don't know that."

He didn't, but Jono refused to believe this was a fight they would lose. Despite everything standing against them, Jono wasn't going to back down when giving an inch meant giving up the world.

"If we weren't a threat, the Dominion Sect wouldn't be trying so bloody hard to take us out."

"Well, they've succeeded in the sense that my job is fucked, and what federal coverage I could get us is no longer available."

"So what do we do?" Wade asked.

He had a box of Pop-Tarts in his lap and was steadily eating his way through it. It was his second box since they'd arrived, and Leon had a third waiting on the kitchen counter for him. Jono hoped they had more in the pantry. Wade was prone to stress-eating right now, and that got expensive.

"We wait to see what, if any, charges come down like Danai advised yesterday," Sage said.

"You sure that's the best option?" Emma asked.

Sage frowned. "It's the only one we have right now. Youssef's death changes everything. Estelle got ahead of the story before we could, effectively changing the narrative of the past few months. All the attacks might have been perpetuated by her and her pack, but she put on a good show yesterday, and the media ate it up."

Patrick set his glass on the table and leaned back against the sofa, pressing the heels of his hands against his eyes. "Every single case I've worked on since last June is now open to being thrown out by the courts, and that includes the shine case from last August that directly impacts Estelle and her god pack."

"Fuck," Leon said. "Every case?"

Patrick dropped his hands, staring up at the ceiling. "I have a fucking *bias* when I shouldn't."

"Everyone has biases," Sage said.

"They're not supposed to be overt in a federal job. The SOA's Legal department is going to be working overtime addressing every single case I've touched since I arrived in New York last year."

Jono tightened his hold on Patrick's hip, dragging him closer. Patrick didn't try to stop him. "What about the ones concerning the hunters in New York?"

Patrick grimaced. "*Every* case is subject to review now, especially the ones where you are involved."

"So, what? Estelle gets away with murder?" Wade asked.

Marek sighed. "Sure sounds like it."

"What are we going to do about it all?" Emma asked.

Patrick opened his mouth, but Sage raised her hand, cutting him off to answer for him. "We can't talk about that."

Emma frowned. "We need to be prepared."

"*Our* god pack needs to be prepared. That's confidential information we've discussed with our attorney and no one else at this time. To keep attorney-client privilege, we can't tell you what our defense is going to be."

"No one's been charged with anything yet."

"The court of public opinion begs to differ," Patrick muttered.

Emma let out a frustrated sound. "Then what can we *do*?"

"We'll need you to keep an open channel with all the other packs under our protection. Danai said our communications are evidence, so going forward, we'll need you to act as our intermediary. We'll meet with you every day if we have to," Jono said.

"Of course," Leon said, nodding along with Emma. "Does that mean you need some time off from the bar?"

Jono sighed. "Might be for the best right now. The media has been a bloody annoyance since our suit fitting got interrupted."

"We could close the bar until things die down. It'll be safer for everyone right now, especially if the packs will be calling us to get in touch with you."

"Don't close the bar," Sage said, not looking up from her laptop. "Closed means Jono can't work, and that might impact his visa."

Leon made a face. "Right. Forgot that could be an issue. All right, so we'll keep the bar open. It's not like we've had a lot of business since the hellfire bomb attack."

"We'll still pay you, Jono," Emma said.

Patrick snorted. "At least one of us will get paid."

"We have tithes," Jono said.

"I don't know if I should use them."

Jono turned to look at him, but Patrick wouldn't meet his eyes, choosing instead to lean forward and grab his drink again. Jono reached for his wrist, holding on with loose fingers, prompting Patrick to freeze.

"Don't. Please."

He wasn't sure if Patrick would listen. Jono was well acquainted with Patrick's methods of coping—cigarettes and alcohol and keeping everyone at arm's length. Jono had worn away Patrick's walls over the months, convinced him to give up smoking, but alcohol was still something he reached for to soothe the stress of their lives. He'd gotten better about it, Jono could admit, but there were times, like today, when Patrick poured himself enough to serve three people.

Jono thought Patrick would fight him on it, but he only heaved out a sigh and sat back again. He slouched on the sofa, leaning toward Jono rather than away. Jono tightened his hold on the other man and didn't let go.

"The tithes are there for us to use," Jono reminded him.

Sage glanced up from her laptop, eyeing them. "It's too late to deny you're our alpha. Unless that's what you want?"

Jono didn't breathe for the ten seconds it took for Patrick to say, "No. Pandora's box has been opened, so to speak. We can't shove it all back inside. But any move I make is going to be scrutinized and used against us."

"We're *all* being scrutinized. Despite Estelle's pack being the aggressor, we're taking all the blame. I don't think that's going to change for a while."

"Think we can get another meeting with the crisis PR company today?" Jono asked.

"I'll call and find out, and loop in Danai. Considering a crisis is their job, they should be available."

Sage set her laptop on the coffee table and went to retrieve her mobile from the dining room table where she'd left it after breakfast. Jono let her take the lead on that. They hadn't sent out a statement about anything yet on Danai's advice, but the PR company would hopefully be able to craft *something* for them that wouldn't open them up to a bigger legal mess. Jono felt they needed to get their side of the story out there, though how much good that would do them at this point was debatable.

Sometimes silence wasn't golden.

"You said you saw Youssef at the Met in the exhibit room where the trishula was? Do you think he knew what they had planned?" Emma asked.

Patrick sighed, the scent of whiskey on his breath coming through. "Who knows? The trishula isn't like the Morrígan's staff. Shiva can apparently pick up any trishula in the world and it'll become his weapon. Whether or not it was Shiva who actually wielded it against Youssef is unknown at this time, and will likely remain unknown."

Wade opened up his last packet of Pop-Tarts from the box he had with him. "Do you think that god is on their side?"

"I don't know. I've never had to deal with the Hindu pantheon before."

Jono would prefer if fewer gods were involved in this mess rather than more. They already had to deal with the possibility of Hades being in New York. Jono didn't like that arsehole, and neither did Fenrir.

"I think the bigger question is why is everyone in New York? It can't be just to take you out, can it?" Emma asked.

Jono wasn't sure how to answer that. He glanced at Patrick, who was picking at a ragged fingernail.

"Taking us out would clear the playing field," Patrick eventually said.

"They haven't taken us out," Jono said.

Patrick shrugged. "My job is hanging by a thread, they keep targeting you, and at some point, some kind of charge is going to stick that will affect your visa. If we're separated, that halves my power."

Unspoken went the fact that their soulbond was illegal, and if it was discovered, Patrick would be charged with a capital crime for interfering with someone else's soul.

Jono swallowed tightly. "Maybe that's the point."

Patrick grimaced, gaze sliding away. "Maybe."

Jono didn't like being a target. He liked it even less when the man he loved was in the enemy's crosshairs.

JONO WOKE up Sunday morning to an empty bed. He ran a hand over cool sheets and dialed up his hearing. He could hear Patrick's heart beating in the kitchen, a steady metronome that he'd always find comforting. Jono stretched until his spine popped before shoving the duvet off and getting out of bed. He'd slept naked last night, so he fetched a pair of joggers from the dresser and headed for the kitchen.

Jono found Patrick standing in front of the coffee maker, dressed for the day in jeans and a T-shirt. He was barefoot, having left his dagger and mobile in the bedroom, dark red hair messy from sleep. Jono wrapped his arms around Patrick's waist from behind and kissed the top of his head.

"Did you get any sleep last night?" Jono asked.

"Not much."

They'd spent yesterday afternoon in a long meeting with Danai and the PR company, taking the conference call at Sage's flat, in a room warded for silence. It had been a bloody headache, but they'd finally released their statement refuting Estelle's accusation. How much good it would do them remained to be seen.

"Want me to make you a fry-up?"

The coffee maker beeped, and Patrick set about pouring himself a cup. "Sure."

He didn't sound thrilled about breakfast, but Jono knew Patrick hadn't eaten much yesterday. A meal would do him good. Patrick stayed out of his way but didn't leave the kitchen. His presence soothed Jono, who stole a kiss when Patrick stole a piece of bacon.

Jono was finishing scrambling the eggs when the flat's threshold pulsed in such a way that even he felt it. He dropped the spatula, a shiver coursing down his spine as Patrick's head snapped around.

The heavy knock on the front door was all the warning they got.

"Police and FBI! Open up!" someone shouted.

Jono turned the hob off. "Don't answer the door."

Patrick set his coffee mug down. "They'll batter it down if we don't."

"You don't know if it's really the police out there. It could be hunters. It could be the Dominion Sect."

"Then I'll shield us."

Patrick moved to leave the kitchen, but Jono grabbed his arm. "Patrick. *Don't.*"

Someone pounded on the door again. "Open up!"

"We need to let them in," Patrick said quietly.

The dark circles beneath his green eyes stood out starkly on his pale face. Jono was reminded Patrick hadn't gotten much, if any, sleep last night. It made him wonder if Patrick had anticipated something like this happening, if he'd tossed and turned last night because of the possibility.

Jono unclenched his fingers after a moment and followed Patrick to the front door. He was glad to see Patrick had conjured up a mageglobe, the hand holding it tucked behind him, out of sight. At least he was being cautious.

"I'm opening the door," Patrick said loudly.

Jono was ready to yank him out of the line of fire as Patrick undid the lock and pulled the door open, magic making his skin itch from the shield that settled close over both of them. Jono peered over Patrick's shoulder at where Casale stood on the landing, a pair of ESU officers flanking him, one of them carrying a small battering ram. The fourth person crowding the landing was a man in a dark suit who smelled human to Jono's nose. The FBI badge hanging from his neck was impossible to miss.

Casale's gaze was shuttered when he looked at Jono before shifting his attention to Patrick. The FBI agent in the suit raised his hand, a folded piece of paper held between two fingers.

"SOA Special Agent Patrick Collins, I have a warrant for your arrest," the man said.

Jono couldn't smell a damn thing coming off Patrick, but he could hear the way his lover's heartbeat spiked like a hummingbird's.

"What's the charge?" Patrick asked.

"The murder of Youssef Khan."

"*Bollocks*," Jono snarled. "Patrick didn't kill anyone."

Casale didn't so much as glance at Jono when he spoke. "Are you going to let us in, or are we going to do this the hard way? The SOA sent me a mage just in case, even after I told the SAIC that wouldn't be necessary. I told the FBI the same thing. I hope you won't prove me wrong, Collins."

The mageglobe burning in Patrick's hand faded away to nothing, and he let his arm fall back to his side. The shield surrounding them dissipated, taking with it the scent of magic. "Is the warrant only for me?"

Casale nodded. "Jonothon hasn't been charged."

The *yet* lingered in the air between them all. Jono ground his teeth so hard one of them cracked.

"Then let's get this over with."

Patrick stepped backward, forcing Jono to move as well. He watched as Casale and the ESU officers marched into the flat. They were followed by people in suits and jackets with FBI printed on the back. Everyone separated and started going through the flat in a way that clearly showed they were looking for something.

"Do you have a search warrant?" Jono snapped.

The FBI agent who seemed to be in charge held up another

folded piece of paper. "Right here."

Jono snatched it out of the man's hand, his quick motions causing the ESU officers to point their guns at him. Jono ignored them as he opened up the search warrant, skimming the legal language. Enough time spent around Sage meant he could parse some of it, but not most of it.

"You have the bloody murder weapon. What more do you need?" Jono asked, glaring at Casale.

Casale didn't answer him, and Jono realized bitterly that the other man wouldn't. Casale's job was to protect New York City, and Jono would always be the enemy in some way by virtue of the werevirus running through his veins.

"Turn around and put your hands behind your back," the lead FBI agent said.

Patrick wordlessly complied, not reacting when the man snapped handcuffs as well as two bracelets around his wrists. The bracelets stank of magic, and Patrick's scent started to finally bleed through the air, his shields abruptly going down. Jono figured the cuffs had to suppress magic in some way if Patrick was forced to alter his shields. Patrick's mouth twisted in displeasure as he stared at Jono.

"Call Danai, then call Sage," Patrick said, ignoring the agent reading him his Miranda rights.

Jono nodded, his gaze falling to Patrick's bare feet. "Let me get your shoes."

"You'll stay right there," the FBI agent ordered.

"It's a pair of fucking *shoes*. I'm not arming him, and you aren't walking him out of our home in front of the media in bare feet," Jono snapped.

"You don't give the orders here."

"You can take your sodding attitude and get the fuck out of my face."

Jono was furious and afraid—for Patrick, and what this all meant for their pack. The threshold wrapped around the flat tapped into his emotion and read it as a threat for the first time ever. He didn't have magic, but the magic surrounding their home reacted to protect them.

A deep hum ripped through the air as a bright light flashed in the corners of Jono's eyes. Pressure filled the air before sliding off him like water. Patrick appeared equally unaffected, but the same couldn't be said for everyone else in the flat.

Power ripped through their home, dragging everyone who had entered it right back out to the landing. It didn't care about being nice, and quite a few people were banged into walls or doorframes during their expulsion. It took seconds to clear the flat of everyone except Jono and Patrick. Even the mage the SOA had sent along couldn't stop the threshold from barring the police and FBI.

Patrick stared at where a couple of FBI agents were sprawled on the landing, others having been shoved down the stairs to the landing below. Pained groans and people swearing filled the air. Patrick turned his head to stare at Jono, lips twitching at the corners with a humorless smile.

"You probably shouldn't have done that," Patrick said.

Jono snorted. "I didn't do anything. I'm not the one with magic."

"No, you just live here."

Jono headed for the bedroom, rocking to a startled halt past the doorway, the smell of ozone bright and sharp in his nose. He stared at the god wearing a jacket with FBI printed across the back who hadn't been chucked out of the flat by the threshold.

"What the bloody fuck are *you* doing here?" Jono hissed, keeping his voice low.

Hermes closed the nightstand drawer on Patrick's side of the bed, holding up the small, warded iron box that contained the broken-off bit of the Morrígan's staff to wiggle it at Jono. "We'd wondered where this had gone."

Jono ducked into the closet to retrieve Patrick's combat boots. "Don't you dare remove that for the feds."

"I'm hiding it, along with the Greek coin and his dagger."

"You better give them back *after* the feds leave."

"And if I don't? They don't belong to you."

Jono wasn't aware of moving, but he suddenly found himself standing in front of Hermes, his hand wrapped around the god's throat, Fenrir's teeth in his voice.

"If you take what does not belong to you, I will be displeased, cousin," Fenrir hissed.

"You kept a piece of the Morrígan's staff and never told us. What else are you hiding from your allies, Fenrir?" Hermes got out, seemingly unperturbed in the face of Fenrir's wrath.

"Nothing."

Fenrir bled out of Jono, giving him back control. Hermes smirked, his gold-brown eyes bright with amusement as Jono released him. "Go hand Pattycakes off to the authorities while I play with his phone."

Jono wanted to punch the god. Fenrir rumbled his agreement in the back of Jono's mind, but they didn't have time to wipe the smirk off Hermes' face. He turned on his heels and returned to the living room.

Patrick hadn't moved from his spot in front of the door. The FBI agent who had cuffed him stood on the landing now, glaring at him, unable to enter. Patrick ignored the demands to leave the flat, clearly waiting for Jono to return. The SOA mage standing beside the FBI agent had a mageglobe burning in one hand, but the threshold was holding against whatever she was trying to do. Jono didn't know if it was due to Patrick's magic or Hermes' presence that was keeping everyone out, but he was grateful for the reprieve.

Jono knelt and helped Patrick into his combat boots, lacing them up with deft fingers. He curled his fingers around Patrick's calf and tipped his head back to look up at Patrick. There was so much he wanted to say, but none of it could be spoken in front of the authorities except for one single truth.

"I love you," Jono said as he stood.

Patrick's gaze never wavered. "I'll come back."

Jono wanted to believe that, despite everything tearing them apart. He kissed Patrick firmly on the mouth before letting him go. Patrick licked his lips, squared his shoulders, and turned to walk out of the flat, into the hands of the authorities. The threshold let him pass over it with a flicker of magic, but when the SOA mage tried to step inside the flat, she was pushed back.

The FBI agent who'd handcuffed Patrick scowled at Jono, one hand gripping Patrick by the arm. "The search warrant still stands. We still require admittance to the apartment."

Jono scowled at him. "You can send a new group of arseholes up and see if they have any luck coming inside."

He wasn't going to make it easy on the police or the FBI, but neither was he going to obstruct anyone else. Jono knew there was nothing incriminating in the flat, and anything that could be perceived as a threat was being kept safe by Hermes.

"Stay where you are. I'll be sending up more agents."

The FBI agent yanked on Patrick's arm, hauling him down the stairs and out of sight. The SOA mage followed. Jono had to stop himself from going after them, absolutely gutted that Patrick was leaving in handcuffs, charged with a murder he didn't commit.

"He'll be all right," Hermes said from behind him.

Jono didn't turn around. "You don't know that."

"No, but he can't pay his soul debt if he's locked up, and we gods aren't happy with the interference of demons."

Jono shoved past Hermes to go retrieve his mobile so the feds didn't take it. He wondered if he could keep Patrick's. "We aren't happy with the interference of gods."

"The two of you never would have met if it weren't for us."

Fate was a road leading to a future with endless possibilities, but maybe Hermes was wrong. Whatever choices Jono made in some other life, he wanted to believe they would always lead him to Patrick.

10

THE METROPOLITAN CORRECTIONAL CENTER WAS COVERED IN protective wards and containment spells in equal amounts. Patrick knew that much, even if he could no longer sense the magic embedded in the foundation of the jail, not with the spelled bracelets he wore that restricted his magic. All jails were built the same, and he'd passed through enough in his career to know their safety requirements.

He was usually on the other side of the bars though, not sitting in an interrogation room on a shitty Sunday with his wrists cuffed to the table, waiting for Danai to arrive. Patrick shifted in the hard plastic seat, trying to get comfortable, knowing it was a lost cause. The guard standing in the corner tightened his grip on his pistol but didn't tell him to stop moving.

The cuffs rattled against the spelled bracelets. He'd been stripped of his clothing and put in a white prison uniform during processing before being placed in a segregated cell away from the general population. The cell was warded, the magic in the walls giving him a headache. With his magic muffled, Patrick couldn't adjust his personal shields to account for the magical oversight.

The only reason his shields were even still up was because of Persephone's anchors burned into his bones.

The door opened, and Patrick watched two men in dark suits enter, each of them carrying a briefcase. No one else followed them inside, and Patrick sighed, resolving to stay silent until Danai arrived. He'd been arrested that morning, but it was difficult to judge what time it was now when he was exhausted from lack of sleep, getting arrested, and unable to relax his guard. He hadn't seen a clock since his processing.

The man who sat down first looked to be in his early forties, with dark brown hair and eyes, a stern mouth, and a no-nonsense attitude shared by his companion. His suit was expensively made, tailored with a precision that reminded Patrick of the initial suit fitting he'd gone to for Sage and Marek's wedding. He bit the inside of his cheek, wondering if he'd even get to see the ceremony now.

"Patrick Collins," the man said, omitting Patrick's job title. "My name is Preston Strauss. This is my co-counsel, Louis Ackerman. We're assistant US attorneys for the SDNY Department of Justice."

Patrick stared at them and said nothing in the face of their introduction.

Preston smiled blandly as he pulled a folder from his briefcase and set it on the table. "I understand you have invoked your right to an attorney and have retained counsel. We'll wait until they arrive, unless there's anything you'd like to tell us?"

Patrick snorted at that statement and slouched in his seat.

Preston's expression never changed. "You'd do well to think about ways to help yourself, and help us. You're looking at life in prison if you don't."

Patrick was well aware of the charges against him, but they weren't enough to get him to talk without his lawyer present. They sat in silence for what his internal clock said was maybe ten minutes or so before the door was pushed open again.

Danai stepped inside, carrying her own briefcase, dressed in a stark black pantsuit and pale gray blouse that wouldn't be comfortable in the high summer temperatures outside. She looked ready to go to war, judging by the flat look she gave the assistant US attorneys as she took the seat beside Patrick.

"Did they try to get you to talk?" Danai asked as she pulled out a legal notepad and pen.

"Yeah," Patrick drawled.

"Did you say anything?"

"No."

"It's in your best interest if you do," Preston repeated.

"My client is innocent until proven guilty, despite the charges your office has concocted against him," Danai said sharply.

"There's no concocting when the evidence speaks plainly."

"We'll see about that."

Preston flipped open the folder and bypassed the crime scene photographs of Youssef impaled on the trishula in favor of a lab report depicting graphs and readouts Patrick was familiar with. The report was pushed across the table. Danai drew it closer so they could both review it since Patrick's hands were restricted in movement.

"What is this?" Danai asked.

"Results of an energy scan conducted on an artifact. The process can record a magical signature if done early enough at a crime scene where magical traces are still viable. It's missing a few pages, but that's what it is," Patrick said before Preston could explain.

They were difficult to come by, because not every police department had access to those kinds of machines, and the results weren't always precise. The PCB had them on hand, and it looked as if Casale had wasted no time sharing what evidence his people had uncovered at the crime scene with the feds.

"It recorded yours, to be exact, Patrick," Preston said.

Patrick looked up to meet the other man's sharp-eyed gaze. "It's wrong."

"The PCB scanned the stolen trishula at the crime scene. They requested the SOA run the results of it against your signature the agency has on file. It was a perfect match."

"It's never a perfect match."

Preston gestured at the report. "Tell me that's not your magical signature?"

"Don't answer that," Danai said.

Patrick looked down at the report, studying the results marked and signed off by an SOA agent and approved for release by the SAIC. His stomach roiled, bile creeping up his throat. Patrick had to force his hands flat against the table to stop them from shaking.

He knew what his magical signature looked like when distilled into scientific numbers and percentages, in graphs that could never completely encompass a person's magic. Like a polygraph test, the scans were disproportionately relied on in criminal cases when one was acquired. The results allowed for a margin of error, and that's where doubt crept in.

The conclusory evidence on that piece of paper was close, but not accurate. It was the closeness that worried Patrick. Replicating a person's magical signature was nearly impossible. It came down to a person's magical strength, their affinity, their very *soul*. Matching something different from your own magic would always leave revealing traces behind of the differences—like fingerprints, no two magical signatures were alike.

Not even twins, but they came closer than anyone else.

Patrick forced his breathing to stay even with long practice. Since Chicago, he'd kept the threadbare tie to his sister's soul locked down, walled off, and buried deep.

Maybe that hadn't been enough, especially after Paris, when the Morrígan's staff had sought to cleave his soul from his body in exchange for a resurrection. Srecha's blessing had ultimately paid the price required, but the sentience of sort that lived in the staff had still left its mark on him. Ethan must have discovered the connection in Hannah's soul and used it to target him.

"Youssef Khan died Thursday, between one and two o'clock in the afternoon," Louis said, staring at Patrick. "Where were you at that time?"

"Don't answer that," Danai said to Patrick, all her attention on the two attorneys. "My client will not be pressured into a false confession while I'm sitting right here."

Patrick bit his tongue, trying not to twitch. If that time of death proved to be accurate, then Youssef had been killed while he'd been meeting with Lucien and Ashanti. He wondered if someone had followed him to Ginnungagap, if they'd attacked Jono to flush Patrick out and drive him to the one person whose secret Patrick couldn't afford to give up.

Lucien was his criminal informant, and the master vampire's diplomatic immunity had been approved by the government. Patrick's ties to Lucien weren't the problem. It wasn't even Ashanti's secretive presence on American soil. It was the fact both vampires could walk in daylight, and that was a myth that could not afford to become fact. It would too easily spin out of control, painting every Night Court in existence with a false ability, and plunging the preternatural world into chaos.

Fear was a motivating factor in every massacre perpetuated against everyone and everything in the world. Patrick refused to have that blood on his hands, even if Lucien *was* a fucking bastard.

"We scheduled this meeting to give your client a chance to make things easier on himself," Preston said.

Danai's voice was frigid when she spoke. "And I told you on the phone we had nothing to say. The meeting is over. I require time with my client without government interference."

She slid the lab report back across the table, and Preston picked it up. He tucked it away in the folder and placed it all back into his suitcase, seemingly unsurprised at Danai's pushback.

"It's always a pleasure, Danai."

She arched one dark eyebrow, disdain dripping from her lips. "I can't say the same, Preston."

The assistant US attorneys left, as did the guard when another waved him out. Danai waited until the door shut before letting out a harsh sigh.

"You sound like you know them," Patrick said.

"I've tried several cases in the SDNY court where Preston was the prosecutor. He works out of the Office of Public Corruption division and is as hard-nosed as they come," Danai said.

Patrick clenched his hands into fists, fingers throbbing from how tightly curled he held them. "So what now?"

"You're being charged with murder under flimsy evidence, a hate crime due to Youssef being a werecreature, and obstruction of justice due to your position as a federal agent."

"Is that all?" Patrick asked with a wince.

She gave him a thin smile. "Honestly, you're not the worst case I've handled."

"It kind of feels that way, at least for me."

"Your arraignment is set for tomorrow. I'm doing everything I can to get you released on your own recognizance. Aside from that, I'll be requesting the court issue a writ for habeas corpus et animum for a necromancer to raise the dead for a deposition."

Patrick had no idea how that would play out, but he didn't have any hope of getting to walk free. "How much will my bond cost?"

If it was in the millions, no amount of tithes would be able to cover that, not that Patrick would ever touch anything but his own money for something like this—money which was nowhere close to seven figures.

"Federal courts don't issue cash bond."

Which was a nice way of saying a jail cell became your home away from home.

"Do you think the court would be more willing to release me if there was money on the table as collateral?"

Danai sighed. "We can do a secured bond if you like. Marek already made it clear he'd be willing to pay for it, but I'd counsel against requesting one."

"It would probably go over well in the court of public opinion."

"That's not where you're being tried."

Patrick raised an eyebrow. "You and I both know that's not true."

The court record might be what mattered when it came to his freedom, but his reputation was already being torn to shreds.

"Very well. I'll request a secured bond at your hearing."

"Great." Patrick blew out a breath. "Do you know where the body is being held?"

"At the morgue in the PCB. Why?"

Patrick nodded, glad it wasn't in the hands of the SOA yet. "See if you can't keep it there. I trust Casale to keep the body untampered with."

Danai raised an eyebrow. "But not your agency?"

"Ethan Greene was a former SOA special agent. He left supporters behind when he went on the run. The director and those who held the position before her have spent years trying to remove Dominion Sect members and sympathizers from its ranks. The agency isn't clean. I'm not saying the NYPD is clean, but they don't have the reach of a federal agency. A PCB in any city was never going to be worth the Dominion Sect's time to infiltrate."

"You sound like you're familiar with the man."

Patrick had to choke back his laughter so he wouldn't get sick. "I've handled cases for the SOA where he and the Dominion Sect turned out to be the perpetrators. I fought him directly in the Thirty-Day War."

"If that's the case, then we'll need to look into the angle that you were framed for getting too close to them for reasons related to national security. It wouldn't be the first time something like this has happened." Danai wrote on her notepad a reminder in what looked like her own personal shorthand. "I'll reach out to Casale with our concerns after I leave. The last thing we need is contaminated or missing evidence."

"Right." Patrick uncurled his fingers to scrape his fingernails against the tabletop. "How's Jono?"

"Worried, like the rest of your pack."

"Have there been any more attacks against them?" Danai hesitated, which told Patrick all he needed to know. "Fuck."

"Not against Jono and your pack directly, but some of the packs under your protection. From what I understand, your arrest and the spillover of the god pack civil war is bringing unwanted attention from the public to all the packs, and several are thinking about leaving."

"Permanently?"

"No, only until this all dies down."

Patrick laughed, no humor in the sound. "That's not going to happen."

He hoped Jono could convince everyone to stay. If packs started leaving, that would be a blow to their leadership, not that Patrick's arrest on a false charge wasn't already. More than that, it would be a loss of territory they'd have to scramble to hold onto.

"I anticipate discovery will happen quickly whether or not you are released."

Patrick couldn't keep the bitterness out of his voice. "You really think that will happen when I'm up for murder?"

Danai turned in her seat to face him, expression serious, but her voice was kind. "I'm working on gathering letters of support to bring to the hearing tomorrow. My partner is in the midst of that outreach right now while I meet with you. I'll be heading to the office after I leave to continue preparing. I'm not saying it's an impossible task to get you out of jail, just for you to have a little faith."

The problem was, he didn't.

Patrick sighed, knowing his freedom was in her hands, and there was nothing else he could do except go back to his cell after she briefed him in-depth on the charges against him.

Monday dawned hot and muggy, but Patrick was awake well before the lights turned on in his cell block three hours before his hearing was scheduled to start. Patrick drifted through his monitored shower and the shitty breakfast in a haze, scratching at the skin beneath the spelled bracelets that kept his magic in check.

The containment spell didn't interfere with his soul, but it would short-circuit his ability to focus and call on his magic. Any hint at reaching for his magic would induce a painful shock, the force of which would escalate depending on the strength of the spell he tried to cast.

As a precaution against his status as a mage, every guard assigned to overseeing Patrick was required to be a magic user. Mages were the most powerful, but the least numerous. The only reason the sorcerer currently on duty would be able to take him out was because of the bracelets.

Patrick wanted to burn the damn things.

He was taken to a room where a crumpled suit was laid out on a table, along with a pair of shoes. Patrick recognized it as one he kept in the back of the closet, and he bit his lip as he realized Jono must have given it to Danai.

"Get dressed," the guard in the room with him ordered.

Patrick had spent nearly ten years in the military; getting dressed in front of an audience wasn't anything unusual. The guard undid his handcuffs and oversaw Patrick getting dressed to impress, since that was the only reason he could think of why Danai had delivered him a suit.

Getting processed out of the jail for transport for the courthouse didn't take long. Apparently being high-profile meant the correctional officers had to keep to the schedule. Patrick left under guard, wearing a bulletproof vest over his suit jacket, which he thought was laughable. If Ethan wanted him dead, it would be by way of magic, not something as pedestrian as a gun.

Following protocol, every officer escorting him to the court-house was a magic user. Even through his shields and the spelled bracelets, he could recognize what they were. Passive magic some-times wasn't strong enough to trigger a spell, and the soul wound he carried wasn't something that could be blocked.

Patrick stared at a spot between the two officers on the oppo-site bench in the transport van, wondering how long it would take to get to the courthouse. He hadn't eaten much breakfast, and what food he'd managed to swallow sat like a rock in his stomach. Sweat trickled down the back of his neck and beaded at his hairline.

The van eventually slowed to a halt, and Patrick held still as one of the officers undid the chain that connected his handcuffs to the floor. The van doors opened, and Patrick exited like a crim-inal beneath the flashes of dozens of cameras and countless shouted questions from a crowd of reporters. He kept his face impassive in front of the prying media, trying his best to ignore the fear eating at the back of his mind at being the center of atten-tion in public.

Patrick had spent over two decades hiding in one way or another—under a new name, in a uniform, and behind a badge. Getting marched into the courthouse beneath a sea of cameras went a long way toward negating all of that, and he wondered if that was the point, if this was what Ethan wanted.

All their family's dirty secrets dragged into the open for all the world to see.

The cacophony of voices faded once Patrick entered the court-house. The police with him led him around the security check and through the halls. Patrick kept his gaze focused straight ahead and not on the attorneys, clients, and court staff present for other cases being held that day.

"In here," one of the officers said when they finally reached a set of doors on the fifth floor.

A pair of FBI agents stood guard outside the courtroom.

Patrick flexed his fingers as one of the doors was opened, and a police officer went in ahead of them.

The first thing Patrick noticed upon entering the courtroom was his pack. Jono, Sage, and Wade had claimed the bench behind the defendant's table, where Danai sat. With them was Marek, but Patrick didn't see Emma or Leon. The four of them were on their feet and staring right at him as Patrick walked down the aisle. A curl of shame ran hot through his chest at them seeing him like this, but he couldn't change the situation.

"All right?" Jono asked him as Patrick passed their bench.

With the police between them, Jono didn't try to reach for him, not that Patrick was in any position to receive comfort. "Been better."

"This is bullshit," Wade muttered, arms crossed over his chest and a scowl on his face.

Patrick held still as an officer unlocked his handcuffs but not the spelled bracelets. He let the officer unstrap the bulletproof vest, and Patrick shrugged out of it, tugging at his suit jacket to try to get rid of some of the wrinkles.

He scanned the courtroom, taking in the atypical number of police and federal agents present—some SOA, the majority FBI— and Estelle sitting on the bench behind the prosecutor's table with Nicholas and several other members of her pack. He'd missed them on the walk in, too focused on Jono and the others. All of them carried demons in their souls except for Estelle, and he wondered about that discrepancy and what it meant.

"Don't look at her," Jono said, breaking Patrick's concentration. "She's not worth your time."

Patrick wrenched his gaze away from Estelle and back to the people who mattered. Jono smiled tightly, rage embedded in the corners of his mouth, but the love in his eyes was what shored Patrick up. The distance between them wasn't much, but the police officer not part of the court staff situated near the defendant's table was a silent warning for Patrick not to get close to his pack.

He wanted to, badly, but Danai settled her hand on his shoulder. Patrick turned to face her, eyeing the stack of paper situated near an open black binder full of tabs and documents.

"I didn't think my case had generated that much paperwork so far," Patrick said as he sat down.

"I have your copy in my briefcase. You'll be allowed to take it with you."

"Back to jail?"

"That's not what we're aiming for."

The bailiff exited the door leading to the judge's chambers right then, drawing everyone's attention. "All rise for the Honorable Talibah Mohamed."

Patrick stood, along with everyone else who was seated. As the woman in her long black judge's robes exited her chambers, Patrick was hit with the crackle of ozone—electric, immortal power that cut through his shields and the spells keeping his magic in check for a split second. A god's power would always be stronger than any spell a mortal could cast, and it was like a sucker punch to the gut as the immortal judge walked into the courtroom.

Patrick heard Jono suck in a breath but otherwise didn't say anything as the judge stepped up to her bench. She was a slim woman with medium-brown skin, a sharply featured face, and black hair that tumbled past her shoulders in thick waves. She looked young to be presiding over such a prestigious court, but Patrick knew anything was possible when gods were in the mix.

He just didn't know which god, which side of this damn war, was sitting on the bench, prepared to rule over his life.

"You may be seated," the god masquerading as Judge Mohamed announced in a voice that rang through the courtroom.

Patrick would've sat, except Danai touched his elbow and subtly shook her head. He remained standing, as did the US attorneys.

"Criminal cause for arraignment in the United States of America versus Patrick Collins," the clerk said before rattling off a string of letters and numbers for the case number. "Counsel, please state your appearances."

"Preston Strauss and Louis Ackerman for the United States. Good morning, Your Honor," Preston said.

"Good morning," the judge replied.

"Danai Belvedere of Belvedere and Elliot for Patrick Collins," Danai said. "Good morning, Your Honor."

"Good morning." The judge then turned her attention to Patrick, and he felt pinned by eyes that held no humanity in them. He wondered if anyone else noticed. "Please state your full name for the record."

Patrick swallowed, giving the legal name he'd gone by for the past twenty-two years. "Patrick Collins."

"Thank you. This is an arraignment for you, Mr. Collins. I'm going to read the indictment, which is brief." She looked at the paper on her desk and flipped over a page. "Count one being murder in the first degree of Youssef Khan, alpha werewolf of the New York City god pack, whose body was found in Brooklyn with your magical signature on the missing trishula you were charged with investigating.

"Count two being a hate crime act committed against a person of the preternatural community, as the death did not happen inside a federally recognized challenge ring. Count three being obstruction of justice due in part to your position as a federal agent overseeing cases brought against the murdered individual in question and using your position to gain standing for your god pack."

The judge paused and looked up, staring at Danai. "Ms. Belvedere, have you discussed the charges set forth in the three counts with your client?"

"I have, Your Honor," Danai said.

"Does your client wish to enter a plea at this time to the charges in the indictment?"

"Yes, Your Honor. He will plead not guilty to each count."

"All right. A plea of not guilty will be entered. I understand you are also representing the second god pack staking claim to New York City as a whole and individually. Does your client understand the inherent conflicts of interests involved with that?"

"He does. He is willing to waive it for his defense."

"Very well. Is there discovery?"

"Yes, Your Honor," Preston said. "We will be sending it out to the defense shortly."

"The defendant invokes his right to a speedy trial and requests a necromancer to call the soul of the victim back from the afterlife for a deposition," Danai said.

"The government objects to that request," Preston said.

"The government is reminded the defendant is guaranteed a speedy and *fair* trial." The judge looked over at Danai. "Submit the writ or a motion. The court will set a hearing accordingly if it's the latter. Let's move on to bond."

"Your Honor—"

"Any motion submitted to the court, the government has a right to oppose. I understand the government is requesting detention without bond?"

"Yes, Your Honor. The defendant is a flight risk."

"The defendant is not a flight risk, Your Honor," Danai countered. "He is a veteran who diligently served his country in the Mage Corps for years before joining the Supernatural Operations Agency. He's put down roots since his transfer to New York City and has no reason to flee the jurisdiction. His monetary assets are limited."

"The government is against releasing the defendant for the reasons in the indictment, Your Honor. As to monetary assets, he has access to funds tithed to him by other factors, one of his pack members is engaged to a billionaire, and several known acquaintances are multimillionaires."

"None of which means if money was offered, it would be taken. The defendant is dedicated to his job and the country, Your Honor.

He has no intention of fleeing and every reason to stay. He is willing to submit a secured bond in the amount of one million dollars to prove it."

The judge looked at Danai. "The defendant's letters of support were considered by the court, as well as the confidential reports submitted under seal by the SOA and the US Department of the Preternatural."

"What reports?" Preston said, voice going sharp before he belatedly smoothed it out. "Your Honor, what reports is the court referring to?"

"National security issues will not be read into open court, Mr. Preston. Suffice to say the court rules the defendant will be released on his own recognizance if the secured bond is met at one million dollars. He will be required to hand over his passport."

Danai nodded. "Thank you, Your Honor. The secured bond will be paid today."

"Your Honor, the government strenuously objects to the court's decision," Preston said, disbelief bleeding into his voice. "The defendant is charged with murder and is a danger to society."

"The court's decision is not changing," the judge replied coolly, that hint of ozone growing stronger.

"The government requests restriction of movement for the defendant to Manhattan."

"The defendant will need permission to be in Washington, DC," Danai countered.

"The defendant will be restricted to movement within the five boroughs of New York City, travel between that city and Washington, DC, and within the nation's capital as a whole." The judge picked up her gavel and knocked it against the block on her bench. "It is so ordered."

"Thank you, Your Honor," Danai said.

Preston echoed the formal platitude, but he didn't sound like he meant it. When Patrick glanced over at his side of the courtroom, he could see the angry disbelief on both the attorneys' faces. He supposed it wasn't every day someone charged with murder was allowed to go free before trial. Behind them, Estelle's god pack were scowling at the judge, but none of the demons riding their souls bothered to speak up.

Judge Talibah Mohamed—a goddess who was maybe, just maybe, on the side of all the heavens—stood and left the bench, retreating to her chambers.

Danai let out a quiet breath before closing her binder. "That went better than I thought."

"What now?" Patrick asked.

"Marek is financing your secured bond. We'll get it paid, and you'll be processed out of jail. I'll pick you up in a couple of hours."

An officer approached, the bulletproof vest in one hand and handcuffs dangling from the other. Patrick glanced back at his pack for a brief moment, seeing their eyes on him, before he was taken into custody once more.

11

"Can I throw rocks at them?" Wade asked, peering through the blinds at the mob of press waiting on the sidewalk below the flat.

"No," Jono said.

"What about flowerpots?"

"We don't have any, but even if we did, no."

"What if I singe them? Just a little bit?"

"And have that be a breaking news story? No, Wade. You are not allowed to singe the press."

Wade stepped away from the window, grumbling under his breath. "*Fine.*"

Jono could understand Wade's frustration, because he didn't like the media following them around either. Being treated as if they were a sideshow in a circus made Jono want to lash out, but they couldn't. Every move they made was being watched, which restricted them from retaliating against Estelle. Jono figured that was what she'd wanted, and he hated it.

He'd had to clean up the flat after the police and FBI ransacked it Sunday. They'd ended up not taking much—Patrick's mobile, his agency-issued laptop, and every file from his desk. Hermes had wandered around getting in Jono's way to keep him from snapping at other agents. When everyone had finally left, Jono had found Patrick's dagger, the lone Greek coin, and the broken-off piece of the Morrígan's staff in its warded iron box on the bed, with the immortal nowhere to be found.

The flat had stunk of strangers for hours afterward, driving Jono mad. Even with Wade staying over, it had taken time for the intrusive smell to fade away. Their pack was buddying up as a precautionary measure, and with Patrick having been in jail, Wade had volunteered to stay with him last night. He hadn't made up his mind yet if he was going to stay another night or sleep at Sage's home.

Sage planned on doing more wedding planning stuff when she got home, despite everything going on, and Jono would rather not be in the midst of that. He wasn't sure Wade would either. Sage was currently curled up on the sofa, glued to her laptop. She'd been on a conference call with Tiarnán earlier that Jono had barely paid attention to, but he knew they'd have to meet with her boss eventually. The alliance ran both ways, and Tiarnán had need of them.

Marek was sprawled beside Sage, staring at the television but not really watching it. He'd paid Patrick's bond out of his own pocket, not dipping into pack money, and Jono knew there was no way they'd ever be able to repay him for that generosity. He knew the money would get returned if—*when*—Patrick was found not guilty, but the fact that Marek hadn't thought twice about paying it had made Jono so incredibly grateful for his friends.

"I want Patrick to get here so we can eat," Wade said as he flopped down onto the armchair. "I bet he's hungry. Prison food always looks gross in movies."

"Have we found something you won't eat?" Sage asked, not looking up from her laptop.

Wade frowned thoughtfully. "Maybe? Not like a jail could hold me. I could've busted Patrick out, now that I think about it. One tail flick—"

"There will be no destroying federal buildings," Jono interrupted. "Stop taking after Patrick."

"Someone has to until he gets back."

"Which should be soon, so no need to plan a jailbreak when it's not needed."

They'd gone with Marek to pay the bond, but Danai was the one to have picked up Patrick from jail. Jono had wanted to, but the news was already filled with talking heads railing against his release while charged with murder. The talk of double standards for federal agents or police officers compared with the average citizen was getting a lot of traction on the airwaves.

All in all, it would've been a spectacle, one Danai had told them all to avoid, which was why they'd come here. Emma and Leon were back at their place, trying to stay under the radar while keeping an eye on PreterWorld and other social media sites to see what sides people were taking. Jono didn't envy them that job.

Between fielding calls from the packs under their protection, Jono had cooked up supper, but not knowing when Patrick would arrive meant everything was covered and staying warm in the oven. Jono went into the kitchen to check on the food again to make sure it wouldn't get too dried out. He was in the process of pulling bread out of the cupboard when the background sound of the crowd on the street changed pitch. He dropped the bread on the counter and left the kitchen.

Sage had abandoned her laptop for the window, peering through the blinds at the street below. "He's here."

Jono wanted to run downstairs and clear Patrick a space through the reporters, but Sage had impressed on him earlier the need to keep a low profile. He opened the front door of the flat and waited, nearly breaking the doorknob in his impatience.

Patrick's heartbeat filled his ears, and Jono's shoulders loosened when he got the first breath of that familiar bitter scent. Then

Patrick rounded the bottom landing, still in the suit from earlier, a plastic bag containing the clothes and shoes he'd been arrested in clutched in one hand.

"Pat," Jono said, staring at him.

The naked relief in Patrick's tired face was all it took for Jono to meet him halfway, stopping in the middle of the stairs to drag him into a tight hug. Patrick dropped the bag on the step he stood on, tucking his face against Jono's shoulder and letting out a deep, shuddering breath. Jono buried his nose into Patrick's dark red hair, smelling harsh soap and a multitude of other scents that had embedded themselves into freckled skin where they didn't belong.

Patrick's grip on his shirt was tight enough to stretch the fabric, but Jono didn't care. All he cared about was getting to hold the man he loved and never wanting to let go.

"Fuck, I've missed you," Patrick mumbled into his skin, trying to get closer.

Jono pressed a hard kiss to his skull before taking a deep breath. "Couldn't sleep without you."

Patrick laughed, the sound choked out and shaky. His fingers dug into Jono's back before finally easing up. He shifted on the step, missing the edge, his weight tipping backward. Jono tightened his arms to keep Patrick from falling.

"Made you dinner," Jono said, brushing a kiss against Patrick's cheek.

Patrick pulled back enough that Jono could see his face and the shadows under his eyes. "Prison food is gross."

"I told you," Wade said from their flat's landing. "You should've let me break him out."

Patrick laughed tiredly, and Jono kissed the sound away. Patrick let him, one hand cupping Jono's stubbled jaw.

"You need a shave," Patrick murmured.

"You need a kip." Jono bent down to retrieve the plastic bag with the clothes and shoes. "Is Danai coming up?"

"No. We're meeting with her tomorrow though. Setsuna is

flying down in the morning for it."

Jono maneuvered Patrick around in the stairwell, urging him to climb with a hand to his lower back. Patrick made it to the landing, and Wade didn't wait any longer before hugging him and lifting him off his feet.

"Put me down," Patrick grumbled, but he still hugged Wade back.

"Next time, I'm breaking you out," Wade promised.

"Here's hoping there won't *be* a next time," Sage said. "Let Patrick get inside so we can feed him."

Wade released Patrick, and they all returned to the flat. Jono locked the door behind them, and the scent of Patrick's magic filled the air as he cast a silence ward. Quiet followed a burst of static, blocking out the world. Jono sighed, pleased to have the flat put to rights again.

"I need a shower," Patrick said, rubbing at his eyes.

Sage wrapped her arms around him and hugged him, rubbing his back for a few seconds. Then she released him and pressed a quick kiss to his cheek. "Go shower. We'll get dinner ready."

She didn't scent mark him, but Jono knew she wasn't the only one itching to press their pack scent back into Patrick's skin. He didn't smell like any of them anymore, only where he'd been —prison.

Jono and Sage worked on getting dinner out of the oven, reheated where needed in the microwave or stove, and set up on the dining table. They only had four chairs, so Wade grabbed the one from Patrick's desk in the guest bedroom. It was a tight fit, but Jono almost preferred that after rattling around the flat alone for the past day or so.

Patrick finally came out, smelling like the soap and shampoo he used, the harshness from before washed away. Jono spent a good solid minute pressing his scent into Patrick's skin, and then it was Sage's turn. Between the two of them, they covered Patrick in pack scent, erasing the memory of its absence.

"You done?" Patrick asked, but a smile tugged at his mouth.

Jono kissed it away. "For now."

They joined Marek and Wade at the table, and Wade hadn't filled his plate yet. He handed Patrick the serving tongs for the steaks with a flourish.

"You go first," Wade said.

It was his own version of care, and Jono didn't bother hiding his smile. The rest of them didn't serve themselves until Patrick had filled his plate first and started digging in. Patrick ate with a sort of single-minded focus that told Jono he hadn't eaten much while locked up. Stress probably played a factor in that, as well as whatever had been served. But magic users needed to be fed, and he made a mental note to make some of Patrick's favorite dishes for the rest of the week.

No one spoke, the companionable silence that settled over the table broken only by the comforting heartbeat echoing in Jono's ears from his left. Having Patrick back settled the ferocious ache he'd carried around since the arrest, and Jono didn't want to let him out of his sight.

He could've done without Hermes ruining his good mood.

"Doesn't this look cozy," the god said as he waltzed out of the bedroom.

Jono made a face at the burst of ozone that ruined the taste of perfectly good steak in his mouth. "Fuck off."

"Is that any way to greet a guest?"

"Guests are invited. No one invited you," Patrick said.

Hermes smirked. "Lucky for you I don't need an invitation, Pattycakes."

Patrick set down his fork and knife, twisting around on his chair. Jono glared at Hermes over the top of Patrick's head. "What do you want?"

The immortal wasn't wearing the FBI uniform from Sunday, dressed once more in his typical torn jeans and band T-shirt. His dyed-green curls looked a little faded, dark brown coming in at the roots, and it was that color which more closely matched his gold-brown eyes.

"Your dagger is safe," Hermes said.

"I saw it on my nightstand," Patrick said.

Hermes raised his hand and uncurled his fingers, revealing the carved wooden raven resting on his palm. "This does not belong to you."

"It doesn't belong to you either. Put it back in the box I had it in."

"Fenrir warned you to leave it alone," Jono reminded the god.

Hermes tossed the piece of the Morrígan's staff from hand to hand. "You never told us you broke the staff, Pattycakes."

"Srecha gave me her blessing. What did you think was going to happen?" Patrick asked.

Jono's gaze strayed to Patrick's left hand for a second, where his skin had carried that goddess' burning mark in Paris.

"If the staff is broken, does that negate some of its power? Shouldn't you gods be happy about that?" Sage asked.

Hermes snorted. "What a quaint way of viewing things."

"Return the raven to Patrick."

The smell of ozone got stronger, and Jono looked across the table at where Marek sat, his hazel eyes gone completely white. He didn't know which Norn was speaking through his friend, but Jono wished they hadn't joined the conversation. Marek didn't need to lose any more colors.

Hermes shot Marek and the goddess stealing his voice and eyes a dirty look. "It doesn't belong to him, cousin."

"Neither does it belong to you. Return it. I will not ask again."

Jono wondered if Hermes was going to disobey a direct order from one of the Fates, but in the end, the messenger god tossed the carved raven into the air and it disappeared. "Fine."

"It better be back in its warded box," Patrick warned.

"I know better than to ignore a request by one such as Urðr."

Jono snorted his disbelief of that. "Why are you here?"

"I've a message to deliver. It's what I do."

"Try email next time. Or give us a ring."

"So you can ignore me? Where's the fun in that?" Hermes laughed, but he was the only one to do so. "Hera has a warning for you both."

Patrick tensed in Jono's arms. "Are she and Zeus returning?"

"They're enjoying the summer in Santorini, but they still have ties here. The Crescent Coven will always pray to her."

Hermes stepped closer, and Jono couldn't stop the growl he let out. When the god reached for Patrick, Jono grabbed his wrist and didn't let go, ignoring the electric shock to his body the touch brought on.

"Don't," Jono growled.

Hermes twisted his wrist, easily breaking the hold. When he turned his hand around again, tiny, dried-out white blossoms were piled on his palm. Patrick sucked in a sharp breath, apparently recognizing the remnants of flowers Hermes poured into Patrick's lap.

"The cardinal points were overrun with blossoms before they had the life sucked out of them, and it is not our doing. Someone else is interfering with the flora on this island. The parks think it is winter when it is summer."

"What are those?" Wade asked right before he sneezed, nose tucked into the bend of his elbow. "Ugh. Smells like magic."

Patrick touched one of the flowers with a fingertip, frowning at them. "They're cliff roses. Hermes gave me a bunch last summer as an apology bouquet. Bushes of them started growing out of the ground in areas where we placed Greek coins to contain Ethan's spell."

"It wasn't an apology bouquet," Hermes said.

Patrick ignored him. "Prospect Park carried some strange magic inside it when I went to investigate Youssef's murder scene. I didn't think anything of it since it had nothing to do with the murder."

"Are you certain about that? The cliff roses were made with magic, created to be unobtrusive. They no longer are. Brooklyn could've been another target."

"What do you want me to do about it? The SOA took my gun and badge. I can't investigate anything right now, and we have our own problems, in case you didn't notice."

"We are aware of what is going on."

"Yeah? Then who was it that freed me from jail? Because I was charged with murder, and getting released with a charge like that never happens."

"*You are useless to us if you are locked up. Maat agreed to ensure your continued freedom,*" Urðr said through Marek.

Patrick froze. Jono curled his arm around the other man to flatten his hand over Patrick's heart, feeling scar tissue through the thin fabric of his sleeping shirt.

"Which god is that?" Jono asked quietly.

Hermes rocked back on his heels, gaze half-lidded. "Egyptian."

Jono tightened his hold on Patrick, knowing how he felt about that pantheon being attacked and used during the Thirty-Day War. The flash of bitter guilt that washed through Patrick's scent made Jono press down on his chest harder.

Jono glared at Hermes. "Are you done playing errand boy?"

"For now."

Hermes took a step back and disappeared through the veil as only a god could. The sharp scent of ozone faded with his exit, as did the all-encompassing white of Marek's eyes. He slumped forward in his chair, holding up his head with both hands as he groaned.

"Fuck," Marek muttered, expression twisted with pain.

"I'm sorry," Patrick said.

"It's not your fault I'm a seer."

Sage turned in her seat and placed her hand on the back of Marek's neck. "Do you need Victoria?"

Marek swallowed loudly. "Yeah."

Sage looked across the table at them, mouth twisting. "I'll take him home."

Patrick pulled away from Jono, getting to his feet. "I'll cast a look-away ward so you don't get hassled by reporters."

It took a couple of minutes for Sage to gather their things and then carefully lead Marek out of the apartment. Jono didn't want them to walk to their car alone, not with the media still on the street and risk of an attack by Estelle's people, but Sage had only shaken her head at him and promised to ring him when they made it home.

Wade didn't leave the table, still happily eating his way through the food. He stuck his fork into another steak and dropped it on his plate. "I'll clean up when I'm done eating."

"Cheers," Jono said, before steering Patrick into their bedroom.

Patrick sprawled on the bed while Jono got undressed, stripping down to skin. Then he crawled onto the bed and lay down on top of Patrick, pressing him down into the mattress. Jono tucked his face against the warm skin of Patrick's throat, breathing in the clean scent of pack.

"I don't want to lose you," Jono murmured.

Patrick's arms wrapped around his torso, holding him tight. "I wish I could say you won't."

But they both knew how the gods liked to play with their lives. This latest mess was further proof of that.

Jono sighed heavily and rolled them onto their sides, tucking his head beneath Patrick's chin. Lying in bed with him, listening to his heartbeat, should've been comforting, but the stress of an unknown future was starting to become impossible to ignore.

"How do we fight this?" Jono asked.

"We take the hits and keep going."

The weariness in Patrick's voice made Jono hold him tighter, unable to stop wondering if their time together was coming to an end none of them could see.

12

"This is quite a mess you're in," Setsuna said.

Patrick eyed where she sat across the conference room table from him in Danai's law firm. Setsuna looked tired, and he wondered how many political attacks she'd taken since his arrest. He'd read through a handful of news stories painting him in a negative light before Jono had taken away his temporary phone so he'd actually eat breakfast.

The food Jono had made him sat like a rock in his stomach. As nice as the gesture was, and as much as Patrick missed eating food that wasn't made in a jail kitchen, his appetite was nosediving. Stress made everything taste sour.

"You can't be surprised this happened," Patrick said.

Setsuna pursed her lips, glancing at where Jono sat next to Patrick on his side of the table. "I'm not. I warned you of the risks, but it wasn't my place to stop you."

Jono's grip on Patrick's thigh tightened, his words coming out sharp. "Not like you could."

This wasn't how Patrick had thought Jono and Setsuna would ever meet. His preference would've been they never met in person at all, but that was no longer an option. They were both too stubborn and hardheaded, neither willing to give an inch when it came to what they thought was best for him. Sighing, Patrick settled his hand over Jono's and shot Sage and Wade a pleading look where they sat farther down the table.

Sage frowned but didn't give voice to her opinion while Wade very loudly chewed on the chip he shoved into his mouth.

"Coming here won't put you in a good light with everyone back in DC," Patrick said.

"Despite the calls for my resignation from political talking heads, I have the support of the president. We know what's at stake even if the agencies coming after you don't," Setsuna replied.

Jono scowled. "That does fuck all for Patrick's standing with the public. And who's to say the FBI won't be coming after you?"

"Let's wait for Danai to get back so we can figure out a way to fight this," Patrick said tiredly. He knew today wasn't going to be easy, and he already had a headache. The more he could put off making it worse, the better.

They settled into an uncomfortable silence that was only broken when Danai returned to the conference room, a file cradled in one arm. She gave them all a polite smile before focusing on Setsuna.

"It's nice to meet you, Director," Danai said as she sat down.

"I wish it was under better circumstances, or not at all," Setsuna said.

"Don't we all? I understand you have some documentation that you think might help with Patrick's defense. Before we get into that, I'd like to go over Patrick's whereabouts during the time Youssef was killed."

Patrick grimaced. "I told you. I was meeting with one of my CIs."

"And I told you I'm going to need a name. It's important for establishing an alibi."

"Which CI?" Setsuna asked.

"You know which one," Patrick said flatly.

Danai glanced at him, then at Setsuna, before sighing. "Stonewalling me, as your attorney, is not going to help your case any."

"His CI is a matter of national security," Setsuna said.

"Is this the same information your agency submitted to the court under seal on Patrick's behalf, along with the military? I still haven't received a copy."

Setsuna tilted her head slightly in Danai's direction. "Your lack of security credentials has been an issue. We ran an extensive background check on you over the weekend. As soon as you sign the corresponding forms and agreements, you'll get your copy of the information in question."

"You did a federal background check on me in one weekend without my consent?"

"The US Department of the Preternatural helped, but yes. As to consent, your fingerprints are already a government record from when you passed the bar, and you've gone through others for travel purposes."

"I still didn't consent to it," Danai said coldly.

Setsuna opened the briefcase she'd arrived with. Patrick watched as she pulled out a stack of files, several in sealed envelopes stamped with faded ink stating *Certified Copy*. She organized them into different stacks before handing over a fairly thick one to Danai.

"Sign these so we can continue discussing Patrick's defense."

Danai eyed the height of the stack, one corner of her mouth twitching. "It'll be an hour."

"Your soul is safe."

"I'm still reading every word."

It didn't take an hour, more like thirty minutes, and no one talked while Danai reviewed the documents in front of her and signed off on each one. Then she handed them back to Setsuna, a displeased look in her eyes.

"Start talking, and you better have something worthwhile to help my client," Danai said.

Setsuna folded her hands together on top of the table and addressed Danai. "Patrick cannot tell you who he was meeting with at the time of Youssef's death. That is a nonstarter, and information that will not be revealed, even under seal."

"If he has a valid alibi—"

"He won't tell you. Neither will the government."

Danai clenched her jaw before looking at Patrick. "This is not in your best interest."

"Believe me, I know," Patrick said, shrugging stiffly.

"Which means we must go a different route, and the only likely avenue of success is the magical signature the US Attorney's Office incorrectly believes is Patrick's," Setsuna said.

Danai leaned back in her seat, tapping the tip of her pen against her yellow legal notepad. "Why wouldn't it be his?"

Patrick's heartbeat ratcheted up to an uncomfortable speed as he stared at Setsuna. "No."

Setsuna looked at him with eyes that held no pity, but also no warmth. "This is the only way to get your case dismissed."

"Murder charges are rarely dismissed."

"They can be if it is proven a defendant was framed."

Sage got up from her seat by Wade to take the one on the other side of Patrick. She took his hand in hers and squeezed it gently. "If we can force the US Attorney's Office to produce the trishula as well as the body, and have a third party perform a forensic analysis on the magical signature results compared to yours, there could be enough of a difference to set you free."

"Magical signatures can't be faked," Patrick said.

Setsuna picked up a Redweld bucket filled with documents, along with a thick, sealed package whose clear top covering made it possible to read the face page of the pleading. She handed both to Danai.

"Magical signatures are difficult to duplicate, but those with familial blood ties are closely related, and there is nothing more similar than that of twins, identical or not," Setsuna said.

Patrick closed his eyes, biting his bottom lip until he tasted blood. Jono's warm fingers curled over his chin as the metallic tang washed across his tongue.

"Don't," Jono said quietly.

"If this gets out, it'll require a review of my soul. We can't—" Patrick broke off, turning to look at Jono.

His tie to Hannah was buried deep, walled off, and if he could cut it out completely, he would've done so already. Letting the government dig into his soul would possibly reveal that tie, yes, but it also risked revealing the soulbond that connected him to Jono, and that was a capital offense in the eyes of the law. He might escape one murder charge only to be sentenced to death a second time for messing with someone else's soul.

"We'll find a way around that," Jono said quietly, thumb skating over Patrick's lips.

"These are family court records and juvenile records," Danai said slowly, gaze riveted on the stack of documents she was flipping through. "These—"

She broke off, eyes flicking from side to side as she absorbed the information Setsuna had given her. Patrick's stomach twisted as he watched her read what could only be the record of his past: the police report concerning his mother's murder, the eventual death certificates the Salem medical examiner's office signed off on for Patrick and Hannah Greene, the name change order that had stripped him of his past, and quite possibly the restricted report of his and the Hellions' actions at the end of the Thirty-Day War that revealed Ethan was alive.

Patrick Greene had survived the horrors of what had happened in a Salem basement only to die at Persephone's feet. Patrick Collins had been born in Washington, DC, a false history provided by the federal government as a form of witness protection giving him life.

The gods had tasked Setsuna with keeping him hidden from his father, and that false-named protection lasted right up until the Thirty-Day War. Patrick knew he couldn't hide forever, but he'd lived twenty-two years with a last name that felt more like his than the one on his original birth certificate ever would.

Danai finally stopped reviewing Patrick's past and lifted her gaze to meet his. He couldn't read the look in her eyes. "This could free you, but it will make your life difficult."

"It's already difficult," Patrick said.

"Is all of this documentation what was submitted under seal?"

Setsuna nodded. "Most of it, yes."

"Then here's what we're going to do." Danai tapped her pen against her legal notepad again, staring at Patrick. "I'm going to submit a motion to unseal and a motion to dismiss for defective indictment, arguing that you were set up by your father for Youssef's murder and it was done using your twin sister's magic. I'll draft a declaration from this paperwork for you to sign, and I'll do one for Setsuna as well."

Setsuna picked up her phone, presumably to make a reminder for herself or send an email. "I'll have the SOA's Legal department review both declarations and send you any modifications."

"Fine, but I'll need a quick turnaround on your end for signatures. The US Attorney's Office will fight the motion, because that needs to be their position, but I'm hopeful the evidence will make them rethink the case. I'll send a Brady demand for their lab report today and then start on the writ for habeas corpus et animum for the necromancer. We'll get it served, and if they fight it, we'll submit a motion to the court. We'll have a third-party forensic firm review the report against the one the SOA has on record for you as soon as we receive it."

"How long will it take you to file the motions?" Sage asked.

"No later than the end of the week." Danai pointed her finger at Patrick. "We'll be focusing on the motion to dismiss, but if it isn't granted, we'll need to revisit your whereabouts during the murder."

Patrick shrugged, knowing that was another fight he'd have to face if it came down to it. Giving up Lucien and Ashanti's ability to walk in daylight was a nonstarter. He could maybe play off meeting with Carmen, but if traffic cameras caught anything of the others arriving, there went his alibi. The FBI was most likely doing a deep dive on his phone and figuring out his GPS record if they'd even gotten through the encryption and security features yet. Jono had said Hermes had probably messed with it, and Patrick hoped the god hadn't done anything that would get flagged.

Patrick wasn't sure when or if he'd get that phone back, but Sage had presented him with a new one that morning, the line held under her plan. His name wasn't linked to it in any way, which wouldn't deter the FBI whenever they found out about it. Patrick needed to rebuild his contacts from memory, though he was reticent to call anyone without the proper security and burner apps on the phone.

"I would advise that you stay out of sight of the media for the next few days," Danai said.

"We have pack responsibilities," Patrick said.

"The both of you are magnets for the media right now. You'll endanger any privacy the packs under your protection would want to keep. Call them if you have to, but refrain from in-person meetings."

"If Estelle and her god pack initiate another attack in our territory, we're not going to stand by and do nothing."

"Getting into another fight risks your bond being revoked and the police coming down hard on Jono. The mayor isn't happy with the fighting happening between the packs. It doesn't matter that you're fighting to defend yourselves. The public doesn't care about that. They only care that their commute is ruined and the streets aren't safe. You want to earn good PR points? Don't fight."

"That's not possible," Jono said. "Fighting is how we handle disputes."

"Then do it in your challenge ring."

"Like that's going to happen," Wade muttered loudly from his side of the table. "We don't even have one."

Jono grimaced. "We'll do what's best for our pack."

Danai didn't seem thrilled about that answer, but Patrick agreed with Jono. Their pack had to come first, especially now.

They spent another hour in the conference room, with Patrick forced to revisit moments of his life he'd rather forget about forever. Danai was brutally kind in her interrogation of his past to secure his future, but Patrick felt as if he'd been flayed open to the bone by the end of the meeting.

"I think that's everything I need for now," Danai said, gathering up all her paperwork. "I'll be in touch if I have any further questions. Expect to hear from me on Thursday about your declaration."

Patrick reached over and snagged her pen, writing out his new contact information. "I have a new number until I get my phone back. Since I'm not working, feel free to call me anytime."

"You haven't been fired," Setsuna reminded him.

Patrick scowled at her. "You took my gun and badge and put me on unpaid administrative leave. That's as close to fired as you can get."

"If the charges are dismissed, you'll be taken off leave."

"That's a pretty big if."

"On leave or not, you'll still be required to appear before whatever hearing Congress sets up regarding all of this. They haven't picked a date yet, but they will sometime soon." Setsuna started organizing the documents she was keeping and putting them back into her suitcase. "The truth coming out will change your standing amongst your peers, but it won't change your employment with the agency as long as I am the director."

"Your position isn't permanent."

"The president still backs me, which means I stay, and so will you."

His badge made things easier when it came to following the gods' orders. Paying his soul debt would become a lot harder if he didn't have the government backing that would open doors. He knew that even if he got it back, none of his fellow agents would ever trust him again. They'd see him as dirty, and any chance at getting promoted or retiring with the SOA had been irrevocably damaged by the charges levied against him.

Jono curled his hand around Patrick's, his touch warm. Patrick glanced at their joined hands, knowing that whatever happened, Jono would be right by his side, no matter what. If he could no longer work as an SOA special agent, then leading their god pack would become his job until he could find something else.

That all hinged on them *keeping* their god pack. With everything going on, Patrick knew the stakes were even higher, and the risks were getting more dangerous.

But they weren't backing down, and if it took finally coming clean on who he was to stop Ethan, then so be it. He'd kept enough secrets over the years, buried enough truth to survive. Time for some of it to see the light of day again.

13

TEN O'CLOCK AT NIGHT ON THURSDAY IN BROOKLYN WAS HOT AND muggy, but the darkness provided some bit of cover from prying eyes. Patrick's look-away ward helped ensure no one bothered them on their walk to Prospect Park.

Jono glanced at Patrick as they walked down Vanderbilt Avenue toward the Grand Army Plaza entrance. He was only half listening to the conversation Patrick was having with Danai on his new mobile, who was apparently still at work finalizing the brief. Jono had left his mobile at home to hide the fact they were in Brooklyn.

"We're on track to file tomorrow morning. I'll have our PR coordinator reach out to our contacts with some of the news stations to get a statement out. If it involves a live appearance, did you want to join in?" Danai asked.

Patrick hunched his shoulders, and Jono wrapped his arm around them, despite the heat. It might be creeping closer to midnight, but that didn't mean the weather was any cooler.

"No. If the case gets dismissed, maybe later," Patrick said.

"Then if you trust me to speak for you, I will."

"Just don't put words in my mouth."

"I'm your advocate, not your enemy."

Patrick let out a heavy sigh, tugging on the brim of his baseball cap. Despite them driving over to Brooklyn and it being well past sunset, he hadn't removed it since it did a good job of hiding his dark red hair.

"I know."

"I'll call you tomorrow after I've handled everything on my end. Normally I wouldn't seek out the news, but we need to change the narrative, and I won't be saying anything that we aren't stating in our filing." She paused, her voice gentling a little. "I would advise keeping a low profile over the weekend. The docket is public record, and every interested news agency is going to be accessing the motion and underlying evidence once the word is out."

"Understood."

They ended the call, and Patrick tucked his mobile into his back pocket. He leaned into Jono as they walked, the lit-up Soldiers' and Sailors' Arch growing larger as they approached the plaza. The police presence from last week had long since disappeared, though patrols of Prospect Park had been upped after Youssef's murder.

"The park still feels weird," Patrick muttered.

"Think it's Ethan?" Jono asked.

Patrick shook his head. "I don't know. Whatever it is, it's sucking the life out of all the plants, and that's definitely not normal."

"A god?"

"Hard to say, but we can't rule it out."

Jono wished the Brooklyn Night Court had chosen a different spot to meet at, but Jono knew the vampires weren't about to offer up their territory's inner sanctum as a bargaining spot. The media attention Jono and Patrick brought with them these days wasn't something the preternatural world particularly enjoyed. It had served to keep Estelle and her god pack in check, but Jono knew that break from attacks wouldn't last long.

"We should've parked closer," Patrick said as they waited for the light to change so they could cross the street.

"If there'd been a parking spot, I would have. As it is, we're in a red zone," Jono said.

The government plates on Patrick's Mustang would hopefully ensure he wouldn't get towed. No guarantee that wouldn't happen though, especially with all the negative news stories about him specifically and their pack generally getting spread around.

Their god pack's reputation was getting hit hard. So far, the packs under their protection were choosing to stay with them, but Jono knew that solidarity was tenuous unless he and Patrick could prove themselves worthy of leading.

The light changed, and they crossed the street, the arch softly lit against the night. The statues on top were grand enough, but it paled in size to the Arc de Triomphe in Paris.

"Not sure it's a good idea to return to the scene of the crime like this," Patrick mused.

"Wasn't your crime," Jono grunted.

They still passed over the site Youssef's body had been dumped at. The kill site was still nowhere to be found since Patrick hadn't committed the murder and couldn't tell anyone anything.

They entered the park, Patrick's look-away ward gaining them some privacy. He didn't bother to cast any witchlights, so it was Jono who led the way through the park to the Vale of Cashmere. It was usually a thick pocket of greenery surrounding a pond and was utterly dark. Right now, the greenery was withered as if winter had come early.

Jono's enhanced eyesight enabled him to make out the area better than a human could. He kept Patrick's hand in his, guiding him forward into the dark. The buzz of mosquitos hummed in the air. Jono didn't care if they bit him since he'd heal in seconds, but Patrick started swearing and slapping at his arms and neck.

"Goddamn bloodsuckers," Patrick said.

"That's no way to talk to your betters," a voice shot back from the dark.

The undead smell of vampires drifted through the air, coating the back of his throat. Jono rocked to a halt some distance from the water, dialing up all his senses. A second later, dark blurs that Jono could barely make out slipped through the tree line and slammed to a halt on the brick pathway they stood on.

Patrick finally called up his magic to give them a little light to see by. The mageglobe that flared to life near his shoulder cast a pale blue light in their immediate area. The illumination reflected off eight pairs of eyes staring at them from the shadows.

Jamere was the master vampire of the Brooklyn Night Court, though he could've passed as a high schooler if one ignored the jagged fangs he flashed in a parody of a smile. Originally from the Caribbean, he'd come to New York City after the Civil War ended. People were fooled by his young appearance, but Jamere had been protecting his territory for over 150 years. Jono would never underestimate him.

Patrick glared at the master vampire. "You aren't our betters."

"We're just the ones you're begging for help," Jamere said.

"Our god pack doesn't beg."

"Maybe you should start."

"We're here to talk about what happened in your territory last week in accordance with our alliance," Jono said.

Jamere sauntered forward, dressed in basketball shorts and an oversized T-shirt, his sneakers making no noise against the brick walkway. "Here's the thing about that alliance. None of you pray to our mother anymore, so I don't think we owe you our help."

"You're that stupid to go against Lucien?"

"He doesn't rule my Night Court."

"But *I* rule all my children, including you," a dangerously amused voice said from the shadows.

Jono had met Ashanti only once, that night in Ginnungagap

after Patrick had returned from overseas, but he would never forget her voice. The mother of all vampires slipped free of the dark like a shadow, all midnight skin and eyes, her hair and clothes the only bright spots on her. The clack of her ironshod bone hooks on the brick echoed softly in the thick muggy air as she approached their group.

Behind her strolled Lucien and Carmen, the only two to escort her to Brooklyn. The rest of Lucien's Night Court had apparently stayed in their territory. With the Dominion Sect and hunters running amok, everyone had to be on guard. Ashanti's presence in the five boroughs was apparently still a well-guarded secret only held within the Night Courts and their god pack. They were all trying to keep it that way for now.

If word ever got out that she was in the United States, Jono knew it would be a bloody mess. Lucien had bargained with the government for a century's worth of diplomatic immunity and border crossing. It pertained only to his Night Court. Ashanti was someone Jono knew no government would be pleased to have in any of their cities.

Patrick had been the one to call Lucien and ask them to come, figuring rightly that Jamere would protest the alliance. Jono would've preferred Ashanti stay far, far away from them. He didn't trust the goddess, didn't trust how Patrick reacted to her presence —like she *could* be trusted, simply because she'd been the one to teach him how to sharpen the edges of his life to survive as he grew.

Jono didn't want Patrick to feel as if he owed her anything, but guilt was a poison sometimes, eating away at rational emotion. Ashanti's resurrection couldn't erase the four years Patrick had grieved for her. All Jono could do was remind him that their future was worth fighting for, no matter the ghosts that followed in their wake.

Jamere's smirk disappeared as Ashanti joined their circle, replaced with a reverence Jono had only ever seen on the faces of religious fanatics. He inclined his head in deep respect at Ashanti, arms spread wide in a half bow, before taking a step back as his Night Court clustered close.

"Mother," Jamere said.

"Child," Ashanti replied silkily. "There are hunters and demons in our territory. I want them gone."

"We will kill them in your name."

"Good. Now tell me what happened here last week with the wolf."

It probably would've been like pulling teeth to get answers out of Jamere if he and Patrick had faced the master vampire alone. Letting Ashanti give the order opened up doors they'd always find shut to them without her help.

"There wasn't a fight. We'd know if one took place. The hunters haven't been subtle when it comes to their attacks." Jamere gestured at the bare trees and pond surrounding them. "One of mine always patrols the park. They didn't see the drop, but they saw the body pinned like a bug beneath the Arch. They reported it to me, and I ordered them to leave it alone. The dead wolf stank of magic, and it wasn't worth getting tied to werecreature problems by moving it."

"Did any of that magic come from the park?" Patrick asked.

Jamere shot him a condescending look. "We aren't made to handle magic. The wolf was dead, and we stayed clear."

"The cliff rose bushes that grew last summer on the cardinal points overran their planting locations and then started dying. When I came to look at the body last week, Prospect Park felt off, magically speaking. It still does," Patrick said, looking at Lucien.

"Are the ley lines affected how they were last summer?" Lucien asked.

Jono knew that Patrick's public record stated he was a mage in name only these days due to damage to his soul. With the soulbond that tied them together, he could once again tap into a ley line, but neither of them was going to announce that fact in front of Jamere and the Brooklyn Night Court.

"The nexus under New York City has been under strict monitoring since then. I haven't been notified of any changes."

Lucien's lips curled up in disdain. "Doesn't mean it hasn't been tampered with. The damage done last summer was due to your agency's failings, remember?"

"You're not saying anything we don't already know."

"If the Dominion Sect is back in New York, there is a reason for it. That they have partnered up with demon-driven hunters is not unusual, merely an annoyance," Ashanti said.

"That annoyance is going after my packs," Jono said irritably.

"Then perhaps you should eradicate the threat."

"Killing Estelle right now will make the charges against Patrick worse, even if we handle it in the challenge ring, which we aren't doing. The goal is to clear Patrick's name and keep our territory. If the alliance we have with the Night Courts stands, then we're here to ask for their help in keeping an eye on our packs and protecting them from hunters."

"We aren't responsible for your mess," Lucien sneered.

Jono glared at him. "If you want to stop Ethan, then you'll help."

Lucien's black eyes narrowed, but he stayed where he was when Ashanti raised one hand in a commanding gesture. Of all the times they'd faced off against the notorious master vampire, Jono had never seen him so deferential before.

Ashanti stared at Jono, the taste of ozone growing stronger on his tongue. "I told Patrick the alliance between our sides would remain intact. We expect aid to be reciprocated when asked for."

Jono raised his chin, never blinking. "We keep our word."

Ashanti's lips parted in a smile. "Good. My children will begin hunting tonight."

At that order, Jamere inclined his head again before leaving, the breeze of his passing fading after a few seconds. Jono wondered if the vampires would come to hate the order to aid them, or if any would attempt to disobey Ashanti. Knowing what he knew about the mother of all vampires through Patrick, Jono assumed their pack would have support until Ashanti ruled otherwise.

Ashanti shifted on her bone hooks, gliding toward where they stood. Jono took a step forward, Fenrir clawing at his soul. The smile on Ashanti's lips told him she was aware of Fenrir, but the god's presence didn't seem to bother her.

"So quick to defend Patrick," she mused.

"He's pack, and he's mine," Jono said, refusing to look away from the black holes that were her eyes. Patrick's magic reflected in them like tiny bits of blue-white flame, stars in a night sky no different than the one above them dimmed by light pollution.

"Your packs prayed to me."

"Not anymore. Not since you came back."

He was done praying to the gods and kneeling before their altars. Love was the only altar Jono would ever worship at from here on out, and Patrick would be the only one to hear his prayers.

Ashanti's smile got wider, revealing the dull iron fangs that looked like jagged mountains in her mouth. "A pity, but not a problem since I am here."

Patrick came to stand next to Jono, their fingers brushing. "If Jamere said it was a body dump that no one saw happen, then Ethan had to have traveled through the veil to do it. I don't know what the traffic cameras caught that night, but they don't have me on any feed. It would've been in the charges if Ethan was able to get a glamour to stick like that."

"Do the cameras have anyone on the feed?" Jono asked.

Patrick shrugged. "No idea. Danai will probably ask for it in the next round of discovery. But it could also be guilty knowledge information, in which case, the US Attorney's Office will fight to keep from revealing it."

"If you're imprisoned again, that helps no one," Lucien said.

"You think I don't fucking know that? We're working on it."

Patrick was free due to a goddess' interference. There was no guarantee how long immortals could bend the legal system to favor Patrick. Jono only hoped their efforts lasted long enough to clear his name.

"Go home. We will keep watch over your pack territory. If need be, I will contact Persephone to ensure your freedom," Ashanti said.

Patrick went rigid beside Jono. "Don't do me any favors."

"She owns your soul debt. Mortal laws can never interfere with that, no matter what your judges, juries, and executioners believe."

"Her help isn't ever free. Whatever price she'd give me this time, I won't pay it. So don't ask her for anything on my behalf."

Ashanti's expression wasn't one Jono would ever call kind, but she showed a sense of almost human understanding no other god had ever offered Patrick. "You can't outrun this."

Patrick barked out a harsh laugh, the sour stench of old pain rising through his bitter scent. "I know. I tried, and it got me nowhere."

Ashanti raised her hand to his face, and Jono wanted to slap it away. He didn't, knowing any strike against her would be returned a thousand-fold by Lucien. That was a fight they didn't have time for.

She touched Patrick's face, and he didn't pull away; Jono wished he would. "Honed yourself sharp over the years I was gone, did you?"

Patrick swallowed hard enough Jono could hear the sound of it in his throat. "That's what you taught me."

"Then remember not to break."

Ashanti let him go and turned her back on them. She disappeared between one eye blink and the next, preternatural speed carrying her away from them. Lucien and Carmen followed after her, leaving Jono and Patrick alone in a winter-dry Prospect Park at the height of summer.

Jono slid his fingers between Patrick's. "Let's go home."

The light from Patrick's mageglobe faded as he drew down his magic, leaving them in darkness. Jono tugged gently on his hand, leading him out of the park and back to the car.

The long drive home was made in silence, and Jono didn't try to break it. Whatever thoughts were running through Patrick's mind, he wasn't ready to speak them. Jono wouldn't pressure him to do so. He was looking forward to maybe getting a couple of hours of sleep before Friday morning came with its expected headache.

Estelle waiting for them on the sidewalk in front of their brownstone, carrying a demon in her soul, ensured neither of them would sleep easy that night.

Patrick's magic washed over Jono in a shield he could actually see, raised between them and the enemy come calling at the witching hour. He pulled free his dagger, the matte-black blade erupting in heavenly fire. Jono didn't shift, not yet, but it wouldn't take long for him to change forms. He dialed up his senses, and only then was he able to discern the crackling ozone scent of a god buried beneath the sulfur of demons.

Estelle was guarded by Nicholas and several other god pack members on the sidewalk in front of the apartment building. The gargoyles were lined up on the stoop, refusing them passage with the help of a god.

The tall figure should've been shadowed from the distant streetlight, but his aura was bright enough that it glowed like a halo around his form, illuminating him. The long linen shirt he wore over fitted trousers couldn't hide the blue skin on his throat or the snake that coiled loosely around it like a living necklace, hanging over his shoulders. When he turned his head to watch their approach, the third eye in his forehead blinked out of sync with the other two.

"Fuck," Patrick muttered, not caring who heard him. "I hope Shiva doesn't ask me to get his trishula back from the FBI."

"I can easily find another offering," Shiva drawled.

Jono and Patrick didn't move. Fenrir drifted through Jono's

mind but didn't demand control. The last thing Jono wanted to do was fight the god for bodily autonomy.

"What do you want?"

Shiva's teeth flashed in a quick smile. "Nothing as of yet."

Jono could only hope the god would never ask for anything, but he knew that was wishful thinking. He shifted his attention from Shiva to Estelle and the demon riding her soul. "And you? What the fuck do you want?"

"We're here with an offer," the demon said, the voice tangled in Estelle's familiar from London and the subway, a nightmare that had been aimed at them since the bounty on Jono's head first appeared.

"Andras." Jono clenched his hands into fists, the prick of claws cutting into his palms as he realized what stared out of Estelle's bright amber eyes. "We don't bargain with the enemy."

Andras spread Estelle's hands, the veins beneath her skin tracing black lines through her body as the smell of sulfur burned through the air. "This is your last and final chance to back down. Take it, and leave New York City to us."

Jono forced out a laugh past his clenched teeth. "No."

"You won't win in or out of a challenge ring, no matter your alliances."

"Fuck off. You wouldn't be here if we weren't still a threat."

Andras laughed, the other demons joining in until a chorus of hell rang in the street. "I fear no one."

"You fear the future where you lose," Shiva said, not moving from the stoop. "You fear your savior being born."

Andras snapped Estelle's teeth at the god but didn't move from their spot on the sidewalk. Neither did the other demons. Jono wondered when it was Andras had possessed Estelle, and if it had been before or after Youssef had died.

"Get the fuck out of here before I send you back to the hell you crawled out of," Patrick warned, raising his dagger in a pointed threat.

Andras hissed at him, the sound discordant. "If you refuse to give up the city, then we will see you in the streets."

"We're already there," Jono said with a derisive snort, thinking about all the fighting that had already happened over the months. "New York City isn't yours, and it isn't Estelle's. It's ours."

"You'll die believing that delusion."

"Not tonight."

Which was proven true when Andras and the other demons fled in the werecreatures they possessed, sulfur drifting on the muggy breeze. Jono didn't trust why they had come or the ease with which they had fled. He trusted the god guarding their home even less.

"Are we going to have to go through you to get to bed?" Jono asked.

Shiva stepped down to the sidewalk. "No. Hermes suggested I take my nightly walk around your territory instead of through Central Park."

"Our home. Sure," Patrick said.

More like the walk was done to protect the bit of a goddess' staff capable of raising millions of dead.

Shiva faced them, one hand absently stroking the snake he carried over his shoulders, the beast hissing softly at the touch. The god's three eyes blinked out of sync at them, and Jono found it difficult to meet his gaze, not knowing where to look.

"Do not give them New York City. It is an altar you can ill afford to give up," Shiva said.

"It's a bloody city," Jono said.

"The Dominion Sect used the pyramids in Egypt to bring a hell to Earth. What makes you think they will not use the skyscrapers of this city to perform the same feat? Altars come in many forms. Your god should know that, wolf."

Patrick sheathed his dagger and lowered his shield. "We know."

Jono narrowed his eyes. "You could've helped us out and killed the demon rather than let it go."

Shiva laughed, the sound like soft thunder that Jono hoped wouldn't wake the neighbors. "We gods are not supposed to directly interfere in another god's creation."

"Funny how that's all you've been doing for years," Patrick bit out.

"Ethan risks us all. It is one thing to be forgotten by history, quite another to be eradicated completely. We take offense when it matters. But demons?" Shiva shrugged, the snake coiled around his throat hissing with the movement. "They are one of the dominant stories these days, as am I and my brethren. We have no desire to have angels walk the world."

"But you'll let demons?"

"Demons can be banished. Angels always refuse to leave their prophets' sides. They are aggravating that way."

Shiva turned his back on them and headed down the street in the direction the demon-possessed werecreatures had fled. Jono could only hope the god was going hunting. He pressed his hand to the small of Patrick's back. "Let's get inside."

Patrick nodded jerkily, and Jono led him home, behind their threshold, into the only safety they could find right now—within each other's arms.

14

"WE COULD WATCH SOMETHING ELSE?" WADE ASKED AS HE FLOPPED down into an armchair.

Patrick grunted wordlessly at him, gaze locked on the television in Sage and Marek's home. "You can in the other room."

"I brought you snacks. How can I support you with snacks if I'm in the other room?"

A packet of Pop-Tarts dropped into Patrick's lap, flung from Wade's direction. He glanced down at the silvery foil packet containing two mass-produced pastries and fingered one corner. He wasn't hungry, his stomach too knotted up from stress for him to eat, but the gesture was appreciated.

"Thanks, but it's okay. I'm not hungry," Patrick said, tossing it back with a smile he hoped didn't look like a grimace.

Wade caught it one-handed, his other hand holding two strawberry Pop-Tarts fanned out like playing cards. "I'll eat them for you."

Patrick nodded absently, returning his attention to the television. They'd turned it to a national cable news channel, since that was the one Danai had called earlier to say she'd appear on.

He and Jono had woken up around dawn, hauled themselves out of bed, and driven cross-town to the Art Deco building Marek owned. They'd parked in the garage rather than the street, intent on spending the entire day and rest of the weekend with their friends, holed up away from the eyes of the world.

"Coffee?" Jono asked, holding out a mug for Patrick as he came around the couch.

Patrick took it with both hands so the coffee wouldn't spill. "Thanks."

Jono sat beside him on the couch, holding a cup of tea in his left hand. Patrick slouched a little until his shoulder rested against Jono's, soaking up the warmth radiating off the other man. The day had seemed daunting when he'd first woken up. The only thing making it bearable was Jono and the rest of their pack.

"Tiarnán needs to have a meeting with us today," Sage said as she came down the stairs from the upper level of the penthouse.

"Could it wait?" Jono asked.

"He said it's important. He's asking as an ally and is on his way over right now. If you want me to call him back and cancel, I can, but it sounded urgent."

Patrick took a sip of coffee. "No, let's keep that meeting. I'm going to need a distraction after the news hits. Think he's going to finally ask us to help find whoever is missing?"

"I think it's a little more complicated than that, but we'll find out when he gets here."

Sage had her personal MacBook tucked under one arm and carried a binder in her other arm. Patrick knew the binder contained the master organization of her and Marek's wedding. At some point, he still needed to have his suit fitting, though he wasn't sure if he'd even be able to attend.

"Not like things aren't already complicated enough," Jono muttered.

A chyron started scrolling red across the bottom of the screen as the anchor finished up their current spiel, announcing an update on his murder case.

"It's about to get worse," Patrick said.

The front door slammed open as Emma and Leon hurried through, having run up from their apartment below, preternatural speed enabling them to arrive in seconds.

"We saw it was starting. Thought you could use some support," Leon said as he raked one hand through his dark hair.

"Marek," Sage shouted up the stairs. "It's starting."

Patrick tuned everyone out as they came to huddle around the couch. Wade reached for the remote and raised the volume as the midmorning star anchor, Ryleigh, talked her way into Danai's introduction. Then the screen split, showing the anchor in the studio and Danai in her office on a remote video link.

"We have with us this morning Danai Belvedere, the attorney representing defendant Patrick Collins in the case of Youssef Khan's murder," Ryleigh said with that clear, neutral accent every television personality had. "Welcome, Danai."

"Thank you for having me," Danai said calmly.

"Is it true your office filed a motion to dismiss today in the USDC Southern District of New York? My understanding is that's a rare motion to submit so early in a case. Can you tell us why you think the case has a good chance to be dismissed considering the charges?"

"As you know, my client offered up a secured bond to the court on his own accord and was released on his own recognizance. With the charges levied against him, that decision shows the government's argument isn't as strong as it appears. Considering the evidence we submitted to the court this morning, I believe our defense will prove beyond a reasonable doubt that Mr. Collins is innocent."

"How so?"

"Aside from the fact he was somewhere else completely during the time Mr. Khan was murdered? There is compelling evidence that supports our argument that Ethan Greene and the Dominion Sect have taken a particular interest in Mr. Collins to the detriment of his freedom. Mr. Collins has proven to be a thorn in their side as a special agent for the Supernatural Operations Agency, and as a soldier when he was with the Mage Corps during the Thirty-Day War."

"Being good at your job isn't exactly a compelling argument when faced with murder charges."

"It is when your birth name is *not* Patrick Collins, but Patrick Greene. This is not the first time Ethan Greene has tried to get rid of his son. Framing him for murder is something Ethan would do if it would permanently get Patrick out of the way, and we've outlined the reasons we believe this to be true in our motion to dismiss we filed this morning. It's public record, in case you doubt the truth of my statement."

Danai spilled his secrets with a calmness that Patrick didn't feel at all. The trip-hammer thud of his heart made Patrick's ribs hurt, and he didn't know his hands were shaking until Jono took his coffee mug from him so it wouldn't spill.

The momentarily blank stare that Ryleigh gave Danai on camera disappeared after a few seconds. Patrick wondered if someone was feeding her information through her earwig. Most anchors hated being caught flat-footed on national television.

"I'm sorry, are you saying that Patrick Collins is the long-thought dead son of Ethan Greene?" Ryleigh asked, unable to keep the disbelief out of her voice.

"We explained everything in the motion we filed today. Suffice to say, the government had its reasons to hide him in witness protection for so many years."

"The high priestess of the Salem Coven testified before Congress last month about the dangers of the Dominion Sect. Did she know her grandson was still alive?"

"My client was kept hidden to keep him alive."

"But did Eloise Patterson *know?*"

"That's something only the government can answer. My client was a minor when decisions about his life were made."

The sidestep wasn't neat but designed to act like bait for the media. Danai had warned Patrick the issue of his mother's family not knowing he was alive would become a major story. It was better to have the government handle that explanation while she focused on clearing his name by sowing doubt about the case against him.

Danai didn't let the interview go on for much longer. She deflected questions about Patrick's past by bringing up the government's interference in it, or she teased the evidence in the motion without saying much about it. The tantalizing hints would drive curious parties to access the docket. The tactic of deflection was one Patrick was familiar with.

They'd only entered his juvenile records concerning the name change, copies of the Salem Police Department's police report on the night his mother was murdered, and his sworn affidavit that he was meeting with his CI during the time of Youssef's death. Some of that information had been concurrently unsealed from a previous filing in his case, but not all of it. General Reed's affidavit about Patrick's efforts under orders to support national security against the Dominion Sect had also been unsealed.

That had been a delicate dance, considering the plaintiff in Patrick's case was the United States government. But the affidavit had been cleared up the chain, and Patrick knew it wouldn't have if the Joint Chiefs of Staff hadn't ultimately approved of it on an expedited basis. Legal and political maneuverings made Patrick's head ache, but it seemed he couldn't escape either right now.

The interview eventually ended, with the anchor reluctantly steering it to a close but then promising her viewers they'd have an update on the situation within the hour.

"That's enough time for them to pull the motion from the docket and do a quick review," Sage said as she muted the television.

Patrick leaned over his knees and curled his hands over the back of his neck. Jono's hand settled between his shoulder blades, a grounding touch Patrick never wanted to shake off.

"Breathe," Jono said.

Patrick stared at the expensive area rug beneath his feet and did as Jono asked, forcing air in and out of his lungs. He couldn't afford to have a full-blown panic attack, not right now. If he'd been alone, maybe, but he had his pack, and they let him have his minor freak-out until he got himself under control. When Patrick finally sat up again, Sage was sitting beside him, radiating warmth the same way Jono did, telegraphing every move she made as she reached to take one of his hands in hers.

"I spend twenty-two years keeping my mouth shut about my past, and then we go and spill it all on national television," Patrick said, mouth dry.

"Maybe it was time," Sage said gently. "You've carried those lies long enough."

"The gods were the ones who said I had to change my name in the first place."

"If Maat is presiding over your case, maybe she allowed you to come clean for a reason," Jono said.

Patrick dragged a hand over his face, letting out a hard breath. "Who knows. Whatever their reason, it won't be good."

His phone buzzed on the coffee table, lighting up with Danai's name on the screen. He picked it up and swiped the green icon to accept the call. "Collins. Line and location are not secure."

It wasn't secure for legal reasons, but it was for everything else. Patrick trusted everyone in the room with him, but he wasn't willing to put them in the line of fire when it came to government subpoenas. If he could try to spare them that, he would.

"It's done," Danai said.

"I saw."

"I don't enjoy giving out statements like that. It's not my normal way of doing business. A case should be decided on the evidence, not the court of public opinion." She let out a heavy, annoyed sigh. "The Brady demand and request for writ for habeas corpus et animum went out yesterday. I'll be reaching out to the US Attorney's Office within the hour to request a meeting with them on Monday about the trishula and magical signature. I think you should be present for it if they agree."

"Do you think that's a good idea?"

"We're in the strange position of having the government both prosecute and defend you. They don't have any evidence against you except the magical signature that you say isn't yours. Your ties to the werecreature community admittedly don't look good, but that doesn't mean you're guilty of murder or a hate crime."

"There's still the obstruction charge."

"The SOA's own admittance about Dominion Sect sympathizers over the years is cause enough for doubt in that area, especially if you've always been a target. I'll also speak with Preston about a forensic investigator. I've used several in the past, and so has his office. If we can find an overlap both sides agree on, we might be able to have one appear on Monday, but that's a stretch. Hopefully Preston won't try to stonewall us."

"If you want me with you on Monday, I'll be there."

"Good. I'll keep you updated if it goes forward. For now, lay low."

"That was the plan."

She ended the call, and Patrick put his phone down on the coffee table. Jono and Sage never moved, keeping their hands on him in a show of support he never thought he'd ever be worthy of before he came to New York.

"The media will stake out our flat again," Jono said, sounding irritated.

"What do you mean again? It's not like they ever left," Wade retorted.

"That's why you both packed an overnight bag and are staying here this weekend," Sage reminded him.

Patrick stared at his coffee mug. "I need a drink."

Jono shook his head. "Best not start drinking this early."

Patrick would've argued that whiskey in his coffee wasn't a bad thing when Sage's phone rang, Tiarnán's name flashing over the screen. She picked it up to answer. "I'll buzz you in. Please come up. Our door is open."

Patrick reached for his coffee again, guzzling down half of it before the Lord of Ivy and Gold arrived at Sage and Marek's door. He wasn't alone. The fae lord arrived dressed as if he were going to a human court rather than one in Underhill. Silver hair brushed his shoulders, and his violet-eyed gaze was studiously blank.

A gold-tipped wooden cane was held in a hand wrapped in silver filigree plates and links that lined every knuckle and bone, connecting to a silver cuff. Gemstones flashed against the silver, and Patrick had half a thought to ask him to leave the silver designer gauntlet outside.

Trailing after him was a tall, lithe fae woman with pale pink eyes and dark green hair braided back away from her face in deference of the hot weather. Delicately pointed ears were adorned with numerous tiny gold hoops. Unlike Tiarnán, Deirdre wore no silver jewelry into werecreature territory.

Tiarnán's gaze strayed to the television, which was still on, if muted. "I've been made aware of this morning's news on the drive over."

"Yeah, so was the entire country. What's so important you got summoned back to the Seelie Court?" Patrick asked.

Tiarnán tapped his cane against the floor, and magic flowed from the tip in a wave that washed through the apartment. Like a silence ward, but powered with fae magic, he created a bubble of privacy that told Patrick they weren't going to like the problem that had brought him here.

Tiarnán folded both hands over the top of his cane, gaze sweeping the room. "Cernunnos is missing."

Patrick blinked. "Come again? Wasn't he in Dublin?"

"Yes. And now the Horned One is unaccounted for, yet the parks here in New York reek of his magic."

While in London back in June, Patrick had met with Órlaith, the Summer Lady of the Seelie Court and granddaughter to the goddess Brigid. She'd been in Dublin, working with Cernunnos, though he hadn't met the god at the time. Maybe he should have, if only so he knew what they were facing here.

"Are you asking us to help find him?" Jono asked.

Tiarnán opened his mouth to respond, but he never got a chance to reply. Marek made a noise that didn't sound as if it came from a human throat—twisted, mangled, and riven with agony. Sage was on her feet in an instant, her warmth disappearing as she raced to her fiancé's side. Patrick and Jono followed.

Leon got there first, cushioning Marek's fall, holding his friend's head in his lap while Marek arched against the magic coursing through his body. Ozone spiked in the air, and his hazel eyes were a searing white in his face. His face twisted in agony, fingers curled into claws against the floor, and the voice that came out of Marek's mouth wasn't his *or* the Norns', but something else entirely unearthly.

Patrick clamped his hands over his ears, the sound so incredibly painful he thought his brain would bleed out of his ears and nose. The pressure in the air around them became an unbearable weight that drove him to his knees and tore the breath from his lungs so he couldn't even scream.

"You face a hell you cannot outrun if what you sacrifice is not enough."

The presence of whatever had spoken through Marek abruptly disappeared, leaving Patrick gasping for breath against the excruciating pain stabbing through his head. He leaned over, digging the heels of his hands against his eyes, trying to stop his optic nerves from wanting to burn out his vision. Vertigo made his stomach twist uncomfortably as bile slid up his throat and past his clenched teeth, out his nose, burning hot and acidic.

Someone rolled him to his side, onto his back, and the world shifted all around him, colors melting against the back of his eyelids. Hands tried to pull his away from his face, but Patrick knew if he opened his eyes, he'd go blind. It was a strange thought to have, but the instinct clawed at him in a way he refused to ignore.

He thought he heard someone shout his name, but he couldn't be sure through the tinnitus echoing in his ears, as if he stood inside a huge bell while it rung. He took a breath, tasting bile, smelling it, when it was suddenly replaced by the scent of flowers and fresh grass. The richness of spring filled his lungs, chasing away the pain and the noise that echoed through his body like a furious thunderstorm. It left him weak-limbed and heavy-headed, breathing as if he'd run a marathon.

Slim, warm fingers pulled his hands away from his face with implacable strength. "Open your eyes."

Patrick didn't want to, but he could never disobey the goddess who owned his soul debt.

He forced his eyes open, seeing Persephone kneeling on the floor near his head, the dark curls of her hair falling gently around her freckled face as she leaned over him. Gold-brown eyes stared down at him, seeing straight through to the soul she owned inside of him. Patrick blinked, the colored spots floating across his vision fading until all he saw was the hint of her aura like a halo around her body.

"What?" Patrick croaked out, not wanting to move for maybe a decade. He didn't think Sage would mind if he took up space on her floor. The cleaners could work around him.

"Human ears aren't meant to hear an angel sing," Persephone said.

Patrick blinked slowly, wondering if he misheard her. "Angels?"

The Greek goddess and queen of the Underworld smoothed her fingers over his forehead, taking away the lethargy that had seeped into his bones. "It seems the Choirs are finally taking notice of our war. Ashanti was right to reach out to me."

"Shiva's going to hate them," Patrick slurred.

"Pat," Jono growled. "Look at me."

Patrick's gaze strayed slowly away from Persephone's face to where Jono knelt by his hip, one hand gripping his knee. When Patrick finally focused on him, Jono reached over to frame his face with one warm hand. Those wolf-bright blue eyes searched his before Jono let out a heavy sigh of relief, shoulders slumping.

"Let's get you cleaned up," Jono said.

Patrick swallowed, tasting bile, and made a face. His skin felt weirdly sensitive, and everything sounded muffled, despite Persephone's healing. Patrick didn't fight Jono's pull, letting himself be guided to a sitting position. The world tipped in a way that should've made his stomach churn, but it didn't.

Jono gently guided him to his feet, and Patrick leaned heavily against him. His shirt stank of acid, but the absence of pain was a curious blank spot throughout his body. Patrick moved his head to the side, still letting Jono's shoulder hold him up. He spied Marek lying on the floor, head pillowed in Sage's lap, white-faced and eyes closed, with Emma and Leon kneeling next to them.

"Marek?" Patrick asked, the syllables slow to leave his tongue.

Sage carefully smoothed aside Marek's hair, not looking up. "The Norns put him to sleep for the moment. Persephone took away his pain."

Her voice hitched with a hint of fear Patrick rarely heard their dire express. It made him want to dig deeper into what was going on, but Jono steered him away to the guest bathroom on their level. Patrick got sat on the toilet seat, divested of his filthy shirt, and wiped down with a warm washcloth.

"Here's his clothes," Wade said, holding a bundle of fabric in his arms where he stood in the doorway.

"Cheers," Jono said, taking the shirt.

Patrick rubbed at his face, feeling as if his brain was finally starting to reboot itself. "I can dress myself."

Jono arched an eyebrow but didn't argue, merely handed him the shirt. Patrick pulled it on slowly, then took a moment to just rest, body a heavy anchor that wouldn't move.

"What happened?" he asked through gritted teeth.

"Marek got hijacked and our brains were blended. We healed, but you didn't," Wade said.

Jono pressed a kiss to the top of Patrick's head. "Scared the bloody hell out of me, the way you were screaming and sicking up. Thought you were having a seizure."

"Felt like it," Patrick said slowly. "Persephone said it was an angel?"

Jono's mouth thinned to a hard line. "I don't know what it was, I just know I don't ever want to hear it again."

Patrick nodded agreement before shoving himself to his feet. Jono reached to steady him even though he was in no danger of keeling over, and Patrick didn't shake off his touch. Jono dug up a bottle of mouthwash from beneath the sink, and Patrick gargled until all he tasted was mint.

They left the bathroom together, with Wade hovering nearby, a worried expression on his face. Patrick waved for him to follow them back to the living area, where someone had drawn the curtains on the windows overlooking Central Park and turned off the television.

It was dimmer than it had been, but not dark. Marek had been moved to the couch rather than his bedroom. Sage refused to let him go, her attention on him and not the goddess wandering through their home, leaving the scent of spring in every corner. Emma and Leon hovered near the pair, both of them tense.

Patrick watched Persephone with a wariness he hated but couldn't escape. The pale blue sundress she wore swayed around her knees as she walked. Her strappy white sandals had no heels, bright against the tan of her skin. Persephone looped back to them, and Patrick couldn't help the way he pressed back against Jono for support.

Because for all that she owned his soul debt, for all that Fenrir's claws were sunk deep into Jono's soul, they had each other, and Patrick didn't have to stand on his own anymore. Jono wrapped an arm around his waist and didn't let go, fingers holding on tight.

"You need to pay your soul debt," Persephone said.

"You're telling me something I already know," Patrick said.

She came to a stop in front of him, and Patrick met her gaze without flinching. After a moment, Persephone reached out and settled her hand against his chest, right over his heart. Jono stiffened against him, a soft growl falling from his mouth.

"Don't touch him," Jono bit out.

Persephone stayed where she was, her hand a pressure against his scars and the nerve damage there. In some areas of his chest, he could feel the scrape of fabric over skin. In others, there was nothing.

"Just because we gave you to him doesn't mean he's yours," Persephone said, speaking to Jono while keeping Patrick in her sight.

"Patrick *is* mine."

Persephone's lips curved in a smile that held no comfort in it. "Then fight the demons overrunning your streets."

"If we challenge Estelle now, it'll make Patrick's case worse."

"Maat will handle that. The legal maneuverings against Patrick will be dealt with."

"I don't trust you lot to handle *anything* when it comes to Patrick's life."

"His life doesn't belong to you."

"That's where you're wrong."

"What do you want?" Patrick interrupted before they could really go at it.

Persephone lifted her hand to touch her fingers to his jaw, drifting over the arch of his cheekbone. Every brush of her fingertips brought with it a tiny static shock. "I came to ensure you could still fight."

"Even if I was dead, you'd probably hold me to my soul debt. Nothing's changed. I'll still do what you require."

Because it was the only way to reclaim his life, in whatever shape this fight ultimately left it in—whole, in pieces, or gone entirely.

Persephone let her hand fall away. "If angels are looking this way, you will need more protection than your pack can give you. I will reach out to my cousins."

The thought of more gods coming around made Patrick want to bang his head against the wall. "Or you could not."

"It is as much for your protection as ours." Her bright gaze flickered over to Tiarnán. "Perhaps they can aid in searching for Cernunnos and ask the Horned One why he's interfering with the cliff roses and the land over the nexus here."

Tiarnán's grip on his cane tightened ever so slightly. "What is happening to the greenery in New York City is not our doing."

"It may not be yours specifically, but it is fae magic seeping into the earth and changing it. We left the cliff roses where they bloomed as a precaution against further magical interference of the nexus. They act as a shield, and someone is undermining it by killing them off."

Persephone sounded displeased by that fact, but the warning in her words left a chill to the air in the apartment—a hint of the season that always drew her to the Underworld.

"If the Horned One is a prisoner of the Dominion Sect, then we must find him. That is why I am here," Tiarnán said.

Patrick winced, not liking that possibility at all. "Not sure how much help we'll be if the media is watching our every move. I don't have the backing of the government right now, and I'm not supposed to investigate anything."

"We are still allies. Your state of personal affairs will not negate that."

"Then we'll do what we can, but don't get pissed at us if we're handicapped by outside forces."

What kind of help they could give, Patrick didn't know. His hands were tied by the court, and that wasn't something he could ignore. Not when his entire identity was being ripped apart to satisfy a nation's curiosity. On top of that, they still had to deal with Estelle and her demon-infested god pack, and Patrick knew that problem wasn't going to end in anything but bloodshed.

15

"A GRAVEYARD, HUH?" PATRICK ASKED, POKING AT THE HAM-AND-cheese omelet on his plate. He wasn't really hungry but knew he had to eat before his midday meeting with Danai and the assistant US attorneys.

She was scheduled to pick him up soon, which was why he was dressed in a suit and tie on a Monday. His dagger was sheathed at the small of his back rather than his right thigh, marring the line of his suit jacket, but he didn't really care. He might not have his gun and badge anymore, but there was no way he was going anywhere without his dagger.

Across the dining table, Marek clutched his coffee mug with a white-knuckled grip. The seer had slept for twenty-four hours straight after his vision, waking Saturday morning with every shade of blue having faded to gray. Patrick and Jono had found him that morning standing at the windows overlooking Central Park on the first floor with Sage, staring at a sky whose color he could no longer see.

Being a seer was lucrative financially, but money couldn't buy sanity or a cure for blindness. One day, Marek's life spent as a vessel for the Norns was going to drive him insane and suicidal. He'd been spared nearly a year of no true visions simply because too many Fates were fighting over a future none of them could clearly see.

It appeared that had changed.

Guilt meant everything had tasted sour in Patrick's mouth over the weekend as they waited out the crushing media attention on his case. His presence in Marek's life was a curse he'd never be able to apologize for.

"Yes. I think Ethan was there," Marek said tiredly.

"Anyone else?"

Marek shook his head.

"Can we trust this angel's vision when all the other gods of fate have seen sod all?" Jono asked.

Wade snorted before shoveling a huge bite of sausage into his mouth. "It liquified our brains. I'm going with no."

"It was a Throne," Marek said, lifting one hand to rub at his forehead. "It was made up of wheels and eyes, and I think it cracked the inside of my skull with its voice."

"You aren't a prophet," Patrick said.

Marek smiled wanly. "At this rate, I don't think it matters. I'm a seer, and this is what I was born for, and it's what I'll die as. I saw a graveyard, which means there's some kind of ending we're now running toward."

Patrick winced, knowing there was only one way to pay his soul debt, and this fight would only end with one or more of them dead. Ethan's actions had created a rift between all the gods of the heavens and hells, and his story, his myth, wasn't one Patrick could afford to be anything but a footnote in history.

"Bollocks," Jono said. "It's not going to end however you saw it."

Marek shrugged, and Patrick knew believing in a future that might not be true was setting them all up for heartache, but he couldn't help it. Part of him wanted to believe that he and Jono and their pack would come out of this mess together, so he didn't try to argue that Jono was wrong.

"Are you heading back to the apartment?" Patrick asked, turning his head to look at Jono.

"Not sure the rats have cleared out."

"Maybe the gargoyles will have eaten them," Wade said hopefully.

Patrick rolled his eyes. "No one is eating the press. That goes double for you."

"I wasn't offering. I bet they taste as bad as demons do."

"Just be safe. Goes for all of you."

Jono nudged Patrick with his elbow. "You too."

Patrick tapped at his phone to get the time, seeing that Danai would be arriving soon. He was the only one going to the meeting, while Jono and Wade were most likely heading home together. Sage was working remotely upstairs, refusing to leave Marek's side after the weekend. Not that Patrick blamed her. Their wedding was in a little under two weeks, and they still had so much to finalize on top of the civil war happening within the werecreature community. The gods dropping a vision onto Marek was another stressor they could all do without.

Aside from Marek's vision and trying to lie low, Patrick had been unable to stop watching the news over the weekend. So he'd seen when the national and international media had descended on Salem, Massachusetts, attempting to get a statement out of everyone on his mother's side. Eloise Patterson had yet to appear before the cameras, though many Salem Coven members had gotten between the media and his family with a surprising amount of hostility.

Patrick was waiting for the moment his grandmother appeared on camera. He wasn't sure what he wanted to see when that happened—his family fighting to reach out to him, or casting him aside in the wake of Ethan's actions.

Wade finished the last sausage on his plate and then eyed Patrick's remaining food. "You going to finish your omelet?"

Patrick silently slid his plate across the table to Wade, who happily stabbed it with his fork.

"You should've eaten more than that," Jono said.

Patrick shrugged. "Wasn't really hungry."

His phone rang before Jono could worry further about his eating habits, Danai's name appearing on the screen. He swiped to answer it, putting the phone up to his ear.

"I'm two minutes away in a black Escalade," Danai said.

"You don't strike me as someone who'd own that kind of car," Patrick said.

"I have a preference for fast and sleek. I'm using my firm's car-hire service with a driver this time."

"I'll be downstairs. Hopefully you weren't followed by the press."

Danai made a noncommittal noise before ending the call. Patrick shoved his phone into his suit pocket and pushed his chair back, getting to his feet. He locked down his shields with a single thought, the weight of them settling into his bones. Jono followed him to the front door, keeping him there with a lingering kiss.

"Be safe. Tap a ley line if you have to," Jono said when he finally pulled back.

Patrick licked his lips and nodded. "Not sure that's a good idea if the government might be looking at my soul."

Jono curled warm fingers around Patrick's chin, holding him still for another kiss. "Do it anyway."

"Now you sound like Wade."

"I heard that," came Wade's muffled shout from the dining table.

"Finish my breakfast," Patrick yelled back. Then Patrick tugged at Jono's wrist, twisting it to press a kiss against his knuckles. "I'll come back."

The worried line Jono's mouth was pressed into didn't soften. "I love you."

Patrick left because he had to, but he carried his pack's support with him for the fight ahead.

Danai's vehicle pulled up in front of the building when he made it downstairs, and Patrick didn't waste any time climbing into the back with her. Her designer tote bag sat between her feet, heavy with a case file, and she held a brief in one hand that she'd apparently been reviewing on the drive over.

"Ready?" Danai asked as her driver stepped on the gas.

"No other choice but to be, right?" Patrick replied.

Danai gave him a slight smile. "Not a ringing endorsement."

Patrick shrugged, reaching for his seat belt to snap it into place. "I'm not the lawyer. I'll do what you tell me to do."

He'd learned enough from having Sage as their dire that letting the legal minds take the lead in situations like this was the only way to go sometimes.

They took Fifth Avenue, passing by a withered Central Park along the way to the US Attorney's Office in Downtown Manhattan. Danai didn't initiate any conversation. He wasn't sure if that was because of the driver, or if she had all the information she needed for the upcoming meeting. Either way, Patrick was just along for the ride.

Until he wasn't.

They put Central Park behind them in favor of the dense high-rises that made up the iron jungle of Manhattan. The light stayed green as they drove through the intersection of Fifth Avenue and Fifty-Second Street. The one-way traffic on the cross-street should have stopped.

It didn't.

Patrick had been looking ahead for trouble when a streak of movement out of the corner of his eye caught his attention. The sound of an engine rumbled through the air, cutting through the noise of tires burning rubber against asphalt even as the recognition of hell filtered through his magic.

"*Go!*" Patrick snarled. He ripped his shields out from beneath his skin, casting them wide enough to cover Danai and her driver.

The driver hesitated, instincts honed for New York City traffic and not war. The hesitation lost them an easy escape.

The car on the cross-street T-boned their vehicle on the right side. Metal crunched and tore with an ear-piercing sound, the force of the crash sending their vehicle skidding across the intersection. The dark-tinted windows shattered on the right, glass clattering over Patrick's shields. He looked out through the damaged window at the man behind the wheel of the other car, seeing a black-veined face with shadowy eyes staring back at him.

The hunter didn't bother getting out of the car, merely pulled out a tactical pistol and started shooting. The bullets slammed against Patrick's shields, sparks of pale blue magic flaring up at every impact point. He could feel the magic embedded in the projectiles—military-grade spells that would've broken through his shields if he hadn't been trained to hold them up at a baseline defense to withstand the attack.

"What is happening?" Danai shouted, a thread of hysteria creeping into her usually calm voice.

"I think Ethan's pissed I'm airing our family's dirty laundry," Patrick said.

He leaned forward far enough to yank his dagger free of its sheath, white-hot heavenly fire flickering around the matte-black blade. He sliced through his seat belt, then Danai's, before leaning between the two front seats to free the driver. The man was white-faced with shock and still scrabbling for the door, unable to reach the handle through Patrick's shields.

Outside on the surrounding street and sidewalks, pedestrians screamed as they ran for cover inside the surrounding luxury stores. A few were taking the risk to hunker down near those doors and windows, as well as the cars on the street that had come to a sudden stop, in order to record what was happening on their phones. Survival instincts were lacking in part of the populace, as far as Patrick could tell.

"If I get murdered in broad daylight, Jono is going to kill me," Patrick muttered under his breath as he strengthened his shields.

The bullets had stopped, but only because the hunter was reloading. Patrick used that lull to conjure up a mageglobe, fill it with raw magic, and send it directly at the hunter. The resulting explosion engulfed the car in flames that couldn't touch them through his shields.

"Get out of the car," Patrick ordered.

He expanded his shields through the damaged frame of the vehicle, allowing Danai and the driver to exit on shaky legs. The driver tried to run for it and ended up slamming against Patrick's shields with a groan.

Patrick grabbed him by the arm and turned him around. "You run now, you're just going to die."

"I don't get paid for shit like this!" the man cried out.

"And the government stopped paying me to do this shit, but we'll ignore that."

Patrick looked back over his shoulder in time to see the explosion of negative light as the demon left its host in a swirl of incorporeal energy. The hunter himself was screaming his way out of the wrecked car, body encased in magefire.

"Oh god," Danai said in a thready voice. "I think I'm going to be sick."

Beyond the burning car and hunter, dark shapes blurred through the stalled cars in the street. Recognition was a punch through Patrick's magic—werecreatures, and lots of them.

"No time for that," Patrick told her, right as more gunfire opened up from the sidewalk, spelled bullets slamming into his shield.

He conjured up another mageglobe and tossed it at the god pack werecreatures coming their way. It exploded on the ground, rapidly expanding into another shield that curved between them through the intersection, latching onto the corners of the surrounding buildings on either side of the blocks. It wasn't his best defense, but it would do for now.

Then he shoved the driver down Fifth Avenue, figuring Danai was the more levelheaded of the two and wouldn't need to be led. "Run!"

"Where?" Danai asked, stumbling into a run in her high heels, tote bag slung over her shoulder. It was too hot to risk running barefoot on asphalt, so Patrick didn't ask her to kick off her shoes.

Patrick opened his mouth—and instead of words coming out, it was an ugly sound of pain. He swore, agony throbbing through his head from the magical hit that cracked the shield between them and the god pack. He looked over his shoulder, gaze landing unerringly on the mage who'd levied the attack.

Zachary splayed his tattooed hands against Patrick's shield, a dozen mageglobes forming against pale blue magic. Arrayed around Zachary were snarling werewolves, bright amber eyes practically glowing in monstrous faces before inky blackness overtook the color. Interspaced between them were Krossed Knights, the hunters carrying guns. The smell of hell hung heavy in the summer air from the demons riding over a dozen souls beyond the shield in the street.

The odds weren't good, but the Dominion Sect and their allies had made one glaring mistake—they'd attacked within a block of hallowed ground.

"Get to the cathedral!" Patrick yelled.

He pulled back his personal shields, giving his charges room to run. Danai raced forward while the driver veered left, looking for safety in the nearest store. Patrick swore but let him go, knowing panic was driving the man and there was no breaking through it.

Patrick shoved his fear down deep, reached through the soulbond connecting him to Jono for the ley lines that ran through the earth below, and tapped the closest one. External magic burned through the soulbond, powering Patrick's defense so the shield didn't break on Zachary's second attack or even his third.

Patrick's head throbbed with every hit that carved damage into the shield. The fourth shattered the shield, but by then, Patrick and Danai were past the Cartier store and St. Patrick's Cathedral was within sight.

The flow of traffic meant the one-way street was clear of vehicles as he drew down his scattered magic, leaning hard on the soulbond. Distantly, he was aware of Jono's fury through it, but Patrick couldn't worry about him right now.

A multitude of howls had him spinning on his feet, dagger clutched in one hand and half a dozen mageglobes forming around him. He filled each one with a strike spell, despite the illegality of using it on domestic soil, in a major city, while surrounded by civilians. If he didn't buy them time, they'd never survive.

He thrust his left arm forward, the pale blue spheres streaking toward the oncoming god pack. The mageglobes slammed to the ground and exploded like bombs, catching some of the werecreatures within the blast radius. Their howls cut off as the explosions shook the ground, crashing against the red-black magic that cut through Patrick's. Zachary's attempt at shielding meant most of the god pack members survived the attack, though some weren't so lucky.

Patrick spied two werewolves ripped to shreds on the street from his attack, neither of them whole enough to shift back to human and save themselves. The demons riding their souls fled the now useless bodies in flashes of negative light.

A mageglobe arched through the air from Zachary's position back near the intersection, malevolent magic capable of incinerating an entire building. Considering they were surrounded by skyscrapers, that would have a number of casualties Patrick refused to allow.

He threw a trio of larger mageglobes at Zachary's, looking to contain rather than eradicate. Patrick wasn't the best at defensive magic, but that was the only kind he could use here.

Zachary's spell exploded within the confines of Patrick's containment shield, shredding through the layers. The brunt of the blast was initially contained, and what broke through Patrick's magic blew out windows on either side of the block rather than entire buildings. The god pack werecreatures surged forward with the hunters right behind them.

Patrick raised another shield, feeling the foundation of it waver as he turned and ran after Danai. He'd bought them seconds, but seconds weren't enough. Patrick caught up with her at the intersection of Fifth Avenue and East Fifty-First Street, the terror on her face something he never wanted to see again.

St. Patrick's Cathedral in all its gothic glory loomed against the summer sky, bracketed in the distance by the skyscrapers of Midtown Manhattan. Traffic was a mess, people panicking from the sound of explosions, and a fender bender had already happened on the cross-street. The iconic building was at risk of being damaged, and if he ruined Sage's backdrop for her wedding photographs, she'd never forgive him.

Patrick pointed at the cathedral. "Get inside! The demons can't follow you there."

Danai clutched at her tote bag and didn't argue, merely cut through stalled cars for the safety of the cathedral. Patrick stayed on her heels, trying to ignore the screams filling the air that couldn't drown out the snarl of the god pack.

Danai stumbled on the steps leading to the cathedral, going to her knees. Patrick got both feet on the step beside her when magic exploded behind them with such intensity that heat roiled through the air. The only reason Zachary's magic didn't touch them wasn't because of Patrick's shields, but the priestly magic and holy prayers sunk into protective wards built into the foundation of the cathedral. That defensive magic was called forth in the face of a demonic attack with a *crack* that made Patrick's ears pop.

He spared a glance over his shoulder at the cathedral, licking at the sweat that beaded on his upper lip. Glittering lines of protective wards burned into existence against the gothic stone architecture, running up the walls to the flying buttresses and the two towers.

Patrick could honestly say he'd never cared for the hypocrisy of the Catholic Church when it came to magic, but it came in useful right then. The cathedral's own shielding lay dormant except in the face of a direct threat to its infrastructure. The shields pulsed, nearly invisible in the air except for a faint shimmer of gold where Zachary's magic had been brought to heel.

The werecreatures who'd attempted to flank them around Zachary's attack ran through the dissipating magic, coming right for them. Then they abruptly jerked back away from the shielded concrete steps as if they'd been burned. Smoke drifted up from their paws where they'd come into contact with the holy ground that extended beyond the cathedral's shield, the demons in their souls unable to stand before the prayers.

Patrick bared his teeth at them, still clutching his dagger in one hand. "Hallowed fucking ground, assholes."

Breathing hard, Patrick pulled Danai to her feet and pushed her up the steps, never taking his eyes off the werecreatures and the hunters squaring off at the demarcation of the shield. He heard her footsteps fade as she fled for safety and didn't move to follow her.

"You can't outrun us," Nicholas said, blood falling from his fingertips to the sidewalk below.

"Doing a pretty damn good job so far," Patrick shot back.

Something slammed into the ground to his left, and Patrick jerked, a mageglobe sizzling into existence near his elbow. He snapped his head around, ready to fight, a silent command trigger cutting through his thoughts. Then he saw the gargoyle that had landed on the steps, cracking concrete, and stayed his hand.

Another gargoyle flung itself off the cathedral, landing by the first, and those weren't the only ones. More gargoyles flung themselves off the cathedral, others crawling over building façades across the street as they answered some silent call. Apparently the city's gargoyles were taking the attack against the cathedral as a personal affront.

Patrick pointed his dagger at Zachary. "Your assassination attempts need work."

Zachary glared at him through the dissipating smoke and light of his magic, hunters backing him in the street, none of them willing to breach the cathedral's shields.

"Who said anything about assassinating you?" Zachary shot back.

And oh, wasn't *that* a terrifying thought?

"Your hunter back there aimed for my face."

Zachary smiled. "He aimed for your shields."

Patrick stepped closer to the cathedral's shields, the heavenly white fire twisted around his dagger's matte-black blade growing brighter. The gargoyles crouched on the steps flung themselves through the shield, the magic not impeding them at all. They charged the werecreatures, their stone bodies capable of withstanding the claws and teeth of werecreatures better than human flesh.

Patrick raised his dagger, ready to press the edge of it against the shield to carve himself a hole to fight through, when a vicious howl ripped through the air. Zachary wasn't the only one who looked back the way they'd come on Fifth Avenue. Patrick didn't have the best view of the street, but the group of werecreatures racing toward them had him breathing a quick sigh of relief as the soulbond pulled taut with Jono's close proximity.

Jono and Sage led the charge, with what had to be most of the Tempest pack right behind them. The god pack facing off against Patrick and the gargoyles were forced to reorient themselves to deal with the oncoming werecreatures.

Patrick pushed his dagger through the shield, the prayers in it opening up a way through for him without bringing down the shield or breaking the protective wards. He slipped through the opening in time to see Zachary spin up a mageglobe and throw it at Jono and the others. Patrick didn't hesitate to throw his own at the other mage's attack, knocking it off its trajectory.

The resulting explosion ripped a hole in the asphalt closer to the other side of the street, but not through bodies. Zachary turned to face Patrick rather than the god pack that slammed into the demon-infested group he stood in the center of. His red-black shield flickered in the sunlight like bloody flames as Patrick readied another mageglobe, calculating the risks of another strike spell.

Then a furious, deep voice rang through the air, leaving the demons howling in protest.

"*Satanam aliosque spiritus malignos, qui ad perditionem animarum pervagantur in mundo, divina virtute, in infernum detrude.*"

The commanding Latin that was the start of a Catholic exorcism prayer came from the cathedral's steps. Patrick looked over his shoulder at where the cardinal in his ordinary black dress with red piping stood in the doorway, hand raised in a commanding gesture. The power in his exorcism prayer was as much a weapon as any spell Patrick had in his repertoire.

The melee of werecreatures, hunters, and gargoyles abruptly broke apart as the demons collectively pooled their power to drag their hosts and Zachary through the veil. Jono snapped his teeth on empty air, an aggravated growl leaving his throat as his massive head swung toward Patrick.

"I'm fine," Patrick said, ignoring how hard his heart was beating. He flexed his fingers around the hilt of his dagger before slipping it back into the sheath against his lower back beneath his suit jacket.

Jono twisted through agitated gargoyles, the sound of grating stone making Patrick's ears hurt. When he was within reach, Jono headbutted Patrick in the chest hard enough he was forced to take a step back.

Patrick buried one hand into Jono's thick fur, tugging on it. "You got here fast."

Jono huffed out a snort, licking blood off his fangs. His bright blue eyes lacked the shine of Fenrir being in control, which Patrick was grateful for. He was even more grateful that Jono had gotten to him in time.

"I had thought all the news stories of hunters and demons were exaggerations," the cardinal said as he came down the steps.

Patrick swallowed against the fading taste of hell in the back of his throat. "They weren't."

"I see that now, my child."

The rote paternalism made Patrick scowl, but he bit back his retort in favor of getting eyes on the surrounding area. He no longer sensed any threat through his magic, but that didn't mean it wouldn't return. If Ethan was willing to attack him in broad daylight, uncaring of the civilian casualties, there was the risk he'd do it again. Zachary's pointed threat about not wanting Patrick dead wasn't something he could easily shake off and ignore.

The distant sounds of sirens wailed through the air, growing closer. Patrick let his hand fall away from Jono to gesture at the cathedral.

"Let's get inside."

Even as he spoke, the protective wards started to disappear on the cathedral walls, the shimmer of gold fading to nothing as the shield came down now that the threat was gone. Patrick turned to face where the cardinal stood on the steps, the older man staring at the sea of gargoyles and werecreatures milling about on Fifth Avenue.

The cardinal shifted his attention from the gargoyles to Patrick and Jono. He studied them with a bland expression on his face, judging them how men of faith always judged the world. Patrick thought the cardinal would find them wanting. Most people of the larger organized religious denominations felt that way toward magic users and the preternatural community. If those groups weren't trying to save them, they were trying to eradicate them. Religion of all sorts was the underlying bedrock of most wars, along with control of resources and the need to get rich.

"Come inside and rest," the cardinal offered after a moment.

Whether the generosity was due to being filmed by bystanders or out of the cardinal's own sense of care, Patrick wasn't about to say no. He needed to check on Danai and his pack, and he'd rather do that out of view of the public eye if at all possible.

"Hope this mess doesn't impact my release," Patrick muttered under his breath as he started up the steps, Jono right by his side in wolf form.

16

ST. PATRICK'S CATHEDRAL WAS A HUSHED PLACE OF WORSHIP, ITS stained glass windows throwing colorful light across worshippers kneeling in prayer in the pews. No one sat at the massive organ situated above the front entrance, but the quiet hum of voices whispering for guidance was like a muted song.

The white columns and soaring vaulted ceilings high above were lined with Latin prayers that sparkled at the very edges of Patrick's peripheral vision. He doubted mundane humans would ever see the magic laid down into the stone of the place. He wondered if the Pope made select allowances for the Catholic Church's cathedrals across the world, or if it was done on the sly by the local men of faith who presided over their flocks.

Either way, the prayers had saved his ass today, so he was inclined to ignore the hypocrisy.

"Collins."

Patrick looked away from the ceiling, head snapping around at Casale's voice. He twisted in his seat on the long pew near the back of the cathedral and close to the entrance. Beside him, Jono did the same, one hand settling over Patrick's hip in a proprietary manner.

The scowl on Jono's face wasn't friendly at all. Considering the last time they'd faced Casale together Patrick had been arrested, he could understand Jono's unfriendly attitude.

At least they'd be facing the police in decent clothes. Everyone in his pack was dressed in clothes they could fight in. Wade had been told to stay behind with Marek while everyone else ran to help Patrick once he'd yanked on the soulbond. Only after Emma's pack had returned home did Wade gather up extra sets of clothes and hitch a ride to the cathedral to deliver the outfits to Jono and Sage. He'd entered under the glare of media cameras, and Patrick had hated putting him through that.

Wade's identity as a fire dragon wasn't known publicly, though it was acknowledged in some political circles. After Paris, when he'd shifted mass in front of French government magic users to save them from getting torn to pieces by millions of zombies, Wade had been careful about where he showed his face. Walking a media gauntlet wasn't the best way to keep a low profile, but he'd refused to let anyone else deliver the clothes to his pack.

Wade was currently wandering around the nave after having disappeared for a while. Patrick had half a thought to warn the priests tending to frightened followers who still didn't want to leave the cathedral that Wade had sticky fingers. If some of the shiny religious objects went missing, well, Patrick would tell Wade to clean his apartment again.

"Come to arrest me for a second time?" Patrick asked, not bothering to hide the bitterness in his voice. He'd thought he had a pretty decent working relationship with the PCB, but that had come to a screeching halt with the charges levied against him.

Casale shook his head, coming to a stop beside their pew. Danai, sitting across the wide aisle from them with Sage, barely looked up from her phone when she said, "I would advise against you further speaking to the police, Patrick."

"I'm not here to arrest him," Casale said.

"I've already given my statement about what happened to detectives out of the PCB. So did Danai," Patrick said.

Jono scowled. "We all have."

"I know." Casale let out a heavy sigh. "I'm here to talk to you about your civil war."

"That's pack business, not police business."

Casale arched one dark eyebrow and jerked his thumb in the direction of the cathedral's doors that led out to the street. "It's everyone's business when Collins' car gets hit and he's chased down Fifth Avenue by werecreatures."

"It wasn't only werecreatures chasing me. We've been telling you for months that the Krossed Knights and other hunters are a problem," Patrick said.

Casale nodded, a troubled look crossing his face. "I know, but we can't arrest people without probable cause."

"Why not? You did that with Patrick," Jono said caustically.

"And maybe we were wrong, but the evidence still points to Collins."

"Not for much longer," Danai said, finally putting her phone away. "We're due at the US Attorney's Office still, and the PCB promised us an escort there since my car-service vehicle is now evidence in a crime. Let's get going."

"Ramirez and Guthrie are waiting outside."

Patrick didn't immediately move, keeping his attention on Casale. "What are you going to do about Estelle? Because none of those god pack members were ours, and they didn't care at fucking all for the safety of the civilians of this city."

"We'll be taking her statement and questioning her on her pack's actions. I don't like the alliances she's made," Casale said slowly.

Patrick tried not to scrape at the wooden pews with his fingernails. "You could've done that before we reached this point. Because now? They all have demons in their souls, same as the hunters. Your people better go with someone who knows how to exorcise demons. Maybe ask the cardinal if he wants an excuse to deal with some sinners. He came in pretty handy in a pinch."

Casale grimaced at that warning, but he didn't brush it aside. "I'll see if the cardinal has anyone he can spare. I'd ask my wife, but I don't want to risk anyone from her coven. They aren't mages, and it seems the Dominion Sect is making trouble in New York again."

Angelina Casale was a priestess for the Crescent Coven, a group of magic users who worshipped Hera. That goddess had acted as the coven's high priestess to herself last summer before leaving the country for Greece once Zeus was rescued. Despite her absence, the coven continued to pray to her, providing faith and worship to give Hera memory and life.

"But you'll risk the people working under you?" Jono asked with a faint sneer.

"That kind of risk comes with the job, and they're trained for it. Angelina's coven members are not." Casale shook his head. "It wasn't personal what we did, Collins."

Patrick had made his share of arrests over the years, so he knew it wasn't supposed to be personal. Considering his arrest had tipped him headfirst into a past that lived in his nightmares, he wasn't willing to be charitable when it came to Casale's awkward and misplaced non-apology.

"It never is. That doesn't mean you aren't making a bigger fucking mess than it needs to be. You and the FBI both," Patrick said.

"You'd have done the same if I was standing in your shoes."

Patrick shoved himself to his feet so it was easier to look Casale in the eye. "If you were standing in my shoes, you'd be the one with a homicidal father gunning for your ass, and not me. I didn't kill Youssef. If my pack was going to fight them, it would've been in a challenge ring. I thought you'd have a better opinion of me than that."

"Please don't make statements like that to the police," Danai said, giving him an irritated look.

"It won't be held against him," Casale said.

Patrick snorted. "Watch your people's backs when you go into that other god pack's territory. Don't brush aside my warnings like you have been."

Despite the ruined professional relationship, Patrick didn't want anyone to die because of negligence.

Casale nodded slowly. "You should know that we've received reports from multiple covens that every single park in the five boroughs looks as if winter has come early."

If it was fae magic like Persephone thought it was, Patrick hoped it didn't have anything to do with the Morrígan's staff. The last thing they needed was zombies ruining everyone's commute. They had enough problems with demons and werecreatures as it was.

"If it's a local magical problem versus a crime, shouldn't the PCB handle that outreach and not the SOA? I don't have a badge right now, remember? It got taken, along with my gun."

"Then consider it a friendly exchange of information."

"You were real friendly when you were knocking on the door to our flat looking to arrest people," Jono growled as he gently pushed Patrick out of the pew.

Casale raised an eyebrow at him. "Going to hold that against the PCB forever?"

"Don't tempt him. Jono lives for grudges," Patrick warned.

Jono snorted his opinion on that before steering Patrick around Casale, heading for the exit. "Wade, we're leaving."

Patrick looked over his shoulder and did a double take as Wade came running down the center aisle, a red, square, rigid cap sitting ludicrously on his head. He didn't look guilty at all, and his pockets definitely bulged with stolen goods.

"Put it back," Patrick told him.

Wade gave him a defiant look. "No! It's red, and I like red."

"It's not yours."

"Finders, keepers."

"You didn't find it, you stole it."

Wade crossed his arms over his chest, the cap slipping sideways on his head. "Who's to say the door wasn't unlocked? You weren't there."

Sage came up behind him and plucked the cap from his head, tossing it onto an empty pew. "No stealing. Come on, we're going home."

Wade rolled his eyes and shoved his hands into his pockets. "Whatever. I'm hungry. All they had back there were dry crackers."

Casale pinched the bridge of his nose, looking like he was trying not to laugh. Patrick managed to keep a straight face because Wade's hoarding habits were an everyday occurrence, and he'd learned not to encourage Wade with things like this.

"I better not find out you're hoarding crosses," Patrick said.

Wade smirked as he walked past them. "In these pockets? I don't think so."

Considering the way Wade shifted mass, Patrick knew it was a distinct possibility he could be hiding extremely large religious iconography in his pockets.

"Might be useful against demons," Jono mused.

"Only if he believes in that god," Patrick said.

Wade snorted, a hint of smoke drifting out of his nose, the acridness impossible to ignore. "Hell no. Gods are just trouble."

Jono tugged on Patrick's arm. "At least we're raising him right."

Patrick rolled his eyes. "He's nineteen. He could raise himself."

"Doubtful. He'd be living off Pop-Tarts and Hot Pockets if he tried."

"Breakfast of champions for college students everywhere."

"I'm not in college," Wade said over his shoulder, nearly to the entrance.

"Not yet. You need to finish your HSE Diploma first."

Wade still didn't know what he wanted to do in regards to

higher-level schooling, but Patrick wanted him to know he had options. Sage had promised to cover his school costs out of her own personal pockets so they didn't have to touch the tithes. The idea of college still left Wade a little uneasy, as if the thought of being away from the pack wasn't something he was ready for, but Patrick knew one of these days he'd have to spread his wings.

Sage brushed past them, giving him a brief smile as she squared her shoulders for facing the crowd outside. "Good luck. Come by for dinner afterwards."

"I will," Patrick said, rolling his shoulders to settle his suit jacket a little better. His clothes had lingering traces of the hells embedded in the fabric, and he knew no amount of dry cleaning would fix that.

Jono grabbed his hand and raised it to his lips, brushing a kiss over the back of his knuckles as they passed through the high arch of the cathedral doors and into the hot summer day. "I love you. Be safe."

"I'll come back," Patrick promised, tongue tracing out different syllables behind his teeth. He wanted to believe the words slipping free of his mouth were true, that everything going on wouldn't further separate them.

"I'm heading back to Emma's to get the car, and I'll pick you up after your meeting. Ring me when you're finished."

"Okay."

He ignored the cameras pointed their way, letting Jono go because he had to. Patrick guided Danai down the steps toward where Detective Specialists Allison Ramirez and Dwayne Guthrie stood near an unmarked police car on Fifth Avenue.

Allison gave him a slow nod at their approach. "The chief said you needed a ride."

"Not to a jail cell at the police station," Patrick said.

"We know."

Dwayne scrutinized him in silence before shaking his head. "It's all a fucking mess, Collins."

"As thrilling as this conversation is, we have somewhere to be," Danai said pointedly.

Patrick sighed, not looking forward to the upcoming meeting, but got into the car with Danai anyway. He couldn't fight the inevitable, after all.

"You certainly know how to stage some theatrics," Preston said.

"Did you really just say I *staged* the attack on Fifth Avenue?" Patrick asked, his tone bypassing disbelief and going straight to *fuck you sideways*.

"I was referring to Danai's news conference last week."

"Sure you were."

"Stop antagonizing my client, Preston. You agreed to this meeting," Danai said.

Preston's jaw twitched. "The US attorney approved it."

Patrick wondered if there had been some sort of disagreement between the assistant US attorneys and their overseeing partner, or if the gods had once again influenced the proceedings somehow. Considering they were having the meeting at all, he figured that was more likely. It wasn't every day the government responded to a demand so quickly, or that a forensic investigator could be retained on such short notice.

They were in a large conference room on the sixth floor of the U.S. Attorney's Office for the Southern District of New York. A court reporter and videographer were set up in the corner, though neither was recording anything yet. At the far end of the table sat a pair of witches from a third-party forensic investigation firm. They were present to compare the lab report on the magical signature found on the trishula to Patrick's.

The US Attorney's Office had brought their own mage, who would be capable of telling if the results the witches came up with were in any way tampered with, either by the forensic group or

Patrick. His official file said he was a mage in name only, and maybe Preston thought his deficiency was enough to ensure Patrick couldn't hide anything from them.

Considering he had a soulbond and a tenuous connection to his sister in his soul, and anchors burned into his bones by a goddess, Patrick had every incentive to lie through his teeth, perjury be damned. He didn't want to possibly escape one capital charge only to be hit with another.

Danai pinned Preston with a hard look. "We're ready if you are."

Patrick would never be ready for something like this, but he had no choice but to comply. It wasn't a court-ordered review of his soul, but that didn't matter. Danai might have served the subpoena for the trishula and the lab report, but the need for the truth wasn't going to go away, and the sooner he got this test over with, the better.

Preston signaled to the court reporter and videographer. "Let's get started."

Everyone was sworn in for the record, statements of everyone's identities were given, and it wasn't long before Patrick was facing down the two forensic witches. One opened her laptop, and the other opened the transport case in front of her. She extracted a handheld device that looked similar to a radar gun used to check speed.

Fredricka, as she'd given her name a few minutes earlier, gave him a brief smile. "I'll be measuring your aura's energy output for your magical signature with this. It won't harm you."

"What do you want me to do?" Patrick asked.

"We'll need you to drop your shields and conjure a mageglobe how you normally would. I'll ask you to do it a couple of times to get different readings. Please wait for my instructions on when to cast and when to draw down your magic."

Patrick flexed his fingers beneath the table. "All right."

He lowered his shields completely, not missing the way the

witches twitched in their seats and how the other mage leaned back, an uncomfortable expression crossing his face.

"Oh," Fredricka said, squinting at him.

"Soul wound," Patrick said, trying not to bite off the words. "If you've seen the news, you'll know how I got it."

The damage he'd sustained, both as a child at Ethan's hands and at the end of the Thirty-Day War, was evident in the feel of his magic when he didn't have his shields up—it was uncomfortable for other magic users to be around. Setsuna had used that as an excuse from when he came on board the SOA to never assign him a partner. He was supposed to keep his head down, but the cases he'd handled over the years hadn't helped with that.

"Right." She cleared her throat while her partner continued tapping away at the keyboard of the laptop. "Let us get a couple of reads on you now for a baseline before you cast your mageglobe."

It took them another minute to reconfigure whatever they had to on their end. Then Fredricka gave Patrick a polite nod and pointed the scanner at him.

"This won't hurt," she promised.

Patrick stared at the scanner, noticing the shine of the laser on the flat end of it. "Sure."

It took about five minutes for them to get whatever baseline readings they needed before Fredricka nodded at Patrick. "We're ready. Please cast your mageglobe."

He did so with a silent command, magic pouring out of his soul into the burning ball of pale blue power that hovered in front of him over the conference table. Fredricka alternated aiming the scanner at him and his mageglobe for several minutes. Patrick tried to ignore the way the other mage monitored the proceedings, the foreign magic stifling him with no shields to guard against the focus.

Patrick fought back a grimace, staring at his mageglobe. He hoped that whatever results the witches and their tests came up with, it would all match what was in his records and not with what the government had on file wrapped around the trishula that had killed Youssef. His magical signature had been recorded when he first joined the SOA. Too much had happened between then and now for Patrick to be certain the results would be the same.

He was glad no one in the room was a werecreature; they wouldn't be able to smell his fear or hear how fast his heart was beating. That wasn't to say no one else in the building was a werecreature, but if they were, he hoped they were under his pack's protection.

After ten minutes, Fredricka finally put the scanner down. "All right, we have what we need. Give us about thirty minutes to give you a preliminary report."

Patrick blinked at her. "That quick?"

"We have your SOA records saved to file, and running the comparison program doesn't take long. Certifying the report will need to wait until we get back to our office, but the preliminary results don't take long, and both sides of this case requested an expedited answer."

Preston looked at the mage. "Was there any attempt at tampering?"

"No," the mage said after a long pause.

Preston didn't appear happy about that statement, but he didn't argue against it. He looked as if he wanted to, judging by his scowl.

"Let's take a break," Danai said.

After the court reporter and videographer designated a break for the record, Danai got to her feet. Patrick let his mageglobe fade to nothing, drawing down his magic even as he raised his shields. The way the witches and mage seemed to lose tension in their shoulders proved they hadn't been comfortable around him for the duration of the test.

Patrick got up and followed Danai out of the conference room for the office set aside as their space for the meeting. He closed the door behind them and watched Danai take a seat in the chair behind the desk.

"How are you holding up?" he asked.

Danai snorted. "Shouldn't I be asking you that?"

He studied her face, noting the faint streaks of dried sweat near her hairline from her run down Fifth Avenue to safety, her wrinkled clothes, and her now scratched, incredibly expensive shoes. The subtle hints of disarray did nothing to detract from the clear-eyed stare she gave him.

"It's just another day for me."

"If this is how exciting your life usually is, I think I'd like a vacation."

Patrick barked out a laugh. "I'm owed one, believe me."

Danai cracked a smile. "Then let's make sure you get it."

Something tight loosened in his chest. Yes, they were paying her an exorbitant amount of money to defend him in court, but Patrick had a feeling any other lawyer would've never left the cathedral with him—would've walked away and substituted out over fear for their life. Except Danai hadn't, and he was starting to think that maybe he wasn't just a paycheck to her, but a wrong to be righted.

Like Sage, she seemed to live for that challenge, and Patrick knew he was as challenging as they came in some ways.

"Think a preliminary report will change Preston's mind?" he asked.

"Hard to say. It's preliminary, which means there's still some wiggle room for a wider set of findings, but the forensic investigators are meant to be neutral."

Patrick nodded, resting his hands on the back of the empty chair in front of the desk, letting it hold up his weight. "People can be bought off."

"I'm aware of that, but I don't think that will happen here. I've used this firm before, and they have a rock-solid reputation."

"All right."

He settled in the other seat and pulled out his cell phone to update his pack on what had happened. He kept his phone on silent so the usual beeps of an avalanche of text messages didn't annoy Danai. Twenty minutes later someone knocked on the door. Patrick straightened up from where he was slouched in the chair and put away his phone.

"Come in," Danai called out.

Preston opened the door, gaze sweeping over them. "They're ready."

"Will the meeting be over once they give us the preliminary report?" Patrick asked.

"Yes," Danai said before Preston could say otherwise.

Patrick texted Jono on the way back to the conference room, getting a response almost immediately that he was parked nearby. Considering what had already happened today, that wasn't exactly safe, but Patrick had known arguing with Jono back at the cathedral was a migraine waiting to happen.

They entered the conference room again, where the two witches sat huddled around the laptop, scanner put away and three sets of printed-out pages in front of them. Danai and Patrick took their seats again, as did Preston and the other mage. The court reporter read everyone back into the record, and Preston took the lead.

"What did you find?" he asked.

Fredricka gathered up the papers, handing one set to Danai, one to Preston, and one to the court reporter to enter it into the record as an exhibit. "On their face, the magical signatures are similar on many certain levels, but vary in others, which is typical in familial cases. The variances were strong enough to conclude they are not identical, especially with Mr. Collins' soul wound taken into account."

Patrick would've let out a sigh of relief, except he knew it meant nothing if the charges against him weren't dropped.

Preston frowned down at his copy of the reports. "Are you certain?"

"This corroborates the underlying evidence in our motion," Danai said pointedly.

"This doesn't clear him of murder."

"The facts don't lie." Danai turned her attention back on Fredricka. "How long for the official certified report to be released?"

"We can have it to you by Wednesday," she said.

"Thank you."

Preston still didn't look happy about the results, but he didn't argue it on the record. It didn't take long to close out the meeting after that. While the court reporter and videographer started to pack away their things, Fredricka came around the conference table to shake first Preston's hand, then Danai's, and finally Patrick's.

"Thank you for allowing us to provide you with our service," she said.

She squeezed his hand gently in a too-pointed way, causing Patrick to drop his gaze, attention snagging on the slender gold signet ring she wore. Stamped on its flat face were Egyptian hieroglyphics that Patrick couldn't read, but it didn't matter. He knew whose name they had to spell out.

Fredricka gave them all a professional smile as she released his hand, never letting on that she worshipped a goddess born in the hearts of an ancient culture that still considered the Nile River a waterway of life.

Gods were meddlesome, but in this case, Patrick would let it slide.

"I look forward to what the government decides to do with this evidence, Preston," Danai said as she picked up her tote bag.

"Get home safe, Danai," Preston said, sounding like he meant it.

Patrick followed Danai out of the office and to the elevator bank down the hall. She pressed the call button and sighed deeply. "That went well."

"Yeah." Patrick pulled out his phone and checked the screen, seeing that Jono's latest text said he was circling the block. Patrick shot off a quick text for him to pull up front. "Do you have a ride home?"

"I was going to take a taxi."

"Nah. We'll drive you home. I'd rather know you got there safe after today."

"Thank you."

The doors to the elevator slid open, and they stepped inside, taking it down to the lobby. Jono had pulled up in front of the government building and was ignoring the security guard gesturing for him to move.

"We're leaving," Patrick called out.

The security guard looked over his shoulder at them then did a double take. Patrick was getting real fucking tired of those.

Jono leaned across the seat to open the passenger-side door, eyes hidden behind a pair of aviator sunglasses. "Are we driving Danai home?"

"Yeah."

He got in the back seat, ceding the front passenger one to Danai. Once they were buckled up and the door was shut, Jono stepped on the gas, pulling away from the US Attorney's building.

"How did it go?" Jono asked.

"Wasn't my magical signature."

Jono snorted. "Could've told the lot of them that. Didn't need a bloody false murder charge to reach that conclusion."

Patrick laughed and laughed and didn't stop for two blocks.

PATRICK WOKE UP WEDNESDAY AFTER DAWN WITH HIS FACE PRESSED against the nape of Jono's neck, arm slung over Jono's hip, sweaty from body heat despite the air-conditioning keeping the apartment cool. He drew in a deep breath, taking in the hint of Jono's cologne that lingered on his skin. Patrick had missed that comforting smell while in prison—had missed sharing a bed like this when he'd only been doing so for a little over a year.

He hated thinking about the possibility he'd never get this again.

"It's too bloody early for you to be this anxious," Jono said, voice coming out slow and sleepy, having probably smelled Patrick's current mental state since his shields were down.

Patrick kissed the knob of Jono's spine, sighing softly. "Sorry."

"What has you worried now?"

Patrick bit his lip, too many thoughts like a storm rumbling through his mind, but the only one that mattered right now was the warning Zachary had given him at the steps of the cathedral on Monday.

"I think Ethan is after me," Patrick said.

Jono shifted in Patrick's arms. The mattress dipped a bit as he turned over onto his other side. His black hair was sleep-messy and falling into his eyes. Patrick pushed it off his forehead with gentle fingers. Jono hooked a hand over Patrick's hip, thumb rubbing circles against his hip bone. They were both naked, the sheet pushed down to Jono's waist, putting the expanse of his broad chest on display.

Jono frowned. "He's *been* after you."

"No, I—" Patrick grimaced and rolled onto his back, staring at the ceiling because it was easier than looking Jono in the eye. "Nicholas said they weren't trying to kill me."

"They purposefully crashed a car into yours. They *shot* at you," Jono said slowly. "How is that not trying to kill you, and why didn't you tell me this before?"

Patrick winced at the hint of anger in Jono's voice. "Sorry. I've had other things on my mind. I wasn't trying to hide it from you."

A warm hand curled over his shoulder, pulling Patrick back onto his side so he was looking at Jono again. "You don't need to apologize for being stressed, but this is *important*. If Ethan is targeting you for who the bloody fuck knows what this time, that's something the pack needs to know."

"I'm telling you now."

Because they'd long since promised not to lie to each other or hide important information in some misguided attempt to protect each other. Patrick hadn't meant to keep this from Jono; he just hadn't found a good time to tell him.

Jono sighed thickly, settling his hand back on Patrick's hip. "I'll tell Sage. You should probably tell Setsuna. The government knows you're a target, but there's a difference between *wanting* you and wanting to murder you."

"You want me."

"Yes, but there are some days you're so bloody stubborn I think about murder. It'd be purely out of love though."

Patrick huffed out a startled laugh, watching the way Jono's mouth curved into a smile. He trailed his fingers down across Jono's jaw, the prickle of a beard starting to come in scratching against sensitive skin. Jono blinked at him slowly before closing the scant inches between their mouths to kiss him. Patrick parted his lips, ignoring the taste of morning breath in favor of kissing Jono, because there'd been a time the other week he hadn't been sure he'd ever get to again.

Jono bit lightly at his bottom lip, the faint sting making Patrick's cock twitch with interest. "Not going anywhere. Won't let you go either."

Patrick couldn't bring himself to voice the fear that *he* might, and so kissed Jono again, because that was better than thinking about everything in his life he couldn't control. Jono let Patrick set the pace of the kiss—quick and hard, needy in a way Patrick only ever was with him.

Jono responded with just as much want, but the touch of his hands was careful and soothing against Patrick's body. One slid down his thigh and curled around the back of his knee to hike his leg over Jono's hip, pulling them flush together. Their cocks slid against each other, and the dry friction drew a groan from Patrick.

"Gonna make a mess of you," Jono promised.

Patrick hummed agreement, in no way capable of arguing against that. Jono had fucked him every single day since he'd been released from prison. Patrick couldn't smell the scent of Jono on his own skin, but he didn't care. It was a mark that he was pack, and he'd never say no to that or to Jono.

They both had a day packed with meetings, but in the soft morning light of their bedroom, their responsibilities faded away in favor of slow kisses, shared breath, and the warm slide of Jono's slick fingers jacking them both off together. It was easy and warm and gentle, Jono in no hurry even when Patrick pressed biting kisses against his collarbone.

"Please," Patrick gasped out, rolling his hip into Jono's grip, toes curling at the heat spreading through his belly.

Jono dragged his thumb across the swollen tip of Patrick's cock, licking his way back into Patrick's mouth without bothering to speak. He didn't need to, not when his touch said everything and more.

When Patrick came, it was with Jono's name on his lips, body arching into a touch he'd always crave, feeling anchored in place for the first time in weeks. Jono rolled him over onto his back, grinding their hips together until he came with his teeth pressed against the edge of scar tissue stretching over the jut of Patrick's collarbone.

The sticky, warm mess smeared between them meant they'd need to shower soon, but Patrick was content to stay where he was, pressed down into the bed by Jono's weight, breathing in a sense of safety he didn't want to give up.

It was long minutes later when Patrick finally found the where-withal to speak. "I have a meeting I need to get to."

Jono nuzzled his throat, licking at the sweat there. Patrick shivered at the touch. "I'll make you breakfast."

"Shower first."

"All right. Five more minutes though."

Eventually, they rolled out of bed and cleaned up, with Patrick dressing in jeans, T-shirt, and his combat boots. After Monday's attack, he'd sworn off suits unless he had to appear in court.

Jono was at the stove frying up some bacon, and Patrick was tapping his fingers impatiently as he waited for the coffee to finish brewing when his phone rang. Pulling it out of his pocket, he answered because it was Sage.

"Yeah?" he asked.

"Turn on the news. Your grandmother is finally giving a statement," she said flatly.

Patrick froze, fingers curled in the air above the counter for a second before he slowly made a fist. "Okay."

He ended the call and hoped Sage didn't mind the curtness of his actions. Jono removed the pan from the hot burner and left the kitchen ahead of Patrick to turn on the television. Patrick joined him in the living room and tried to steady his breathing as the picture filled the frame of their large flat-screen television.

He didn't remember his grandmother's house in Salem—the memories long since buried beneath the life he'd lived—but the scene on the news channel seared itself into his mind.

The house was two stories, situated next to a body of water, the yard open and blooming in the middle of summer. Standing in front of it, arrayed on the sidewalk beyond the property line, was a group of people Patrick could see himself in. Whether blond or red-haired, he saw bits of his own face in theirs, the profile of his nose, even his height. For all that he had his father's eyes, the rest of him, he realized right then with sudden clarity, was very strongly influenced by his mother.

Eloise Patterson was a slender woman at the age of eighty, with bony shoulders the silk of her blouse settled lightly on. Her fair skin was wrinkled around her eyes and mouth, her hair a pale red that spoke of the genetics that had been passed down to Patrick, though her current shade was probably a dye job. She appeared poised before the cameras, her eyes clear, but her voice was riven with steel when she spoke, a cut-glass, genteel accent that sounded nothing like him.

"I speak for my family, as well as for the Salem Coven which we preside over. I am aware of the information recently come to light about my grandson and granddaughter. My family have previously reached out to government officials to confirm the truth of the matter. It is with great grief that I confirm my grandchildren, who we thought taken from this earth twenty-two years ago, are indeed alive, and we were kept in the dark," Eloise said.

She paused, swallowing loud enough the microphones caught the noise. Her gaze swept over the people gathered in front of the house that viewers couldn't see, but judging by the number of microphones set up on the podium, there was a large news crew present.

"Despite the national security issues that stem from Ethan Greene's traitorous acts, this is, at the very heart, a private family matter. We will not play it out before the cameras to satiate public curiosity." Eloise stared directly into a camera, her blue eyes shimmering lightly with unshed tears. "However, it would be remiss of me to not use this moment to reach out to my grandson. Patrick, if you are watching, please understand we didn't know. If we—if *I* had known, rest assured, there would be nothing on this earth that would have kept me from you."

Patrick didn't know he was holding his breath until Jono wrapped both arms around him from behind, lips brushing against the shell of his ear. "Breathe, Pat."

He let out an explosive gasp, lungs burning. Patrick stared at the television screen, the sound of reporters calling out questions a buzz in his ears as he watched his grandmother step away from the podium and head back to her home. The rest of his family—people who had to be aunts and uncles and cousins—put themselves between her and the cameras, escorting her into the safety of her home.

"If she tries to ring you, will you pick up?" Jono asked long minutes later after the scene had cut away to an anchor and Patrick had gotten himself under control.

"My old phone is still in evidence lockup," Patrick said, throat working hard to get the words out.

"Pat."

"I don't know. I can't think about this right now."

It was too much in a way—the reality that the family he'd been kept hidden from wanted him back, even after all these years. Even after what he was being charged with. Persephone had delivered him into Setsuna and Ashanti's hands as a child, and he'd gone knowing he could never look back. He could never dream of a reunion, of a home, if he wanted to stay alive, so he hadn't.

This wasn't something Patrick was ready for, if he ever would be.

Maybe that made him a coward or worse, but he had other, more immediate problems he needed to deal with. Getting in touch with his grandmother was at the bottom of his list right now. It had to be.

Patrick twisted around in Jono's arms, rising up on his tiptoes to kiss him hard on the mouth. "You promised me breakfast before my meeting."

It was a brutally obvious plea to change the subject, and Jono went along with it, letting Patrick ignore his past for a little longer.

"The director is concerned about your safety," Henry said.

"I know. It's not like there's much she can do," Patrick said.

"She suggested we put a security detail on you."

"Oh, fuck no. I'm still on unpaid administrative leave. She can worry about my ass if the agency decides to pay me again."

It was Henry's job to handle threats against the agents who worked beneath him, but Patrick wasn't going to put this mess on him. The SOA was already besieged on all sides, and none of that was Henry's fault.

Coming back to the New York City field office had still been difficult and awkward. Patrick had held his head high through all the stares and the whispers that trailed in his wake as he'd cleared his way through security and been given an escort up to Henry's office. He couldn't move around the building with the freedom he used to have. He might be out of jail, but the murder charge still hung over his head.

"It's my understanding that the PCB is working to get a handle on the hunter issue and to bring the remaining alpha of the New York City god pack in for questioning about her pack's actions against you on Monday."

"The only New York City god pack is mine."

Patrick met Henry's gaze with a challenging one of his own. He knew his standing within the werecreature community was causing hell for the SOA and all the cases he'd touched since last June, but he refused to let them ignore his pack.

Henry's expression didn't change. "I'm sure the PCB will keep you apprised of their findings."

Which was a nice way of saying the SOA wouldn't. Patrick wasn't surprised.

"I said I'd come and speak to the legal department about some of my cases. If there's nothing else you need to update me on, then I'd like to get started with the lawyers," Patrick said.

He hadn't brought Danai because it didn't seem like something he needed her for. Patrick knew most of the cases he'd handled for the SOA since being transferred to New York weren't influenced by his standing within his pack. The ones that were, well, those had also been directly or indirectly the focus of Ethan and the Dominion Sect. He would know better than she would what he could and could not talk about regarding his work.

"The conference room on this floor is set up with the case files, and the in-house lawyers are waiting for you. I also have this for you." Henry opened his desk drawer and pulled out a plain white envelope. "The director convinced the congressional subcommittee to overnight it here so I could deliver it to you. We couldn't be sure your mail wasn't being tampered with."

Patrick wanted to burn the envelope. "It's not a subpoena."

If it was, a process server would be the one to hand it to him. Henry nodded slowly. "You aren't being served."

That didn't make it better.

Patrick reached for the envelope, studying all the official markings that said it came from the House of Representatives. He slipped his finger under the flap and ripped it open. Pulling out the thick bond paper with its embossed seal up top, he quickly read its contents.

Really, he should've burned it.

"I'm assuming I can't ignore it?" Patrick asked, thinking about Setsuna's warning when she'd been in New York the other week.

"If you choose to ignore the requested summons, then that's your argument to bring up with the director."

Patrick smiled humorlessly as he folded the letter back up and set it on the desk. "Don't shoot the messenger, right?"

Before Henry could reply, Patrick's phone rang. He ignored the irritated look on Henry's face and pulled it out of his back pocket. Danai's name came up on the screen, and he answered it.

"Collins. Line and location are not secure," he said.

"I take it you aren't home," Danai said.

"No. I'm at the SOA's field office downtown. What do you need?"

"If they have a television, I'd advise you to turn it on. Any news channel will do. The US Attorney's Office is set to make a breaking news announcement on your case in about fifteen minutes. We both received the final report from the forensic investigation firm this morning via courier."

Patrick froze in his seat, a feeling of déjà vu washing through him. "Did Preston call you?"

"No. I have it set up so I get notified about any breaking news Google hits on you or your case. The announcement is rolling through major news sites right now."

"Fucking great."

"Do you want me to stay on the line?"

"Yes."

Because while he didn't need her guidance on his past SOA cases, he definitely needed it for this.

He muted his microphone pickup and looked across the desk at Henry. "The US Attorney's Office is making an announcement about my case in fifteen minutes."

In response to that, Henry turned on the television in his office, the channel already set to a news station.

"I'll call the director and inform her of the situation," Henry said.

Patrick left him to it and unmuted his side of the line on his cell phone. He didn't want to put it on speakerphone since he wasn't alone. Two minutes later, while Henry was on the phone with Setsuna, Patrick's phone started vibrating from a slew of incoming texts in the pack group chat right as it beeped with an incoming call from Sage. He sent her call to voicemail and shot off a single text.

I KNOW. DANAI CALLED.

Patrick ignored whatever texts came in after that, keeping the phone on his ear as he stared at the empty stage in the US Attorney's Office's press room. He wondered when the reporters had been notified, because there were a lot of them seated in the room already. Maybe there was a press pool always on standby there.

A little less than fifteen minutes later, the door to the right of the low stage opened and a small group of people in suits stepped out. Mostly men, but a couple of women were there as well. Patrick spotted Preston, but he wasn't the one to stand in front of the podium, bracketed by several flags.

US Attorney Mia Santiago rested her hands against the wooden riser, staring directly into the cameras. She'd carried nothing with her to the stage, which made Patrick think it was going to be a short news conference. His stomach twisted at that implication, but he didn't give voice to his concerns, not while standing in Henry's office.

"After reviewing and evaluating new evidence in the case against Patrick Collins and considering the surrounding national security issues, it is the United States government's decision that it will drop all charges against the defendant," she announced, getting right to the point.

Patrick didn't register anything else she said after that, staring at her face on the television and tracking the way her mouth moved, but his ears were full of static. It didn't seem possible to go from being charged with murder to exonerated in such an incredibly short amount of time when he *knew* a case like his meant he should still be in prison.

How much godly interference had it required to reverse the government's decision? Worse, how many gods were secretly pulling the government's strings?

"Collins," Henry said, gently touching his shoulder.

He jerked, finally hearing the way his ragged breathing sounded between them. The conference was still happening on the television, but Patrick turned his attention to Danai.

"—listening to me? This is fantastic news, Patrick," Danai said, her voice warm with relief.

"Yeah, I'm here," he got out.

"I'll make a follow-up call to Preston once this news conference is over, but it looks like the decision came from above him."

"What do you think made them change their mind? Because we both know the government rarely does something like this."

"Yes, but you forget you *also* had the government defending you. It's a strange occurrence to be sure, but I think the national security interest, your signed declaration about where you were during the time of the murder, and the lab report on your magical signature were the deciding factors."

Patrick thought about Maat and her role as his judge, the forensic investigation witch who worshipped her, and decided it might've been based on evidence, but the reversal had ultimately been decreed by the gods to keep him out of jail.

"Okay."

"I'll call you after I speak with Preston and hopefully get some more information and what the timeline is to have your personal effects returned." Her voice gentled, coming out quiet. "Go home to your pack when you can. I'm sure they'll be thrilled about this."

"I need to be in DC tomorrow for a congressional hearing."

"Do you want me to come along?"

"No, it's okay. Setsuna always has her own set of lawyers for these kinds of appearances."

"Have they reinstated your position as a special agent?"

Patrick grimaced. "No, but that might change."

He realized he could have his job back if Setsuna was able to offer it again, but his position would always be looked at with suspicion because of his ties to the werecreature community. Even if the SOA ethically walled him off from taking any cases dealing with werecreatures, his bias would always be a problem. It would always be a sticking point in the courts.

"I'll let you go," Danai said.

She ended the call, and Patrick let his arm fall down to his side, still clutching his phone. He stared at the television, trying to refocus on the last bit of the press conference but finding he'd missed a good chunk of it. It didn't matter. He'd rewatch it later online if he had to.

"I'll call the director and update her on what's happened," Henry said.

Patrick's phone vibrated in his hand from a text, and he glanced at the screen to see a notification from Jono. He unlocked the phone and was glad Henry wasn't looking his way as he read the text, because he couldn't stop himself from wincing.

Brigid is demanding a meeting tonight in Central Park.

"Fuck," Patrick muttered softly under his breath, feeling a headache coming on.

18

"You shouldn't go," Jono said as they trudged through Central Park for the entrance to the hawthorn path.

Patrick shot him an exasperated look. Despite it being well after sunset, Jono could see that the circles under his green eyes were a little darker than normal thanks to the witchlights guiding their way. Patrick hadn't been sleeping well, and Jono half wished he'd take one of Victoria Alvarez's sleeping draughts to get some rest tonight. At this rate, Jono would have better luck getting Wade to stop snacking than to convince Patrick to slow down.

"Have you ever ignored a congressional request? Because let me tell you, ignoring it only makes it worse. They come back with subpoenas, and if you ignore *those*, you get tied up in court for months on end. I'm a little sick of dealing with the courts right now," Patrick retorted.

So was Jono, but the tide seemed to be turning. The police and two federal agencies were turning their attention to Ethan and continuing to search for Youssef's killer now that it was clear Patrick hadn't been the one to murder the arsehole. A BOLO had been issued for Ethan in the northeastern states, while the

INTERPOL red flag was still active. Jono, like Patrick, didn't think Ethan was in Europe.

Mayor Doyle Ferbenn, while refusing to issue a curfew like he had during December when the Wild Hunt was on the loose, had made it clear that Estelle's god pack should restrict themselves to their territory. The PCB had increased patrols through Hamilton Heights, and for once, none of the packs under his and Patrick's protection had reported skirmishes within their own territory. It seemed every pack was lying low to take the heat off their community as a whole.

Jono knew the reprieve wouldn't last.

The rival territory claims still existed between their god pack and Estelle's. Nothing short of a challenge ring fight would change that. With the charges against Patrick in the process of being dismissed, that took away one of the reasons for not bringing the fight to Estelle's doorstep. With the current public scrutiny and the daylight attacks that had happened already, the werecreature community couldn't afford any more bad press. Neither could Jono's pack afford to let Estelle remain in New York City.

On top of their citywide pack problem, they needed to support their alliance with the fae and keep Patrick out of Ethan's hands. Their current situation was all around a bloody headache.

"I still don't like it," Jono said.

"It's not like I'm going alone. Sage is coming with me," Patrick said.

Jono looked over his shoulder at where Sage and Wade trudged along the path behind them. Late evening meant the sun was below the horizon, and twilight had faded to night. The summer heat hung over the city like a heavy blanket beneath the night sky.

"Don't you have a meeting with your florist tomorrow?"

From behind them, Sage let out a heavy sigh. "I do, but I switched it to Friday afternoon since the hearing is only happening tomorrow."

She'd been smelling like stress when Jono could catch her scent at all lately. She was supposed to have all next week off for the wedding. Worry over Patrick and Marek, on top of planning her wedding while in the midst of a god pack civil war, had left Sage pulled in too many directions. No matter what happened, Jono was going to make her and Marek take their honeymoon.

Jono looked ahead again, eyes unerringly finding Tiarnán and Deirdre farther up the path. They'd put Bethesda Fountain and Bow Bridge behind them, and the Lake was a pool of black that glinted like obsidian through the shadowy bare trees surrounding them. They were heading into a place that should've been all dense greenery that served as the transition point to the hawthorn path that connected Tír na nÓg to the mortal world. Instead, the path was lined with bare trees and filled with dried leaves.

At least this time they weren't being chased by the Sluagh.

Tiarnán's magic had shielded them since they met up at the corner of Fifth Avenue and East Seventy-Second Street. The fae magic smelled strangely floral to Jono, but reminding him of nothing grown on Earth. It grew stronger the closer they got to the hawthorn path. Jono reached for Patrick's hand, their fingers sliding against each other as he got a good grip. He didn't want what had happened the last time they came this way to occur again.

A soft golden glow appeared up ahead, growing until the trees and bushes around them appeared drenched in sunlight when the only thing overhead was the moon. They broke through the tree line, following the hawthorn path to that strange in-between area that wasn't quite past the veil, but wasn't quite anchored to the mortal plane.

The Spring Queen of the Seelie Court and a goddess in her own right stood in the center of the path, surrounded by an escort of fae warriors. Brigid's red hair was the color of the sun at dawn, with fire flickering at the tips of the long curls. Her dark blue eyes met Jono's unerringly, gaze full of power he only ever saw in immortals.

Her gown this time was the same color as her eyes, the blue rippling like waves. A cape made out of flower blossoms was draped over her shoulders and pooled at the ground around her feet. Brigid's crown of twisted silver and gold filigree had hawthorn flowers woven through it. The scent of spring hung heavy in the air, but beneath it was the sharp burn of ozone that always lingered around a god.

On either side of her stood a pair of immortals that had Patrick making a startled sound so low Jono wouldn't have heard it if he was human as Tiarnán bowed to his queen.

"Gerard," Patrick said, surprise bleeding into his voice. "What are you doing here?"

Captain Gerard Breckenridge offered up a smile that was more like a grimace. "Hunting."

He hadn't changed much since December, but then, Jono knew he never would. The name Gerard went by in the mundane world was an alias. Ireland still awaited Cú Chulainn's return when he finished his duties here in the United States.

"That god you're missing?" Jono asked.

Gerard glanced at him and nodded. "Yes. I'm on leave with the Department of the Preternatural and working with Órlaith to track Cernunnos' passage through the veil from Dublin. We're not having very much luck."

"Probably because he's somewhere here in New York, and it's full of iron," Patrick said.

"Which is why we are meeting you here," Brigid said, her voice as fiercely powerful as always.

Fenrir stirred in the back of Jono's mind at the sound of it, the god's awareness burning through Jono. While his pack and the fae gods standing before them were aware of who Jono carried in his soul, Tiarnán was not. Jono weighed the risk of what the reveal would cost them, but in the end, he let Fenrir have control.

"Your wayward elder is causing trouble, cousin," Fenrir said through Jono's mouth as the god let go of Patrick's hand.

The brightness of Brigid's aura dimmed in Jono's eyes with Fenrir's help. Brigid didn't seem surprised Fenrir let his presence be known, but Tiarnán did a very obvious double take before he got himself under control.

"Cernunnos has always been a law unto himself."

"The Greeks are displeased he interferes with the magic they laid down around this island. It is not yours to destroy."

"Considering the Greeks are why we are here, I have no sympathy for their position."

"We do not have time to fight amongst ourselves."

Brigid gifted Fenrir and Jono with a look that could've frozen the Hudson River at the height of summer. "Then tell the Greeks to stay out of our way. Cernunnos takes precedence for us."

"The parks are withered as if it were winter and they reek of magic like his, Your Majesty. The magic hasn't faded, which means he hasn't left," Tiarnán said.

"Is he the one sucking the life out of everything green in the city?" Patrick asked.

Brigid's gaze cut away from Jono's, pinning Patrick with a hard look. "The Horned One would not risk our standing and memory with mortals by damaging the land unless forced to."

"Are you sure about that? Because you gods are all about meddling, and it seems he's already doing it."

Gerard winced. "Collins."

The exasperated tone was one Jono understood well when it came to Patrick. Jono loved the man, but Patrick attracted trouble and started fights without even trying.

Órlaith touched her hand to Gerard's elbow before meeting Jono's gaze, Fenrir refusing to blink. "When Cernunnos missed the Lughnasadh ceremonies, I went looking for him at his home and found it ransacked. Hellfire had scorched the threshold, and the inside was tainted by blood magic, cast by the same mage who took me last year."

"Zachary," Patrick bit out, echoed by Fenrir's growl that was half Jono in the sound.

"Hellfire?" Sage asked sharply. "The only god we know of who uses that is Hades, and the Dominion Sect is making a mess in New York City right now."

Give me control, Jono demanded.

Fenrir receded with a huff, Jono's nerves reacquainting themselves with his brain as he got control of his body. He turned his head to look at Patrick. "You said you think the Dominion Sect is after you. Can you think of a reason why?"

"Other than me dead?" Patrick made a face. "I don't know."

"Ethan wouldn't have come back here without a reason. If you're the reason, then the problem can only be one thing."

The full-body flinch that hit Patrick had him shifting on his feet. Jono reached for his hand again because Fenrir wasn't there to force him to let go.

"What do you mean they're in New York for you?" Gerard asked sharply.

"Have you seen the news?" Patrick asked.

Gerard slowly shook his head. "I've been past the veil once I sent your lawyer my letter of support."

"Thanks for that, by the way."

"Answer my question, Collins."

"Hunters and the other god pack crashed a car into the one carrying Patrick and his lawyer on Monday in broad daylight. Zachary made it clear they wanted to take him alive," Jono said grimly.

"Yeah, to *kill* me," Patrick stressed.

Gerard had a particularly murderous look on his face. "Not on my fucking watch."

"You and everyone else in our pack," Sage said.

"What's Cernunnos the god of?" Wade asked. Everyone looked at the teenager, who stared back at them with an annoyed expression on his face. "What? I got bored in my last history class and stopped paying attention around the time we learned about the Dark Ages. They don't really teach about myths that have all of you in the stories."

"Cernunnos presides over nature, guides all beasts, and gives life when it is begged for, but life has to come from something. It is never given freely. There is always a trade," a familiar accented voice said from the shadows.

Out of the corner of his eyes, Jono saw Brigid stiffen, her blue eyes widening as a piece of the surrounding shadows slipped out of the trees and into the light. Ashanti flashed them all a sharp-fanged iron smile as she approached, lifting her chin in a challenging way in greeting to Brigid. Being shorter than the Spring Queen didn't detract from her power, and the increase of ozone on the air made the back of Jono's throat itch.

"I had heard you were nothing but dust," Brigid said into the heavy silence.

Ashanti ignored the way the fae warriors drew closer to their queen, hands tightening on their bladed weapons. "You know the way my story goes."

Brigid nodded slowly, never taking her eyes off Ashanti. If Jono didn't know any better, he'd say she was wary. "I am sure your children are pleased you walk this earth again."

It was a clear statement that the ruler of the Seelie Court was *not* pleased. Gerard, for his part, didn't seem perturbed by Ashanti's presence even if Órlaith was.

"Oh, fuck," Patrick breathed out, drawing everyone's attention. "Cernunnos is a fertility god."

The sudden way all the blood drained out of Patrick's face had Jono stepping closer to him. "Pat?"

"Why would that be a problem?" Gerard asked.

Patrick opened his mouth, but nothing came out. Jono answered for him, meeting Gerard's gaze with a sickly grimace. "Ethan performed a fertility rite in Chicago earlier this year with Freyr's help. We believe Hannah's pregnant."

Brigid leveled a flatly displeased look in Jono's direction and the god he carried in his soul. "And you have the gall to lecture me about interference, cousin?"

"Oh, *fuck*," Gerard said, staring at Patrick.

"Perhaps the fertility rite in Chicago wasn't enough," Sage said after a fraught moment of silence.

"Macaria has been bound in a mortal body for over two decades. The flesh you carry on your bones is not capable of containing a godhead in perpetuity," Brigid said.

Jono tightened his grip on Patrick, pulling him closer. "So, what? You're saying Hannah is dying?"

Brigid gave him a pitying look. "The twin the hells took died years ago."

"She's a walking corpse, I *know*, but it's one of your pantheon that's trying to keep her alive," Patrick spat out.

"An act done under duress."

"You don't know that."

A fury like a hurricane spanning a continent flashed across Brigid's eyes. Jono thought the only reason she didn't lash out in the face of Patrick's continued disrespect was Ashanti's presence. The mother of all vampires had come to stand on Patrick's other side, a coldly powerful presence that seemed to kneecap Brigid's rage.

"If Cernunnos is giving aid to the Dominion Sect, whether of his own free will or not, the more pressing question is what do they want you for, Patrick?" Órlaith asked.

"You said it yourself," Jono said, jerking his chin in Brigid's direction. "They're twins."

Patrick's expression remained bleak. "And I'm still tied to Hannah."

Órlaith's expression wasn't pitying, but it was close.

"There has always been power in bloodlines," Ashanti said. "In twins."

Patrick let out a harsh laugh that Jono never liked to hear.

"Persephone said the same thing once."

"She wasn't wrong."

"Perhaps we do not need to hunt for Cernunnos if we can find him through your ties to your twin," Brigid said.

"No," Jono growled.

Brigid stared at him, gaze implacable. "Your pack owes us for the support we have given you. I want Cernunnos found. If you can find him through Patrick's connection to his family, then do so."

"They aren't his family."

"Blood does not lie."

"And I fucking said no."

"This is not negotiable if you wish to keep our alliance and your packs safe."

Patrick was silent in the face of her demand. His lack of an argument told Jono he expected to have to obey the gods. Not for the first time did Jono want to strangle every last bloody one of the fuckers.

"You want us to somehow track Hannah through Patrick? He doesn't have an affinity for blood magic, and messing with souls is illegal," Sage said.

"Ah, but I do." Ashanti tilted her head to the side, studying Brigid. "Take care with your demand, cousin. It is one of yours who aids the hells, after all."

Brigid's mouth curved at the corners, sharp and threatening. "As you have yourself over the centuries."

"I am as I was made. I can be nothing less."

Vampires didn't have souls, but Ashanti had a godhead. Jono wondered what sort of power Ashanti carried or was able to externally access, and how much of it—if any—she'd passed down to her children over the years outside of walking in sunlight.

"If you want them to hunt for Cernunnos, I'll stay and help," Gerard said, inclining his head toward Brigid in a sign of respect, but his voice was firm and unwavering in his decision.

"I'll keep searching through the veil for any traces he might have left behind. There's enough that it brought us here to New York. We will hope there is more," Órlaith said before Brigid could protest.

"Very well," Brigid said after a moment, never looking away from Jono. "Do we have an accord?"

"Not much of a bargain in an order, but if it'll keep you lot on our side, then yes," he said. They'd been pushed into a corner he didn't think even Sage could argue them out of, so there was no sense in trying. "We'll help you find Cernunnos."

There were so many ways that promise could get twisted, but Jono didn't have time to carve out any more amendments to it. Fenrir didn't seem concerned, at least not over the bargain, and Jono had no qualms breaking a promise made to a goddess if it meant keeping Patrick safe.

Fuck the gods and all the twisted lies buried in every last one of their promises. If they wanted Patrick, they'd have to go through Jono first.

"Good hunting," Brigid said.

The Spring Queen turned on her heels and marched back down the hawthorn path with her escort, disappearing into a distant fog that swallowed them whole. Gerard and Órlaith remained where they were.

"You never said Ethan was after you," Gerard said to Patrick.

"That status quo hasn't changed for years," Patrick said tiredly.

"This is different if they're trying to do a stop and grab in the middle of Manhattan."

"Let's get off the hawthorn path before you two start arguing. I want some sleep before we fly to DC tomorrow," Sage said.

Gerard frowned. "Why are you going to DC?"

"Congressional hearing," Patrick said.

Gerard shared a look with Jono, raising an eyebrow in a silent question that was easy enough to interpret. The witchlights reflected oddly in his silver eyes, but his expression was clear enough to read.

"Estelle is still a problem. I can't go with him," Jono said.

Gerard nodded decisively. "I'll go then."

"Wonderful. You can help keep him out of trouble," Sage said as she started back the way they'd come.

"Don't I get a say in this?" Patrick asked.

"No," Jono and Gerard said in unison.

Órlaith tugged Gerard into a deep kiss. "I'll continue our hunt and will let you know if I find anything."

"Be safe," Gerard said, brushing the back of his knuckles over her cheek after they parted.

"Always."

Órlaith headed in the direction Brigid had gone, and the rest of them put the hawthorn path behind them. It took less than a minute to return to Central Park proper, with Tiarnán leading the way. Even though they hadn't gone past the veil entirely, they'd lost some amount of time. Jono's mobile put it a little past midnight, which definitely meant Patrick and Sage wouldn't get enough sleep before needing to get up to catch their flight out.

"If Patrick's twin is in New York and sick, wouldn't she be in some hospital?" Wade asked from up ahead.

"Private home care would be my best guess, which means she could be anywhere," Gerard mused.

Ashanti had yet to leave their group, though Jono could smell other vampires in the park around them, waiting for her return. "If you're going to DC, you would do well to retrieve something for me. It will aid us in tracking Hannah through your blood and soul if it comes down to it."

Patrick's expression twisted, color having returned to his face. "Jono agreed to finding Cernunnos. I didn't agree to what you're suggesting."

"*Weapon,*" Ashanti reminded him with all the gentleness of acid.

Jono noticed Patrick's flinch because he was looking, and he scowled at Ashanti. "Leave off."

The flash of iron teeth was easy enough to make out in the glow of witchlights Patrick had cast to help them see in the dark.

"There is a spell book I left in the Library of Congress sometime during this country's Industrial Revolution. Bring it to me," Ashanti told Patrick.

"Do you know how many books are in that place? How the hell do you expect me to find it?" Patrick protested.

Ashanti slipped her hand into the pocket of her skirt and pulled out a carved wooden figure half the size of her palm. It took a moment for Jono to see the shape of the elephant head in the design, and how the tusks weren't made of lighter wood, but of crystal filled with dark fluid held inside a tiny space.

The artifact smelled of magic and blood, none of it good.

"This will locate the spell book."

Patrick took it from her after a moment, rubbing his thumb against one wide ear on the elephant's head. "Like a dowsing rod?"

"If you must compare it to such useless magic, then I suppose that works."

"Dowsing rods work."

Ashanti curled her fingers around Patrick's wrist. "Retrieve the spell book."

Patrick sighed heavily, giving in. "Guess it's a good thing I'm going to DC."

"Thought you gods were supposed to be all-powerful and all-knowing? Didn't think you'd need a book for that," Jono said, not bothering to keep the mockery out of his voice.

Ashanti laughed, low and rough, the sound some bit of the nightmare she was to people. "I have forgotten more than you will ever remember in ten lifetimes, wolf."

Ashanti disappeared before Jono finished blinking, gone in a streak of darkness that blended into the night around them. The scent of the undead went with her.

"Don't antagonize her," Patrick said, his shoulder brushing against Jono's arm. His pockets weren't big enough to hold the small, carved elephant head, so he held it in his left hand with loose fingers.

"I'll stop when you stop defending the shit positions she puts you in. I don't bloody care if she taught you how to play word games with gods. She was a terrible teacher, because you're shit at looking out for yourself," Jono said.

"That's why Jono is good for you, Razzle Dazzle," Gerard said from up ahead.

Patrick made a face. "Fuck off."

But he didn't move away, only stepped closer to stay by Jono's side, hand reaching for his. Jono held on to Patrick and refused to let go.

19

Thursday afternoon found Patrick running on coffee and spite by the time he finished with the closed-door congressional hearing before the Committee for Magical Enforcement. He should've felt better that it was over, but all he felt was *tired*.

"That didn't go as terribly as I thought it would," Setsuna said as he approached where she sat in the rows of chairs behind the low wall separating the audience from the front of the room.

Most of the seats were empty; only those with the appropriate security clearance had been allowed to be present. Gerard was one of them, though he'd opted to sit with members of the military rather than with other politicians. Sage had been relegated to the hallway outside and hadn't minded the separation in order to guard the only way out.

"I don't know if your bar for shitty political maneuverings is set too low or too high," Patrick said as he buttoned up the front of his suit jacket, having turned his back on the raised dais of seats the senators were leaving.

"Perhaps a mix of both."

Patrick's head hurt, as it always did after going through one of these hearings. He felt more flayed open than usual, if only because the entire four-hour hearing had revolved around the information about his past now recently come to light.

It made him want to find the nearest bar so he could order an entire bottle of whiskey and see how long it took him to reach the bottom.

It was a fleeting thought that Patrick let go after a few seconds of wishful dreaming. Jono wasn't there to tell him no, but Sage was, and he'd gotten better over the months about not using alcohol as a crutch for his emotional state. Blunting his emotions didn't mean they went away. His VA-assigned therapist had ultimately been right about that. It didn't mean he couldn't wish to forget the last few hours.

"Let's get out of here," Patrick said, jerking his head in the direction of the door.

Gerard peeled away from the cluster of military brass who'd opted to sit in on the hearing. He wasn't in uniform, but he was in a suit. It helped him blend in with everyone on Capitol Hill, despite being a god.

"I'm surprised you didn't murder anyone. Some of those questions were close to being out of line," Gerard said. Patrick glared at him, and Gerard laughed. "Too soon?"

Patrick elbowed him sharply in the side. "*Yes.*"

The US Attorney's Office was scheduled to file the dismissal of his case today. Danai would notify him the second they did. Patrick wouldn't feel in the clear even after the case was closed. His reputation had taken a hit he couldn't ever fully recover from.

"I'll get the paperwork pushed through regarding your reappointment to your former position," Setsuna said as they headed for the door.

He wondered about the optics of the swiftness she was pushing, but Patrick wasn't going to complain about getting back his badge and gun. Now, if only the US Attorney's Office would return his cell phone, work laptop, and everything else the FBI had taken from his apartment and handed over to them.

Mostly, he wanted his phone back. Considering Preston hadn't sent Danai a demand for his passcode, Patrick wondered if they were able to break the encryption and access everything on it.

Gerard lengthened his stride to open the door for them and froze for a split second. It was long enough for Patrick to reach for his dagger sheathed against the small of his back. Guests weren't allowed weapons in the heart of their nation's government, but his gods-given dagger had gone undetected at security.

"Cousin," Gerard said in a cool voice as he exited the hearing room.

Patrick looked over Gerard's shoulder and found Sage facing off against the same goddess who had allowed him to walk out of jail the other week when she masqueraded as a federal judge. The political aides and other observers waiting outside seemed oblivious to the standoff, passing by them without a single glance.

Maat, dressed in a vivid emerald-green pantsuit, looked away from Sage, and Patrick forgot how to breathe. The weight of her gaze was nothing like before, stripped of whatever play at humanity she'd acted out on the bench.

"How does freedom taste?" Maat asked, her voice rich in a way it hadn't been in the courtroom. There was power in law, and she embodied the wealth of it right then.

"Uh, good?" Patrick managed to get out.

Gerard stepped between them, and it felt less like his entire life was being judged in an instant. Patrick let out a heavy breath and stepped into the hallway after Setsuna.

"This is not your homeland," Gerard said.

"The refugees who call this country's cities home believe otherwise," Maat said. "I am not here for you, but for the one who owes us."

Patrick let his hand drop away from the hilt of his dagger as he stepped around Gerard to face the Egyptian goddess. "This isn't really the place to chat."

The senators on the subcommittee were seconds from leaving the hearing room, more political aides were coming to meet them, and as soon as the reporters figured out the hearing was over, they'd be clamoring for statements. Patrick was surprised they hadn't arrived already, but he figured Maat probably had something to do with that.

The goddess turned on her high heels, the dangling gold ostrich feather earrings she wore flashing beneath the lights. "Then you and I will take a walk."

Sage looked as if she wanted to argue, but Patrick shook his head at her. She snapped her mouth shut before crossing her arms over her chest. "I'm supposed to keep an eye on you."

"We're still doing that," Gerard said, nodding at Patrick. "Go. We'll be right behind you."

Patrick looked at Setsuna, who merely tapped her cane on the floor.

"I need to speak with General Reed. Call me when you're finished," Setsuna said.

Patrick nodded and hurried after Maat, who hadn't bothered to wait while they figured out if it was safe to follow a goddess. He caught up to her at the end of the corridor, not paying much attention to the people crossing their path. Most were focused on their phones or whatever senator they were following since they were in the Senate's wing of the Capitol Building.

The complete disregard for their presence came down to magic. Patrick had been in the center of enough media scrums recently to know that his appearance right now was enough to incite one. That no one gave them a second glance proved godly manipulation was at play.

Maat led him out of the air-conditioned Capitol Building to the main rear exit that opened up onto the National Mall. He followed her down one of the two massive staircases that led to the ground on either side of the building. The grass stretching outward between them and the Washington Monument three-quarters of the way down the length of the park was lushly green, the trees lining the pathways providing shade in the muggy heat. It looked nothing like the parks back in New York City.

Patrick discreetly tugged at the collar of his shirt, already feeling sweat trickling down the back of his neck. He cast a cooling charm on his suit jacket, but it only did so much beneath the hot summer sun.

Maat appeared unbothered by the heat, head held high as she walked at a pace that was less a jog but wasn't quite a slow walk. She didn't speak until they passed the National Gallery of Art on their right.

"You should have stopped your father in Cairo," Maat said.

Patrick had to consciously not grind his teeth. "I'm aware of that."

She didn't speak for another minute, staring straight ahead, chin tilted up proudly. "My brethren and I ultimately survived, despite your inaction."

"We broke the spell."

"A worthless action if we gods remain a target even now."

"I've been trying to *fix* that, but it's a little hard to do when I'm locked up." Patrick breathed sharply through his nose. "Thank you for that."

"You are useless to us if mortal laws bind you to a sentence that is not yours to serve."

"Yeah, I know. I still wasn't looking forward to jail."

"We are looking forward to an end, however it goes." Maat turned her head slightly to look at him, her eyes the color of earth nourished by the Nile. "My ruling helped pave the way to clear your name. It does not clear your reputation."

Patrick wasn't worried about his reputation surviving—it was more important *he* survived.

"An angel gave a seer a vision of a graveyard. It's the first solid sign of the future he's had in over a year," Patrick said.

"We bury bodies, and we bury memories. We will bury the world if we must, in order for a different one to rise in the echo of its passing." Maat looked forward again, never breaking stride. "It is the way of things, as inevitable as the Nile floods."

"Bodies come back when raised. So can memories. What's to stop someone else trying again if Ethan fails taking on Macaria's godhead as his own?"

"The whole of the world cannot remember what is forgotten by everyone."

Patrick frowned, glancing at her. "If one of your kind has that power, why haven't you attempted it before now? Why make me fight this war for you?"

"Because Persephone is a mother above all else, and Macaria is intertwined too deeply with your family's blood to risk wiping the world's memory." Maat came to a stop, finally facing him on the path shaded by tree branches overhead. The National Mall was full of people, but they were impossible to see beyond the fiery glow of Maat's godhead that burnished her skin. "She will not leave her daughter to die, and some of us die so easily these days. We cannot afford the loss of one even as forgotten as Macaria."

"Half you gods want her dead by virtue of aiding Ethan."

"But that half is not the one you owe."

Patrick was quiet for a long minute, refusing to look away from Maat. "Macaria is killing Hannah, isn't she?"

He wasn't speaking of his twin's soul, because he knew nothing but madness remained in her mind. But her body still breathed, was still capable of carrying life even if it could barely contain a stolen godhead. He wondered what that stress was doing to her unborn child, wondered how much support she needed to see that child eventually born.

"Twenty-two years is a slow way to die," Maat said.

Patrick closed his eyes, shame and regret and guilt coursing through him. Shielded as he was, he knew Sage wouldn't get the scent off him. It wasn't anything he wanted to be comforted over, because Maat was right. All of this could've maybe been avoided if he had only pulled the trigger when he'd had Ethan in his sights back in Cairo all those years ago at the end of the Thirty-Day War.

But if he had, he never would've known Jono or Sage or Wade. Never would've gained a pack and a family. Patrick would've remained alone, and he wondered, right then, if maybe it hadn't only been shock that had stayed his finger on the trigger, but fate.

If there was one sure thing he'd learned over the years, it was you couldn't outrun fate.

"Pay your debt, Patrick," Maat said as she turned and walked away from him. "You owe us an end to all of this."

He watched her leave, the muggy air rippling around her as Maat slipped through the veil in the way only gods could, no one the wiser. The smell of ozone faded, replaced by freshly cut grass that made him sneeze.

Fast footsteps behind him made Patrick turn, watching as Sage and Gerard hurried closer on the path, dodging around a family with kids and a jogging stroller. The scowl on Sage's face was tinged with anger. "I couldn't hear a word you were saying."

"I didn't cast a silence ward," Patrick protested.

"That was all Maat. What did she say?" Gerard asked.

"Nothing new. Pay my soul debt. Kill my family. The usual."

His words lacked humor, and Gerard reached out to grip his shoulder, giving him a friendly squeeze. "At least you're free."

"Feels like I keep owing the gods for everything in my life these days."

It wasn't a good feeling.

Sage sidled close and looped her arm through his. Patrick automatically bent his arm at the elbow so she could hold on. "Let's call Setsuna so we can get that damned book before the Library of Congress closes."

Patrick conjured up a tiny mageglobe, hiding it in against the palm of his left hand. He cast a silence ward before pulling his phone out of his pocket to call Setsuna without the usual protocol of multiple tries. She picked up after the second ring.

"We're done. I'm supposed to be thankful the gods interfered, which is fucking stupid, because they've been interfering since I was eight," Patrick said.

"You have your freedom," Setsuna said.

"I'm not in jail, sure, but I still owe them. That's not freedom."

"It's enough. General Reed tells me Eloise has reached out to the Department of the Preternatural demanding answers about their role in taking you from her family and demanding contact information for you. She's been doing the same at the SOA since the revelation of your identity hit the news."

"What are you two telling her?"

"Nothing at this time." Setsuna paused, the quiet on the line interrupted only by soft breathing for a few seconds. "She left her personal number and asked that we pass it on to you. We did not give her yours."

"My actual phone is still with the US Attorney's Office back in New York. I need to figure out when I get it returned to me."

"That's not an answer."

"I don't have time to deal with this. I have other problems I need to worry about."

"Eloise won't stop reaching out until she gets in contact with you."

Patrick couldn't put into words how much he wasn't ready for that. "I need to go."

"Think about it, but if you do choose to contact your family, be careful."

"What? You think they're like Ethan?"

"No. I just don't want to see you hurt."

It was a confession that cut through Patrick's anger and emotional uncertainty in a way that left him momentarily at a loss for words. Setsuna was rarely so blunt in her support over the years.

"They can't be as bad as Ethan," Patrick said.

Sage snorted beside him. "No one is as bad as Ethan."

"It's not their perceived association with Ethan through your mother that I'm worried about. It's complicated." Setsuna huffed out a tired sigh. "I'll run interference as much as I can until you're ready to speak with them, if that's what you ultimately want to do. They might head to New York City though, so be aware of that."

Patrick scowled. "I hate having everyone know where I live."

Beyond the privacy, it was a safety issue Patrick still had to deal with. Gargoyles were well and good against mediocre burglars, but they'd do nothing against someone of Zachary's magical strength or Ethan's deviousness. It had taken Shiva to hold off demons the other night.

"Handle what you need to here in DC and then get back to New York. I'm working on reinstating your position with the SOA."

"That's not going to make a lot of people happy."

"My job is to keep this country safe, not keep people happy."

Setsuna ended the call, and Patrick shoved his phone into the inner pocket of his suit jacket. Gerard eyed Patrick over the rims of the aviator sunglasses he wore.

"Let's get that book and then get the fuck out of here," Gerard said.

"Yeah," Patrick said, not wanting to spend the night in the hotel they'd reserved just in case. He'd rather fall asleep in Jono's arms than in a Marriott by himself.

***

THE LIBRARY OF CONGRESS consisted of three buildings, the most recognizable one being the Thomas Jefferson Building. As the research arm for the federal government, it was located on a block in front of the Capitol Building. Its stone façade was unremarkable in a city area where granite and marble made up the majority of neutral tones around the National Mall. The preservation wards etched into its walls could be found on most of the monuments calling the heart of the nation's capital home. These wards were different, in that they were meant to keep intact the delicate paper and historical relics kept inside the Library.

Housed and protected within its walls were upward of thirty-eight million written works in over four hundred different languages. The largest library in the world was a place that had carried countless whispered conversations over the centuries, and Patrick contributed to that storied history with an unrepentant "Fucking *shit*, but this is getting us nowhere."

Sage didn't even look away from the shelves she was perusing on the other research landing, critically eyeing the titles on the bindings. "You're the one with magic. Shouldn't you be able to find the book through a spell?"

Patrick scowled from his own research landing, glaring at the books before him. "Half the books on this floor are warded with magic for safekeeping. Outside magic isn't allowed."

"You're using an outside voice," Gerard said from the other end of the African & Middle Eastern Reading Room.

"Oh, fuck you."

It was well past closing, and the only reason they had access after-hours was due to Gerard's ties to the military and a direct request from General Reed to allow them entry. Patrick's government connections were nonexistent still, and they'd have been kicked out at closing if he'd been the one to ask.

They weren't making the last flight out back to New York tonight, and he was still pissed about that.

Sighing, he looked down at the carved elephant head in his hand, touching his thumb to the tip of one tiny crystal tusk. He'd been surprised the tusks hadn't been made out of ivory, but once he figured out the liquid inside was blood—probably Ashanti's—the artifact's construction made more sense.

So far, the subtle, insidious magic layered over the artifact had drawn them to this room. It had taken walking through all the many hallways, rooms, and archives of the library before they'd been pulled into the African & Middle Eastern Reading Room.

Patrick couldn't sense any magic in the room, but that didn't mean the book they were looking for wasn't there. Ashanti's magic didn't stem from a human soul but a godhead, and the book they were searching for could've been made with the same sort of power. Which should have made it more noticeable, but nothing was standing out.

Sighing, Patrick turned away from the shelves and took the stairs down from the research landing to the floor. The bookshelves attached to individual research landings were separated by windows. The blinds had all been closed, but the orange glow of streetlamps seeped through a couple of them. As he passed one of the windows on his way back to Gerard, the elephant head vibrated subtly in his hand.

Patrick rocked to a stop, looking down at the artifact for a moment before turning his attention on the surrounding books. The shelves on the nearby research landings were some they hadn't checked out yet, except the vibration hadn't happened near the stairs, but in front of the window. He tracked his gaze higher to the balcony that surrounded the reading room lined with shelves and shelves of more books.

"Find something?" Gerard asked from his spot near the wooden archway in the center of the room that bridged both sides like an elegant catwalk.

"Maybe," Patrick said.

Patrick made his way to the narrow set of stairs on the other side of the archway that led to the balconies. He climbed up and headed for the same area he'd felt the artifact vibrate. Patrick looked up at the shelves in front of him, gaze skimming over titles that had no meaning to him. The carved elephant head never stopped vibrating; Patrick could feel the hum it gave off in his teeth.

Holding the artifact in front of the shelves, he started from the bottom and slowly moved it over the spines of the books. He wasn't sure what he was looking for—he still couldn't sense any magic beyond the faint pulse in the artifact—but *something* was there.

Ultimately, the book Ashanti had left behind so long ago wasn't made of magic at all, but blood would always call to blood.

On the top shelf, set high enough that Patrick needed to climb the shelves to reach it, was a slim book that nearly made the artifact shake out of his grip. Patrick left the carved elephant head on the shelf in favor of removing the small book. It slipped free easily enough, the cover old and faded, looking as if it should've been in an environmentally sealed case rather than the open air of the reading room.

Getting his feet back on the balcony floor, Patrick studied the cover of the book, frowning at the feel of the leather. As he stared at it, an oily sheen of magic rippled across the front, taking with it the glamour that made it appear like an historical text.

The leather was a dull tan that had wrinkled at the corners. The edges of the paper became yellowed and ragged, aged in a way that spoke of decades spent on a shelf. Patrick carefully opened the cover, frowning as he stared at the handwritten calligraphy listing out the title in a language he couldn't read. The ink wasn't ink, but blood, and it made him wonder if the leather was human skin.

"Aw, fuck," he muttered. Of course Ashanti would be in possession of a book on blood magic.

"What is it?" Sage asked from the floor below, her head tilted back as she looked up at him.

"It's a spell book containing illegal magic."

"Not surprising, considering who owns it."

Patrick jumped up to grab the carved elephant head from the

top shelf. As his fingers dragged it off the shelf and into his palm, recognition punched through his magic with sickly force. He swallowed the taste of hell, twisting around to face where the threat stemmed from once his feet were back on the floor.

At the end of the reading room, framed in the open doorway, stood the stuff of nightmares.

"*Soultakers,*" Patrick snarled, shoving the artifact into his pocket so he could reach for his dagger sheathed at the small of his back.

20

Patrick ran for the stairs that led back down to the reading room's floor, book held tight in one hand, dagger trailing white-hot heavenly fire in the air behind him. The trio of soultakers that had either been summoned through the veil or eaten their way through screamed as they staggered toward where Sage and Gerard stood.

The soultakers' screams were reminiscent of tearing metal and made Patrick's ears pop. The sound of cracking glass told him the windows were going to break soon.

"Get to the other exit!" Patrick shouted as he raised a shield between them and the demons.

"We can't leave the fucking soultakers behind when we still have security guards in the library," Gerard yelled back even as he and Sage ran to his position.

Patrick's feet hit the floor hard. "The damn things will follow us. That's what they do."

Gerard glared at him and twisted his free hand in the air, the crackling pop of displaced air the gesture produced revealing the

Gáe Bulg. The sleek weapon had a pole made out of bone topped with a long, notched blade. The magic pouring off it made Patrick's hair stand on end.

Or that could've been the presence of the soultakers.

"You aren't fighting them in close quarters," Gerard snapped.

Patrick conjured up a mageglobe, knowing the damned demons would eat his magic and drain him dry if he gave them half a chance. His dagger, on the other hand, was the safer option.

"You have a better idea?"

Sage shoved them both with preternatural strength, forcing them into a stumbling run. "Yes. We get the hell out of here to a more open area, and I tear off a couple of heads."

While a tank was good, and Patrick's dagger could turn the demons to ash, Sage in her weretiger form was strong enough to rip the heads off the demons if she could stay out of reach of their dangerous mouths and never-ceasing hunger for magic and souls. It was a risky attack, and the only time she'd done it successfully had been with the support of other werecreatures last summer. Patrick wasn't willing to risk her, not when he had a weapon that could kill the demons.

Sage hadn't shifted yet, but she had kicked off her high heels and torn her skirt on either side of her legs for more maneuverability. The soultakers had halved the distance between them, their toxic, whiplike tongues lashing through the air in front of them.

The trio slammed through the entrance opposite the one the soultakers had appeared in, racing into the hallway. Patrick's shield lasted a couple of seconds more before he felt the vicious bite on his magic as the soultakers ate away at his defense. He let the defensive ward go and severed his connection to it, letting the soultakers eat what they'd already gotten their teeth into while he drew the rest back into his soul.

"I want a tank," Patrick said, trying not to whine.

Gerard tossed Patrick an exasperated look over his shoulder

before his attention shifted farther behind them. "Not even the president has the authority to request tanks be deployed in down-town DC."

"The government should change that."

"Keep running."

The sound of clawed feet scraping against the floor behind them had Patrick listening to Gerard. Adrenaline and fear crawled through Patrick's veins as he ran, the smooth soles of his oxfords sliding along the floor when he tried to take the corner at the hallway intersection without slowing down. His shoulder slammed against the wall, and he propelled himself right back off it, staying on Gerard's six.

Most of the lights in the Library of Congress were off; only a handful of dim recessed lights in sparse locations lit the way. Visiting hours had ended well before the sun had set, and it was dark outside. Despite knowing they only had to worry about security guards inside the building, it was everyone else outside that would eventually become a problem.

"We can't contain three soultakers by ourselves," Patrick said, breathing hard as Gerard led them to the exit with unerring strides.

They didn't have the support to do that, not like they'd had on the Skellig Islands last December. Back then, they'd had the entire Hellraisers bolstered by Gerard's fury, and Wade in the sky as aerial support. Here, it was only the three of them, and the last thing Patrick needed was another fight in the middle of a major city to get picked apart on the news.

"We'll have to try," Gerard said.

They burst through a set of doors and nearly bowled over a security guard.

"What the hell?" the guy exclaimed, fighting to keep his footing as Sage grabbed him by the arm and yanked him along.

"No time to explain," she growled.

Sage hauled the man along with easy strength as they pitched themselves down the stairs that led to the first floor of the Great Hall, marble pillars flashing by as they ran. They'd just reached the ground floor when the soultakers screamed so loudly Patrick's ears ached. The security guard let out a sound of wordless terror, fumbling for his sidearm. Sage swatted his hand away from the gun and headed for the front entrance across the marble floor.

They never made it.

A fiery arc cut through the air, materializing as a sword at the last second. Gerard spun his spear to stop the attack as hot metal bit into the bone pole, but the *Gáe Bulg* didn't break.

The figure stepping out of the veil wouldn't have been out of place at a party on an expensive yacht sailing the Mediterranean Sea. Tanned skin looked bronzed beneath the dim after-hours lighting. The gold-brown eyes were dark holes in a face many artists had carved into marble over the centuries, framed by curly brown hair. The high-fashion clothes would've looked better on the runway rather than the dreary DC streets where black was the only color in town some days.

Gerard spun his spear to parry the sword to the side before cutting the notched blade toward the other god's head. "Ares."

The Greek god of war ducked out of range of the attack, wielding his sword like an extension of himself. "Here I thought you'd still be past the veil on the losing side, Cú Chulainn."

"I dare you to say that to Brigid's face," Gerard growled.

Ares laughed, the sound booming in the vast open space of the Great Hall. The soultakers screamed again in response, and Patrick swore when the security guard gave in to his instincts and tried to make a run for it. He didn't get far before a knife thrown by Ares buried itself in his back.

"*Fuck*," Patrick snarled, knowing they didn't have time to stop and help the man. At this rate, he'd be fodder for the soultakers coming down the stairs behind them.

Patrick put himself behind Sage, facing the oncoming demons, but he didn't raise a shield. The matte-black blade of his dagger was impossible to see beneath the white-hot heavenly fire burning over the prayer-infused metal.

The three soultakers staggered off the stairs, their bipedal bodies showing glistening bone through stretched and blackened muscle. The gaping maw of their mouths took up most of the space on their heads. They had no eyes, but it was their never-ending hunger that made the demons formidable hunters and difficult to kill.

Patrick conjured up a mageglobe and filled it with raw magic. It acted like a beacon for the demons, drawing their attention to him rather than the clash of weapons and swearing happening from where Gerard was fighting Ares.

"I can shift," Sage said, radiating heat from right behind him.

"Not yet," Patrick said.

She growled, the sound more animal than human. *"Patrick."*

"I'm not leaving Gerard."

He'd never leave his pack, and he'd sure as hell never leave his former captain. Patrick finally raised a shield between them and the soultakers, shaping it into a wall. He pushed Sage back as the demons sank their metal fangs into the shield. The vicious tug of magic siphoning away from his soul started right behind his ribs, making it difficult to breathe for a second.

Sage grabbed his arm and yanked him backward. Patrick nearly tripped over his feet, but her preternatural speed ensured he didn't lose his footing completely. Ares' sword cut through the air where they'd just stood, the blade sinking into the floor from the force of the blow.

Patrick twisted his head around, seeing Gerard alive but bleeding from a slice across his torso. It wasn't a mortal wound, but it definitely looked like it hurt.

Sage never stopped moving as she raced for the exit, dragging

Patrick along with her. "Drop your shield. I don't want them draining you."

Patrick held it up a few seconds longer, long enough for Gerard to take up their six before he tore his magic apart, taking back the portion that wasn't between a soultaker's teeth. He could feel the rest of it get siphoned away, the drain in his soul an ache he felt in his bones.

The scrape of metal over tile had Patrick glancing back in time to see Gerard swing the spearpoint of the *Gáe Bulg* in an underhanded arc. Fire erupted, the heat of it scorching as Gerard used it to keep Ares at bay.

Sage bypassed the empty security checkpoint at the main entrance of the Library of Congress and slammed through the front door. She didn't bother using the handle, merely shouldered through the glass with preternatural strength. Patrick's personal shields kept him from getting glass shards in the face, pieces crunching beneath his oxfords.

"I'm not dressed for this fight," Patrick said.

"None of us are," Sage snapped.

She pitched them toward the stairs that led to the wide brick-and-stone landing that branched out on either side to yet more stairs that would take them to the street. Patrick's feet barely touched the steps on the way down, but his knees felt it when they finally made it to the empty sidewalks below.

Patrick jerked his arm out of Sage's grip, managing to get free only because she let him. "Stop. *Stop.* We aren't leaving without Gerard."

Sage spun on her bare feet, mouth twisting into a snarl to reveal teeth so sharp her lips bled when she spoke. "They're after *you*, and I *refuse* to let them have you. We can't stop."

Patrick opened his mouth to argue when a soultaker's scream ripped through the air, the sound eerie and macabre, echoing over the city sounds. Then a flash of light exploded on the landing they'd just left. Patrick managed one step toward the stairs when

Sage got a grip on the collar of his suit jacket and yanked him back.

"*No,*" she snapped, giving him a hard shake.

Patrick shoved the spell book against her chest, forcing her to make a grab for it. "Hold this and don't lose it."

"*Patrick.*"

She still took the book from him, and Patrick conjured up a dozen mageglobes, pouring his magic into them as the hellish taint got worse. It scraped against his magic, leaving an acidic taste in the back of his throat. He swallowed against it and turned to face the street and the greenery spread in front of the Capitol Building and the threat there.

A curl of red-black magic flashed between the trees, and Patrick gripped his dagger tighter. He raised a domed shield around where he and Sage stood, ignoring the way his head throbbed from the effort. Sage followed his gaze, lips peeling back from her teeth.

"Zachary," she growled, nostrils flaring.

A soultaker screamed, the sound too close for comfort, and the weight of the demon that dropped onto the shield made Patrick flinch. He looked up into the gaping maw of the soultaker, watching as it bit into his magic and started sucking it down.

"Can you tap a ley line?" Sage asked.

"Jono isn't here," Patrick said.

"We're closer than Chicago. Can you?"

Patrick hesitated before shaking his head. "I think we're too far."

The soulbond was drawn tight between them, but not as tight as when he'd been half a country away. That still wasn't a distance he could easily overcome. The only magic he could rely on was his own, and the soultakers were currently feasting on it.

Another explosion of magic on the landing above ended with a body crashing into the street. Patrick's breath caught in his throat, fear an icy grip on his voice, throttling it. But the figure who'd broken asphalt on his crash-landing wasn't Gerard like he feared.

Ares lay in the street, the *Gáe Bulg* protruding from his midsection. The Greek god of war was immortal, but even he would have a difficult time shaking off a wound like that. A flash of movement out of the corner of his eye proved to be Gerard, the fury surrounding him an almost palpable thing. He was running toward Ares, but before he could make it to the other god, a shockwave spell rolled through the street in their direction.

Gerard dived for the ground, trying to find purchase. He couldn't afford to stand still though, not with a soultaker chasing after him. Patrick aimed a mageglobe filled with raw power at the soultaker, hoping to distract it. The shock-wave spell hit his shield a second later, cracking it with the help of the soultaker still chewing its way through.

"I need to let it in," Patrick said.

"That is a *terrible* plan," Sage snapped.

"Trust me."

She glared at him, holding the spell book so tight her fingernails cut into the old skin that made up the cover. "You're why I'm getting gray hairs in my thirties."

"It makes you look distinguished."

"It makes me want to strangle you."

Sage pressed her back against the barrier, out of the way of the soultaker doing its best to gnaw its way through Patrick's shield and straight to his soul. He readjusted his grip on his dagger, positioned himself as far outside the soultaker's head as he could get, and ripped the shield apart from the inside out.

The soultaker crashed to the ground, tongue lashing out, searching for a meal. Its clawed feet scraped at the cement as it jerked upward, trying to stand. Patrick didn't hesitate to stab the dagger straight into the back of its head with all the force he could muster.

Heavenly white-hot fire burned its way along the edge of the blade through the soultaker's dense skull as if it were made of paper. Thick, tarry fluid welled up around the matte-black blade as the soultaker convulsed against the ground, jackknifing so hard it nearly snapped its spine. The scream it let out was a death knell that shattered the nearby streetlamps, plunging their area into a darkness lit only by magic.

All the prayers in Patrick's gods-given dagger burned the soultaker to ash, its body crumbling to nothing. Patrick checked the forward thrust of his dagger before it could scrape against the cement, the silvery words of countless prayers floating across the blade. Its power didn't fade, the threat of its magic burning bright in the night like a beacon.

The reprieve lasted only a couple of seconds. Sage grabbed him by the shoulders and dragged him out of range of the mageglobe streaking their way. Patrick sent a pair of his own to intercept it on instinct. The resulting explosion was so bright Patrick couldn't see in the aftermath. He wrapped a shield around the two of them in time to prevent the third soultaker from overtaking their position.

"I am not dying here in DC when my wedding is next week," Sage growled.

Patrick blinked rapidly, trying to get rid of the colored dots dancing across his vision. The dots were replaced by flares of magic that erupted from his shields as bullets ricocheted off it.

"They're trying to box us in," Patrick said.

Hunters in dark clothing had stepped free of the greenery in front of the Capitol Building and were advancing. Zachary's magic was easy enough to make out, burning malevolently against the dark.

"I think it's working."

Sage's words came out grim, but Patrick could only spare so much for her worry when a soultaker was draining his magic. He poured more magic into the shield, knowing that it was only going to be eaten. But he needed to buy them time, enough so they could regroup and hopefully go on the offensive.

Gerard dove out of reach of the soultaker harassing him, rolling close to where Ares lay on the street. He grabbed the bone pole of his spear, pressed one foot against the other god's chest, and yanked it free with inhuman strength.

Ares screamed, the sound almost animalistic in its agony. It looked like Gerard yanked out some of Ares' intestines when he removed the *Gáe Bulg*, but they got shaken off. He spun the spear, magic forming a glowing arc around him that distracted the soultaker long enough for Gerard to retreat to their position.

"Is Ares dead?" Patrick called out.

"No," Gerard replied, sounding grimly annoyed about that.

"Is he dying at least? Please tell me he's dying."

The magic flickering over the notched blade of the spearpoint was enough light for Patrick to make out Gerard's face. It also made him a target.

The strike spell was familiar to Patrick's senses—the way it burned through the air from close proximity, Zachary's magic laced through with hints of hell. With a soultaker feasting on his own magic, Patrick wasn't sure his shield would hold against the hit.

The god stepping in between them bolstered his weakness with a ferocity that reminded Patrick of Ares' initial rage.

Gods of war were always a vicious sort.

Montu was no different.

The Egyptian god of war dropped down from above to land in front of them on the street rather than the sidewalk. Patrick didn't know whose side Montu was on, not until the god thrust one arm toward Zachary's spell to counter it with enough power to melt asphalt.

The strike spell exploded harmlessly against the shield Montu had raised in front of him, human magic no match against a god's power. Patrick hoped whatever amount of prayers that sustained Montu these days was enough to turn the tide.

Montu looked over his shoulder at them, eyes a searing gold in his dark face. "Get him out of here, Hermes."

Patrick opened his mouth in protest. "No, wait—"

"Too late, Pattycakes," Hermes said into his ear as a strong hand landed on his shoulder. "We can't let them have you."

His magic was ripped apart as Hermes dragged him through the veil. The pain whited out his vision, but he still felt Sage's free hand curl tight around the lapel of his suit jacket, refusing to let go. Gray fog exploded around them, and he let go of the bits of magic the soultakers were eating, feeling it drain out of him like a broken pipe before it was welded shut.

The tearing separation left Patrick lightheaded, or it could've been getting dragged through the veil at a disorienting speed. Either way, when his feet finally touched solid ground, it was inside the apartment he shared with Jono, the soft glow of dawn creeping through the windows.

They'd been dragged out of DC well before midnight on a Thursday night, and here it was Friday morning now. Patrick's head throbbed with a headache from being magically drained and the anger bubbling up at being taken against his will someplace he didn't want to be.

"Why the *fuck* did you do that?" Patrick snarled as he rounded on Hermes, forcing Sage to let him go. "You left Gerard behind!"

The Greek messenger god appeared unconcerned in the face of Patrick's fury. "You're a target."

Patrick got in Hermes' face, shaking off Sage as she tried to pull him back. "I've been a target my whole fucking life. You don't fucking leave a man behind, Hermes!"

"Cú Chulainn will be fine. You wouldn't be if they had taken you."

Patrick snarled wordlessly in Hermes' face, ready to argue, when a heavy knock on the front door derailed his focus. Sage stepped out of his way, still clutching the spell book. Patrick approached the front door, trying not to tense up. The last time they had unexpected guests, it hadn't ended well for him.

"Yeah?" he called out.

"Collins? It's Detective Ramirez," Allison called out. "There's been an incident concerning Jonothon."

The twisting in his chest wasn't his magic, but the soulbond, pulling painfully tight as Patrick reached for it and held on with everything he had, searching for proof of life. It wasn't broken, and when he tugged on it, he felt an answering pull coming from the other side.

Patrick looked back at Hermes as he settled his hand on the dead bolt. "You better get our things from the hotel in DC and bring them back here."

He'd have to get Setsuna to handle their checkout, but right now, Patrick was being torn in two different directions—how the rest of the fight had ended in DC and what had happened to Jono in his absence. If he had to deal with the cops again, he'd give his phone to Sage and have her call Gerard.

Patrick refused to believe his old captain was anything but alive.

Hermes smirked, staring at him with half-lidded, gold-brown eyes. "Say please."

Patrick ground his teeth. "Are you fucking—"

"Patrick," Sage interrupted sharply, glaring at him.

He scowled, bowing beneath the order in her tone. "*Please.*"

Sage passed Hermes on the way to the bedroom to hide the spell book, shooting him a venomous look. "Don't make me gut you."

"Feisty," Hermes said with a chuckle.

"She'll do it," Patrick warned.

"She could try. But since you asked so nicely, I supposed I can swing by DC."

Hermes stepped backward, slipping through the veil and disappearing from sight. Patrick breathed out harshly before yanking open the front door. Allison and Dwayne both stood on the landing, waiting expectantly.

"Jonothon is fine," Allison assured Patrick.

"Brooklyn isn't," Dwayne drawled.

Patrick closed his eyes and took a deep breath. "What happened?"

JONO WOKE IN AN EMPTY BED EARLY FRIDAY MORNING TO HIS MOBILE ringing loudly. The bedroom was dark when he answered, the time on the screen indicating dawn was over an hour away. Austin Capaldi's name flashed across the screen, and Jono became instantly awake.

"Yeah?" Jono answered as he sat up in bed.

Austin's breathing was heavy over the line, his heartbeat not even close to steady. "There's been an incident."

Jono was already shoving the sheets off his body. "What happened?"

"Keira stopped by after hitting the clubs in Manhattan. She had a fucking demon in her soul."

The chill that washed through Jono's body made his teeth scrape together. "Bloody *fuck*. Is everyone all right?"

"We got her contained. Sven's wife is a sorceress in the Crescent Coven. They live on the same floor as we do. Roxie managed to contain Keira and the demon, but we need Patrick."

Jono yanked on a pair of jeans, mobile pressed between his

cheek and shoulder. "Pat is still in DC for a congressional hearing. He's flying back today."

Austin swore, stress bleeding into his voice. "Then what do we *do*?"

"I'll let you know when I get there. Can Roxie keep the demon contained?"

"So far, yeah."

"Call her coven and see if any other magic users can come help her out."

"Will do."

Jono ended the call and got dressed in record time. As he laced up his shoes, the door to his bedroom opened and Wade leaned inside, yawning hugely but already dressed.

"Demons?" he asked.

"Demons," Jono grunted.

"Ugh. I'm bringing mouthwash."

"I wasn't going to ask you to eat any."

"Yeah, but I usually have to, so this time I'm coming prepared."

Jono didn't argue, just let Wade leave with the mouthwash. They were out the door of the flat less than a minute later, clattering down the stairs to the street at breakneck speed. The Mustang was parked out front, and Jono was behind the wheel in seconds.

Rush-hour traffic hadn't started up yet, but they'd be going against the flow of it. Jono got on the road and dialed Emma before he even made it to the corner while Wade blearily tried to buckle his seat belt.

"Yes?" Emma asked, sounding wide-awake despite the early morning hour.

"One of Austin's pack members came home with a demon in their soul. I'm heading to Brooklyn. I want you there as well," Jono said.

"Mother*fucker*. Patrick's not back yet?"

Jono's grip tightened on the steering wheel. "No."

"Right. Fuck. I'll wake up my pack."

She ended the call, and Jono kept driving. Wade cracked his jaw through a few more yawns before waking up completely. The mouthwash got stashed in the glove compartment as Jono edged past the speed limit.

"Do you think a sorceress is going to be strong enough to get a demon out of someone's soul?" Wade asked.

Jono grunted. "Don't know."

Wade slouched down in the seat and stretched out his legs. He didn't say anything more, just pulled out his mobile and unlocked it. A minute later he did a full-body jerk, leaning forward against the seat belt so hard it locked into place.

"Holy shit!" he exclaimed. "Someone attacked the Library of Congress in Washington, DC, last night."

Jono very nearly drove out of the lane. "*What?*"

"News says it was a demon attack. Gerard is quoted in the article saying the Dominion Sect was behind it."

Jono's chest tightened as he pulled at the soulbond, spots dancing across his vision at how deep he went. He couldn't feel a damn thing, and that frightened him more than anything. He had to remind himself he'd felt the same sort of emptiness when they'd been past the veil.

Jono stabbed at the dashboard, tapping at the screen there to get to the mobile-linked options so he could tell it to "Ring Patrick."

The sound of ringing filled the car for a long few seconds before it finally clicked over to voicemail. He kept it brief.

"Heard the news. Give me a ring."

Jono took a deep breath and tried to still the pounding of his heart. The fact that Gerard hadn't called him yet meant Patrick was probably not in immediate danger, and that Gerard was most likely holed up with his higher-ups with no way to get a message out. If something had happened to Patrick, he liked to think Gerard would've told everyone to fuck off while he let Jono know.

"Patrick hasn't texted the group chat," Wade said, sounding and smelling worried.

"I'm aware."

"What do you think happened?"

"I don't know."

Wade went quiet after that, seeming to realize Jono didn't have any of the answers he was looking for. Jono wished he did. He wished he knew where Patrick was.

I'm not letting him leave the city without me again.

Sage could hold their territory if they had to go beyond the five boroughs. No bloody way was Jono letting Patrick waltz off on his own after this, not with the Dominion Sect still after him.

The drive to Brooklyn took less time than it would in an hour or so when commuters started to get on the road. They got to the apartment building that most of Austin's pack lived in, seeing someone already standing on the sidewalk outside. The woman waved them down, and Jono braked to a stop in the street beside her. She slipped between two parked cars as Wade rolled down his window. Jono got a good whiff of her scent—Austin's pack, her own, and nothing remotely hellish.

"Turn into the parking garage and I'll let you in. Austin had us move his car so you could park there," she said.

Jono nodded and followed after her to the driveway entrance that led to the apartment building's car park halfway down the block. Jono parked where she directed and got out. "Emma's on her way."

The woman tilted her head to the side, brow furrowed. "I'll move my car, then. You head upstairs."

Jono and Wade walked at a swift pace to the front door of the building, getting let in by another one of Austin's pack. The stench of sulfur hit his nose the second he stepped inside, and his lips curled at the smell. He hoped it was only Keira they needed to deal with. Handling more than one demon-infested werecreature without Patrick would take some work.

Jono had been to Austin's territory before and knew the way to the flat. He wasn't surprised to see other pack members in the hallway standing guard, but he couldn't hear anything coming through the cracked open door of Austin's flat. The scent of magic was stark in the air—clean and floral, like expensive perfume. He assumed it was Roxie who had cast a silence ward, but it turned out it wasn't her.

"What are you doing here?" Jono demanded as he entered the ransacked apartment.

Casale looked their way but didn't move from his wife's side. "Angelina got a call for help from within her coven. I wasn't about to let her go alone. Where's Collins?"

"In DC."

"Fuck."

Angelina Casale looked the same as she had last summer when Jono had first met her in Hera's home, the heart of the Crescent Coven. That particular group of magic users had been formed to pray for Hera, and even with their goddess now in Greece, they still worshipped her from a different shore.

Angelina barely glanced at Jono, all her attention on the young woman dressed in a tight minidress, her broken high heels cast aside within the pentagram Roxie must have cast. The witch in question stood at one point of the star, her athame held perpendicular to the floor. Magic ran like water through the athame into the containment spell she had cast, lighting up the lines of the pentagram.

Sulfur settled in the back of Jono's throat like rot. He swallowed against the taste and stepped up to the circle encasing the pentagram, knowing better than to cross it. The demon that had taken over Keira's soul stared out of her eyes, veins black in her face like pulsating worms. She smiled, and her pretty features twisted into something horrific.

"I do like wolves," the demon grated out. "They've a particular feel one doesn't get with mundane humans."

"Get out of her," Jono snarled.

"Make me." A cackling, raspy laugh fell from Keira's mouth, making Austin flinch from the other side of the pentagram. "Oh, that's right. None of you have the power to force me out, and you won't hurt this meatsuit."

Jono stayed silent in the face of that truth, studying the demon wearing Keira's face. It was a shame Spencer Bailey didn't work out of New York. Jono could've done with the soulbreaker's power right about then.

"The Catholic Church is sending an exorcism team," Angelina said in a calm voice that drew the demon's attention.

Casale stepped closer to his wife as the demon snapped Keira's teeth at her.

"Those fools can do nothing," the demon hissed.

"Anything's worth a shot," Austin growled.

Jono thought it odd that a witch had called for the Church, but he supposed demons made strange bedfellows. "How long until they arrive?"

"Hopefully soon. I was the one who put in the call to the archbishop," Casale said.

The demon snarled loudly, the sound not even close to human, but nowhere near the otherworldliness of an angel singing. It lunged at Casale but was thrown back by the containment spell, Keira's skin sizzling on her bare arm where it had touched Roxie's magic. Even as Jono watched, the skin started to immediately heal, the werevirus taking care of the wound.

Demons riding werecreatures' souls was a horror Jono had never wanted to face down in his own city. London had been bad enough. Youssef being dead was one good thing in this whole mess, because if he weren't already burning in hell, Jono would murder the arsehole the same way he was going to murder Estelle for doing this to their people.

The demon leaned forward, grinning against the heat of the

magic, the skin there cracking as it spoke with Keira's voice. "You think this meatsuit is the only one we stole?"

Jono's heart missed a beat, a chill running through his body. He stared the demon in the eye and bared his teeth. "If you think I won't fight to get back anyone you've taken, remind Andras what we did to the bastard in London."

The demon narrowed Keira's eyes. "We'll do the same to Ethan's son."

Jono snarled, the sound drowned out by the howling in the streets outside the apartment building. Austin did a full-body twitch before he raced for the door, a blur of preternatural speed. The demon in Keira's body threw back her head and laughed.

"Fuck you," Jono snarled.

The demon smiled, nothing human in the expression. "You can't win this war."

Jono ignored that taunt, turning instead to face Wade. "Stay here. If the sodding thing breaks free, sit on it."

The demon scoffed even as the pentagram grew brighter. "I'll eat the boy's heart."

Wade smiled, red scales pushing through the skin of his face as his eyes turned molten gold, pupils thinning to slits. Fire flickered behind his teeth, smoke drifting out of his nose. "Not if I eat you first. It's almost time for breakfast, and you should know I'm always starving in the morning."

The demon widened Keira's eyes, the flicker of surprise there enough for Jono to think Wade was an unexpected complication they hadn't been prepared for. Considering what had happened in Paris, Ethan should've known. If he wasn't warning his supposed allies, then that spoke of a discord they could possibly exploit.

Angelina poured her magic into Roxie's spell, taking it over. Then she nodded at the younger woman. "Go with him."

Casale unholstered his pistol, mobile in his other hand, in no hurry to leave his wife's side. "I'm calling in the PCB."

"Don't get in my way," Jono warned.

"Keep some of them alive. You still need proof, remember?"

Jono waved off the suggestion as he took Roxie by the arm and left the flat with her at a speed that made the walls seem to bleed color beneath the hallway lights. She cast a shield right before he crashed them through the front door of the building, protecting her from the impact. They exited into a veritable bloodbath on a once quiet Brooklyn street. Jono left her on the porch to join the fray.

Roxie expanded her shield into a wall that kept the silver bullets aimed in their direction at bay. Jono was already changing form as he headed for the fight. The pain lit up his brain for a single second before it turned off, nerves rerouting the signals as his body twisted and broke. His clothes ripped, shoes peeling apart from the shift. Blood spattered the pavement as he shifted with brutal speed into his wolf form, the world spinning as his vision settled into something new.

Fenrir rose up from the depths of his soul, awake and furious and wanting to kill. Jono kept hold of his bodily autonomy despite the snarling demands of the god.

We give up your presence now, then we lose our only edge, Jono snapped as he picked up speed to escape the *pop pop pop* of silver bullets aimed his way.

Roxie had shielded him from the sides, but she hadn't been able to shield directly in front of him due to not knowing who was friendly and who wasn't in the fight happening on the street.

Austin's pack was getting outflanked and outgunned by Estelle's demon-controlled god pack members and the Krossed Knights. Patrick wasn't there to defend with his magic, and while they had Roxie, she wasn't combat trained. She'd stay where she was and help as much as she could, but it wouldn't be enough.

So Jono tossed back his head and *howled*, pouring command into his voice the way he'd done with Ronaldo at the bar and others who'd needed help changing form over the last year. Only this time, he twisted the call for every werecreature beholden to his god pack within a five-mile radius to *come help*.

He felt the answering call from dozens of werecreatures deep in his soul and in the clear, early morning air. The power of it reverberated through his bones—or that might've been the impact of crashing against Nicholas with lethal intent. Jono drove him to the ground, the both of them twisting and snarling, trying to get the upper hand. Nicholas smelled like sulfur, and his blood tasted like the bitterness of hell when Jono sank teeth into his side, ripping out a chunk of fur and flesh.

Nicholas snarled loudly, snapping his teeth at Jono's face, but Jono jerked out of reach. Then Nicholas heaved them both off the ground, demon-backed strength paired with his own a force to be reckoned with. Jono leveraged himself away from the other were-wolf in order to land on his feet rather than his side.

Nicholas growled at him, the bright amber of his eyes replaced with an inky blackness that looked wrong. The demon hissed a cackling laugh through a throat not meant to make that sound. Jono licked blood off his fangs and lunged for Nicholas' throat. Nicholas met him halfway, the two of them tearing into each other's skin with a viciousness that left the asphalt slippery with blood beneath their paws.

Pained howls followed the echoing sound of guns firing. Not all the bullets found their target, but enough did. Jono snarled in pain when one found its home in his back right leg. The searing pain of silver poisoning burned deep, scratching at his concentration. The wound wouldn't heal, the bullet wouldn't be pushed out, not with silver in the mix.

Nicholas took advantage of the tiny break in Jono's focus to get in a lucky swipe near the wound. Jono let out a pained snarl as blood soaked his fur, the hot sting refusing to fade.

Jono slashed at Nicholas, who jerked back and kept moving, but Jono didn't follow. He wasn't about to get led to the slaughter, but staying in one spot was almost as bad. The Krossed Knights had them surrounded in the street, and Roxie's shields weren't enough of a defense. None of Austin's pack were retreating back to the apartment building where too many innocents resided. Too many lives would be at risk if they searched for shelter inside, but they had to get the wounded out.

Sirens filled the air in the distance, coming closer at an ear-shattering pace. The sky above was nowhere near as dark as it had been when he and Wade had driven over from Manhattan. The sun was rising, which meant the Brooklyn Night Court wouldn't come to aide them, treaty or no treaty. The vampires wouldn't risk their undead lives in the onslaught of the coming daylight. Ashanti had been very clear about that. The only other alliance they had were the fae, but they were off hunting their missing god still, and Jono knew they couldn't be counted on for a last-minute rescue.

A vicious warning howl suddenly rent the lightening sky, and Jono knew reinforcements were finally on the way. But they were all still stuck out in the open, trying to keep Estelle's god pack between them and the hunters and the weapons pointed in their direction. Fenrir's presence was a heavy weight of *wrath* that Jono knew he couldn't hold back for much longer, and honestly wasn't sure he wanted to.

The decision was taken out of his hands when the heavy beating of war drums echoed in the air like thunder, the rhythm something Jono felt in his bones. The pulse-pounding beat was joined by a deep, sonorous sound of a conch shell being blown, bringing with it the crashing power of waves that crossed the oceans. Fog exploded on the Brooklyn street, carrying the salt scent of the ocean and the rot of death baked beneath a tropical sun into an urban jungle.

Everyone startled, the fight lurching to a sudden stalemate as they all attempted to orient themselves to a new threat. Jono didn't know who or what was arriving, and he panted for breath, wondering if this fight was going to end in a loss after all.

Then Fenrir sank his teeth into Jono's awareness, imparting an answer to a question that was only half-formed. *Night Marchers. The ancestors of Pele's children.*

The ghostly line of warriors from the echo of a time gone by marched out of the veil beneath the flicker of torches and into the trailing edge of darkness retreating from the dawn lining the eastern horizon. The mainland wasn't home to their memory, not the way the Hawaiian Islands were—pinpricks of land in the vast Pacific Ocean—but these shores would welcome them the same way they'd welcomed Fenrir and all the other gods over the centuries.

The torches grew brighter as the ghostly ranks of warriors got closer. A battle cry echoed through the fog, loud and fiercely powerful as the Night Marchers overtook a Brooklyn street to clear the way for a god who was more solidly real than they were and far, far more dangerous.

Ozone crackled through the air, overshadowing the smell of sulfur like a tsunami. Jono swallowed, tongue tingling from the taste as he watched the god march forward.

The vibrant red loincloth tied around the god's hips was the length of a skirt and split along the sides, hitting to midthigh. The color stood out against rich brown skin tanned by a tropical sun. A feathered cloak layered with plumage plucked from tropical birds was a burst of color that couldn't soften the scowl on the god's wide mouth. The feathered helmet he wore was similarly adorned, while the wooden spear he clutched in one hand was lined with shark teeth.

The hunters and enemy werecreatures turned to face the new threat, but their weapons and silver bullets couldn't hurt the ghostly dead, nor the god who led them. The Night Marchers, however, could harm the living, and they seemed to know who was the enemy and who was not. They glided through the fray, choosing their targets with brutal precision. Several werecreatures were speared through the heart, the flash of negative light proof enough the demons saw the fight as a losing one.

The odds got even worse for the other side as the Davenport pack finally arrived, Amelia in the lead, her people coming from both directions. Their wolf forms ranged in size and color, but they all shared a similar rage. The hunters took aim at them rather than the ghosts, but the shooting didn't last for long, not when they had to protect themselves against ghosts who couldn't die but could kill.

Since the god and his ghosts weren't trying to kill the packs under Jono's protection, he focused all his attention on Nicholas. The arsehole was trying to retreat into the fray, looking for a way out, and Jono refused to let him. He lunged after Nicholas, ignoring the pain throbbing in his hind leg and lower gut. The silver poisoning was spreading, but right now the more pressing need was sinking his fangs into the enemy.

Nicholas or his demon sensed Jono coming, twisting on four legs to meet Jono's attack. Nicholas snarled, a hint of amber flickering across black eyes. Jono wondered if the demon was prepared to flee, or if Nicholas was panicking and pushing through the control. Either option was acceptable as he aimed for Nicholas' throat again, because it meant he was afraid.

Jono had put the other man on his knees once before and forced him to show throat. Tonight he was willing to rip it out.

Fenrir let him have control, blocking the pain so Jono could focus on the threat. The demon riding Nicholas' soul might be in the driver's seat, but Jono refused to let it win this fight. He slammed into the other werewolf, driving them both to the ground. Nicholas' claws raked his side again, the pain vicious heat against his ribs before Fenrir pushed it aside. Jono kicked out with his good leg, catching Nicholas in the stomach, ripping through skin.

The wet sound of tearing flesh was drowned out by Nicholas' howl, the sound louder than the ghostly drums beating around them from the Night Marchers. Teeth scraped over Jono's muzzle, and he bit back, tasting bitter blood on his tongue. They rolled over the asphalt, crashing against a parked car and rocking it back on two wheels. Jono got pinned in against metal, but he braced himself against the car to kick himself free. He rolled fast and hard to get back to his feet and turned to find Nicholas trying to run *again*, and fuck it all, but the bastard's cowardice was annoying.

Nicholas didn't get far, skidding to a halt when the Hawaiian god stepped into his path and pointed the shark-teeth-encrusted spear at him. The god said nothing, but his intent was clear— Nicholas was going nowhere.

At the end of either block, police cars turned the corner with tire-squealing speed, lights flashing and sirens blaring. Some of the werecreatures started to peel off from the melee, seeking to escape. Jono launched himself at Nicholas before he could attempt to do the same, landing on his back and sinking his claws into the other man's body. He clamped his jaws around the back of Nicholas' neck, biting down until he tasted blood and his teeth scraped against bone.

Nicholas sank to the ground, shuddering as Jono increased the pressure over his spine. For a moment, Jono thought he'd have to snap Nicholas' neck to get him to stop fighting. But then an explosion of negative light nearly blinded him, the taste of sulfur overwhelming in his mouth and lungs. It abruptly faded as the demon escaped to a safety its host would never find. Nicholas let out a raspy whine before his body moved against Jono's in the way that spoke of a shift.

Jono didn't let up his hold on the other man, even when Nicholas finally lay beneath him as human, naked and covered in blood. Jono's claws still scraped over rib bones as his teeth cut skin on either side of Nicholas' skull in a pointed warning. Fear was a sickly scent Jono usually hated to smell, but in this instance, it pleased him.

"I yield," Nicholas pleaded.

"Hold fire!" Casale suddenly shouted over the snarling sounds of the fight still happening around them. *"Hold fire!"*

Razor-sharp shark teeth lining wood that smelled like the sea passed across Jono's vision as the Hawaiian god made his presence known. "Do you want the kill, or shall I take him with us?"

Jono removed his teeth from Nicholas' head, lifting his own to meet the god's powerful gaze. He needed a voice to answer, and so started to shift despite the agony involved. He rolled off Nicholas, knowing the god wouldn't let the other man run.

Shifting was difficult this time around, the silver poisoning in his system hindering the transformation. Fenrir pushed him through it, and Jono let out a gasp once his mouth was human, left leg buckling beneath him, stomach a shredded mess. He went to one knee, gritting his teeth against the blood flowing down his body from the gut and bullet wound. He could feel the bullet still in his body, a heat deep in his flesh that wouldn't come out.

"Ta for your help, but who the bloody fuck are you?" Jono ground out.

That wide, expressive mouth curved into a hard smile. "I am war's blessing. You may call me Kū."

"*Jono!*" Wade shouted from behind him. "Jono, are you all right?"

He craned his head around, watching as Wade raced toward him. "What happened to the demon upstairs?"

"Still contained, but you sounded like you needed help."

"Had it covered, mate."

Wade snorted as he made it over, casually placing his foot on Nicholas' back and leaning his considerable, if hidden, weight on the other man to keep him in place. The sound Nicholas let out was definitely pained. Wade appeared lean in human form, but looks could be deceiving. His ability to shift mass meant Nicholas wasn't going anywhere except to jail if Jono had anything to say about it.

"Sure you did," Wade said.

Around them, the police were advancing, weapons drawn, as the Night Marchers disappeared with the first rays of dawn breaking free of the eastern horizon. Kū looked at Jono, tapping his spear against the asphalt.

"Persephone asked for my aid to bridge the hours between night and day. Where I go, the echo of the past follows. The Night Marchers escorted me across the Pacific and a continent because I do so love a good war," Kū said with a smile that promised nothing good.

Jono jerked his head toward Nicholas. "*This* war isn't yours. It's mine."

Because he knew, after this morning—after all the other vicious, underhanded fighting Estelle had instigated—there was no winning this unless one of them was dead. There was no denying his spot in the challenge ring, not after this.

"Until twilight, then."

Kū disappeared, stepping through the veil and taking the fog with him. Jono ignored the surprised shouts that lingered in his sudden absence.

"Jono," Casale called out as he approached, pistol in hand. "I assume you're pressing charges this time? And do I need to get you seen to by the EMS?"

Jono pressed a hand over the ragged skin torn across his stomach. The bullet hole in his thigh let out another spurt of blood as he shifted on his knees. He didn't care that he was naked, but he didn't want anyone to get close who didn't have the proper protection against the werevirus in his blood.

"I'll press charges, and so will everyone who fought with me tonight." He inclined his head at the aftermath of the fight surrounding them. "Is this proof enough for you?"

Casale grimaced, gaze skating away to take in the bodies on the street, the wounded in need of medical attention, and the police coming forward to deal with it all. "I doubt this is going to make anyone happy, but you weren't in the wrong."

Jono would've responded, except a sudden sharp tug in his chest made him gasp. He hunched over as the soulbond pulled tight, squeezing his eyes shut as he was *finally* able to sense Patrick again.

"Jono?" Wade asked worriedly.

He slid his bloodied hand up his chest to press it over his heart and took a breath. He wasn't about to give voice to the soulbond's existence, not when they were surrounded by the police. Instead, Jono raised his head and gave Wade a cautious nod.

"Need to give Pat a ring," he said.

Relief settled on Wade's face, the red scales finally fading beneath his skin. "He's going to be so mad you got hurt."

Jono rasped out a laugh, choking on pain. "Yeah."

He didn't care that Patrick would be pissed at him for bleeding all over the street. Jono was just happy he could sense Patrick again through the soulbond. Knowing he was alive was all that mattered.

"Hey now, don't pass out," Casale said, catching Jono by the shoulder when he slumped forward.

"Not going to." Jono swallowed, grimacing at the taste of blood and lingering sulfur on his tongue. "Need my mobile."

It had been in his back pocket when he'd left the flat earlier, but Wade pulled it free from the front pocket of his own jeans and wiggled it in Jono's direction. "Here you go. I kept it safe before you left for the fight."

Jono smiled wanly. "Sticky fingers."

Wade sniffed haughtily and tossed it to him. "I'll have you know my fingers are perfectly clean."

Jono caught it, smearing blood over the screen. He unlocked it and scrolled through his contacts until he reached Estelle's number, thumb hovering over the call icon.

Casale's grip tightened ever so slightly. "Let the PCB handle it."

"You tried. Nothing's changed." Jono drew in a harsh breath and hit Call, forcing his lungs to hold steady with Fenrir's help. He watched as Wade casually kneeled on Nicholas' back and covered his mouth with one hand to keep him from speaking. The line picked up three rings in. "Estelle."

The faint pause told him she didn't think he was supposed to live to see the dawn. When she spoke, Andras wasn't in her voice at all. "Jonothon."

"You wanted that challenge ring fight? You'll get it."

"Ready to finally die?"

Jono laughed, the sound ugly and vicious. "Whatever bargain you made with Andras won't save you. I'll take control of New York City when I leave your body on the ground."

He ended the call before she could protest the inevitable, breathing through the pain cutting its way through his nerves.

"You fight her now in the condition you're in, you'll lose," Casale said quietly.

"No, I won't," Jono said as Fenrir growled in the back of his mind, the god's presence a promise of support he had no qualms now about using.

2 2

of Jono, critically eyeing the slash wound on his stomach that was slowly healing.

Jono cupped Patrick's jaw with one hand, glad he was finally within touching distance. "That's my job, love."

"Can you not talk about murder where I can hear?" Casale asked tiredly.

Jono managed a weak chuckle, hissing at the way his still-healing skin pulled from the motion. The bullet had been removed from his thigh by an FDNY EMS, but the silver poisoning had been addressed by Victoria's healing potion. She'd left her nursing shift at the hospital and had come straightaway to Brooklyn to help. She was currently tending to those of Austin's pack who had survived the fight and had no plans to leave any time soon.

A couple of Austin's pack members were missing, taken by demons and removed from the fight when the bastards had left their original hosts in the face of the Night Marchers' approach. Jono vowed to get them back, the same way they'd managed to bring Keira back with the help of the Catholic Church's exorcism squad.

She was currently resting in Austin's bed, surrounded by pack members, and Jono knew that was a trauma he'd have to figure out how to help her handle. Just one more failure added to his list as a god pack alpha.

Warm fingers touched his throat before sliding up to brush over his lips. "Hey. None of that now."

The soulbond hummed between them like tuning forks. Jono didn't mind Patrick was parsing his emotions through it—he did it enough to the other man through scent reading.

Jono shook his head, the motion dislodging Patrick's touch. His mouth twisted into a grimace that pressed tight against his teeth. "This shouldn't have happened."

"Which part? Estelle not caring about the packs under her protection? Her alliance with hunters? Our packs getting hurt? The entire fucking civil war because she's power-hungry the same way Ethan is? There was no stopping any of it." Patrick made a face as he sealed the pressure bandage back over the wound. "Although, if I'd gotten here faster, I could've stopped you from issuing a challenge until you were fully healed."

Jono caught Patrick's fingers in his own, giving them a squeeze. "You came. That's all that matters."

He'd come through the veil, dragged back to New York by Hermes, which Jono didn't approve of. Gerard had been left behind to tackle the aftermath of the attack at the Library of Congress. One god of war had gone after Patrick, and another had been sent to aid Jono. The irony wasn't lost on him; there were many sides to every war, after all.

Austin's flat had become ground zero for communication with the police. The entire street had been cordoned off while CSU gathered evidence from the fight dressed in hazmat suits. Several hunters and rival god pack werecreatures had been arrested while others had been carted off in body bags. Wade had let Nicholas go only after the other man was put into warded handcuffs and been injected with a sedative that would keep him from shifting.

Police had taken everyone's statements while medical treatment was administered. Some, like Jono, had been shot with silver bullets, and the poisoning was difficult to overcome. Even with Fenrir to steady him, Jono still felt weaker than normal and mildly sick to his stomach. The wounds would close, but they'd leave bruises behind that would take at least a day or more to heal. None of it would fade until the silver was fully flushed from his system.

"When did you tell her the challenge would happen?" Sage asked from where she was carefully sorting through the debris in the living room for anything that could be salvaged.

Jono licked his dry lips. "I didn't."

"Don't go after her today," Casale warned.

"You don't get to dictate how and when we fight. We have a right to settle this in the challenge ring."

"There's been enough damage to the city this month already. Let me at least plead your case to the mayor so we can get a curfew in place. The less collateral you have to deal with, the better."

"She sent demons to steal the souls of the people under my protection. I'm not willing to let her think that's acceptable by *waiting*."

"You've waited this long already, what's twenty-four hours more?"

That stung, mostly because Jono knew Casale had a point. They'd been biding their time for months and months, trying to shore up their weaker position with alliances and convincing other packs to join them. But they'd reached a tipping point that had started in the subway and would end with Estelle out of power.

"He's right," Sage said quietly. "Get the mayor on our side for this. We need some good PR."

"That's why we hired a PR company," Wade muttered around the large bite of the microwaveable sandwich he'd heated up in the kitchen. He'd been steadily raiding Austin's kitchen, and Jono had a feeling he'd owe them several grocery shop runs.

Casale sighed heavily, hands on his hips. "Give me time to get the mayor on your side."

"You had months, the same way we did. We don't need you pleading our case to the mayor when we can do it ourselves. Get us a meeting with him today. That's all you need to do," Patrick demanded, craning his head around to look at Casale.

Patrick's anger was bright and bitter on Jono's tongue. He swallowed against it, never letting go of his hand. "You asked for twenty-four hours, and as a courtesy, we'll give it to you. But that's it. This ends tomorrow."

"Yeah, because if it keeps going to Wednesday and Sage misses her wedding, she'll kill us," Wade added.

"Try Monday. Patrick has his final fitting that day," Sage said, aiming for lightness, but they all knew how she felt about her wedding getting disrupted.

Jono pushed himself to his feet, ignoring the way Patrick tried to get him to remain seated on the broken sofa. He winced at the way his muscles pulled in his torso and thigh at the motion. The scrubs the EMS had given him were slightly too small, but he didn't care that he looked ridiculous. All he cared about was going home with his pack, but they weren't done here yet.

Casale eyed him with an unreadable look, but the other man smelled like a mix of exasperation and worry, not anger.

"You know Estelle is going to deny she had anything to do with what happened here today. She'll place all the blame on Nicholas, and he'll take it because he's loyal to her. You want peace within the werecreature community here? Then get us a meeting with the mayor," Jono said in a low voice.

Jono would prefer to drive over to Estelle's territory right then, knock on her door, and tear out her throat. It didn't matter he was weaker than he normally was due to silver poisoning. Politics was about trying to placate everyone and pleasing no one in the end.

Except it would please *him* to know Estelle would no longer be a threat, because she'd be fucking dead.

"I'll make a call," Casale said, choosing to walk away rather than continue the conversation.

"Can we go home now?" Wade asked.

Jono wanted to stay and keep an eye on the New Rebels and Davenport packs, but he also wanted to lie down for a kip and let Victoria's healing potions have their wicked way with him. He'd been spoiled over the years with his preternatural ability to heal quickly. Dealing with lingering pain made him short-tempered, something he couldn't afford to be right now.

"We'll be all right," Amelia said from her spot on the one dining room chair that hadn't been destroyed by the demon in Keira.

"The media isn't going to leave this area for the rest of the day," Sage warned.

Amelia shrugged one slim shoulder, the borrowed shirt not the best fit. They were all in clothes purloined from the closets of Austin's pack members. "I don't mind guarding Austin's territory for him while his pack heals."

It wasn't an offer she would have ever made while under Estelle and Youssef's rule in the past. Jono was glad the packs who'd switched loyalties were settling into a new normal that allowed them to be friendly with other packs and not look for claws in their back.

"We need to get going. You need rest," Patrick said as he stood.

He offered his hand to Jono, who took it without hesitation. Jono looked at Sage. "We should give a statement to the press."

"No. Absolutely not," Sage said.

"We've never presented our side to the public in person. I think it's time."

"We have a PR company for a *reason*."

"Yes, and if we fuck it up, we'll pay them to fix it."

Sage glared at him, arms crossed over her chest. "As your lawyer, I'm entirely against this course of action."

"Duly noted. We're still going to have a chat with the press."

They made an odd-looking group on their way out of the apartment building and to the perimeter of the crime scene. Patrick and Sage were still in their clothes from yesterday, dirty and torn from the fight at the Library of Congress. Wade was in jeans and a T-shirt, and Jono was barefoot in scrubs. It wasn't the put-together look Sage would've wanted, but Jono thought it made them look less polished and more human overall.

The hastily put-together podium for updates given by the police was absolutely overflowing with microphones. Jono's enhanced hearing picked up the way the media voices got louder as all the reporters realized who was coming their way.

"Do you even know what you're going to say?" Patrick asked quietly.

"No," Jono said, but he had an inkling.

The cameras were all pointed their way as the officers keeping watch let their pack pass under the Police Line – Do Not Cross tape. The questions started before they were even at the podium, and Jono ignored them all.

He braced himself against the wooden riser and leaned over slightly as the other three fanned out around him. "Can you lot hear me? Brilliant. First, I want to say I'm sorry everyone on the street here were woken up this morning by the attack on innocent people, but I won't apologize for the way the packs under my protection defended themselves against hunters, demons, and Estelle's people.

"Every single attack against me and mine over the last few months have been perpetuated by her god pack. Estelle, and Youssef when he was alive, never had the decency to come at us face-to-face. They always sent proxies from their own people or hunters. There's a bounty on my head she's funded since earlier this year. She's sold her own people to vampires to stay in power before. She's made deals with demons and is too much of a coward to face us herself. That ends now."

Jono swept his gaze over the assembled crowd of reporters, sunlight reflecting over the cameras. "I issued her a challenge, as is my legal right. So, if you're listening, Estelle? We'll settle the claim for New York City once and for all so its citizens can quit walking about in fear. No one will mourn you when I put you in a grave, the same way no one's mourned Youssef."

He could hear Sage's indrawn breath, even if it was too soft for the microphones to pick up. Not that her annoyance mattered. Murder in a challenge ring wasn't considered a crime, and Jono had every intent of leaving her body in the ring.

Jono pushed away from the podium, ignoring the veritable wall of sound that erupted around them as the reporters started shouting questions at him again. A few were even for Patrick, who ignored them with a cool, neutral expression on his face. They turned their backs on the media, heading back the way they'd come.

"Announcing you're going to murder Estelle on national television is not the best way to get the general public on the side of our pack," Sage said through gritted teeth.

"Sod what the public wants. I want Estelle dead. She's done enough damage to us and this city. If the police won't put her down, I will," Jono replied.

"Maybe it's the month of bad news," Wade mused as he pulled a candy bar out of his back pocket.

"For Estelle."

"Idiots," Sage sighed.

Patrick slung his arm over her shoulders, giving her a comforting hug. "Look at it this way. We deal with Estelle and her pack this weekend, and your wedding is in the clear next week."

Sage was too proper to sulk, but she did side-eye Patrick something fierce. Jono laughed, despite the pain humming beneath his skin. "Let's head home. If we're meeting with the mayor today, I'm not bloody doing so in scrubs."

It was one thing to go in front of news cameras and show the cost of fighting in the preternatural world while dressed in scrubs, quite another to do the same whilst bargaining with a politician in power. Appearances meant everything these days, and Jono had gotten better at playing the political game.

JONO STEPPED out of the shower and wasn't surprised to find Patrick waiting for him in the bathroom, holding up a towel for him.

"Casale called," Patrick said as Jono took the towel from him. "The mayor is willing to meet with us before he announces the curfew for the city under an emergency order."

Jono wrapped the towel around his waist, reaching for the medicine cabinet and the deodorant there. "Didn't think we rated an emergency order."

"It's us coupled with my now dismissed case and the Dominion Sect. The mayor wants people off the streets."

"Can't say I'd argue that."

"Sage said you need to wear a suit."

Jono sighed, thinking of how it was going to irritate his still-healing wounds. "I'd like to argue that."

"You're wearing a suit!" Sage yelled from the living room.

Patrick wrapped his fingers around Jono's wrist, and he let himself be led out of the master bathroom adjoined to their bedroom. "Come on. It's hours until we need to meet with the mayor. Let's get some sleep."

"Can we afford to?" Jono asked, thinking about everything that had happened and the fight still ahead.

"I'm not letting you fight Estelle sleep-deprived. Get on the bed. You're hugging me until I feel less murderous that she tried to execute you in an ambush."

Jono smiled wanly. "That'll take more than a few hours."

He still lay down with Patrick, the towel dropped to the floor once he dried off. Patrick remained in his clothes, suit jacket and tie somewhere else in the flat. He burrowed close to Jono once they were on the bed, hands gentle next to bandages still covering Jono's bullet and gut wounds.

"I'm healing," Jono promised.

"I should've been there."

"You were facing down Ares in DC. I'm a bit more worried at how many gods are coming after you right now."

"Gerard bought us time. He'll fly back here tomorrow, and I'll pick him up from the airport."

"How is he?"

Patrick sighed, his breath ghosting over Jono's collarbone. "Exhausted, I think. Fighting Ares took a lot out of him. He's a demi-god, for all he's immortal. It's a different level of power compared to others."

"Still took down a god of war."

"Yeah, well, he was pissed."

"Understandable." Jono yawned, letting his eyes shut. "At least he's alive."

"And dealing with all the politics I left behind when Hermes dragged us through the veil. I'll owe him for that."

Jono stroked his fingers over Patrick's upper arm. "Sleep, love."

They slept through the middle of the day, tangled up in each other, their mobiles in Sage's capable hands. Jono woke up hours later to afternoon sunlight pouring through their bedroom window and Patrick staring at him from the pillow they shared, propped up on one elbow.

"Watching me sleep?" Jono murmured.

"Favorite pastime."

"Thought that was getting into trouble?"

Patrick rolled his eyes before leaning over to kiss him softly on the mouth. Jono raised a hand to splay it over the back of Patrick's head, keeping him there. When they broke the kiss, Jono brushed his lips over the edge of Patrick's jaw.

"I love you," he said softly.

Patrick hummed quietly, pressing his forehead to Jono's and exhaling slowly. He didn't say anything, but the quiet metronome of his heartbeat and the way his scent spiked was an answer in and of itself. Jono knew that Patrick would keep his promise and always come back to him.

"We need to get ready," Patrick finally said.

Jono sighed and watched as Patrick rolled away from him, fighting against the urge to keep him there in bed. "Right. Challenge and all that bloody nonsense."

"It's your own fault for announcing it on the damn news."

Jono wasn't going to deny that, but neither did he regret it. Sometimes you had to get your hands dirty, whether with blood or with politics.

Not that there was much of a difference between the two these days.

Patrick had exchanged his dirty and torn suit for clothes that didn't smell like a soultaker had rolled in them. His jeans and T-shirt were definitely more comfortable, even with his leather jacket thrown over them. He'd upped the cooling charms on the jacket to stay as comfortable as he could. Despite the heat and humidity outside, he wanted the extra bit of protection the jacket gave him with its embedded wards.

Jono, however, was in a suit, and Patrick was staring at the other man so hard as they walked to their car that he almost tripped on the sidewalk.

"Eyes ahead, not on my arse," Jono said with a chuckle.

"Your ass is better to look at."

"Focus, love. We need to convince the mayor we're the better option."

"In that case, we should've taken Sage with us."

She was long gone by then. Wade had left with her to meet with Marek and their wedding planner to deal with the florist. The pair had stayed through his and Jono's nap before leaving, and now it was closing in on 1800 on Friday evening. The mayor had his press conference scheduled for the top of the next hour, and they were meeting with him thirty minutes before it started. So long as they weren't ambushed in the streets, they'd be on time.

If they *were* ambushed again, he was going to be really fucking pissed.

Nothing was amiss with the Mustang, and Patrick got behind the wheel. Once Jono was buckled up, he started the engine and pulled into the street, heading downtown for City Hall. Patrick knew the way without GPS, though they had to fight through some lingering rush-hour traffic to get there. Friday night always had more cars on the street, especially during the summer.

Street parking was restricted due to security concerns. As Patrick circled the block to get to the underground parking entrance, he noticed the small City Hall Park that was usually in full bloom with flowers and greenery this time of the year looked as if winter had come early.

"That's different," Jono murmured as they drove past.

"It's like all the other parks in the city."

The trees were bare of leaves, the grass was brown, and the dirt beneath bushes was littered with dried leaves. The lingering feel of magic that Patrick had sensed in Prospect Park the other week was present here as well.

"What do you think Cernunnos is doing with all this magic?" Jono asked.

Patrick chewed on his bottom lip, stomach twisting in the way it always did when he thought about Hannah. "I think whatever was done to her in Chicago needs shoring up. Why else would Ethan require the aid of a second fertility god?"

Jono settled his hand on Patrick's thigh, drawing him away from the thoughts swirling through his mind. "It's not your fault."

Patrick pressed his lips together, saying nothing. Jono kept his hand where it was until they'd cleared security at the underground parking garage and Patrick had found a spot, turning off the engine. Then Jono reached up to curl his fingers around Patrick's chin, turning his head around. Patrick let himself be led, because it was Jono guiding him, and he'd never fight the other man.

Jono kissed him on the mouth, warmth seeping through his touch. "You're not alone in this. I want you to remember that."

They had a pack, and they had each other, and it was more support than Patrick had ever had for his entire adult life, because Jono knew his secrets. Jono knew *him*, and that made all the difference when everything that made Patrick who he was kept being torn down. Except the bones of Jono's support were made of a fierce belief that would never be shaken or broken.

"I know," Patrick said.

They left the car behind them—protected with magic— and followed the signs to the elevators. The only buttons available were the garage levels and the ground level. Access to City Hall was restricted in the areas they could go as members of the public.

The weight of the magic built into the foundations and walls of the place pressed down heavily on Patrick's shields. The protective wards here were threaded through with active offensive spells designed to trigger in the event of an attack. The combination wasn't unheard of in major government buildings, but there was something in the air that made Patrick's shoulders tighten. Jono appeared just as on guard as they made their way to the security check-in at the lobby

"Doesn't feel right," Jono muttered under his breath. "Doesn't *smell* right."

The security guards on duty spotted them and waved them over. Patrick no longer had an SOA badge to produce as his ID, so he handed over his New York State driver's license instead, while Jono presented his green card.

"The mayor is expecting you, but he's still in a meeting. We've been instructed to escort you up to his office's reception area, and one of his aides will be with you shortly," the guard said.

It wasn't out of the ordinary, but Patrick still kept his guard up, shields at the ready as they passed through hallways and an elevator to get up to a higher floor. The bustle of City Hall had slowed for the day, the lack of people enabling their footsteps to echo in the air. Jono stayed right by his side as they followed the security guard to a grand wooden door carved with runes along the edges that had been made decades ago.

The magic in the door didn't react when pushed open. Patrick and Jono entered a reception area that would've looked better in a contemporary art museum than City Hall. The furniture was sleek and thinly designed with no embellishments, the glass tables were weirdly shaped, and the area rug beneath the reception space was a mix of color with no pattern to it.

"Someone will be with you shortly," the guard said before leaving.

The door closed behind him, and Patrick tried not to feel as if they were being locked in. He'd had enough of that while in jail.

Jono drew in a deep breath, making a face as he did so. "Smells bloody awful."

"The magic?" Patrick asked.

"Not sure."

Patrick let his fingers stray over the hilt of his dagger, reminding himself it was within reach. "I don't think anyone will notice bloodstains on this rug if it comes down to it."

There wasn't much to look at in the reception area, but Patrick still cased the area. The wards were old and layered, renewed yearly, but not dangerous unless you were. The decorations on the shelves were generic pieces, but there were also framed photographs of Mayor Doyle Ferbenn posing and shaking hands with other people throughout the course of his job.

Patrick leaned closer to one at eye level, staring at the redheaded man through narrowed eyes. His curly hair was more on the orange side and neatly trimmed. His suits were stylish if a little loud when it came to patterns, and his smile was wide, pricking at Patrick's memory.

He'd seen that face before, he realized, in the shadow of the Gap of Dunloe amidst a winter fight.

It was as if a shroud lifted from his mind, memory washing clean, sharpening the god's features into a visage no one would take as mortal. Patrick nearly bit through his tongue, shock flooding his veins.

"Pat?" Jono asked worriedly.

The door opened, allowing a blonde woman to enter, ozone crackling through the air with her arrival. Patrick yanked his dagger free of its sheath and conjured up a mageglobe as he turned to face her. White heavenly fire burned along the edge of the matte-black blade, drawing the goddess' attention. Jono growled, low and harsh, mouth twisted in fury.

"*You*," Jono snarled.

"I see you remember me," the immortal said with a face devoid of emotion even if her eyes were dark pools of rage.

She kicked the door shut behind her, the wards activating on some unheard order. If the more recent layers were hers, then she was the cause for the strangeness of the magic. But it meant they were trapped in a cage with no way out, facing off against a murderous goddess.

"Hard to forget the audience watching me get tortured last summer."

She was the mayor's aide Jono had recognized months ago, Patrick realized. It made him wonder who else on the mayor's team was immortal.

The goddess shrugged carelessly, her clothes fashionably trendy, even as her glacial beauty wasn't something a mortal woman could ever obtain. Jono stepped closer to Patrick, bringing with him a warmth that offset the coolness that had settled in the reception room.

"You gods really need to get out of politics," Patrick said.

Her mouth curled at the corners, jaw elongating in a way that allowed all her sharp teeth to shine in the light. "I am an Erinyes."

"Still a fucking immortal."

Most people knew the Greek Erinyes as Furies, deities who undertook vengeance against men. Patrick didn't know which one they were trapped in the room with, but he didn't trust the glint of insanity in her eyes one bit. Lack of prayers maybe, or too long walking alone through the centuries. Whatever had made the Erinyes unstable wasn't something her worshippers could fix.

Patrick would've wished her worshippers had prayed her into a grave right about now.

The Erinyes stepped forward, her aura breaking free with a blinding blast of light that made spots dance in front of Patrick's eyes. Despite not being nearly as well-known or powerful as the major gods in her pantheon, the Erinyes still carried a godhead.

She was still a threat.

Patrick raised his shield between them, tapping a ley line through Jono's soul to power the defensive magic. He slammed the flat side of his dagger against the barrier, holding the weapon between them and the immortal hell-bent on murdering them.

The explosion of power she directed their way sent furniture flying into the walls, knocking everything off the shelves. Bookcases splintered, but the wards never broke, glittering brightly around them like stars. Patrick ducked his head against the eye-searing light that burned around them, hoping the heavenly magic in his dagger could hold up against the fury directed at them.

Jono pressed his hand between Patrick's shoulder blades, bracing him against the force aimed their way. "I'll shift, and we'll go for her throat."

Fenrir being willing to murder another god wasn't unheard of, except the Erinyes wasn't of his pantheon. That was a mess Patrick wasn't sure the Greek gods would be willing to ignore with everything else happening.

Patrick tried to blink the spots out of his vision before he realized it wasn't his eyes that were the problem, but the wards surrounding the reception room. He turned his head and squinted at the walls, watching sigils fade to nothing, the magic disintegrating. If the Erinyes noticed, she didn't seem to care. All her rage and power was still focused in their direction, Patrick's dagger all that stood between them and getting burned to ash a janitorial crew would have to sweep up.

The floor shook beneath their feet like an earthquake, breaking the Erinyes' attention enough that her attack faltered. Her stormy blue eyes went wide when she finally realized the wards were no longer holding.

"What—?" she began.

Her words were cut off by the door exploding inward with enough force to send her flying. She crashed to the other side of the reception room, sprawling on the floor with wooden shards embedded in her back and thighs. She bled red, but the wounds wouldn't kill her. If Ares could survive Gerard's attack, she could survive this. Maybe it had something to do with the way their myths were told, the way their stories ended, but he doubted the Erinyes would die from something so mundane as shrapnel.

"Tisiphone," the Dagda said as the Celtic god entered the reception room. "They were never yours to murder."

Patrick thought it was a little ironic that the Erinyes who punished crimes of murder had tried to take them out.

"*That* bloke is the mayor?" Jono asked, his fingers digging into Patrick's back, ready to haul him away it felt like.

"Ferbenn," Patrick said, not dropping his shields. "I should have realized."

The Dagda inclined his head slightly in their direction. "One of many names I am known by."

First Maat as a federal judge, and now the Dagda as a mayor of one of the world's most prominent metropolises. Patrick hoped no other immortals were masquerading as people in positions of power, but he had a feeling that wasn't the case.

The wards came back to life, powered by the Dagda's magic. The shattered door reformed itself, pieces pulling back into a whole, including the ones embedded in Tisiphone's back. The immortal arched against the pull, scrabbling at the floor with sharp fingernails as the wooden shrapnel slid free.

Patrick didn't lower his shield, keeping his dagger at the ready. The Dagda might have put Medb in her place last December, he might be the Morrígan's husband, but none of that meant the god was on their side.

The wards spread across the door, interlocking in place with a magic that felt far different from the sort Patrick had noticed earlier. The Dagda crossed the room to where Tisiphone was pushing herself up on her hands and knees. He held out his hand to her, but she knocked it aside, sharp teeth bared in a snarl.

"Back off," she spat out.

The Dagda stayed where he was, watching her with a cool-eyed gaze, his aura outshining hers. Tisiphone finally sat upright, kneeling amidst the mess of the reception room. She tipped her head back and stared at the Dagda, eyes unblinking in her face.

"You should have let me kill them," Tisiphone said.

"Murder is your livelihood, but I promised you guidance when you came to me," the Dagda said.

Patrick passed his fingers through his mageglobe, lowering his shield even if he didn't lower his dagger. The Dagda had proven he was mostly on their side of the fight, unless he'd drastically changed his mind. Considering the company he kept, it was a distinct possibility.

"She watched Ethan torture me," Jono growled.

"Tisiphone was prayed into existence to murder. Torture is near and dear to her heart," the Dagda said.

"Not hearing a bloody apology, you arsehole."

"I have nothing to apologize for, and neither does Tisiphone."

"How long has she been working for you?" Patrick asked.

"As my aide?" The Dagda stepped around Tisiphone to reach his office door. "Since I became mayor of this grand city."

"That's not what I meant."

"Persephone asked a favor of me years ago when she discovered Hades was attempting to recruit her pantheon for Ethan's gain. We needed some way to keep ahead of the Dominion Sect and find my wife's staff since you were incapable of paying your soul debt."

"Fuck you," Jono snapped out before Patrick could.

The Dagda ignored the insult as he entered his office. "I offered Tisiphone a place to ply her trade with no one the wiser in exchange for information on what Ethan was planning."

"You let her murder people in New York City in exchange for spying on Ethan?" Patrick asked incredulously. "You knew what she allowed to happen to Jono and you didn't try to stop her?"

"The wolf had yet to be given to you as a weapon. His life was inconsequential at the time."

"*Careful with your words, cousin,*" Fenrir bit out in Jono's voice.

The Dagda's voice drifted back to them from his office. "We keep our kind close and our enemies closer, cousin. I did what had to be done. The risk was acceptable."

Patrick scowled. "Not to me."

Tisiphone struggled to her feet, wavering through the motions. "Hera and Zeus are not my keepers. I made my own choices."

"Murdering us wouldn't help you."

She raised her chin to a proud angle. "We are not bound to the strictures of our myths when the world barely remembers us."

"Choosing Ethan won't save you."

Tisiphone smiled, teeth cutting into her lips, turning her matte lipstick shiny like gloss. "I have never needed saving. Humanity has prayed to me with their darkest desires. I give what they themselves are not capable of with their own hands. Estelle could not wield the trishula that took her husband's life, so I did it for her after the Dominion Sect coated it in your twin's magic."

Patrick jerked at her words. "*You* stole the trishula?"

Tisiphone's lips parted on words she never spoke, not when Hermes' hand wrapped around her throat. The messenger god slipped free of the veil behind her, framed in the office doorway, his gold-brown eyes meeting Patrick's over Tisiphone's head.

"This is a dangerous game you play, Tisiphone," Hermes said in a falsely gentle voice. "Persephone is highly displeased with your actions."

"She is not Zeus. I do not answer to her," Tisiphone forced out around his steely grip.

"She holds his attention better than you ever will."

The Dagda came back out of his office, holding a portfolio on his hand. "Stay your hand, Hermes. I still need my aide."

"You have plenty, and she is not to be trusted."

"Which is precisely why I have kept her close all these years."

Hermes stepped aside, dragging Tisiphone with him. "Hera has summoned her home to Greece."

Tisiphone's eyes widened at that statement, and she struggled in Hermes' grip. The messenger god shoved her to her knees with a casual show of strength that sounded as if it broke bone.

"Her absence will not go unnoticed by Ethan," the Dagda warned.

"Then your wife will need to find some other way to unearth clues on her staff's whereabouts."

Patrick didn't flinch beneath Hermes' glare when it was directed his way, but only because he was used to being the focus of a god's heavy attention. He knew that Hermes was probably talking about the broken-off piece of the Morrígan's staff. It seemed he was keeping that fact a secret for them still.

Patrick wondered what they'd owe him in the end for his silence.

"Would she know where Ethan is right now?" Patrick asked.

"What say you, Tisiphone?" Hermes asked, shaking her how one would shake a dog.

"I have not been privy to his presence since before the summer solstice," she rasped.

Patrick glanced at Jono. "Is she lying?"

"No," he bit out, Fenrir gone from his voice.

"Fuck."

There went that avenue of hope of finding Cernunnos.

"We'll be going now," Hermes said in a voice that would never be pleasant.

He dragged Tisiphone through the veil by the throat, her feet kicking in protest as she clawed at his hand. They disappeared, leaving Patrick and Jono alone with the Dagda in the wreckage of the reception area.

"We came here because Casale said the mayor wanted to enact a curfew. Are you still going to do it?" Jono asked.

"Are you still insisting on fighting the demons that have overrun the City?" the Dagda shot back.

"You already know the answer to that."

"Then I will enact the curfew."

"Great. While you're at it, clear out Central Park. We're going to need it."

Patrick eyed Jono. "We are?"

"We don't have a challenge ring, and I refuse to fight in the one Estelle controls. If we make Central Park neutral territory and designate it as the challenge ring, that will sort the problem."

"The public won't like it," the Dagda said.

"I don't bloody care."

"Very well." The Dagda's eerie, otherworldly gaze landed on Patrick, and he tried not to flinch beneath the weight of it. "Your dagger is useful, but it will not be enough against what waits beyond the veil."

Patrick thought of Ilya and the millions of dead the necromancer had stolen out of Paris when he retreated at the end of the fight beneath the Eiffel Tower. "Is that where the dead are hiding?"

"For now."

Patrick really didn't need that nightmare to become another reality, one ruled over by Ethan. "Duly noted."

The Dagda gestured expansively at the reception room, magic

spilling from his fingertips. The damage was undone in an eyeblink, everything pieced back together again so deftly one would be hard-pressed to find evidence of the brief fight they'd endured.

"You need to be ready for a reckoning," the Dagda warned.

"I know."

"You know nothing of worth. Our myths always end, in one way or another. Our lives ebb and flow with the prayers that sustain us and bury us. We are an echo of what we once were. Ethan will build his hell, but you must turn it into his Armageddon, his Ragnarök, his myth's ending, because gods are never born or reborn easy, and dying is harder than you think."

It was a warning, one Patrick had heard before, just spoken by different voices, using different words.

Jono turned his back on the Dagda and reached for Patrick to manhandle him around. "Sod your bloody talk of fate. Announce your curfew so I can put Estelle in a grave."

Patrick allowed himself to be led out of the reception room, the door opening beneath Jono's hand either because of Fenrir or the Dagda's will, he didn't know which.

"Bloody *fucking* gods," Jono swore as they left the mayor's office behind.

Patrick could only nod in agreement.

24

"I said no tomatoes," Wade grumbled as he dug through the paper bag holding six breakfast bodega sandwiches

"Eat your vegetables," Patrick ordered, keeping his eyes on the road.

"They should give me a discount next time for messing up my order. I wanted extra meat and extra cheese. Look, now the bagel is all soggy from the tomato."

Wade held the breakfast sandwich up to Patrick's face so he could see. He turned his head and stole a bite, tearing through the toasted bagel and getting crumbs on the center console. Wade's eyes widened in affronted disbelief as he yanked his sandwich back and cradled it close to his chest.

"That was *mine!*" he hissed.

"Figured you didn't want it anymore since you were complaining about the tomatoes," Patrick mumbled around the large bite he'd taken.

Wade scowled, then took the largest bite he could to keep his meal from being eaten by anyone else. Patrick laughed, trying not to spray crumbs everywhere.

Gerard's flight was scheduled to land in forty minutes, and they were driving to pick him up from LaGuardia. He had to travel by mundane means rather than the veil due to the scrutiny aimed their way. The fight at the Library of Congress had been difficult to explain away and extricate himself from, especially since Patrick and Sage and been unceremoniously yanked through the veil. Their absence had been noted, and Patrick had a feeling he'd be called back to Washington, DC, at some point soon.

So long as it wasn't during Sage's wedding, he'd deal with it.

The curfew order had come down last night for the weekend, and people seemed to remember when the Wild Hunt had stalked the city's streets in December. Midmorning on a Saturday should've had more cars on the streets, but traffic was strangely nonexistent. Patrick noticed more taxis and delivery trucks than anything else.

Jono was back in Brooklyn with Sage, following up on Austin's Rebel pack and the Davenport pack. The attack hadn't gone over well with the public, but there'd been some sympathy for their position, and Danai was ruthlessly leveraging that with the crisis PR company they still employed.

They were driving down a cross-town street when his phone rang, Danai's number coming up on the dashboard's screen. He answered it with a touch of his finger. "Please tell me they aren't going back on the dismissal."

"No. Your case remains dismissed," Danai said.

Patrick released the stranglehold he had on the steering wheel while Wade slowly lowered his breakfast sandwich away from his mouth. "Great. What can I do for you?"

"I'm calling because I just spoke with Preston. Your personal items, which were held in evidence by the FBI, have been relinquished to the US attorney's office. They're ready to release them into your custody and control. I know it's a Saturday, but he's at the office downtown and is willing to meet with you to return them."

Wade frantically shook his head, spraying crumbs over his lap. "Bad idea."

Patrick was well aware of what had happened the last time he'd tried to meet with the US attorneys, but he also really wanted his phone back. "I'm on my way to the airport and haven't hit the bridge yet. I can spare ten minutes to pick up my things, but that's it."

Wade banged his head against the headrest and stuffed the breakfast sandwich into his mouth so he wouldn't protest. Patrick was distantly proud about his control, so long as he didn't choke.

"I'll call Preston back and let him know you'll be there within the next thirty minutes or so. You'll most likely be put on the security list like before."

"Have them put Wade down as well."

"That shouldn't be a problem. Just be prepared so show some identification for both of you. Drive safe, and have a good weekend."

"You, too."

Patrick ended the call and jumped right into an argument with Wade.

"This is a bad idea," Wade repeated.

"I want my phone back," Patrick countered.

"Have them mail it to you. Better yet, have them mail it to Danai, since they called her first instead of calling you."

"They called her because she's our lawyer. We're going."

Patrick took the next available right, turning onto Park Avenue South to head downtown instead of to the Queensboro Bridge. Wade groaned before shoving another bite of his breakfast sandwich into his mouth. He wiped his greasy fingers on his jeans before freeing his phone to text one-handed.

Patrick's borrowed phone buzzed in his pocket. "Are you updating the group chat?"

"Jono needs to know you're being dumb," Wade retorted.

Right on cue, Patrick's phone started ringing. It connected to the Bluetooth in the Mustang, and he scowled when Wade reached over to accept the call on the dashboard's screen.

"Why the fuck are you meeting with that arsehole?" Jono demanded.

"They're giving me back my phone," Patrick said.

"You *have* a mobile."

"It's not mine, and I need mine back. I need to know if they managed to hack through the encryption security on it."

"Hermes said they wouldn't."

"I don't trust that fucker."

Jono swore quietly. "I'm still in Brooklyn. Can't you wait until after you've picked up Gerard?"

"It's a twenty-minute detour at most. Gerard won't care if I'm a little late. He'll get coffee somewhere outside the terminal and wait."

Jono let out an aggravated sigh, but Patrick wasn't about to turn back around. "Ring me when you're finished so I know you're okay."

"If I don't, Wade will."

"I told him not to do it," Wade said.

"We know how well that works with him," Jono mused.

"It doesn't."

"Hey," Patrick protested.

Wade quickly shoved the last bite of his breakfast sandwich into his mouth so he wouldn't have to answer and picked up another, unwrapping it with deft fingers. Patrick rolled his eyes.

"Be safe," Jono said.

"We will be."

The call ended. Patrick kept driving, and Wade kept eating. By the time they made it to the US Attorney's building, Wade had finished his food, the bag crumpled on the floormat between his feet.

They parked in the garage adjacent to the US Attorney's Office for the Southern District of New York and took the stairs rather than the elevator down to the ground level since they were only one level up. Patrick led the way to the front entrance of the building, wondering if they'd have to flag down a security guard to get let in. When he tried the glass door, it was unlocked.

"Smells okay," Wade muttered just loud enough that Patrick could hear.

Patrick nodded absently, shields locked down tight and dagger close at hand. They went to the security desk and got put through the rigmarole of handing over identification and getting directed to the proper elevator to take up to the sixth floor.

The reception desk was empty when they arrived in the lobby area of that floor. There was a small bell on the desk that Wade went about tapping over and over so that the ringing sound was nonstop.

Patrick shot him an annoyed look. "You can stop."

"I'll stop when someone comes out," Wade said, hitting the bell faster.

Patrick was about to take the bell away and toss it out of reach of Wade when someone cleared their throat from the direction of the hallway leading to the rest of the office. Patrick turned and met Preston's gaze as Wade *finally* stopped ringing the goddamn bell.

"You didn't need to ring it. The security guard let us know you were on your way up," Preston said.

"Took you five minutes to come greet us. I wanted to make sure you knew we were here," Wade said, finger inching toward the bell again.

The corner of Preston's mouth ticked downward. "You were heard, and it was barely a minute."

"Do you have my phone?" Patrick asked after shooting Wade a warning look.

Preston gestured for them to follow him back down the hallway. "There's a form we need you to sign. It will only take a moment. You can follow me to the back while your friend waits here."

"Nope," Wade said, coming to stand beside Patrick. "Where he goes, I go. And who's *we*? I thought we were only meeting with you?"

"Ms. Santiago is overseeing the closure of your case. She's in today for some overtime, which is why we called your counsel," Preston said.

Wade stuck close to Patrick as they were led deeper into the workspace, bypassing empty offices and cubicles. Nothing appeared out of the ordinary, nothing tipped his magic off, and Wade didn't react to any threat that Patrick's mundane senses couldn't pick up. The building was surrounded in wards, just like the PCB and most other government buildings.

Which meant it was all the more shocking to enter Mia Santiago's office and find Hades and Estelle seated before her desk, a demon looking out of Estelle's and the US attorney's face with matching black eyes. Hades held the Trishula of Shiva in one hand, the three prongs at the tip of the weapon glittering with magic that swirled around the room, acting as a barrier.

Maybe the damn thing was a god's weapon after all.

"Hello, Patrick," Andras said, the echo of the demon's voice curling through Estelle's.

"What the—" Preston said, sounding utterly confused.

Patrick grabbed him by the back of his suit jacket and yanked the man out of the doorway, swinging him around to shove in Wade's direction. Preston still felt human to his senses as the punch of recognition that spoke of hell and werecreatures finally cut through whatever magic had kept them all hidden. It would be a fucking nightmare if Patrick got charged with the murder of a US attorney after finally clearing his name.

"Patrick!" Wade yelled, scrambling around Preston, one arm outstretched toward him, ready to drag him to safety.

He got his fingers around the hilt of his dagger, got the blade free of the sheath, when burning ropes of a binding ward wrapped around his body.

Patrick had a split second to make his choice—and it wasn't even a choice.

The gods of heaven had given him the dagger as a weapon, one that could not fall into Ethan's hands. Patrick knew Jono could find him—he *knew* that—but there would be no way to track the dagger if it was stolen from him.

Before the binding ward made it impossible for him to move and cast magic, Patrick snapped his wrist at his hip, sending his dagger spinning away from him toward Wade. Most people couldn't wield it—the magic embedded in it wouldn't let them— but Wade *could*. Wade grabbed it out of midair, not fumbling it at all, gold eyes wide with desperation.

"Patrick!"

Cold hands wrapped around his shoulders, hauling him backward into the room and through the veil in a way that was nothing how Hermes moved through it. His stomach twisted, unable to figure out which way was up or down as the grayness encompassed everything in his vision.

Then he crashed to the ground, breath driven from his lungs, and he found himself staring up into Estelle's face, Andras looking out of her eyes.

He tried to reach for his magic, but the binding ward burned through his nerves like a toxin, his entire body jerking in protest. Andras used Estelle's preternatural strength to press his shoulders to the cold floor, the bones in his joints grating together.

"You will make a wonderful bargaining chip," Andras said in Estelle's voice, lips stretched wide in a smile.

"Fuck you," Patrick spat out, heart pounding so hard he could barely hear his own voice.

The ceiling above looked made of stone in the dim light, the smell of the place like old earth and blood, mixed with the peculiar scent of shifted werecreatures. It took Patrick a long moment to realize he'd been dragged through the veil to the underground stadium that held the challenge ring in Hamilton Heights. Jono had described it once, and it was as trashy as Patrick had thought it'd be.

Hades knelt on his other side, and Patrick's attention narrowed in that direction. Hades' hand was cold when he pressed it over Patrick's chest, shirt rubbing against the scars there. When the god smiled, Patrick was flung down a black pit of memory to Salem and the basement he'd nearly been sacrificed in.

"My wife's wards hid you well all these years, but since you have chosen to no longer hide who you are, it is time to get rid of her blessing," Hades said.

Patrick had thought the pain of Persephone branding his bones with the ward anchors for his shields was excruciating. It had nothing on Hades burning out the shape of them down to his marrow.

Patrick screamed so hard he couldn't breathe at the end, tipping over into a blackness that buried him.

25

Jono was in the middle of discussing territory boundaries in Brooklyn with Sage, Austin, Amelia, and Tiarnán when his mobile rang. Wade's name was on the screen, and he answered it like always.

"They took Patrick!" Wade shouted the second the call connected.

Jono froze, meeting Sage's wide-eyed gaze with his own. "They arrested him again?"

"*No*! The lady lawyer was a demon. Hades and Estelle were in her office, but Estelle had that demon in her. *They* took Patrick. Dragged him through the veil, and I couldn't—Jono, he gave me his dagger and I couldn't *reach* him and I—"

Jono's hands shook—from rage or fear, he couldn't tell—as Fenrir roared to life in the back of his mind. Wade was a frantic voice in his ear, the teenager miles away from them in Manhattan. Jono couldn't let the rapidly rising fear inside him impede his ability to care for his pack.

"Get back to the flat," Jono ground out. "Get behind the threshold. We'll be there soon."

"Jono, I'm *sorry*," Wade said, voice sounding smaller than it ever had.

"This isn't your fault, mate. Not one bloody bit of it." Jono sucked in air through his teeth, refusing to take out his fury on anyone he cared about. "We knew Estelle would never play fair, and this is them being desperate. I want you *safe*, so get your arse back to our flat."

Wade sniffed loudly over the line. "Patrick didn't give me his keys. I can't drive the Mustang."

"I'll send a car to him," Tiarnán said, already on his mobile. "They'll be there in fifteen minutes."

"Did you hear that?" Jono asked Wade.

"Yeah. But, uh, that asshole attorney called the cops, so I don't think I should stay here," Wade said.

"Head to the PCB. Tiarnán's people can pick you up there."

Wade's voice came through the rush of wind over the line as he obeyed Jono's order to move. "You want me to let them know Patrick got kidnapped?"

"No. The PCB has done sod all for us with this mess. We'll handle it how we always do. It's just a safer pickup point."

"Okay."

Wade still sounded scared and distraught, but he was focused on getting to the pickup point. Jono didn't want to leave him without support, but he needed his entire attention free.

"I'm going to conference you in with Sage and drop my side of the call," Jono warned.

"Okay." Wade sniffed again, loudly. "You sure you're not mad at me?"

"No. I'd never be mad at you for something like this. Just stay safe."

Sage had her mobile out, ready to take the call. Jono looped her in and then ended his side, letting her talk Wade down from the panic attack the teen was so close to having.

Jono closed his eyes, ignoring the explosion of voices around him, reaching deep for the soulbond that tied him to Patrick. He'd been able to find Patrick all the times before when they were separated or missing. This would be no different.

It *couldn't* be different.

Except he came up against the same fucking emptiness that always indicated Patrick was out of reach, beyond the veil, and nowhere close for Jono to find.

"Anything?" Sage asked without going into details in front of their audience.

Jono opened his eyes and shook his head. "Not a fucking thing."

Sage's mouth thinned into a hard white line. "We'll get him back. He has a suit fitting on Monday, and he is *not* missing it."

"Estelle and Andras have him. If they're working with Hades—"

Jono bit the words off, rage a violent shiver that streaked down his spine, pulling his shoulders tight.

"Then Ethan is in play. We know," Sage said, not unkindly. "We —no, Wade. It's still not your fault."

Sage went back to focusing on Wade and Jono forced himself to step back from the desire for murder when a target wasn't immediately available. He looked at Austin and Amelia, who were both equal parts shocked and furious.

"I need you to get your packs into Manhattan. Spread the word. Double up in our Manhattan-held territory and wait for further instructions," Jono ordered.

Both nodded grimly.

"Get everyone over the bridges sooner rather than later. We've been warned the barrier from last summer is broken, and I don't know what Cernunnos will be forced to put in its place," Tiarnán warned.

"What barrier?" Amelia asked.

Jono finished typing out a text to Gerard about what had happened and sent it off. He wasn't sure when the other man's flight would land, but at least he'd be warned the second he turned on his mobile. "That whole mess during summer solstice last year. Some of the wards should've been permanent, but shit happened."

"I'm going to wager Estelle happened."

"She's carrying a bloody demon in her soul right now. Every member of her god pack is. Warn our packs about that."

Austin stared at him. "She really fucking did what the London god pack did?"

"Yes," Jono bit out, the sound a growl.

Austin calmly dug out his mobile and unlocked it. "I'm letting my friends back in California know. They'll spread the word among the god packs over there on the West Coast."

"We should warn Naomi and Alejandro in Chicago," Sage said, pointedly holding open the door.

"Ring them after we reunite with Wade." Jono's gaze cut across the room to the others. "You lot keep in contact with Sage, and if you can't get through to her, ring Emma."

"We'll mobilize all the packs," Amelia promised, already typing away on her mobile.

They had hours before the six o'clock evening curfew went into effect, and that was far too long to wait to rescue Patrick. Jono followed Sage out of the flat, Tiarnán right behind them. Deirdre had been standing guard outside in the hallway the entire time, and she neatly stepped into position on Tiarnán's right, just out of range of the cane he carried.

"Get your people as well," Jono said, looking over his shoulder at the fae. "I want them in Manhattan. *All* of them."

"Brigid wanted you to find Cernunnos," Tiarnán said.

Jono's lips curled over his fangs. "We'll worry about that bastard after we get Patrick back."

"You need to—"

Jono spun on his feet, fingers grabbing Tiarnán's tie and yanking him close. The smell of silver was toxic in his nose as Deirdre held a dagger up in a warning a hairsbreadth from Jono's throat. His skin burned from the close proximity, but Jono didn't care. He'd had worse—was *healing* from worse—and he knew they wouldn't harm him.

"Patrick is the only hope your precious goddess has that Ethan won't turn our world into a fucking hell," Jono snarled. "You cast your lot in with the heavens in this war. *This* is the side you fight for. *We* are who you need to support. So shut your fucking gob and call the fae to fight."

Tiarnán lifted his hand, gently easing Deirdre's dagger away from Jono's throat, the fae lord's eerie violet eyes staring right at him. "We made an alliance. We fae will keep it."

"If you do not, my Lord of Ivy and Gold, I will know," a calmly powerful voice said from behind Jono.

He let go of Tiarnán's tie to face Órlaith. The Summer Lady was dressed in jeans and a short-sleeved blouse half-tucked into her dark jeans, her red-orange wavy hair tied back in a tight braid. She had no less than three blades strapped to her person, all within easy reach. The magic swirling around her made Jono's eyes sting, or maybe it was a leftover reaction to silver.

"My lady," Tiarnán demurred, inclining his head her way.

Jono stalked down the hall and paused for a moment in front of Órlaith, catching her gaze. "I thought you were past the veil?"

She raised her chin. "The trail ends in Manhattan, so here I am."

"You're in Brooklyn, love."

Her mouth twitched. "It does not take much for me to cross the river."

"Then pick up Gerard from the airport and meet us back at Sage's flat. She'll text you the address."

"I will bring my love, and he will lead the fae to fight."

Jono patted her on the shoulder as he walked past her, knowing she'd get the job done. Out of all the gods and immortals he'd had to deal with, Órlaith and Gerard were a decent sort. They at least cared about Patrick because he was Patrick, and not because of what he could do for them in the grand scheme of godly machinations.

Jono tried to keep his breathing steady as he and Sage made their way outside, on edge after everything that had happened. They made it to her Bugatti, and Jono got behind the wheel so she could keep her attention on Wade. He had to shove the seat back to make room for his legs, but after a couple of seconds of adjustments, he started the engine and got on the road. Sage synced her mobile to the car's Bluetooth, letting Wade's voice filter through the speakers.

"Are you at the PCB yet?" Jono asked.

"Yeah, I'm waiting," Wade said.

"We should report the kidnapping to the PCB," Sage said.

"I'm pretty sure the attorney guy is already doing that. I left him at the office, and he'd already called the cops."

"Did the US attorney leave with Hades and Andras?"

"The demon did. I think. She was passed out on her desk when I left."

They couldn't be sure, but neither was it Jono's problem to worry about right now. He was holding on to his ability to think by the thinnest of threads when all he wanted to do was tear through the streets until he bit into Estelle's throat.

Sage kept Wade occupied while Jono tried not to hit anyone as he drove them home, ignoring the speed limit as much as possible. They weren't pulled over by sheer luck, and Jono double-parked out front, surprised there weren't any reporters waiting for them. Maybe the gargoyles had scared them off, or not wanting to be collateral damage in a werecreature civil war.

"Wade, we're here. Grab the book Patrick brought back from DC and come down," Jono said.

"Uh, sure," Wade said.

He finally ended the call, and Sage opened the side door to get out so Wade would have an easier time crawling into the back seat. "Where are we going?"

Jono stabbed at his mobile, calling Lucien. "Ginnungagap."

He disconnected the mobile from the Bluetooth, pressing it to his ear. It only took five rings before Carmen picked up the line.

"We made it clear the daylight hours are not our problem when it comes to your packs," Carmen said.

"Andras and Hades took Patrick. Make it your fucking problem and meet us at Ginnungagap," Jono growled before ending the call.

Wade barreled out of the front door to the apartment building, clutching the spell book to his chest. He scrambled into the back seat, long legs kicking the seat as he twisted to get situated. Sage climbed back inside, and Jono stepped on the gas the second the door shut.

"You know this thing is made with human skin? It's gross," Wade said, thrusting the spell book between the two front seats and waving it back and forth.

"We're aware," Sage said.

"Are we giving it to Ashanti?"

"She'll get it if she helps us out," Jono said.

He didn't know what spells were contained in the bloody thing, but whatever she'd written down and forgotten over the years had to be worth something. Yes, she might have needed Patrick for a spell to track Hannah, but Jono was willing to wager there were other spells inside that book she wanted back.

He wasn't sure what price she'd demand for it, or if she'd help them without demanding payment. Jono wasn't taking any chances, not with Patrick's life on the line.

His rage had settled into an icy fury that left him eerily focused in two directions—the meeting they were driving toward, and the soulbond. He kept reaching for that tie to Patrick, hoping that it would reveal his location, but the emptiness at the end spoke of interference or distance he couldn't push past.

Losing his temper would help no one, least of all Patrick.

Estelle did her absolute best to break him when she rang.

"Don't answer," Sage said when he picked his mobile up from the cup holder in the center console.

Jono ignored her and answered anyway, resyncing the mobile to the Bluetooth with a tap of his thumb. "You realize you signed your death sentence by taking Patrick."

"You should have kept a better eye on your weak spot," Estelle said, with none of Andras in her voice.

"Like you did Youssef? Heard you couldn't off the bloke yourself. Had to get someone else to dirty their hands for you. Bloody typical of you and the way you run things, but you won't be running them much longer."

"You're getting ahead of yourself, Jonothon. New York City was never going to be yours, and it won't be. If you want Patrick back alive, you'll give up all the territory you stole and leave the five boroughs behind."

Jono barked out a harsh laugh, wishing he had her neck between his hands and not the steering wheel. "How thick do you think I am? You've got a demon riding your soul. A Great Marquis of Hell at that. No way is he giving up Patrick in a bargain you're offering when you lot are making deals with the Dominion Sect. I challenged you to a fight, and we're going to have it."

"Is this really how you want to die?"

"You can fight me in the challenge ring, or I'll bring this war to your doorstep, and you won't survive that."

She wasn't going to survive to see tomorrow, but he doubted she'd believe it.

"You wouldn't be able to get past the threshold if I ordered it to keep you out."

"I'm the god pack alpha of New York City. That damned threshold will never keep me out."

She was quiet for two seconds, the pause negligible in most conversations, but Jono took it as a win. "I've held this territory for years, and I won't let an upstart like you take it from me."

"Then accept my challenge or forfeit your rank right now."

"You'll never see Patrick again if you persist with this."

"Bollocks. I'll find him, or he'll come back to me."

Whether across the country or through a hell, Jono would go where Patrick was or die trying, and knew his pack would be right beside him.

"I won't have you set foot in *my* territory," Estelle hissed.

"Then I'll meet you in Central Park, in the Great Lawn at sunset, with all the pack alphas present as required by pack law. Consider it a neutral challenge ring, and when I tear out your throat, even Andras won't be able to save you."

"*Before* sunset. Do you really think I'll let you lean into your alliance with the Night Courts?"

"After what happened in Brooklyn, do you really think they're all the help I have to rely on?"

"Then bring your ghosts, and I'll bring my demons, and I'll break you like I have countless sinners since I fell," Andras bit out through Estelle's voice, giving up the pretense that she was even marginally in control.

Fenrir bit at his mind, but Jono held him back, keeping his voice steady when all he wanted to do was scream at the position they were in. "You couldn't do it in London. What makes you think you'll do it here?"

"You haven't seen the horror I can create, but you will, wolf. You will."

Andras' demonic voice abruptly disappeared as the demon ended the call. Jono drew in a deep breath, trying to sort out his racing thoughts, almost too warm from rage.

"Demon of discord," Sage said after a moment. "We can't trust what he'll say the same way we could never trust Estelle."

"I know," Jono ground out.

"Can you find Patrick yet?"

Jono shook his head jerkily, the soulbond quiet and leading to nothing beyond his soul. "No."

"He could be anywhere," Wade said dully.

Jono wanted to close his eyes, wanted to hit something, but he was driving, and he had his god pack and all the others who were counting on him. "I know."

One thing at a time.

They finally made it to Ginnungagap, and Jono pulled into the side alley to park, killing the engine. Lucien's motorcycle was parked by the door, proof he'd come.

"Here," Wade said, passing him the spell book once they were out of the car.

Jono took it, fingers sliding over the skin-covered binding, hating how it felt and how it smelled. The door to Ginnungagap was unlocked, and Jono opened it, ignoring how what lived in the walls crackled at the edges of his awareness, Fenrir wallowing in it.

They met Lucien, Carmen, and Ashanti on the ground floor of the club, all the lights on, and the mugginess from the heat an oppressive blanket that Jono barely acknowledged. Jono couldn't be sure if the taste of ozone on his tongue was from Ashanti or Fenrir, because control was really only a passing thought right then. Fenrir was nothing but the fury of a world ending, after all, and Jono was more than willing to sink into it if it would help him find Patrick.

"Hades and Andras took Patrick, which means you're going to help us get him back," Jono said, glaring at Ashanti.

Lucien licked his lips clean of blood, the bite marks on Carmen's neck only partway healed. It seemed the news had dragged Lucien out of whatever bed he slept in without even a first meal from his human servants.

"Thought that soulbond of yours allowed you to track him?" Lucien asked.

"Not when he's past the veil." Jono held up the spell book for Ashanti to see. "You can go past the veil. Take us through, and you can have this back."

"You don't know which hell or heaven they would have traveled through," Ashanti said.

"I don't *care*. I'd be able to find him if I wasn't here."

"You don't know that, and I will not expend energy on a failed endeavor."

"Then what the bloody fucking worth *are* you?" Jono snarled.

Lucien blurred toward him, and Jono would've taken any blow the master vampire aimed his way if only to get close enough to hurt the sodding bastard, but Wade didn't let him.

Wade yanked Jono aside with brutal draconian strength to get in Lucien's face, fire and smoke flickering between his teeth as red scales pushed through his skin like a wave.

"Don't even think about it," Wade snarled, the rumble in his voice that of something larger than the building they stood in could contain. "You lay a hand on him and I'll bite it off."

"Found your teeth, did you?" Lucien asked, standing toe to toe with the teenager.

"Always had them."

Wade pointedly snapped his teeth at Lucien, the features of his face flattened and reptilian in a way they normally never were. A hint of his true self flickered around him along the blurred edges of his body for a single second, shadow lengthening to a size that wasn't even close to human.

It wasn't enough to get Lucien to back down, but Ashanti's presence kept the pair at a stalemate. Jono thought that was the only reason Lucien didn't antagonize Wade more.

"The spell book was to track where Patrick's twin might be using his blood. I have no use for it now without him," Ashanti said.

"Then I guess you won't mind if Wade burns it?" Jono asked, holding the spell book out to Wade.

The teen swiped it with the ease drawn from a lifetime of thieving habits. He raised it to his mouth, leaning away from Lucien, and blew smoke on it in a threatening manner.

Ashanti's black eyes narrowed, but she didn't move from her position. "I have others."

"Is that how you store your memories? In books so easily burned?"

"I collect many things and leave behind what I think mortals or others might find interesting." Her mouth twitched into a faint smile. "You should ask yourself if what is written on those pages might be useful in a future you can't see."

"Say the word, Jono," Wade said, blowing smoke over the pages, staring down Lucien with supreme teenage arrogance.

Jono didn't know what was in the book, but he knew any hope of Patrick finding Ethan first through Hannah meant he couldn't let Wade incinerate it. Ashanti seemed to understand he'd come to that conclusion, because she smiled in a way that made him want to claw her face.

"I can't take you past the veil. My world is this world, and my children have never known another. Our heaven and our hell exist beneath the same sky you humans sleep under," Ashanti said.

"You were dust," Jono growled.

"And I will be dust yet again. It is how I exist."

"If you let them have Patrick, you forfeit Earth to whatever hell Ethan will turn it into. What will you eat when he's killed us all off? You lose no matter what if we don't get Patrick back."

"So little faith in the weapon I taught him to be."

"He was a fucking *child*."

"He was made the hero in a tale still being written before he was even born. That is a fate he can't outrun, for all that he has tried. I was tasked with keeping him alive, and that is what I have done."

"You've done fuck all if he dies by Ethan's hand. I'll never forgive you if that happens."

"What use have I for forgiveness?"

Maybe she was too inhuman to understand it, but Jono knew Patrick would never forgive him if he killed Ashanti after her recent resurrection. That was the only reason he stayed his hand.

Jono stepped closer, pushing Fenrir to the back of his mind, staring down into Ashanti's black eyes. Despite her diminutive stature, there was nothing fragile about the mother of all vampires. Her games were different than the fae, than Persephone's, than even the Fates. She hadn't lived this long by giving in.

But she'd die a death more permanent than dust if she didn't.

"You won't help us save Patrick out of the goodness of your heart, because you haven't got one. You won't do it out of love, because you've lived so long you've forgotten what love means," Jono said, choosing his words carefully. "I'll love Patrick because you can't, but you'll save him if it means you win in the end."

When it came down to it, the gods couldn't afford to give up on Patrick.

The thing was, Jono never had, and he never would.

"Some battles never last long enough to become a war. Others merely need a spark." Ashanti smiled at him, beautiful and cold, but it wasn't Jono she spoke to as she gestured at the walls surrounding them. "Would you like it back?"

Deep in his soul, Fenrir howled.

26

It took everything Patrick had to open his eyes.

They felt like sandpaper when he finally blinked up at the ceiling of the underground challenge ring, gritty and rough. The view hadn't changed, neither had the binding spell that kept him pinned spread-eagle on the floor. He tried to move his arms and legs and found that he couldn't. The hissing burn of hellfire flickered around his body. Judging by his position and from what he could see, Patrick figured he was lying in a pentagram with hellfire burning along the spellwork lines.

The pressure in his chest felt as if something was sitting on him, but when he dragged his gaze away from the ceiling, he found no one and nothing else inside the pentagram with him. There were people in the seats that rose around the challenge ring, too many eyes staring right at him as if he were their singular entertainment.

He'd had nightmares like this over the years. All that was missing was a soultaker and Ethan. Their absence didn't make Patrick feel any better about his predicament.

The scrape of shoes against dirt had him trying to move his

head, but he couldn't. Patrick had to wait for the person standing just out of sight to come around within his field of vision. When the tall, sharply dressed figure came into view, the nausea in his belly threatened to slide up his throat and choke him.

"We need to stop meeting like this," Patrick rasped as Hades stared down at him here the same way the god had done in Salem all those years ago.

"If you would lie down and die for once, we'd never need to meet again," Hades said coldly.

Patrick would've flinched, but his body didn't obey. "Well, I'm lying down, just not dead yet. Are you here to change that?"

If Jono had been present, he'd tell Patrick not to antagonize the bastard holding him hostage. But it was only Patrick in this nightmare, the soulbond muffled inside him when he tried to reach for it. For a sickly moment, he thought it had been severed, but he could sense the metaphysical wall that had been erected around his soul over the hollowed-out areas where Persephone's anchors had once rested in his bones.

Hades had somehow blocked the soulbond, and Patrick wanted very much to kill him for that.

"I am here to see a future made," Hades said.

Patrick blinked slowly, knowing there were so many ways that statement could be taken. "Where's Hannah? Where's Ethan?"

Hades didn't answer him.

Someone else did.

"Not here," a rough voice said.

Patrick couldn't see them approach, as the entrance to the underground stadium had to be beyond his head. He could smell the creeping hint of ozone in the air though, could hear the scrape of feet on dirt. The instinct to run crawled through him, but Patrick remained trapped on the pentagram, staring at Hades and wondering if this was how he died.

The god that rounded the hellfire outlining the pentagram was taller than Hades, than most of the gods Patrick had met over the years. A loincloth was belted around his waist, the rich green fabric falling between legs that were covered in brown fur and ended not in feet, but in hooves. He was bare-chested, with a golden torque gleaming around his neck.

His eyes were a rich hazel, framed by dark brown hair that fell to his shoulders in a tangle of curls, and his face would've been handsome if he didn't have half his skull exposed. His skin stretched to nothing along the edge of white bone that protruded from the god's forehead. The bone branched out into a dark brown rack of antlers that acted like a crown which stretched wider than his shoulders.

Patrick licked his lips, mouth dry. "Cernunnos."

The god didn't appear as if he was there under duress. Hades made no move to order Cernunnos around; if anything, the Greek god of the Underworld gave ground. Cernunnos moved in a way that reminded Patrick of a predator, despite the deer attributes he appeared with in his true form.

"You could probably win a Halloween contest," Patrick rasped out.

"Samhain was never meant to be treated like the party you mortals turned it into," Cernunnos said.

"Speaking of parties, I've been to better."

Cernunnos tipped his head to the side, his massive antlers nearly smacking Hades in the face. The god slid out of the way with an annoyed glance aimed at Cernunnos, but he didn't say anything. More proof that Cernunnos was here of his own free will.

Patrick licked his dry lips. "Brigid wanted us to find you."

"She worries so, but my life was never hers to rule."

Cernunnos stepped over the pentagram's circle, the hellfire not a hindrance at all. He crossed another line, bringing him into the space where Patrick's left arm was outflung into one point of the pentagram's star. The god knelt, looming over Patrick in a way that made his heart speed up until it was a drum in his ears.

Dualistic gods were just as dangerous as trickster gods in the way their intentions could be twisted. In some ways, they were worse.

"What have you done to Hannah?"

It wasn't the question he meant to give voice to, but it was still one he needed an answer to. Cernunnos reached out and traced one long finger down Patrick's bare arm from elbow to wrist. They'd stripped him of his leather jacket, and he had no idea where it was. The god's touch was warm, almost gentle, but Patrick knew that gentleness was a lie. If Cernunnos meant to save him, the god wouldn't be looking at him as if Patrick was prey.

"What was asked of me to keep Macaria alive. I've taken life so that I can give it," Cernunnos said.

Patrick blinked, the motion dry and painful, thinking of bare branches and fallen leaves at the height of summer. "The parks."

Fingers dug into the tendons of Patrick's wrist, sending tingling pain through the nerves to his fingers. "Yes."

"And me? Are you here to kill me?"

"I am here to take what I need."

Patrick laughed, the sound cutting his throat to pieces. "Of course you fucking are. That's all your side does. You *take*."

"It is your sister I am trying to aid."

"My sister is dead."

The words were bitter on his tongue, all the *what-ifs* of the life they could have had if Ethan hadn't wanted to turn himself into a god nothing more than a fantasy.

"Her child will live, as will Macaria. The life I create for them both will ensure that."

The dull prick of fingernails against his skin became sharper, more painful, turning into claws that sliced deep like a knife. Patrick ground his teeth against the pain as Cernunnos opened up the vein in his wrist, warm blood sliding over his skin to pool in his upturned palm.

"This won't save you," Patrick said, blinking up at the ceiling as he tried to wall off the pain.

"Ah, but it will save Macaria, and that is why I chose to help my cousin."

"Your apartment was ransacked. The threshold was torn apart."

Cernunnos laughed, the sound dry like cracking wood. "People see what they want to see, my own kind included. I came of my own free will."

Patrick would've recoiled if he had the choice. "The fae won't take kindly to that."

"What they want is of no concern to me. What I need is your blood. It is the last essence I require to complete the spell. Twins are useful that way."

Patrick's blood trickled out of his vein, and Cernunnos drew it off his skin and the dirt floor by way of magic older than some nations. His blood floated upward through the air, like backward rain, until at least a pint of it spun like a mageglobe against the god's palm. The blood loss wasn't enough to make Patrick light-headed, but it would be if the god didn't close the wound.

Unless the whole plan was to steal his blood, then let him bleed out and die.

But that didn't sound like Ethan, even if Hades was here to oversee the blood stealing. Hades had stripped him of Persephone's defenses, had hidden the soulbond as only a god could, and while they were surrounded by demon-backed hunters, Patrick saw no Dominion Sect mercenaries.

They were in Hamilton Heights, in Estelle's territory, and she'd been making deals with demons well before she'd drifted into Ethan's orbit. If she was two-timing people, well, that wouldn't be a surprise.

A searing pain burned across his wrist, and Patrick gritted his teeth. He still couldn't move, but he could at least no longer feel blood pulsing out of his vein. Cernunnos stood, looking down at

Patrick while holding his stolen blood in one hand by magical means.

Those inhuman eyes met Patrick's, and the smile on the god's face wasn't meant to be a comfort. "I know how to stay alive in a world that always changes. I do not fear what comes next."

With that said, Cernunnos stepped out of the pentagram and walked away, out of sight. Hades remained, watching Patrick instead of the other god.

"Persephone won't like what you've done," Patrick said.

"Keep my wife's name out of your mouth," Hades ordered.

"She chose me."

"And I chose our daughter. She will understand when this is all over."

"She'll probably divorce you."

The hellfire burned higher, getting hotter, in response to Patrick's jibe. The heat coming off it was hot enough to burn, even if the flames didn't catch him on fire. His skin seared with blisters on his arms and beneath his clothes where his body crossed the spell lines, ratcheting up his breathing.

"I need him functioning," Andras said with Estelle's voice.

The hellfire flared higher for a few seconds before dampening down to a flicker along the pentagram. Patrick let out a harsh breath, blinking tears out of his eyes, trying not to focus on how much the blisters hurt when they popped.

Patrick watched as Estelle and Andras came into his sight, choosing to stand between the bottom points of the pentagram. Estelle's eyes were shadows in her face, veins lined black, a willing host for Andras here on Earth.

Patrick thought about saying a prayer in the face of the demon, but he knew it wouldn't do any good, not without faith to back it. He'd lost faith in all the gods long ago. Praying wouldn't save him. It never had.

"You should know Jonothon challenged us to a fight. We told

him he would never see you again if he chose that route," Estelle said, Andras an echo in her voice.

"I'll always come back to him," Patrick said.

Estelle smiled, the cruel twist of her lips a warning Patrick couldn't run from. "We're counting on that. You see, when it comes to a fight between two rival god packs over contested territory, only alphas may step into the challenge ring."

Patrick's heart skipped a beat, going suddenly lightheaded despite lying on the ground, because he knew—he *knew*—what was coming.

In the end, horror tasted a lot like hell.

27

"Everyone is in place," Sage said, tucking a piece of loose hair behind her ear.

She smelled like pack to Jono—pack, and a vicious sort of rage everyone he'd come into contact with all day had mirrored. Word had spread like wildfire about Patrick's kidnapping and how Estelle and Andras were holding him hostage. Every pack who'd pledged loyalty to theirs had made it into Manhattan and were now currently scattered in and around the southern half of Central Park alongside the fae.

The packs loyal to Estelle had claimed the northern half, but that didn't mean all of them stayed there. Sage had received reports of minor skirmishes already on their side of the park, as well as multiple sightings of Krossed Knights, other hunters, and rival packs stalking their positions farther south. Surrounding all of them had been reports of police beginning to block off intersections in a two-block radius around Central Park.

It was barely half past six in the evening, but the curfew had ensured the streets were emptier than usual. Jono, Sage, and Wade stood at the corner of the Seventy-Ninth Street Transverse, along with Gerard and Órlaith. The entrance to the winter-dead park wasn't barred to them, and Jono was ready to get this fight over with.

"Are we going?" Wade asked, fidgeting in his spot, gold eyes trained on Jono. Red scales pushed through the skin of his throat and the edges of his jaw, his forearms and hands. Wade had quit hiding what he was for this fight, and he was fidgety in a way that spoke of wanting to shift mass.

"Yeah, we're going," Jono said.

"Let's go rip out some throats," Gerard said, holding the *Gáe Bulg* in one hand. He wasn't dressed in armor like some of the fae had been, but in a combat uniform that wouldn't look out of place in the military, despite no identifying patches.

Before they could head into Central Park, a lone police car turned the corner a block away, driving up Fifth Avenue in the wrong direction, lights running but sirens off. It swung diagonally across the lanes and pulled to a stop at the curb near where they stood. Jono was unsurprised to see Casale sitting in the front passenger seat.

"If you're here to try to talk me out of this, you're wasting your time," Jono said as Casale got out of the car.

"Actually, I'm here to give you a warning. If you'd picked up your phone when I called you this afternoon, I wouldn't have had to track your ass down," Casale said.

Jono refused to feel bad about ignoring Casale's calls, not with everything going on. "The PCB hasn't been helpful. You aren't worth my time."

"None of this is helpful." Casale left the car door open and came around the front of the vehicle to stand on the sidewalk in front of Jono. "SAIC Henry Ng says there's activity in the ley lines that isn't sanctioned."

"I can't help you with that."

The one person who possibly could was missing, leaving a gaping hole in Jono's chest, the soulbond drifting into an emptiness he couldn't breach. Some packs had volunteered to try to break into the god pack territory in Hamilton Heights, but Jono had declined. They'd be slaughtered if any Dominion Sect mercenaries and demon-backed hunters had been left behind to guard it. Jono had blood on his hands, and he didn't want any more that he could avoid.

He knew Patrick wouldn't either, once they had him back.

Casale studied him before his gaze shifted to the others surrounding Jono, lingering on Gerard's spear and Órlaith, who bristled with all manner of silver weapons. The smell of it still made Jono's eyes water and body ache in his gut and thigh. Only faint, yellowing bruises remained from the fight in Brooklyn, but some of the damage still lingered.

"We're working with the SOA at the request of the mayor to clear the area around Central Park. At your dire's request, it has officially been designated your challenge ring by way of a mayoral order."

"*Finally*," Sage said.

Considering who was the mayor, Jono thought the Dagda was cutting it close.

"Make sure most of the fighting stays inside Central Park."

"I can't promise that," Jono said.

Casale sighed. "Jono—"

"The PCB held off on investigating Estelle's god pack for too long. You ignored the hunter problem because it wasn't affecting mundane humans, only our communities. You don't get to stand there and dictate how and where we fight when we're the ones putting our lives and reputations on the line to make this city safer by forcing the fucking demons *out*," Jono snarled.

"We haven't ignored anything. Cases take time."

Jono laughed harshly, thinking of the uncanny swiftness of Patrick's criminal case, shepherded along by the hand of a goddess. "You've done fuck all for my people, Casale. This is me not standing on the sidelines anymore, not when Patrick's life is at stake."

"The SOA is aware of his kidnapping. They've indicated they're preparing to deploy a Rapid Response Team."

"I know who has him, and we don't need the SOA's help to get him back."

Jono turned his back on Casale and walked with his pack into Central Park. The Met loomed in the sky off to their right, the skeletal branches of the trees incapable of hiding the museum.

Sunset was an hour away, and if the fight lasted past that time, then the Night Courts would shore up their side. Ashanti had promised her children would show, and Lucien had dispatched his human servants to the other Night Courts to give the order. Fae were support during the daylight hours, vampires for the night, and the softly descending twilight came with the promise kept by a god of war.

Fog drifted through the trees and bushes, blurring out the edges of Central Park. The faint sound of war drums started up, a conch shell blowing a call to arms as the Night Marchers crossed the veil to aid the packs in the street.

"Kū will enjoy the slaughter," Gerard said.

"So long as he doesn't slaughter any of ours," Sage retorted.

Dry, brittle leaves crunched beneath Jono's shoes as they walked down the path running adjacent to the Seventy-Ninth Street Transverse. It curved around the Met, taking them through a short tunnel that ran beneath the East Drive on their way to the Great Lawn. As they came out of the tunnel, Emma and Leon dropped down from above, flanking their small group.

"All your loyal pack alphas are accounted for and waiting on your arrival at the Great Lawn," Emma said.

"Any sign of Patrick?" Jono asked, unable to snuff out the tiny flare of hope that kindled in him, even though the soulbond still felt empty.

Emma shook her head. "None. No one got eyes or scent of him when Estelle's people started showing up."

"Do we really think they're going to bring him if they threatened we'd never see him again if we fought?" Wade asked.

"There's still time to send packs to Hamilton Heights," Leon said.

"No," Jono said, staring straight ahead down the path. "If they don't bring him, I'll find him."

The soulbond had been tied between them by the gods, and if he had to threaten every god in existence to help him find Patrick, then he would.

Jono could just glimpse the Obelisk in the distance through the branches of the trees as he scanned the area around them. The path to the Great Lawn smelled like death, all the life sucked out from the City's green heart. The closer they walked to the Great Lawn, the more that scent started to mingle with the harsh bitterness of hell. Sulfur coated the back of his throat, and when he swallowed, it made him want to gag.

Their path merged with the circular one surrounding the Great Lawn and the baseball diamonds interspersed amidst brown grass. It acted like the demarcation of a challenge ring. Bare trees surrounded the open area, Manhattan's buildings reaching for the sky in the city blocks past the edges of the park.

The low fencing was easy enough for all of them to vault over. A crowd of people stood in the center of the large field, two sides bunched together in ragged half circles. Every alpha of every pack in New York City had been called forth to witness the fight that would dictate their future, as well as every surviving member of Estelle's god pack and some hunters as well.

Her side of the makeshift challenge ring was triple theirs in terms of numbers. That wasn't even counting the demons that had taken over her god pack. Jono forced his heartbeat steady, even if he couldn't hide his rage. Her pack would be forfeit when he won the fight, but he wondered how many had accepted the demons willingly.

The crowd shifted a little at his presence, the spike of relief drifting from his side almost enough to drive the scent of sulfur from the breeze. Fenrir uncurled in the back of his mind, a heavy, vicious presence that hovered over his thoughts.

People on their side shifted, parting enough to give Jono and the others with him room to walk to the front of the group. They spread out shoulder to shoulder in front of their side, and Jono missed Patrick's presence like he'd miss his heart if it ever left his chest.

Across the dead, brittle grass that separated them stood Estelle. She didn't appear as the grief-stricken woman who'd shown up for the television cameras. This was a woman who had cheated her way to power at the expense of everyone else, including the man she'd married.

"The challenge is for werecreatures only," Estelle called out, standing with a casual slant to her slim shoulders.

"You've called demons out of hell and into those under your protection. You've made bargains with hunters. You can't blame Jonothon for calling upon his alliances," Órlaith said, not bothering to raise her voice since everyone could hear her.

"This is not your fight."

"You made deals with the Dominion Sect. You *took* Patrick. It's all our fight," Jono growled.

Estelle raised her chin, a smile playing on her lips he didn't trust at all. "It's a fight between alphas. No one else is allowed to interfere."

"Bullshit," Wade coughed out.

"Where's Patrick?" Jono asked, ignoring Wade, some of his desperately chained fury breaking free.

"Oh, you chose to fight. You chose *them*—" Estelle gestured at his side of the circle. "—over the man you loved. You won't get him back."

Fenrir growled through Jono's mind, the sound vibrating through his bones, settling in his gut. Fury was a storm Jono was more than willing to let guide him through this fight. "I'm going to kill you."

"You can try, but you will fail. Now, let's finish this, you upstart bastard."

Jono stepped forward, aware of all the eyes on him as he stalked to the invisible center line that separated their two sides. He stopped there in the center, surrounded by people he trusted and people he'd sooner see buried in a grave on Hart Island—unclaimed and unloved and utterly forgotten.

Jono wasn't backing down from this fight—he couldn't, not when Estelle knew Patrick's whereabouts. He'd spent years in exile in New York City, barred from forming a pack until Patrick came along. They didn't have a pack without him, and Jono wasn't going to stop until he had Patrick back.

Estelle didn't move from her position at the edge of the circle, surrounded by her supporters. It was only as Jono stared at her, the distance halved with where he stood, that he realized the only one staring out of her bright amber eyes was Estelle. Jono narrowed his eyes as he drew in a deep breath, trying to parse her scent beneath the almost overwhelming scent of hell that surrounded him.

"Are you going to stand there and forfeit?" Jono asked.

Estelle laughed, bright and cruel, as the crackling scent of ozone suddenly punched through the sulfur and multitudes of pack scent. "Only alphas can fight for god pack territory and control of a city when it comes to war between god packs. That pack law hasn't changed in centuries. But there's nothing in our laws that dictates which one must fight, just that they be an alpha."

The crowd behind her parted, pulling back, ceding space to the god walking toward them. A rumbling growl from dozens of voices went up behind Jono, Wade's voice cutting through the noise.

"Let me eat *that* bastard," Wade called out.

Hades met Jono's gaze with a smirk before he stepped aside to allow the person following in his wake to stand between the god and Estelle, bringing forth a nightmare Jono never saw coming.

Jono stopped breathing, the ringing in his ears drowning out everything else, even Fenrir's howls, as he stared at Patrick.

Black eyes looked back at him in a well-loved face, the familiar green subsumed by the demon riding Patrick's soul. The cant of his head and the twist to his lips were shades of the demon's personality and not his, an arrogance in every line of his body that Patrick had never carried.

"Did you really think I'd leave this city without ruining you?" Andras asked in Patrick's voice.

Sound came back with a snap, Fenrir halting the panicked spiral of Jono's thoughts and emotions in the face of a horror he'd never dreamed of. A rising tide of voices washed over him from the pack alphas who were loyal to him, the distress and anger sour in the air.

Jono finally found his voice, tearing his throat raw when he spoke. "*Get out of him.*"

Andras lifted Patrick's hand, pale blue magic sparking at his fingertips. "You know, I'd forgotten what it was like to possess a witch, but mages are so much more *powerful*, that I'm inclined to stay."

"I did say you'd never see him again if you insisted on fighting. Since you persist in challenging my authority, you'll face Patrick in the ring," Estelle said, almost coyly.

Jono didn't look at her, still staring at Patrick and sinking his awareness into the soulbond, but there was no responding acknowledgment when he pulled on it. Nothing but that strange emptiness at the end of it, which could only mean that Andras was blocking it. Jono wondered if Andras had been possessing Patrick since the first time he tried reaching through the soulbond. The thought made bile rise in the back of his throat.

"That's not how a challenge works," Sage snarled, suddenly by Jono's side.

"Patrick is an alpha. You made him so when you claimed your pack. Loyalty can be shifted, and he's fighting for me now."

"He's not *yours*," Jono snarled, unable to keep the desperation out of his voice.

"He was never going to stay yours, not when Ethan wants his son back," Andras said.

Jono hated the sound of the demon in Patrick's voice, the way the tone was off, the cadence wrong, everything that was Patrick *gone* despite the other man standing right in front of him.

"You can fight him for the right to keep New York City, or you can forfeit, show your throat, and die. All the packs you stole will revert back to me and be punished, or be exiled, no matter what you choose," Estelle said.

She said it with a smile on her face, basking in the knowledge that she believed she'd won without needing to shed a single drop of her own blood.

Andras walked forward in Patrick's body, his stride all wrong, a mageglobe forming against one palm. "Are you going to yield and die to save his life? Or will you fight and lose him and your territory? Because you won't win. You can't break me out of his soul."

Jono watched the body of the man he loved come closer and knew there was no way he could ever lift a hand to him. Estelle had been counting on that, and she ended up being right.

"I won't fight him, but I won't forfeit," Jono said, shoulders tightening as he caught the scent coming off Patrick, one that was all Andras and nothing like what he got when he buried his nose in Patrick's hair.

"A pity. Because I do so *love* a good fight."

The mageglobe streaked forward, almost too fast to track. Jono shoved Sage out of the line of fire, unwilling to see her or anyone else harmed. Jono held out his hand toward it, as if he'd be able to shield himself when he knew he couldn't. The mageglobe slammed into his palm and exploded, the force of the magic tearing through his arm up to his elbow, catching him in the chest and face, knocking him to the ground.

Jono landed on his back, screaming up at the sky for a few horrible seconds before he choked it off. The agony was bright and vicious in his brain before the pain was blunted by nerves turning off. The shift was almost instinctual—his or Fenrir's, Jono didn't know—but it cut off the blood pumping out of his artery at the shredded end of his elbow. Skin grew over the tattered remains, reorienting the veins and arteries to stop the blood loss. The bones in his face and chest rippled, broke, forcing hideously burned skin to smooth out into something less than seared flesh.

He could grow his arm back. If he shifted to wolf and then to human again, it would be as if he'd never lost it.

Jono just needed to *move*.

The shock of losing half his arm didn't hurt nearly as much as the specter of Patrick being the one to give the blow, even though Jono knew it was Andras who had done it, just with Patrick's face.

"Jono!" Wade cried out, falling to his knees, his head blocking out the sky, a frantic expression on his red-scaled face.

Jono pushed back the pain, let it hollow him out, and rolled to his left side, using his one good remaining arm to prop himself up. Wade's hand settled on his right shoulder, shoring him up, as Jono stared at where Andras stood in Patrick's body, another mageglobe burning in his hand.

"Going to lie down and die?" Andras asked with Patrick's voice.

"I said I wouldn't fight Patrick," Jono grunted. "I said nothing about fighting you."

Fenrir's claws sank into Jono's soul, teeth cutting into his thoughts, seeping into every layer of who he was.

Let me out, Fenrir growled.

Jono closed his eyes, and when he opened them again, he didn't have control, but he'd given it up willingly.

Jono knew Patrick hadn't been given that choice.

Fenrir pushed his body to his feet, shaking off Wade's touch. Through eyes he had no control over, Jono saw Estelle's face go slack from shock, while those around her with demons in their souls didn't react.

Andras clenched Patrick's hand around the mageglobe, black eyes narrowing. "I picked apart this meatsuit's memories. I was expecting you well before now, Fenrir."

"*You've been after the souls that belong to me,*" Fenrir bit out in a voice that shredded Jono's throat, power bleeding past his teeth. It tasted like ozone. "*You took what doesn't belong to you.*"

"Souls are my currency." Andras tossed the mageglobe into the air so that it hovered directly in front of Patrick's chest before spreading Patrick's arms. "Your people don't pray to you. Why do you think it was so easy for me to take them?"

"*Do you think I'll let you keep them?*"

"You're half-forgotten, reduced to a spirit rather than flesh. There's nothing you can do to stop me."

Fenrir laughed, the sound horrific enough to give Jono nightmares if he hadn't heard it before. "*Your kind always believes that, and you are always wrong.*"

The shift came hard and fast, ripping through Jono's body, breaking bones and splitting skin with brutal speed, until he stood on four legs in the challenge ring, buried beneath the weight of Fenrir. He didn't fight it, riding the god's awareness with practiced ease.

Except this time was different than all the rest. This time, when his soul cracked open, it mirrored how the rush of magic felt passing through the soulbond and into Patrick's soul, only so much more than that trickle.

Power unlike anything Jono had felt before rushed through him —a deep, unending void that poured out of him like a tsunami, driving everyone but Hades and Andras in Patrick's body to their knees.

The power reminded Jono of every instance he'd stepped inside

Ginnungagap, and what lived inside those walls pressed against his awareness—the yawning abyss. The primordial power of one pantheon's birth that was within shockingly easy reach, cradled in a city of skyscrapers that were altars in and of themselves in some ways, built by countless hands that had prayed to a myriad of gods.

Fenrir threw back his head and howled, the sound calling every pack member in the five boroughs and demanding they acknowledge him—and calling forth something else.

Something from the heavens.

Ginnungagap was a point of creation, a *beginning* that could be found in every myth the gods grew out of.

But a beginning could be anything, to anyone, and when Ginnungagap poured out of Fenrir and filled Central Park, what came through—furiously bright and impossible to look at if one wasn't a god—was a great spinning wheel made up of many eyes.

An angel come down from on high.

2 8

No no no no no!

The mantra floated through Patrick's buried, locked down thoughts as Andras hurled the mageglobe at Jono using his own hand. There was nothing he could do, only capable of watching through eyes he couldn't control as the spell exploded directly in front of Jono, taking off half his arm and burning his face.

Patrick's scream was lost in the tiny corner of his mind he had been relegated to, unable to control his body or his magic. Andras was wrapped all around him, a sickening, hideous presence that caged him in and *laughed*.

Didn't I say I was going to break you? He'll die by your hand, and you'll watch it happen, Andras said, the words an echo felt more than heard in the space Patrick was trapped in.

I'm not the one hurting him, Patrick protested.

Yes, you are. In the end, they always think it's their loved one killing them. He will be no different.

It was a nightmare Patrick wanted to wake up from, to stop, but the horror of it all was that he couldn't. Possession was about control, and Patrick had lost his in the pentagram when Andras had left Estelle's soul for his. Nothing had prepared him for drowning in his own body, with not even the soulbond capable of acting as a lifeline.

His body was a coffin he couldn't escape, buried alive in flesh and bone.

Patrick hated feeling helpless. The worst things happened when he could do nothing, when no amount of fighting would change things.

And he so desperately wanted to change the course of this fight, to save Jono, but he couldn't even *speak*.

Patrick could only watch as Wade appeared by Jono's side, frantic and angry. He could only watch as Jono pushed him aside and stood, Fenrir staring out of eyes gone burning white as his aura exploded with the power of a god. It cracked open, shining like a halo around him. Patrick was distantly aware of the reactions of the pack members behind Jono and within his field of vision, the shock that hit them all as Fenrir finally revealed himself.

Andras had known before then that Fenrir resided in Jono. The Great Marquis had slid through Patrick's mind and memories, looking where the demon had no right to go, sliding through Patrick's life as if Andras belonged when it never would.

Being possessed wasn't something Patrick wanted to ever experience again, and he could've gone the rest of his life, however short or long it might be, knowing what a demon felt like riding his soul.

And then a voice he never wanted to hear again sang through the air—deep, unearthly, and not meant for mortals to listen to and survive sane.

Set them free, fallen, the Throne commanded.

The angel stared at Andras and Patrick with its many eyes, bright enough to burn out optic nerves, the edges of its fiery wheel that spun and spun raging like the surface of the sun. The only reason Patrick didn't go blind was because of Andras. Human eyes with human vision, yes, but the demon was still in control, capable of filtering out the damage.

Fear coursed through Patrick, and it wasn't his—too ancient, too heavy, too filled with bitterness of a long-lost celestial war. The foreign emotion suffocated his thoughts as Andras faced off against an angel floating in a void that threatened to swallow the Great Lawn and everyone in it whole. Beneath that heavenly being stood Jono with Fenrir, the massive wolf unimpeded by Ginnungagap.

The Throne drifted closer, burning like a star. *Leave the mortal flesh which does not belong to you, or I will break you out.*

Andras had taunted Patrick in whispers and screams that the demon would never let him go. For all the demon's hellish tenacity, when faced with a furious angel and an equally furious god wielding a primordial void, Andras did what all demons did.

The Great Marquis of Hell fled from the light.

Andras ripped his presence out of Patrick, and every single shred of the demon that pulled free left acid behind. Patrick screamed, as much from Andras fleeing as from the angel singing in his ears at a level that threatened to permanently deafen him.

Patrick crashed to his knees, body uncoordinated, like a puppet with its strings cut. His nerves buzzed as if he'd been shocked by a Taser. Maybe the aftermath of a demon leaving would be different if he'd willingly accepted Andras the way Estelle had, but Patrick would choose a bullet to the brain than being a meatsuit for a demon every time if that was the choice given him.

The soulbond snapped to life, flooding his soul with Jono's presence again. The sensation made him gasp, its return almost as painful as its absence. Patrick slumped forward, breath stuttering in his lungs as he tried to get his hands to work, to brace himself for the fall, but his fingers barely twitched. Everything *hurt*, and he could feel himself falling as if from a great distance, thoughts still not quite connected to his body.

"Patrick! *Patrick!*"

Wade's frantic shout cut through the bone-aching sound of the angel's voice. Red-scaled hands caught him by the shoulders before his face hit the ground and he broke his nose. He was yanked against a too-warm body, strong arms wrapping around him. Patrick would never tell Wade, but in that moment, the scent of fire was too close to the taste of hell for him. He sucked in a breath anyway, twitching through the aftermath of being himself—and *only* himself—again.

"I have him!" Wade yelled.

Chaos erupted with his shout.

Flashes of negative light burst around them as more and more demons left their hosts. Patrick squeezed his eyes shut against the heavenly light, finally able to clench his hands into fists, control coming back one muscle at a time. The cascade of sensation left him with a headache that skirted migraine level, but he forced himself to breathe through it.

The angel had finally quit singing, but even those few seconds of listening with human ears and no demon in his soul to block the sound left Patrick wanting to puke up his guts. Then fiery heat erupted over his head as Wade roared, spitting flame at someone he couldn't see.

Patrick forced his eyes open, spots dancing across his vision. He tried to orient himself, but everything spun horribly for a moment when Wade dragged him backward with preternatural speed, hands never letting him go. When they settled again, Patrick leaned over and got furiously sick.

"Fucking angels," Wade muttered. "Fucking *demons*. Should've tried to eat him."

"You'd be complaining for weeks about the taste in your mouth. No, thanks," Patrick mumbled.

Wade pulled him into a tight hug, as much as to hold on to him as to ensure Patrick didn't face-plant into vomit. "You're back. Oh man, you sound like you again."

Patrick spat out the bile coating his tongue to clear his mouth, still breathing the sour stench of it, but it was better than tasting hell. "Yeah."

Wade batted at one of Patrick's hands, opening up his fingers. Then something heavy and familiar was pressed against his palm, and Patrick stared down at the hilt of his dagger, the silvery words of prayers drifting across the matte-black blade.

"I kept it safe for you." Wade's voice pitched low, sounding small and bitter. "I'm sorry I couldn't keep you safe."

Patrick curled his fingers around the hilt of the dagger, the world steadying around him. He reached up with his other hand to shakily pat Wade's arm that was still wrapped around his chest.

"I wouldn't want them to have you," Patrick said.

"But—"

"It's not your fault, and it never will be."

"Okay." Wade tightened his hold a little. "I found a new bakery by my apartment. They have really good cupcakes. I'll buy you some."

"Sure."

A streak of orange and black skidded to a stop in front of them, snarling furiously at a pair of wolves trying to get past Emma's shifted form. Sage's tail lashed back and forth before she launched herself into the fray, claws flashing as she took down a pair of god pack members.

"We need to get you out of here," Wade said, dragging both of them to their feet. He slung Patrick's arm over his shoulder, easily taking Patrick's weight.

Patrick's head throbbed with the change in position, but he felt less like his brain was being liquified than the last time the angel sang in Sage's apartment. The Throne still burned like the sun above them, spinning rapidly as demons fled their hosts.

"Where's Jono?" Patrick asked.

"He went after Estelle. Andras left you and went into her."

Of course the fucking demon did.

A flash of magic slammed through a handful of hunters,

sending them flying into the teeth of wolves whose allegiance was to Jono and Patrick. He didn't watch them get torn apart, attention caught on the brutal way Gerard and Órlaith were carving a path toward where he and Wade stood.

"Patrick!" Gerard called out, spearing a wolf that got in his way through the throat. The notched spearpoint severed its spine, and he kicked the body free with a grunt.

Patrick straightened up but then had to duck his head and close his eyes as the Throne exploded in holy light above them. He heard the loud, thunder-like sounds of even more demons fleeing their hosts, leaving the werecreatures behind to face judgment of a different sort.

Estelle's god pack would never be part of theirs. If the werecreatures didn't die today, they'd be exiled if they weren't arrested. He and Jono had given enough warnings to god packs across the country and in Europe that anyone who'd been part of Estelle's would never be welcomed in established territory.

Gerard and Órlaith reached their position and promptly put Patrick and Wade at their backs to guard them. Gerard spared a glance over his shoulder, catching Patrick's eye. "How are you holding up?"

"I'm holding him up," Wade said.

"I'm me again," Patrick said, giving Gerard a salute with his dagger. It was a painful win, but he'd take it. "Cernunnos is working freely with the Dominion Sect."

Gerard swore in half a dozen different languages. Patrick was mildly impressed.

Órlaith gestured sharply with one hand, and a glittering dome of magic formed around them, shielding Patrick and Wade. Sage took up position on the opposite side of the fae, having not gone far after tearing out some throats.

Emma and Leon vaulted over a pair of werejackals who were on their side to join the circle. Patrick was surrounded by his pack and friends, and beyond them, alphas loyal to their god pack started to form a line between them and the enemy—which were still more numerous than their side.

Amidst the bloody melee, Patrick couldn't see Jono at all.

But the soulbond was a weight in his chest again, slowly stitching up the holes Andras had left behind. It gave him comfort and the will to face the fight with his pack. Patrick leaned into the soulbond to tap a ley line—and abruptly pulled back, staggering against Wade.

"What happened?" Wade asked, holding them both up as he snorted smoke out of his nose.

"The ley lines are too unstable to tap," Patrick said.

"Like last year? With the nexus?"

"No, it's—"

The ground jerked. For a second, Patrick didn't know what was happening. Then the shaking intensified, and the only reason he kept his footing was because of Wade.

"Are we having an earthquake? If my shot glass collection gets broken, I'm stealing more," Wade said.

"You're not old enough to drink."

"They have funny designs."

As the earth shook, the Throne disappeared in an explosion of light reminiscent of a supernova. Patrick doubted the angel was dead. Angels didn't *die*, not the way mortals did. In the wake of the angel's disappearance, a different light filled the sky, brighter than the sun tipping toward the horizon in the west.

A building at the southern end of the park, barely seen over the tops of scraggly trees, flashed like a lighthouse. The magic rippled through the air, rolling across the city and through the broken barrier once held up by Greek coins and cliff roses in a flash that had Patrick ducking his face.

The magic left in its wake a scent on the air that made Patrick want to sneeze, like all the summer life that had been sucked out of every park in New York City was drifting down amidst the iron jungle. He remembered what Cernunnos had said, about needing his blood to finish whatever spell was keeping Hannah and her unborn baby alive.

His stomach sank at the realization the god must have completed it. That maybe this whole fight with Estelle had been escalated on purpose. Whatever the reason, the fight in question wasn't over, but neither was it going in their favor.

For all that he felt undone and unmade because of Andras, Patrick was still an alpha of their god pack. He was supposed to fight for the packs they protected, not the other way around. So Patrick reached for his magic rather than a ley line, prepared to join the fight no matter how much it hurt, when a conch shell blew a long, steady note into the sky, like a call to arms.

He hadn't seen the Night Marchers when they saved Jono in Brooklyn, but he saw the ghostly warriors now, charging through the bare trees for the Great Lawn, weapons held high, Ginnungagap providing a shadowy place to fight beneath the fading sun. Some of the hunters and werecreatures broke and ran, not wanting to face the new threat.

"Don't worry," Wade said. "Jono called all the packs to Manhattan. Estelle's people won't get far."

Patrick flexed the fingers of his free hand, took a breath, and forced a mageglobe to form, pouring magic out of his bruised and damaged soul. "They're not going to make it out of the park. Órlaith? Make me a hole."

Órlaith looked over at him and nodded, doing what he asked. Patrick's head pounded, but wavering vision didn't matter when the targets were so numerous. Patrick let his mageglobe fly toward a group of retreating hunters, some part of him wondering if any of them had been in the underground challenge ring in Hamilton Heights, watching him get possessed. It didn't matter, because the hunters didn't get far. When their bodies got ripped to pieces by the magical grenade, the demons they'd sold their souls to fled unscathed.

Deals with the devils never paid out.

29

I want the kill, he told Fenrir as the god spurred his wolf body to a faster speed.

Fenrir's answer was a wordless growl, but Jono knew in this, he would get his way.

Estelle had shifted when her god pack had surged forward, lost in a wave of claws and teeth. Fenrir had her scent, and there was no hiding from a god, with or without a demon in her soul. She carried Andras again—willingly—and Jono would never forgive her for bringing demons to New York City.

Not after what Andras had done to Patrick.

Fenrir raced through the trees and bare bushes, his prey going just as fast up ahead, looking for an escape. Jono saw flashes of movement out of the corners of his eyes—werecreatures fighting, and the ghostly blurs of Night Marchers. Some of the werecreatures tried to intercede on Estelle's behalf, to give her time to escape, but Fenrir was having none of it.

He clawed his way through them without pause, leaving bodies behind.

They were running toward the southern end of Central Park, taking the West Drive rather than the more direct route over Bow Bridge. The hawthorn path was near there though, and the fae had guards in that location. Jono didn't know where she was running to until magic exploded through the air, rippling away from a point too close for comfort.

Cernunnos, Fenrir said, tasting the air with Jono's tongue to parse the magic.

That was another god going on his shit list.

Fenrir put on a burst of speed as they left the trees for Sheep Meadow, the skyline breaking through. Jono could taste the coldness of Ginnungagap between his teeth, the primordial void a companion he didn't mind so long as it was on their side.

They closed the distance between Estelle and Andras and would've taken her down if not for the hellfire that exploded between them, scorching the brown grass. Fenrir vaulted over it, fur getting singed, and faced off against Hades on the other side while Estelle and Andras made a run for it.

"*Move,*" Fenrir growled, voice coming out of a throat not meant to speak in that way.

"No," Hades said, raising his hands that dripped with hellfire.

Before Fenrir could attack, an explosion ripped through the air behind them, Estelle's pained howl mixing with Andras' scream. Fenrir spared a glance in that direction, seeing a small crater in the meadow and a shadow darting forward with preternatural speed. They carried no soul, only a godhead, and ozone crackled in the air like a warning.

A startled expression crossed Hades' face, and the god half turned to assess the new threat and still keep Fenrir and Jono in sight. Fenrir howled, releasing more of Ginnungagap, the primordial void covering Sheep Meadow as it had the Great Lawn. Hades summoned more hellfire to light the area, face washed out in the glare.

"The demon was right," Hades said, voice coming out clipped and uneasy. "You did come back."

Ashanti stalked forward on her ironshod bone hooks, herding Estelle and Andras back toward Jono's teeth with her sheer presence. The malevolence she exuded was primal and vicious, the stuff of nightmares that lived in the dark, what humanity had hidden from for thousands and thousands of years.

A goddess even demons were wary of.

Behind her came Lucien and Carmen, the only vampires Jono could scent. Sunset hadn't arrived yet, which meant the other Night Courts would be the cavalry if they didn't finish this fight soon.

"Did you think I would stay dead?" Ashanti asked with a low laugh, never taking her eyes off Estelle's wolf form.

"I would think you'd choose the winning side for once."

"You'd give Earth over to a madman and let my children starve. I want no part of that story."

"I'm doing it to save *my* child."

"You should have found a better way than stealing what doesn't belong to you."

Ashanti drew closer, watching Andras in Estelle's body with keen black eyes. Fenrir took a chance and lunged at Hades, managing to catch the god's elbow in his teeth. Jono tasted blood, felt the scrape of bone against fangs, before Hades nearly burned his face off his skull with hellfire. Fenrir moved out of the way before Hades' attack could connect, tearing a chunk out of the other god's arm.

Fenrir spat bone and flesh out on the ground, gape-grinning at Hades. Jono didn't mind the taste in his mouth at all. *Walk away, cousin. The wolf we want is not worth your time.*

You should off the bloke, not let him go, Jono snapped.

Fenrir ignored his request, and that was the downside to giving up control—actions he wanted to take never happened. Hades' aura was sickly bright around him, the godhead that gave him immortality continuing to do so. The god glared at them, blood pouring out of the ragged hole in his elbow, the flesh already twisting to seal up the wound.

"*Walk away.*"

Hades looked over his shoulder, not at Andras and Estelle, but at something beyond them, past the trees, in the direction that explosion of magic had happened in. Then he stepped backward through the veil, disappearing from sight.

Fenrir let him go.

What the bloody fuck? You had *him!* Jono railed.

This is not where he dies.

It should be.

He will answer to Zeus. The wolf will answer to me.

Jono scratched at the connection that gave Fenrir control. *This is my kill.*

Soon.

Ashanti had almost reached Estelle, jagged iron fangs bared in a promised threat, when Andras fled her body in a burst of negative light, streaking away through the sky. Ashanti followed the trajectory of his passage with a hungry look in her eyes.

"A pity. I have not fed on a demon in centuries," she said.

Estelle had half collapsed, panting furiously for breath as Lucien and Carmen closed the distance between the trees and their location in a blur of preternatural speed. It was only then that Jono saw the shoulder-mounted grenade launcher Lucien was carrying, the weapon he'd used to stop Andras and Estelle from escaping.

"*Get up,*" Fenrir ordered, power in his words, like a call to the packs, though Estelle would never be pack.

Estelle's wolf form hunched down before she staggered to her feet, head hanging low. She didn't move for a long few seconds. When she finally turned to face them, her eyes were a bright amber once again, Andras no longer in control. She stank of anger and fear, with a lingering scent of hell in the undertones.

Her pack scent was gone.

It took a moment for Jono to understand what that meant, to realize that Estelle's god pack was as good as gone. Whatever claim she'd carried, it had disappeared, stripped away by every choice that had led her to this moment, standing before a god and finding herself wanting in his presence.

Fenrir jerked Jono's head to the side, in the direction they'd come, a clear order in the gesture. Estelle had no choice but to obey, not with two gods acting as her guards. They herded her back to the Great Lawn, her heartbeat getting faster and faster the closer they got, until it sounded as if it would beat right out of her chest.

She knew what was coming.

Fenrir let Jono see the aftermath of the fight that had occurred on the Great Lawn in their absence—torn apart bodies strewn everywhere, others lying whole on the ground, and still more wounded from the fight. He couldn't tell who they'd lost on their side, but he selfishly didn't care about numbers right then, not when he caught sight of Patrick leaning on Wade behind a golden shield.

Some of the packs were guarding people Jono assumed had surrendered, kneeling naked in the bloody grass with their hands behind their backs, fading bruises all that was left of deep wounds. Night Marchers and fae alike were chasing down stragglers at the edge of the Great Lawn and beyond. He knew the streets surrounding Central Park wouldn't be much better in terms of body count.

Take what is yours with my blessing, Fenrir said.

Control returned in an instant, though Jono knew that wasn't what the god meant. He shook his head, and the world didn't settle, not until after he shifted back to human. The change took less than a minute, a brutal tearing of flesh and bone that added to the blood scattered in the winter-dry, brittle grass underfoot.

Jono straightened up, naked and covered in blood, tasting

ozone in the back of his throat and Ginnungagap on his tongue. He licked his lips, staring at where Estelle crouched amidst the bodies of the mess she'd wrought, her back to him. People started to drift over, forming a loose circle around them, a makeshift challenge ring. The golden shield keeping Patrick and Wade safe slowly faded. Jono caught Patrick's eye, the soulbond humming between them, as strong as ever now. As much as Jono wanted to go to him, they still had unfinished business to tend to.

Jono stared at Estelle, aware of all the eyes on him, and pressed his will upon her with the backing of a god. *"Change."*

Power filled his voice, hitting Estelle like a subway train if the way she shuddered was anything to go by. Jono called forth the change in her, stripping her of the animal and replacing it with the human, until she knelt on the grass, back bowed, head hanging down, her fingers digging into dirt.

"Get up," Jono said, power resting along the edges of his sharp teeth, but not biting into his words this time. Fenrir gave him authenticity, but he'd take the authority on his own.

Estelle's shoulders drew up to her ears, and he half thought he'd have to haul her to her feet, when she finally staggered upright, pushed along by pride. She still wouldn't face him, keeping her back to him as the people she had failed to protect drew even closer, prepared to see judgment handed down.

Jono licked his lips, tasting blood. "You've done a lifetime of damage to the packs and this city. You failed to do your duty by them. You failed to keep them safe."

"I kept them safe from humans," Estelle argued in a raspy voice.

"You sold them when you didn't outright murder them by having someone else do it for you. Because that's how you kept your hands clean all these years, isn't it? Paid someone else to dirty theirs. You couldn't even kill your own husband. Had to have an Erinyes do it for you. Youssef died to keep you in power, and he died for nothing."

She turned to finally face him, chin held high, defiance in her amber eyes. It was all a lie, the truth in the way her hands shook by her sides, and the sour fear in her scent that drifted on the muggy evening air. "Keep my husband's name out of your mouth."

"I'll say what I like. You have no authority here. Not anymore."

Estelle flinched at his words, but she didn't lower her gaze, didn't show throat. "I will always be a god pack alpha."

"You aren't anything if you're dead."

He could see it in her face, in her eyes—the terror of a trapped animal with no way out. And like anyone else when faced with death, she tried to bargain her way back to life.

Estelle spread her hands in a beseeching manner that was all an act. "If I stand down, I have the right to exile."

"Bollocks. We owe you no mercy."

Estelle glanced around at the crowd surrounding them, looking for support she would never find again in the eyes staring back at her. "Is this how you'll start your rule? On a pile of bodies?"

"We'll bury the ones that matter and leave the rest to rot in unmarked graves. No one will claim you, if that's what you were hoping."

"Some alpha you are."

"I'm better than you'll ever be, with or without Fenrir."

"I knew we could never trust you."

"Fenrir never trusted *you*," Patrick called out in a raspy voice that made it clear he'd been screaming, long and loud, at some point that day. "None of the animal-god patrons did. You weren't worthy of their blessings, so you went looking to demons instead."

"Don't stand there and talk to me about making bargains when yours are the only reason you made it here today."

"Maybe so, but those bargains will keep our people safe. Yours only put some quid into your pockets," Jono said.

Estelle shifted on her feet, nostrils flaring. She wasn't nearly as bloody as others who had followed her into the fight and survived, which was typical of how she'd wielded her position all these years.

"Do you expect me to lie down and die?" she asked.

Jono stepped forward, spreading his arms wide. "You've spent months trying to kill me. I'm right here."

Estelle had no chance against him, not after everything she'd done, the side she'd chosen, the bargains she'd made. In the end, Jono's god pack had beaten hers through sheer political outmaneuvering, and Estelle was left in the unenviable position of choosing to die standing or on her knees.

Estelle chose to go out fighting, like Jono knew she would. One didn't become a god pack alpha by letting a chance to change the narrative—however minuscule—slip through their fingers. For Jono, it had been taking a meal with Marek and crossing an ocean to find where he belonged.

He refused to give up what he'd fought so hard to keep.

Estelle went for his throat, like Jono knew she would, and he was ready for it, Fenrir slipping through his soul and mind to guide him. Jono used his longer reach to grab her by the shoulder with one hand and her throat with the other, claws sinking into pale, thin flesh that would never carry a demon again.

Jono yanked her close, claws meeting within the warm flesh of her neck, blood flowing down his hand and wrist. Estelle's mouth moved around silent words as she stared at him with wide amber eyes, her own claws scraping over his arms with little strength.

"*Stay human,*" Jono said, Fenrir's power imbuing the order with a command she couldn't hope to fight.

Estelle shuddered in his hold, amber eyes going wide as she realized his will, backed by Fenrir, was something that would break her. Then Jono tore out her throat so deep he could see the shiny white vertebrae of her spine before blood bubbled up to cover the bone.

Jono dropped Estelle like the rubbish she was, watching as she fell to her knees, hands rising to her throat and the blood pouring out of it, jaw tipped down at an unnatural angle with no muscle to support it. Estelle slumped to the side, gravity pulling her down, until she lay on the ground, adding her blood to the mix that had already spilled.

Jono stepped over Estelle, gaze catching on the way her fingers twitched, listening as her heart lost its rhythm. She died packless, powerless, her passing witnessed by the one who stole her mantle, claimed her rank, and sank his teeth in a city that was no longer hers. Some people deserved to see what they lost walk away from them as they died.

Jono hoped Estelle remembered that in whatever hell she ended up in.

No one cheered, but relief was a palpable thing in the air. Sage shifted back to human form while Wade hauled Patrick over to Jono, unaware that Patrick looked as if he could stand on his own two feet, albeit shakily. Patrick's heartbeat cut through the slowly rising voices from the pack alphas who realized they were finally free of Estelle and Youssef. Jono drank him in, unable to look away from the tired green eyes that didn't have a trace of demonic presence in them.

"You're a mess," Patrick said, reaching for Jono before hesitating, hand pausing midair.

Jono knew what that hesitation meant, what was probably running through Patrick's mind right about then, and he was having none of it. Jono wrapped his fingers around Patrick's wrist and reeled him in, Wade gladly giving him up. Jono framed Patrick's face with both hands, breathing him in—the bitterness, the sense of home—lips grazing the corner of his mouth.

"I'm here," Jono murmured.

Patrick's hands found their way to Jono's hips, touch cold. "I'm sorry."

"Let's not start that, love. It wasn't your fault. It wasn't *you*."

Patrick's breath hitched in his lungs, fingers digging into Jono's skin, his voice coming out tired and small. "Sure as fuck felt like it."

And oh, there was so much to unpack in that statement, but this wasn't the place to do it. All Jono could do was assure the man he loved that he didn't blame him for the actions of others done with Patrick's own hands, and never would.

"You would never hurt me, and you didn't."

Patrick's eyes searched his, looking for all the forgiveness and absolution Jono would never deny him. "I came back."

The words ghosted across Jono's lips, like a benediction of sorts, meant to soothe them both amidst the massacre they'd survived. He kissed Patrick with a careful gentleness that left his hands shaking, leaving bloody streaks across pale, freckled skin.

"I know. I'm sorry I couldn't find you."

The confession tore at Jono, words he wished he didn't have to say, but they'd promised not to lie to each other. The soulbond hadn't been broken, but they hadn't known demons could block it. Fenrir had never touched it when the god took over his body.

Patrick wrapped his arms around Jono and hugged him tight. "Even if you can never find me, I'll always come back."

Jono hugged him back, chin resting on Patrick's head, never wanting to let go.

"We factored in the fight, but I don't think we factored in the aftermath," Sage said as she approached, her long hair covering her bare breasts. Other werecreatures who hadn't yet shifted were changing back to human, joining the rest of them standing about in the nude.

"The mayor and Casale promised us a challenge ring," Jono reminded her.

"Yes, and it's our responsibility to bury the bodies."

"We will take our wounded and dead home. The rest may return to the ground. Consider it payment for the interference of our elders," a new voice said, ringing through the air.

Jono lifted his head, looking over at where Brigid strode toward them from the direction of the hawthorn path.

"What do you know about Cernunnos?" Patrick asked tiredly, rubbing at a vivid red line running from elbow to wrist on his left arm. Jono didn't like the look of it, or what it might mean.

Neither did he care for the burn marks that he could see on Patrick's skin.

"It was the Horned One's magic which stole life from this island and gave it to someone else. For that, the roots of your iron city shall be fed," Brigid said, her aura burning bright. The fae guard escort she had arrived with fanned out around her, silver-edged weapons in hand. The metal made Jono's skin prickle.

A wave of green spread outward from the flower cape she wore, rolling across the dead winter grass and returning it to life. The wave picked up speed, crashing into the tree line and moving past it. Jono watched as, in less than a minute, the trees lost their winter dullness and started sprouting leaves, winter turning back to summer.

The grass rapidly grew over the dead, the earth churning like quicksand, as many of the bodies sank into the dirt, swallowed up until not even blood remained. Brigid's magic didn't touch Estelle's body though, leaving it aboveground. Neither did it touch the dead whose loyalty had been to Jono and Patrick's god pack.

Those they would bury and grieve over.

The rest could rot.

"What about the ones in the street?" Wade asked, jumping around a body half sunk into the dirt.

"Those remain for your pack to deal with," Brigid said.

"They'll be evidence," Patrick said, straightening up and pulling away from Jono. He didn't go far, taking Jono's hand in his after another brief moment of hesitation. Jono squeezed his hand lightly, offering comfort.

"We won't claim the bodies that don't belong to us when the police are finished with them," Jono promised.

As for those who'd sided with Estelle and had survived, unless any of them passed muster with Fenrir, Jono was going to start his reign handing down exiles if the lot of them managed to evade jail time.

"It is your city to rule now. I hope you wield that power with a kinder hand than your predecessors," Brigid said.

She didn't sound like she had much hope in that area, but Jono let the subtle insult slide. This was a battle he wasn't willing to fight after the one that just ended.

"We appreciate the alliance you've given us," Jono said, twisting the meaning into a thank you that wouldn't leave them beholden to the fae.

Brigid's gaze never wavered. "It was never meant to last forever."

"I never asked for it to."

"We will guard your borders during the day for a while longer. Consider it payment for what Cernunnos wrought."

Jono wasn't surprised she'd want to clear any perceived debts. The fae hated owing anyone but didn't mind being the ones holding claim to debts. "What did that arsehole do?"

"Kept Hannah alive," Patrick said in a quiet voice that didn't sound like him at all.

His scent was a tangle of emotions that Jono didn't want anyone else to be witness to. Patrick's shields weren't locked down, leaving him vulnerable in a way Jono knew he hated. But it told Jono more than the possession had happened while he was with the enemy, and they weren't in a place to discuss it.

Mostly, Jono wanted to herd Patrick home, put him to bed, and never let him leave the flat again.

"Órlaith," Brigid called out. "It is time to go home."

Gerard and Órlaith came forward through the crowd. The Summer Lady kissed Gerard firmly on the mouth. "I'll finish my duties in the Seelie Court and then return to Dublin. I'll ring you when I arrive."

"Stay safe," Gerard said, lifting her hand to his lips to kiss the back of her knuckles. Streaks of blood were splashed across her clothes and speckled over her skin, but she carried no wounds on her body.

The fae were deadly, no matter what they looked like or what Court they came from.

Órlaith left Central Park by Brigid's side, leaving the scent of summer behind. The greenery of Central Park was startling after nearly a month of winter-like landscape, the life once sucked out of the plants now returned. Jono wondered if the rest of the parks in the five boroughs had been returned to their summer glory, or if it was just this one.

"We'll need to deal with the police and then I'm guessing the press." Sage eyed them before shaking her head. "You'll need clothes if you're going before the cameras."

Jono really didn't want to, but he realized he needed to. He was the alpha of the New York City god pack now, as was Patrick. Except he wanted Patrick squirreled away somewhere safe, which left leading up to Jono right now.

"Let's get everyone sorted," Jono said.

Patrick sighed wearily. "Sure."

"We're getting you seen to first, and then Wade can take you home."

"I'm not leaving you."

The stubborn twist to Patrick's mouth was familiar, even if the fear wasn't, and Jono didn't have it in him to argue. He raised his hand, swiping his thumb across Patrick's lips. "All right, love. But you're staying out of sight of the bloody vultures with cameras."

Patrick nodded, a squint to his eyes that told Jono he must have a headache. "I never got my fucking phone back from the US Attorney's Office, and Andras took the borrowed one."

"Where were they holding you?"

"Hamilton Heights. In the challenge ring."

Territory that was rightfully theirs now as the New York City god pack, but Jono had no desire to set foot on that property.

"We'll let the police handle that crime scene."

Patrick dragged a hand over his face and squared his shoulders, ready to do what needed to be done, as always. "Let's go find Casale. Maybe Sage should call our crisis PR company."

"I can think of several statements we can put out," Sage said, flicking blood off her fingertips.

"I'll let you handle that," Jono said as they started to walk toward the direction they'd arrived in at the beginning of the challenge, Ginnungagap fading around them.

Sage took up position on his right, while Wade glued himself to Patrick's left side. Jono didn't let go of Patrick as they walked, presenting a united front to the other pack alphas gathered around. Some of those alphas would stay behind to ensure the bodies of their fallen would be treated with respect by first responders.

It wasn't the most auspicious start to their rule of the werecreature community in New York City, but power like that never transferred easily. Jono knew they'd rule better than Estelle and Youssef ever could though. He'd regret the blood spilled and lives lost, but not what it brought them.

A chance to breathe.

30

Getting Jono through security in the SOA field office Monday morning took a little more time than Patrick thought it should. He could feel the stares of everyone passing through the lobby, and even if he couldn't hear the whispers, Jono could.

Jono was doing a better job at ignoring the attention than Patrick. He'd left his sunglasses in the car, refusing to hide his eyes anymore in public. He'd dressed in a nice button-down and dark jeans. Meanwhile, Patrick's T-shirt could've done with a tumble in the dryer, and the to-go coffee cup in his hand was as much a crutch as his dagger right then.

He had his phone back, delivered by Danai on Sunday morning when they'd been holed up in their flat. She'd retrieved it from Preston with a police escort out of the PCB just in case. US Attorney Mia Santiago was still hospitalized and recovering from an unwilling demonic possession. From what she'd said, everyone in the US Attorney's Office was undergoing a review of their souls before a cleansing.

Whether or not the government unearthed any other demons

or ties to the Dominion Sect, it still cast a bad light on the actions leading up to the decision to charge him. Danai had said that was in their favor, but Patrick was hard-pressed to see the good in that.

He and his pack had spent Sunday in long interviews with the PCB and the SOA, giving testimony for the various cases coming out of the aftermath of the challenge. Every member of Estelle's god pack who hadn't died were currently locked up in jail awaiting charges if appropriate. If they managed to get set free, they had Jono and Fenrir's judgment to look forward to.

Jono and Patrick had taken pains to claim the Hamilton Heights property as their territory because that was what was expected of them. They wanted absolutely nothing to do with the property Estelle and Youssef had called home, even though it was legally theirs.

Sage was working with her firm to get in touch with the attorney who'd been employed by Estelle's god pack. They needed to work out the legal documents that would ultimately deed a couple of Manhattan blocks to Patrick and Jono. While they didn't want it, they needed to keep it.

Patrick very much did not want to become a landlord. The property taxes were going to be brutal, not to mention the cleaning and cleansing costs associated with purging those buildings of the embedded scent of terror. He had enough nightmares to deal with at the moment.

But the buildings were theirs, rightfully and legally, as proven by how they'd been able to enter the home unimpeded and grant passage to the police and federal agents looking for evidence. The ancient threshold had recognized them as owners, reacting to their presence. They'd stayed long enough to grant access before getting the fuck out of that toxic place.

The PCB was handling the god pack, while the SOA was handling the mess at the Ritz-Carlton. The penthouse in that hotel was the site of a fertility rite the SOA was still investigating. From what Setsuna had told Patrick, it had been reserved by a member of the Wisteria Coven for a guest of theirs. It seemed that family had never gotten over his inability to return their lost child and had been sucked into an alliance with the Dominion Sect.

"You're cleared to proceed," the security guard said, handing Jono a laminated guest pass.

"Cheers," Jono muttered, clipping it to his shirt.

Patrick led him toward the elevators, and they took one directly to the thirtieth floor where Setsuna awaited their arrival. The weekend had been a shitshow. Patrick had skipped going to a hospital for care because there was nothing they'd be able to do. You couldn't heal the kind of damage done to his soul with pills or potions. He'd suffered enough wounds in that area over the years to know what worked and what didn't, and what would never heal.

His VA-assigned therapist had left Patrick a voicemail, saying he was available whenever Patrick was ready to talk. Patrick didn't know when he'd reach out, but he would.

Someday.

Being surrounded by his pack had helped steady him more than anything else. The difference of now compared to when he was younger and alone was starkly apparent. Wade hadn't left his side, claiming their guest bedroom with the very clear intention of turning it into a secondary hoarding space if the number of clothes he'd brought over was anything to go by.

Patrick knew Wade felt guilty about not being able to save him, and that was an issue they'd need to address sooner rather than later. It wasn't Wade's fault, and never would be, but emotions weren't rational in the wake of trauma.

Sage was neck-deep in pack politics and wedding planning, but she still saw them every day. Getting the packs situated after the change in power was never-ending work, and he was forever grateful for her presence. As for the wedding, Patrick had his final suit fitting today after the meeting, and there was no way he'd be missing it. How he'd convince Sage to go on her honeymoon after everything that had happened still had him stumped.

"All right?" Jono asked, hand a warm, steady weight against the small of Patrick's back.

Patrick wasn't sure what he was projecting at the moment, but he didn't mind Jono checking in. "As much as I can be when I'm about to get read the riot act by my boss."

The elevator slowed to a stop, and the doors opened. Patrick knew where he needed to go and led Jono to a conference room. A spare office was set aside for visiting high-ranking officials, but Setsuna had chosen to hold the meeting outside it.

She was waiting for them in the conference room, a silence ward already cast against the walls, her rosewood cane with its carved Shinto shrine resting against the wall. She'd taken the seat at the head of the table, a stack of folders resting near her left hand, along with his badge and semiautomatic HK USP 9mm tactical pistol.

Setsuna studied him with dark eyes, her brow slightly furrowed. "You're not shielded."

Patrick shrugged stiffly before taking a seat halfway down the table. "Hades burned out the anchors Persephone set in my bones. Holding up my shields has been painful."

He'd skipped that defense since regaining control of his body and soul in Central Park. It meant his emotions were an open book to every werecreature coming around, but Patrick couldn't fix that. Not right now.

"Does she know?"

"I'm not in the mood to deal with gods right now, and it's not like I need her shields anymore. I'm done hiding."

Persephone had set the anchors when he was eight to help keep him hidden. She'd reset them last year after he nearly burned himself out before the soulbond came into existence. Both times had been painful experiences, and Patrick had no desire to go through it again.

With his identity revealed to the public, there was no need to hide his magic and soul from anyone who would be searching for him. The world knew who he was, what he was, and where he lived now. There was no shoving all of that back into Pandora's box.

Setsuna's gaze shifted from Patrick to Jono, the faint concern becoming a cool reserve. "You've caused quite a commotion, Jonothon."

"I wouldn't have needed to if the government actually dealt with the hunters back when we warned it of the threat. Don't try to blame us for your failure. We aren't having it," Jono said with a mean smile.

"It's the *we* aspect that is a problem, specifically Patrick's inclusion in it."

"I'm not giving up my pack," Patrick said, looking her dead in the eye.

Setsuna sighed irritably. "I'm well aware of that, as is the rest of the country at this point after what happened Saturday. It's still a problem with your position."

Patrick eyed his gun and badge where they rested on the table. "Are you reinstating me in full?"

"With ethical restrictions. You'll be recused from any case involving werecreatures. If a case you handle leads to anyone with ties to any werecreature community, you will be immediately removed from the case, and it will be transferred to someone else."

"That's a legal headache I can't believe the lawyers allowed."

"The Dominion Sect is still a threat. You are too integral to stopping them to deny you the support being an SOA agent provides."

"And after?"

Setsuna tapped a finger gently against the tabletop. "We'll cross that bridge when we get there."

Patrick turned his head to look at Jono. "That means I'm getting fired."

"I didn't say that."

Jono settled his hand on Patrick's thigh, squeezing gently. "There's enough work running our god pack. Pay is decent. You could even have a holiday."

Patrick snorted out a tired laugh. "I'm still owed airfare and hotel from my interrupted vacation to Maui last year."

"We'll get there one day."

If he crashed and burned out of the SOA after this, it'd be worth it to stay by Jono's side.

Setsuna slid his gun and badge closer to him. "Welcome back, Special Agent Patrick Collins."

He didn't hesitate to reach for them.

"PATRICK."

He jerked awake, pulling free of a nightmare where he was being dragged underwater by some unseen force, drowning while something else crawled inside him and hollowed him out. Patrick blinked his eyes open, staring up at where Jono stood over him next to the bed. The worried frown on his face made Patrick feel guilty.

"Yeah, I'm awake," Patrick muttered, rubbing at his face.

Jono's touch on his shoulder tightened a little, but not enough to wrinkle the button-down Patrick wore. While Jono had showered, Patrick had meant to close his eyes for only a few seconds. Apparently those few seconds had turned into longer, because Jono was now out of the shower, fully dressed, and ready to head out to Sage and Marek's rehearsal dinner.

"I thought you could use a few more minutes, but then your scent changed," Jono said.

Patrick grimaced and shoved himself to a sitting position. Not having permanent shields anchored to his bones that stayed locked down even when he wasn't consciously powering them would take some getting used to.

"I'm all right."

He wasn't, and Jono saw through the lie for the truth Patrick desperately wanted to keep hidden. Jono cupped his jaw, thumb stroking over his cheek with gentle pressure.

"You know I don't blame you for what Andras did," Jono said softly.

Patrick's gaze flicked down to Jono's right arm, the limb whole, but he saw the ruin of it at night when he dreamed. The werevirus meant Jono wouldn't live the rest of his life as an amputee, but that didn't stop Patrick from remembering it was his hand that had thrown the attack spell at Jono.

"I couldn't stop it. I watched it happen and did nothing."

The words were bitter on his tongue, and Jono's insistence that it wasn't his fault couldn't stop Patrick's guilt.

Jono leaned down to kiss him carefully on the mouth, lips firm and warm. "And that's why there's nothing to forgive, so don't apologize. I'll keep saying that until you believe it, for as long as you need to hear it."

Patrick swung his legs over the side of the bed, hoping the dress pants hadn't gotten too wrinkled from his impromptu nap. Sleep had been difficult to come by since Saturday, and tonight was too important to miss because Jono thought he needed a nap.

"I don't want to be late," Patrick said as he stood.

Jono handed him the gray silk tie he'd chosen for dinner that night. "We have time."

The rehearsal dinner was happening hours after the actual walk-through of the ceremony's venue. It had given them enough time to head home and get ready after walking around in the summer heat.

Patrick went to their bathroom to fix his tie, deftly knotting it around his throat. He was adjusting the knot when his phone started ringing.

"Who is it?" Patrick called out.

"It's a number, no name."

Patrick frowned and left the bathroom to grab his phone from the nightstand. He didn't recognize the number. It took a moment for him to realize it had the Salem area code, and when he did, he dropped the phone like it had burned him, breaking out into a cold sweat

"Who is it?" Jono asked with a frown as he buttoned up his suit jacket.

Patrick swallowed dryly. "Eloise."

He stared at his phone like it might bite him. The call eventually rolled over to voicemail. It beeped a minute later with a message notification. Patrick took a steadying breath before picking up his phone again to listen to the message.

"Patrick, this is your grandmother. I'm calling because I don't know if you've seen my press conference, or if Director Abuku has relayed my messages to you. I want you to know that your family misses you, that *I* miss you, and we would really like to meet with you. Please, give me a call."

The message clicked off after she listed out her phone number, and Patrick couldn't decide whether to save or delete it.

"Will you call her back?" Jono asked.

"I don't know."

"It's okay if you don't want to."

"I'm not calling her when we're about to leave for the reception dinner."

"Wasn't suggesting that." Jono took the phone from him and slipped it into Patrick's inner suit jacket pocket. "I'm just saying you don't owe the lot of them anything."

"I don't even know how she got my number."

"Someone probably leaked it."

Patrick blew out a harsh breath, licking sweat off his upper lip. "She said she missed me. How can you miss someone you don't know?"

Jono looked at him with a softness in his wolf-bright blue eyes that Patrick didn't believe he deserved some days. "She knew you once."

"I barely remember her."

"And that's okay." Patrick flexed his fingers against nothing, only stopping when Jono took his hand and held it with a strong grip. "If you don't want to ring her, then don't. You're allowed to have boundaries."

Patrick knew that, he did, but believing it again after being possessed was a struggle. He was tired from sleepless nights, from knowing that Andras had seen every last thought and memory in his head, and there was no defending against that.

The thing about having a demon in your soul was the arrogance meant stuff slipped through. It became a two-way street of brief, haunting moments where Patrick had been a passenger in his own body, trapped in a tiny corner of his mind, listening in on conversations the demon never thought he'd be able to capitalize on.

While the Dominion Sect now knew Patrick had kept the piece of the Morrígan's staff, *he* knew Ethan was running out of time. Macaria's godhead was fraying, Hannah was dying, and Ethan was desperate.

It had been over twenty years since Ethan had bound himself to Hannah to try to control Macaria. Except the godhead had twisted too deep into Hannah's soul to ever be removed easily, and it needed to be channeled through a clean, unmarked soul for a safe transfer into a new host. If Hannah died, then the godhead would disappear, and Ethan would lose the only chance he had at becoming a god.

Babies were blank slates, empty of any possible personality. The perfect vessel to smooth down the edges of a ragged godhead. Ethan had figured out a way to reach his goal, but the baby couldn't survive in a decaying body. Cernunnos might have made it possible to keep Hannah's body alive for a little while longer, but it wouldn't last. Life never did.

They had until Samhain to figure out how to stop Ethan, and Patrick didn't even know where to begin.

"Let's get going, yeah?" Jono said quietly.

Patrick nodded, willing his swirling thoughts and uncertainty to the back of his mind. He didn't want to bring any of that negativity to the dinner; Sage and Marek didn't deserve that on the eve of their wedding.

He slipped his dagger into its sheath against his lower back, smoothed down the lapels of his suit jacket, made sure his hair hadn't gotten totally destroyed from his nap, and followed Jono out of the apartment.

The gargoyles had taken to perching on the stoop and front of the building more than the roof these days. Reporters had stopped staking out the building, but the street was seeing more traffic than usual due to curious people driving or walking by. They'd already had to warn Wade he wasn't allowed to toss things at anyone on the street who annoyed him.

Jono slung his arm over Patrick's shoulders, drawing him close as they walked to where the Mustang was parked. Patrick could smell Jono's cologne, the subtle notes his favorite scent.

"You smell good," Patrick said.

Jono laughed softly, pressing the key fob to unlock the car up ahead. "So do you."

They got into the car, and Jono aimed them in the direction of the restaurant where the rehearsal dinner was being held. The venue—a three-star Michelin affair overlooking a revitalized Central Park—had been closed for the private event. When they arrived, a valet waited to take their keys out front so they wouldn't have to worry about parking.

The door opened before Patrick could reach for it, and they entered a low-lit, intimate space, classical music playing low in the background to dull the echo of everyone's voices.

"You made it!" Sage said with a smile, scooting her chair back to stand and come greet them.

"Wouldn't have missed it," Patrick said.

"Of course you wouldn't." Sage gave him an easy hug, standing taller than him in the stiletto heels she wore that matched her white blazer dress. "Come on, let's get you both a drink."

She led them back to the table that had been set up beneath the chandelier in the center of the room. Wade waved at them, grinning widely, the only one at the table without a multitude of wineglasses at his place setting. Their pack, Emma, Leon, and Marek's immediate family who'd flown in from out of state were all who were attending the elaborate dinner. Patrick and Jono were welcomed with a round of happy *hellos.*

Patrick settled into the moment, wanting to remember it, glad that whatever Andras had done, at least the demon hadn't taken his memories. He laughed and talked with his pack and friends, all of them refusing to talk about work or pack politics. They ate their way through several courses, and if Patrick had more wine than was strictly appropriate, well, Jono hadn't cut him off yet.

Once the second meat course was finally served, and everyone had a chance to taste it, Marek cleared his throat. The easy conversation happening at the table died down as everyone turned their attention to the nearly wedded couple.

"It's apparently tradition for gifts to be given to bridesmaids and groomsmen before the wedding as a thank-you, but since we're all perfectly capable of buying whatever we want, Sage and I decided to pitch in for a different sort of gift with Emma and Leon's help," Marek said, looking at Patrick and Jono.

"Aren't you supposed to do that when you're getting ready tomorrow?" Wade asked.

"We can do it whenever we want. It's our wedding," Sage said.

"What she means is that she helped draw up some legal documents for us and Marek greased the wheels of the government to get it signed off on," Emma said, a smile tugging at her lips.

"Why are you giving gifts? You're in the wedding, you're supposed to get the gifts," Wade said, licking the back of his fork.

"What's the gift?" Jono asked as he buttered a fresh baked roll.

"Since you're officially recognized as the alphas of the New York City god pack by the powers that be, we wanted to make sure you stayed that way," Leon said.

"We aren't giving up our territory now that we've finally claimed it."

Emma leaned to the side to dig through her purse, coming up with a manila envelope. She passed it across the table to them with a bright smile. "Territory is one thing. Visas are another, and we've been wanting to do this for a while now."

Jono leaned forward to take it. "What do you mean?"

"Open it."

Patrick watched as Jono pulled out several sheets of paper, holding them so that they could both see. The documents turned out to be a property deed, business license, and an official-looking agreement. Little stickers saying *Sign Here* were interspersed on various pages, pointing out signature blocks with Jono's name printed beneath the line.

"What?" Jono said, drawing out the word.

"We're giving you Tempest," Leon said.

"Consider it our pack's tithe," Emma added.

"You would not believe the hoops I had to go through to get that liquor license transferred into your name," Marek said.

"Being a business owner and employer means your visa can get upgraded, and it'll make it easier for you to apply for citizenship if you don't want to wait on becoming a naturalized citizen," Sage said.

Patrick gently tugged the documents out of Jono's hands before he crumpled them. "You'd have to give up tea if you become American."

"Sod that," Jono said gruffly. "The US allows for dual citizenship."

"Yeah, but think of the taxes. We already have way too much to pay now. You want to pay it to two countries?"

In answer, Jono turned to kiss Patrick. "I'll pay whatever I need to if it means I get to stay here with you."

The promise tasted sweet on Patrick's tongue, sweeter than the decadent chocolate cake that was eventually served for the dessert course.

31

Sage and Marek's wedding ceremony and reception were being held in two different locations. At the time of reserving the venues late last year, they'd been worried about needing to cross pack territories, risking a fight on their wedding day despite security.

That was no longer an issue.

With Jono and Patrick holding New York City as their territory, acknowledged by domestic and foreign god packs once it hit the news, and backed by Fenrir, they didn't have to worry about an attack from werecreatures during the wedding. Every other threat was fair game, but considering the excruciating focus by the press, Jono held out hope nothing would go wrong today.

Marek, as a true seer, was entitled to federal protection. With everything that had happened and the vision he'd had, the government was picking up the security tab for his wedding. Packs whose loyalty wasn't in question had promised to patrol the blocks surrounding the chosen venues as a precaution.

The guest list was small, less than one hundred, with the majority of invitees consisting of Jono's pack, the Tempest pack, fellow werecreatures, select coworkers from PreterWorld and Gentry & Thyme, several old university friends, and a number of tech company owners. Surprisingly, no one had backed out as a guest at the last minute, despite everything that had happened over the weekend. Sage had even squeezed in two extra settings for Gerard and Órlaith, because money wasn't an issue, and after everything they'd done for the pack, it was only polite to invite them.

The pair's presence meant the flowers Sage had ordered for the wedding, from bouquets to centerpieces to the veritable waterfall set to cover the pergola at the altar on the rooftop garden at Rockefeller Plaza, were blooming brilliantly. The pictures Patrick had texted a few minutes ago from the venue were proof of that. Jono was afraid he'd sneeze at an inopportune moment during the ceremony.

"Well? What do you think?"

Jono looked over at the stairs leading up to the second floor of Sage and Marek's flat, watching Sage walking down them with Emma behind her.

"You look gorgeous," Jono said, taking her in.

Sage smiled brilliantly at him, the couture ballgown falling around her in a cloud of ivory organza, lace adorning the bodice and top of the skirt. It was off the shoulder and sleeveless in deference to the summer heat, and her long hair had been styled back in a sleek ponytail that curled at the ends. The veil was pinned near the nape of her neck, falling around her shoulders. She wore her diamond engagement ring, and more diamonds glittered on her ears and around her throat.

The whirlwind of activity had finally slowed, the makeup artists having departed, though the wedding photographer remained. She was a friend of someone in one of the packs under their protection, a mundane human, but utterly unfazed in the midst of the preternatural community. The woman didn't smell afraid at all, and neither was her partner, who was responsible for photographing Marek.

Marek was already on his way to the venue, having left fifteen minutes ago. Sage was, as ever, perfectly punctual when it came to her schedule. The photographer captured Sage and Emma coming down the stairs, Emma's royal purple dress falling to her knees. The wedding color scheme was royal purple and natural green, and Jono was forever glad they hadn't gone with blue.

Sage did a complete turn to show off the back of her wedding dress, the full skirt swishing softly around her slender frame. Jono smiled at the happiness in her scent, threaded through with excitement. Jono held out the cascade bridal bouquet of purple orchids and white roses interspersed with green leaves.

"Ready to get married?" Jono asked as she took it.

"I've *been* ready," Sage said feelingly.

"She's just happy the planning is over," Emma said with a laugh.

"That, too."

They left the flat for the small limousine waiting for them in the street. The driver had the door open, and Jono helped Sage and Emma into the back before climbing in after them. The drive to Rockefeller Plaza was made in good time, though Sage kept checking in with Jono to make sure they were on schedule. Manhattan traffic being what it was, they'd factored in the start of rush hour to ensure they wouldn't be late for the midafternoon ceremony.

A parking spot in front of the entrance to the building with the rooftop garden at the Rockefeller Plaza had been cordoned off, and attendants were ready to usher them upstairs. Jono ignored the mobiles pointed their way from pedestrians catching their arrival, focused on making sure Sage and Emma exited the limousine safely.

Emma held up Sage's skirt to keep it from dragging on the pavement, only releasing it when they were inside the building. They took a private elevator all the way to the roof, arriving in an open space that could have been used as the reception, except they'd opted to have the meal at the Rainbow Room instead.

Sage's wedding planner greeted them with a smile, not a hair out of place as she clutched her iPad. "We're ready when you are."

"Let's go," Sage said, smiling widely.

The entrance to the outdoor garden area was blocked off by an opaque white tent beyond the glass doors, hiding Sage's arrival from view. Emma set about sorting Sage's dress and veil for the walk down the aisle as the wedding planner spoke into her walkie-talkie to address the DJ for the ceremony.

The soft strains of "Air" from *Water Music* started up, drifting in the air. Jono and Sage stepped out of sight of the tent opening as Emma went first, attendants pulling aside the drapes with gold rope. Once they dropped back down again, Jono extended his arm to Sage, who slipped her hand around the bend of his elbow.

"I'm happy for you," Jono said, leaning over to kiss her gently on the top of her head.

She was pack, and she was their dire, but more than that, she was his friend. Jono hadn't had many of those who counted over the years, but Sage would forever be that and family to him.

"Let's get me married," Sage said.

Jono escorted her to the tent entrance, the drapes getting lifted, and they stepped out into the bright summer day. The aisle between the rows of chairs was made up of white rose petals, the crushed scent of them drifting up as they walked toward the altar where Marek waited, Leon standing as his best man.

The outline of Manhattan's buildings pierced the sky around them, St. Patrick's Cathedral a gorgeous backdrop off to their left. The garden was blooming with an abundance of flowers, the grass vibrant, and the sounds of the city had been quieted by a silence ward.

Sage's grip grew tighter as they closed the distance to Marek, who looked as if he were about to cry. When they reached the altar, Jono let Sage go. She reached for Marek on her own while

Emma adjusted the skirt of her ball gown before claiming the bridal bouquet. Jono retreated to the only remaining empty seat in the front row on the bride's side between Patrick and Wade.

"They look happy," Patrick said in a voice barely above a whisper as the judge appointed for the ceremony welcomed everyone to Sage and Marek's wedding.

"Yeah, they do," Jono said.

He settled his hand on Patrick's thigh, squeezing gently, watching a moment unfold for their pack they hadn't been sure would happen.

Patrick tipped his head in Jono's direction. "What about you? Are you happy?"

Jono tore his gaze away from the altar to look Patrick in the eye, seeing the shadows there that had become more prominent since Saturday. In the wake of everything that had happened, the knowledge of what they still had to face, Jono refused to lose the moments, big and small, that were important.

"I'll always be happy with you," Jono murmured.

Patrick's smile was small but real, brightening his eyes, a wordless promise returned on a beautiful summer day that Jono would always remember.

~~~

The Soulbound series concludes in the epic finale *A Veiled & Hallowed Eve*, available now!

IF YOU LIKE science fiction romance and are a fan of comics and their movie counterparts, check out Hailey Turner's Metahuman Files series, starting with In the Wreckage.

Don't miss out on sneak peeks, exciting news, and more! Sign up for Hailey Turner's newsletter to stay up-to-date on her upcoming books.
~~~

GLOSSARY

Short descriptions of words, acronyms, and phrases used in the story that weren't readily explained in text. Included as well are character names.

Áltsé Hashké: (Pronunciation: Aht SEH hash KEH) Immortal. Diné (given English name: Navajo) trickster god.

Abuku, Setsuna: Witch. Director who oversees and leads the Supernatural Operations Agency.

Academy: K-12 school that teaches magic to practitioners of all affinities and designations. All provide boarding options to students.

Andras: Demon. Ranked as a Great Marquis of Hell. He sows discord in humanity and is in charge of thirty legions of lesser demons.

Ares: Immortal. Greek god of war.

Ashanti: Immortal. Goddess and mother of all vampires. Takes the shape of an Asanbosam vampire out of West African myths.

Bailey, Spencer: Mage. Former combat mage with the Mage Corps, currently a PIA special agent. He is a soulbreaker with the power to put the dead to rest and travels with a psychopomp who takes the form of an ocelot.

Beacot, Sage: Weretiger. A Diné lawyer who works for the fae law firm Gentry & Thyme. Dire to Jono and Patrick's god pack.

Breckenridge, Gerard (Captain): Immortal. Current identity of Cú Chulainn. *See*, Cú Chulainn.

Brigid: Immortal. Celtic goddess associated with fertility, spring, healing, smithing, and poetry. Spring Queen of the Seelie Court. Daughter of the Dagda and member of the Tuatha Dé Danann.

Carmen: Succubus. First known recorded appearance was in Venice, Italy.

Casale, Giovanni: Human. Chief of the NYPD's Preternatural Crimes Bureau.

Cernunnos: Immortal. A Celtic god generally known as the "Horned God" or the "Horned One." He has horns on his head and is associated with stags, horned serpents, dogs, bulls, and rats. He is interpreted as the god of animals, nature, fertility, travel, commerce, and bi-directionality.

Choirs: A descriptive rank. The nine orders of angels, separated into three hierarchies, are listed out in certain versions of Christian lore.

Citadel: United States military academy for magic users. Located in Maryland. All Academies across the nation feed into the Citadel. Mages get automatic inclusion. All other kinds of magic users need recommendations.

Collins, Patrick: Mage. Former combat mage with the Mage Corps, currently an SOA special agent. Has a tainted soul and crippled magic. Is technically a mage in name only due to a soul wound. Co-leader of the god pack he shares with Jono.

Cú Chulainn: (Pronunciation: ku CULL-ann) Immortal. Celtic god and son of the god Lugh. Member of the Tuatha Dé Danann. Irish warrior. Carries the *Gáe Bulg* in fights. Currently hiding under a mortal identity by the name of Gerard Breckenridge.

Dagda, the: Immortal. Celtic god affiliated with life, death, crops, and seasons. Member and king of the Tuatha Dé Danann. Husband to the Morrígan.

de Vere, Jonothon: God pack werewolf. Originally from London, England, currently resides in New York City. Alpha of a god pack he co-leads with Patrick.

Dire: A rank held only within a god pack. The moniker is taken from the dire wolf but has been shortened to account for different werecreature species. Essentially a rank held by a loyal pack member who helps enforce the alphas' orders.

Dominion Sect: A shadowy terrorist group consisting of mundane humans, rogue magic users, immortals aligned with the hells, and other preternatural creatures intent on destroying the veil between worlds so that hell and its denizens can reign on earth. Some members are attempting to steal godheads in order to ensure their hold on power in the new world they hope to create.

Erinyes: Immortal. Also known as Furies. Greek deities of vengeance.

Espinoza, Wade: Teenaged fledgling fire dragon. Part of Jono and Patrick's god pack.

Fae: Supernatural beings who reside in Tír na nÓg. There are lesser or higher fae depending on their status and species. *See also*, Tuatha Dé Danann.

Fenrir: Immortal. Wolf in the Norse pantheon. Patron to a god pack.

***Gáe Bulg*:** Artifact. Cú Chulainn's spear. Translated as "spear of mortal death."

Ginnungagap: Primordial void. Belongs to the Norse myths.

Godhead: Primordial power belonging to immortals that gives them life. The strength of their power can be altered by worship, or lack thereof.

God pack: A pack of werecreatures infected with the god strain of the werevirus. They act as spokespeople for hidden werecreature packs in their territory. They are supported by monetary tithes from the packs under their protection. Very few retain a connection to their animal-god patrons.

Greene, Ethan: Mage. Was a double agent formally employed by the SOA. Is currently a mercenary and allied with the Dominion Sect.

Greene, Hannah: Mage. Currently a vessel. Spiritually deceased.

Hellraisers: A US Department of the Preternatural Special Forces team Patrick once belonged to.

Hermes: Immortal. Greek messenger god and god of trade, thieves, travelers, sports, athletes, border crossings, and guide to the Underworld.

Hernandez, Leon: Werewolf. Partner to Emma Zhang and co-leader of the Tempest pack.

Khan, Youssef: God pack werewolf. Alpha of the New York City god pack.

Krossed Knights: An organization of hunters that formed in the United States centuries ago. An offshoot of European hunter groups that came out of the Crusades.

Kū: Immortal. Hawaiian god of war, politics, farming and fishing. One of the four great gods in the Hawaiian pantheon.

Ley lines: Metaphysical rivers of powers that drain into nexuses.

Lucien: Master vampire. Was a soldier in William the Conqueror's army before being turned by Ashanti. Currently a weapons and magic trafficker. Is wanted by many governments.

Maat: Immortal. Egyptian goddess of truth, justice, wisdom, the stars, law, morality, order, harmony, the seasons, and cosmic balance.

Macaria: Immortal. Greek goddess of the blessed death and Hades' daughter.

Mage: Highest rank of magic users and the only practitioners who can tap external power from ley lines and nexuses.

Mage Corps: Military branch under the purview of the US Department of the Preternatural. Accepts only mages.

Magic: Emanating from and powered by a person's soul. Roughly one-quarter of the world's population has magic. Strength varies, with different titles being bestowed depending on a person's magical reach. Casting is divided into defensive wards and offensive spells.

Medb: (Pronunciation: may-ve) Immortal. Celtic goddess. Queen of Air and Darkness. Ruler of the Unseelie Court. Member of the Tuatha Dé Danann.

Montu: Immortal. Egyptian god of war.

Morrígan: Immortal. Sometimes depicted as an individual Celtic goddess, or more commonly as a triple goddess, of war and fate. She is particularly affiliated with foretelling of death or victory in battle. Often described as a trio of sisters sometimes given the names of Badb, Macha, and Nemain.

Mulroney, Nadine: Mage. Works counterintelligence for the PIA. Is fluent in French and based out of Paris, France.

Nazarov, Ilya: Mage. Necromancer who is the Patriarch of Souls for the Orthodox Church of the Dead.

Necromancer: A magic user who can be of any rank. Their magic has an affinity for the dead, allowing them to raise the dead, control zombies, and manipulate the lingering souls of the deceased. Their kind of magic is heavily restricted in use in the United States and in most countries.

Necromancy: A family of magic that deals with the dead, usually involving blood magic and sacrifices. Predominately illegal or restricted in most countries.

Nexus: Metaphysical lake of power beneath the earth. Usually located in sacred areas or beneath major cities.

Night Court: Vampire group that oversees claimed territory. Headed by a single master vampire. Several Night Courts can exist in the same major city.

Night Marchers, the: Spirits. Hawaiian ancestral warrior spirits that are said to rise from their burial sites or the ocean to march to ancient Hawaiian battle sites or other sacred places. Usually visible on nights honoring Hawaiian gods, such as Kū.

Norns: Immortals. Norse Fates.

Odin: Immortal. Norse god of wisdom, healing, death, knowledge, battle, and the gallows, and is the titular king of the Æsir.

Órlaith: (Pronunciation: OR-lah) Immortal. Daughter of Ruadán. The Summer Lady of the Seelie Court and heir to Brigid. Cú Chulainn's fiancée within the story.

Orthodox Church of the Dead: Religious cultlike group that worships a god of the underworld and offers prayers and sacrifices to Peklabog.

Patriarch of Souls: The high priest in charge of the Orthodox Church of the Dead. They are almost always a necromancer.

Peklabog: Immortal. Slavic god of the underworld who guides the souls of the dead. He is associated with fire, water, snakes, and earthquakes.

Pele: Immortal. Hawaiian goddess of volcanoes and fire.

Persephone: Immortal. Greek goddess of the Underworld and springtime.

PCB: Preternatural Crimes Bureau. A PCB is usually found only in the police departments of major metropolitan areas in the United States. The PCB in New York City is headed up by a bureau chief. The five detective boroughs within the NYPD all field detectives specializing in preternatural crimes through the PCB. The PCB has jurisdiction throughout the five boroughs and its own detachment of cops that work in homicide, narcotics, major crimes, and CSU. The PCB is one of the least manned departments in the NYPD due to the type of cases it handles.

PIA: Preternatural Intelligence Agency. PIA is a national-level foreign intelligence organization overseen by the Secretary of Defense directly through the USDI. The PIA's intelligence operations extend beyond the zones of combat, and approximately half of its employees serve overseas at hundreds of locations and US

Embassies in many countries. The agency specializes in collection and analysis of preternatural-source intelligence, both overt and clandestine, while also handling American military-diplomatic relations abroad. The agency has no law enforcement authority. (Equivalent to CIA)

Psychopomp: Creatures, spirits, angels, or deities that appear in many religions and take many forms. Responsible for guiding newly deceased souls from Earth to the afterlife, whether a heaven or hell. Are used most commonly with necromancy and other magic that has an affinity for souls or the dead.

Shields: Ward. Defensive magic used for protection on a large or small scale.

Shiva: Immortal. Hindu god of destruction and one of Hinduisms principal deities.

Skellig Islands, the: Location. Irish translation: *Na Scealaga.* Rocky islands in the Atlantic Ocean off the west coast of Ireland.

SOA: Supernatural Operations Agency. SOA is the domestic intelligence and security service of the United States that focuses on magical and preternatural crimes and terrorism. Employs human, preternatural, and magically affiliated people to field positions for domestic defense. (Equivalent to FBI)

Sorcerer/Sorceress: Second-highest rank of magic users and moderately more common than mages but are outnumbered by witches and wizards.

Soulbond: A binding of two or more souls to tie people together for magical needs. Illegal under the laws of all governments.

Spells: Offensive magic.

Srecha: Immortal. Slavic dual goddess of fate who appears as a beautiful woman that spins a golden thread. She bestows positive welfare on chosen recipients. When depicted as misfortune, she is known as Nesrecha and appears as an old woman with bloodshot eyes.

Taylor, Marek: Seer. CEO of PreterWorld, a social media platform geared toward the preternatural and supernatural community. His patrons are the Norns.

Threshold: Ward. Applied to a hearth and home for protection to keep out negative magic, spirits, and demons.

Throne: Angel. Third-highest class of angel within the Choirs. Thrones are depicted as a great spinning wheel with many eyes.

Tiarnán: Member of the Tuatha Dé Danann. Carries the title Lord of Ivy and Gold.

Tír na nÓg: (Pronunciation: TEER-na-nog) English translation: Land of the Young. A place in the Otherworld past the veil where the Tuatha Dé Danann and lesser fae reside.

Tisiphone: Immortal. A Greek Erinyes.

Trishula: Artifact. A trident that is a divine symbol within Hinduism, wielded by Shiva.

Tuatha Dé Danann: (Pronunciation: TOO-ah de-danan) Celtic pantheon of gods. They are considered high-status fae.

US Department of the Preternatural: Employs all manner of magically affiliated and preternatural people for military service. Active duty combat mages are seconded to the Army, Navy, Air Force, and Marines and are required to go through BTC and joint training.

Veil: The metaphysical barrier between Earth/mundane plane and other worlds/dimensions/planes, and versions of hell and heaven derived from myths.

Walker, Estelle: God pack werewolf. Alpha of the New York City god pack.

Wards: Defensive magic.

Warlock: Most common rank of magic users. On par with witches.

Werecreatures: Humans who are infected with the werevirus. Can change form into various animalistic shapes. Werecreatures are either infected later on in life or are born with the disease.

Werevirus: An incurable disease that makes those who are infected change into monstrous beasts. Created by an ancient

Roman mage, the werevirus was one of the first recorded instances of magically created biological warfare introduced into society. People are born with the werevirus or become infected through intercourse or blood. Two strains exist: a normal strain and a god strain. The god strain has stronger magical properties which can cause the infected to be susceptible to an immortal patron.

Witch: Most common rank of magic users. On par with warlocks.

Zhang, Emma: Werewolf. Alpha of the Tempest pack.

Zombie: An undead creature consisting of either a skeleton or fresher corpse. They can only be raised by necromancers. Zombies are powered by black magic and souls pulled from the afterlife beyond the veil.

AUTHOR'S NOTES

This book fought me from chapter one, but I eventually won the war on words. I'm grateful to my book village for keeping me on track.

Nora Sakavic, for all your support and friendship amidst the craziness.

Leslie Copeland, for your insight and encouragement and being a great friend through the difficult times.

Lily Morton, for never steering me wrong, for always being there on the other side of the world and the other side of a text message when I needed it most. You're one of my best friends and I can't thank you enough for how you've helped me get through all that life threw at me in 2020.

May Archer, for being there when I needed you through everything. Thank you for your support and friendship.

Lucy Lennox, for your help and compassion and being there when I need it. Thank you so much for being my friend.

Aimee Nicole Walker, for your kindness and help and the distractions I needed during a difficult time. I'm so glad we're friends.

Bear, who continues to be an amazing, brilliant friend. I'm so glad you're in my life.

Last but not least: to my readers. Thank you so much for enjoying the worlds I get to write about so that I can write more. All of you are amazing, and I wouldn't get to do this without you.

I realize that criminal cases *never* happen like this, but I took some authorial license for plot purposes. It's fiction, so enjoy the fastest dismissal of a US criminal case ever. A big thank you to JP for helping me out with US criminal law.

I would be thrilled and grateful if you would consider reviewing *An Echo in the Sorrow* on Amazon or Goodreads. I appreciate all honest reviews, positive or negative. Reviews definitely help my books get seen, so thank you!

Cover design by AngstyG LLC.
Professional Beta Reading by Leslie Copeland: lcopelandwrites@ gmail.com
Edited by One Love Editing
Proofing by Lori Parks: lp.nerdproblems@gmail.com
Proofing by Jenni Lea at LesCourt Author Services

CONNECT WITH HAILEY

Keep up with my book news by signing up for my newsletter and get the free Soulbound prequel short story *Down A Twisted Path* and several free Metahuman Files short stories while you're at it.

Join the reader group on Facebook: Hailey's Hellions

Visit Hailey's website: www.HaileyTurner.com

Like Hailey's author page

OTHER WORKS BY HAILEY TURNER

M/M Science Fiction Military Romance:

Captain Jamie Callahan, son of a wealthy senator and socialite mother, is a survivor.

Staff Sergeant Kyle Brannigan, a Special Forces operative, is a man with secrets.

Alpha Team, the Metahuman Defense Force's top-ranked field team, is where the two collide and their lives will never be the same.

<u>Metahuman Files</u>

In the Wreckage

In the Ruins

In the Shadows

In The Blood

In The Requiem

In The Solace

<u>A Metahuman Files: Classified Novella</u>

Out of the Ashes

New Horizons

Fire In The Heart

M/M Urban Fantasy

<u>Soulbound</u>

A Ferry of Bones & Gold

All Souls Near & Nigh

A Crown of Iron & Silver

A Vigil in the Mourning

On the Wings of War

An Echo In The Sorrow

A Veiled & Hallowed Eve

Soulbound Universe Standalones

Resurrection Reprise

LGBTQ+ Epic steampunk-inspired fantasy:

Welcome to Maricol, where the land will kill you, kinship turns the gears of war, and burning the dead lest they come back to life is the only way to survive.

Infernal War Saga

The Prince's Poisoned Vow

The Emperor's Bone Palace

Infernal War Saga Novella

An Emporium of Hearts

Contemporary gay romance

Short stories previously published in the Heart2Heart Charity Anthologies.

From the Heart: A Short Story Collection

Audible

All of Hailey Turner's books are available in audiobooks. Visit Audible to discover your next favorite listen.

Hailey Turner Audiobooks

Thanks for reading!